LUSO

A Novel About Peter Francisco

This novel is enjoyable to read, historically accurate, and is more than just the story of Peter Francisco, a true American hero. It is indicative of the stories of countless men and women who sacrificed to make us who we are, and it will serve future generations well as a reminder of these great Americans.

—David N. Appleby, former President General, Sons of the American Revolution

The Virginia Giant! The Hercules of the Revolution! There are facts we will never know about Peter Francisco, but his descendant Travis Bowman has written an engaging work of fiction that intertwines a kidnapped boy's search for personal liberty while making remarkable contributions to his new nation's struggle for political independence.

—Dr. James C. Kelly, Director of U.S. Army Museums

This is an amazing story that is larger than life! Peter Francisco was the giant of the American Revolution who stood head and shoulders above everyone else and was wounded multiple times, yet his life was marvelously preserved by the sovereign hand of God Almighty. Travis Bowman's well-crafted novel will mesmerize you.

—Dr. Roger Schultz, Dean of Arts & Sciences, Liberty University

In the Bible, God gave Samson amazing strength which he used to carry out God's will for Israel. In this book, Travis Bowman tells the incredible story of how God gave his ancestor similar strength to carry out His will for America.

—Dean Burris, Senior Pastor, Metrolina Church of Concord, North Carolina

Peter Francisco's story is not just another legend from the battlefields of the Revolution. This truly is the American Braveheart story!

—Robert Whitlow, Christy Award-winning author and film-maker

Without him we would have lost
two crucial battles, perhaps the war,
and with it our freedom.

—George Washington

LUSO

For Love, Liberty, and Legacy

A novel about the Virginia Giant,
Peter Francisco,
soldier of the American Revolution,
by 7th-generation descendant Travis Bowman.

Co-authored by James Warder and Heather Walls

ISBN 978-1-4951-7046-1

Published in the United States by Bequest Publishing.

Previous editions of this book have been published by Bequest with the title *Hercules of the Revolution: A Novel Based on the Life of Peter Francisco.*

Printed in the United States by Lightning Source, Inc.

Editing by:
Heather K. Walls, Lead Manuscript Editor
Linda-Lee Bowman
Kim Cassell

Revival fonts used in titles throughout this book are from the Fell Types collection. The Fell Types are digitally reproduced by Igino Marini.
www.iginomarini.com

Acknowledgements

There are many people in my life that I wish to thank for assisting both directly and indirectly with this book. Please forgive me if I forget to acknowledge the part that you played in this literary work, but know that I am thankful for all the friends and family that have helped over the years.

In memory of Rosalie Francisco Barret, my great-grandmother and great-granddaughter of Peter Francisco, I am ever indebted to her for the phenomenal heritage passed down to me. I appreciate her for raising a great son and then lovingly caring for my mother when she was a young girl.

To Bill and Mildred Barret, Rosalie's firstborn son and daughter-in-law and my grandparents, I am so thankful that you shared Peter Francisco's story with me when I was a little boy. Granddaddy, who passed away in 2003, was a hardworking man and always provided for his family. Grandmother, you are very sweet, and I love to hear you share about events from years gone by. You have an amazing memory! Thank you for raising my mother Linda-Lee to be a nurturing and loving mother.

I want to thank my parents Paul and Linda-Lee Bowman for teaching me to appreciate the freedom that we enjoy in this country. Mom, I am especially thankful for the countless hours that you spent editing and revising this book. Thank you, Dad, for teaching me Godly character and what it means to be a real hero.

Thank you, Michelle—my love and best friend—for your support as I spent so many hours researching Peter's story, then countless more behind a computer putting it into a book. Thank you for always loving me and believing in me despite my failures.

To my boys Austin and Josh, thank you for understanding when I missed a game or time with you so that I could work on this book. You guys are the best sons a father could ask for. Always remember to be grateful for the freedom you have in the United States of America because of those who fought with bravery and honor, as your ancestor Peter Francisco did.

Long before anyone knew who Peter Francisco was, Bruce Nemet believed in this project and assisted financially to make this book a reality. A vision without resources is just a wishful dream. Thank you, Bruce!

Finally, my thanks to James Warder and Heather Walls for working with me for months on end to pen this epic legend. Heather, your feminine touch to this narrative softened Peter's war torn hands so that the love story could be more authentic. Without both of you this story would have never come to life, and my great-grandfather's legacy may have been forgotten.

Preface

Have you ever thought about all the things that you enjoy on a daily basis? The average American owns a home, a car, a computer, a cell phone, a television with over one hundred channels to watch at any given time, and many other things that are considered luxuries in other countries. We shuffle our kids around to different sporting events, and we so easily forget that everything we enjoy came at a price—a high price.

When I was nine years old, my father was stationed in Germany with the Department of Defense, and we lived in a small village for three years. It didn't take long for me to realize that many people from other countries could only dream of living in the United States. That experience began a journey in my own life of understanding how blessed I am to live in the United States of America.

When I was young, my grandmother Mildred Barret told me that I was related to a giant from the Revolutionary War, but I was well into my thirties before I began to research the stories of my ancestor. It wasn't until I visited one of the five Peter Francisco monuments on the East Coast that I discovered the whole story.

Peter's story resonated with me on two levels. First, I realized that I stood the same height as Peter, which put me in his shoes and helped me to see life from his perspective. Second, I have always despised racism, and this story shows the atrocity of determining a person's worth by the color of his skin. But Peter doesn't let that ruin his life and, ultimately, he triumphs over racial discrimination.

I hope you find this story of bravery, strength, romance, and honor about my great-grandfather just as inspiring as I did. More importantly, I hope that it deepens your appreciation for the freedom you enjoy and the blood that was shed for your happiness.

Luso-

A prefix denoting Portuguese language and culture, deriving from *Lusitania,* the ancient name of the province in Roman Iberia corresponding to the medieval and modern nation of Portugal. In colloquial use, "Luso" commonly refers to a person of Portuguese origin.

The long-standing excellent relations between Portugal and the United States can be traced to the roots of a Portuguese immigrant child who grew to be a valiant fighter for independence and a hero of the American Revolution.

—João de Vallera, former Ambassador of Portugal to the United States of America

Photographs:
America Remembers Peter Francisco

The monument in front of City Hall in Hopewell, Virginia, where Francisco was discovered on June 23, 1765, age five, abandoned on a wharf on the James.

Francisco's grave in Shockoe Hill Cemetery, Richmond, Virginia.

Locust Grove, from the early 1790s Francisco's home and farm, in Buckingham County, Virginia. The house was listed on the National Register of Historic Places in 1972 and later fully restored through initiative of members of the Society of the Descendants of Peter Francisco.

Memorial pillar, the "Cavalry Monument," dedicated to Francisco in Greensboro, North Carolina, site of the Battle of Guilford Courthouse, where he wielded the broadsword specially made for him by order of George Washington.

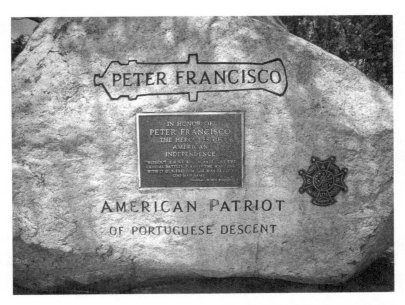

Peter Francisco Square in New Bedford, Massachusetts, with boulder marker commemorating George Washington's high regard for Francisco and Francisco's Portuguese heritage.

Visiting the Amigos da Terceira center in Pawtuckett, Rhode Island, and the monument to Francisco's memory there.

Visiting Peter Francisco Park with its stone obelisk memorial, next to Penn Station in Newark, New Jersey.

Photographs:
Terceira, Peter Francisco's First Home

Descendants of Peter Francisco gather at the church where he was baptized, two hundred and fifty years after his childhood abandonment by kidnappers 2,700 miles away on a dock in the English colony of Virginia.

On June 23, 2015, a new statue was dedicated to Peter Francisco's memory in Porto Judeu, Terceira Island, Azores. The date is significant: it was exactly 250 years earlier that Pedro was found abandoned in Hopewell, Virginia. Guests of honor at the ceremony included João Carlos Tavares, Mayor of Porto Judeu; Paulo Teves, Regional Director of the Azorean Communities; Daniel Bazan, U.S. Consul; and Col. Martin Rothrock, commander of U.S. air base Lajes Field. Eight American descendants of Peter Francisco, including the author, traveled to be in attendance. The new monument stands in front of Porto Judeu's municipal sports arena, itself re-named in honor of Francisco in the same ceremony.

Angra, first of the Azores' medieval ports to be named a city, long a busy and contested station for Atlantic traffic—as the family of little Pedro Francisco, in small nearby Porto Judeu, knew it—and still today a destination of uncommon beauty.

Pedro Francisco, born July 9, 1760, was baptized in Saint Anthony's Church in Porto Judeu. The parish baptismal record was the birth record of the day, and Pedro's is extant. It now resides in the Biblioteca Pública e Arquivo Regional de Angra do Heroísmo, a repository of the island's documentary history. The author was allowed the privilege of holding and examining the records volume, normally kept behind glass for public display.

The baptismal font in Saint Anthony's Church.

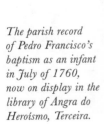

The parish record of Pedro Francisco's baptism as an infant in July of 1760, now on display in the library of Angra do Heroísmo, Terceira.

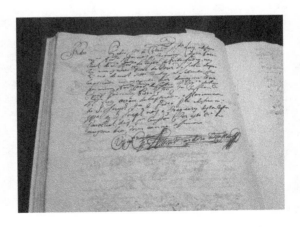

A "return" to Terceira for Pedro Francisco, and a Portuguese and American celebration of his life and legacy.

Above: Some of the attendees (including co-author and editor Heather Walls, far left) at the unveiling ceremony.

Right: The author with Mayor João Carlos Tavares of Porto Judeu.

LUSO
A Novel About Peter Francisco

I.

GIVE ME LIBERTY OR GIVE ME DEATH

ARISING WITH DAWN on that mild morning, the young man readied himself to head for the nearby livery stable to prepare for the short carriage ride from the inn, where he and Judge Anthony Winston had stayed the night before, to St. John's Church, the most prominent building in Richmond. March 23, 1775, would put the otherwise ordinary place of worship on the map of American history in a way that Peter Francisco could not have imagined.

As he exited the inn, Peter looked up and down the main street of the largest town he had ever visited. Having spent most of his life on a secluded plantation, he could scarcely imagine so many people living in one place. *I think the judge said six hundred,* he thought. *I still can't believe I'm really here.* For him, it was like a small taste of a life he could only dream about. A gust of blustery air nearly blew the tri-corn hat off his head, sending it twisting and tumbling freely down the lane, but his quick reflexes kept it securely in place before it could escape. All was quiet. Crickets chirped softly out in the grass. Somewhere in the distance, just barely audible, he thought he could hear the clopping of horses' hooves along the cobblestones. Above the distinct outline of rooftops, tall trees silhouetted the faint blue sky like silent witnesses. Not even a hint of light shone from any of the storefront windows. The entire population still appeared fast asleep.

The solitary figure of this strapping youth—six feet, six inches tall nearing his fifteenth birthday—strode in near silence toward the livery, save the sound of dirt clods crunching beneath his 240-pound body. He was relieved to see that he wasn't the only person in town awake. The stable owner was there preparing for another busy day, expecting large crowds of people again from all over the Virginia colony like those over the last few days who had descended on Richmond, the seat of the Second Virginia Convention.

"Good morning, sir," Peter said, breaking the silence, respectfully addressing the man whose back was turned as he gathered oats for his equestrian guests' breakfast.

Startled, the man turned around to see Peter's immense figure standing in the doorway. "Good morning to you, too. I was just getting ready to feed your two American Cream Drafts. Beautiful creatures they are."

"Yes, they are beautiful," Peter responded. "But you look like you have many horses to feed today, so I'll take care of mine."

The fact that the two horses actually belonged to the judge and not to Peter was of little consequence. From the very first day

Peter had laid eyes on these two equines, he had adored them as if they were his own.

He took a bucket of oats in each of his oversized hands and walked over to the huge beasts. At his height, Peter could look them in the eye. "There, there, now, I've brought you something to eat."

Almost in unison, the horses seemed to greet Peter with a nod as he approached. Each, in turn, nuzzled Peter's face before dipping his massive head in the bucket. "We've a big day before us," he said softly to the horses. "The Judge says we'll be hearing great and powerful things at the church today. Then, later in the week, the judge says we'll be headin' back home to Hunting Tower. Do you miss Hunting Tower? Of course you do," he answered for them.

After they had finished eating, Peter entered their stall and began brushing and rubbing their ivory-colored coats. He loved feeling their well-defined muscles twitching under his deft hand. This closeness of feelings between man and beast was unusual to say the least. Having finished their rubdown, Peter then gathered their collars, bits and bridles and prepared them to be hitched to the carriage in which he and Judge Winston had ridden from Hunting Tower Plantation in Buckingham County. The judge was the local representative to this convention, a pivotal meeting that would change the course of history and waver the allegiance of the recently-reformed Virginia House of Burgesses to their motherland, England.

Most carriage drivers would simply take their horses around to the back of the stable where all the visiting carriages were kept, but Peter decided to wheel the carriage around to the front himself. He grabbed the tongue of the carriage and, as big as he was, easily guided it through the massive doors on the front side of the stable, then returned for the horses. As he began to hitch them up, he noticed Judge Winston walking down the street.

"Good morning, Peter. I trust you slept well," he greeted.

"Yes, sir, and good morning to you," Peter replied.

"Have you had your breakfast?"

"No, sir. I had the innkeeper's wife fix me some biscuits last night, and I'll eat them later. I just thought it best to be ready to go whenever you wanted, seein' as how you don't like to be late for meetings and things."

"You know me well, Peter, you know me well."

Peter had been hitching the horses to the carriage, which now stood ready to take the judge to his destination.

"Excellent, Peter," said Winston. "Then we should be getting on to the church. I have a feeling in my bones that we are about to make history today." With the demeanor of a dedicated servant, Peter opened the door to the carriage, and the judge took his seat. Then, Peter climbed onto the driver's station. Before giving the signal, he reached down beneath his feet to feel where he had placed the sword and pistol the judge had asked him to bring on this trip. They were still there, right where he had placed them only a few minutes before.

"Giddap," Peter prodded the horses in his gentle voice, and the Creams obeyed his command instantly.

For the third day, they rode to the outskirts of town in silence, passing many regal homes belonging to some of the wealthier residents of Richmond. St. John's Church soon came into view, sitting majestically on a hill overlooking the James River. The parish was an imposing structure, adorned in white staves with a massive spire rising out of the vestibule and encasing the large front doors. Completed in 1741, the church was a part of Henrico Parish, a parish that had been established by early settlers in 1611.

A few other folks had arrived early as well. Patrick Henry, the judge's nephew, was talking to two other men who appeared to be of equal substance and stature. Peter didn't know it at the time, but they were Thomas Jefferson and George Washington. At six feet, two inches, Washington was an especially imposing figure, though less so in his reticence, just nodding in agreement as Jefferson and Henry engaged in animated conversation.

History would indeed be made today. After the imposition of the Intolerable Acts on the continental territories by Parliament in 1774, attempting to coerce them into submission, the colonists began to resist. They started organizing themselves against Britain in a series of meetings in Virginia and Philadelphia. The debates at today's convention over the need to establish and arm a militia would set a course that would change the destiny of the New World, but no one here could possibly imagine that. Certainly not Peter.

Among those arriving at the church to occupy seats in the visitor's gallery were Susannah and her father, James Anderson. Peter couldn't help but notice their arrival. Just a single look at Susannah made his heart leap in his broad chest. At least, it felt that way to Peter. Even though their backgrounds divided them socially, their prior encounters had emboldened Peter. Ignoring his knees, which felt like the jelly he often spread on a Sunday morning biscuit, he ambled over to their fully-enclosed carriage. When he had covered the twenty yards' distance, Peter reached up to take hold of Susannah's hand as she stepped down from the carriage. The moment their hands connected, electric warmth shot through Peter's body.

"Why, Peter," she said, "you are always such a gentleman. And how are you today?"

"Seeing you has made me much better already." Peter was almost shocked to hear himself speak such bold words.

Susannah's father had exited the opposite side of the carriage and walked around the back to where Peter and Susannah stood. He noticed that their eyes seemed locked on each other as he tapped Peter on the shoulder. He wasn't entirely sure he liked that, but, after all, Peter had saved his daughter's life.

"Peter, my boy, it's good to see you again. And I see you're wearing the hat I gave you. Wonderful, wonderful."

"Yes, sir," said Peter. "I save wearin' it for special occasions like this."

"Indeed, today should be very special. It will be good to get all this nonsense out of the way at last. Come now, Susannah, we want to find good seats in the church."

As her father reached for her arm, Susannah glanced back. "Bye, Peter, I'll see you later."

Peter's mouth felt like he had been crossing the desert, but still managed, "Good day, Miss Susannah."

He rejoined the judge, regaining his senses and remembering his duties as bodyguard.

Other dignitaries also began to arrive, and soon they were all filing into the church. Judge Winston looked at Peter and said, "You might want to take station near one of the windows today. My nephew intends to address the body with words I think important for you to hear."

During the previous days of the convention, Peter had lingered around the open windows, due to unseasonably mild temperatures, but most of the speeches that he had heard were not very inspiring. Most seemed to favor keeping relations with Great Britain as they were. But Peter knew the position that the judge's nephew would take, and he wanted to hear every persuasive word. At his size, Peter was able to easily make his way to one of the windows. Through it, he could see the judge, Patrick Henry and the two men that Henry had been speaking to earlier. He could also see Susannah Anderson and her father. A flutter of excitement caught in his throat at just the sight of her, for this refined young lady had truly captured his affection.

Various people rose to speak, then returned to their seats. Some of them inspired mild clapping or an audible "Here, here." None of them were very noteworthy until Patrick Henry rose from seat number forty-seven, strode purposefully and confidently to the center of the room, and turned to address the delegates.

"No man, Mr. President," Henry began, addressing Peyton Randolph, presiding officer of the congressional assembly, his tone almost apologetic, "thinks more highly than I do of the patriotism, as well as abilities, of the very honorable gentlemen who have just addressed this House. But different men often see the same subject in different lights; and, therefore, I hope it will not be thought disrespectful of those worthy gentlemen if, entertaining as I do opinions of a character very opposite to theirs, I shall speak forth my sentiments freely and without reserve."

Henry's voice began to rise. "This is no time for ceremony. The question before this House is one awful moment to the country. For my own part, I consider it as nothing less than a question of freedom or slavery; and in proportion to the magnitude of the subject ought to be the freedom of the debate...." Peter watched as Henry began to circle the room, making eye contact with as many delegates as possible, without speaking a word.

"Mr. President," Henry resumed, "it is natural to man to indulge in the illusions of hope. We are apt to shut our eyes against a painful truth, and listen to the song of that siren till she transforms us into beasts. Is this the part of wise men, engaged in a great and arduous struggle for liberty?" With that utterance, the young patriot held out his arms from his sides as if asking the question of all there assembled.

"Are we disposed to be of the number of those who, having eyes, see not, and, having ears, hear not, the things which so nearly concern their temporal salvation? For my part, whatever anguish of spirit it may cost, I am willing to know the whole truth; to know the worst, and to provide for it." Henry's arms dropped to his sides and his shoulders slumped. He stood silent for several moments, and Peter wondered if he was finished. Then, with his arms raised and hands above his head, he looked toward the ceiling and continued, "I know no way of judging the future but by the past. And judging by the past, I should wish to know what there has been in the conduct of the British ministry for the last ten years to justify those hopes with which gentlemen have been pleased to solace themselves and the members of this House."

Peter scanned the room. While some of the listeners just sat impassively, others were nodding in agreement, including Judge Winston, Thomas Jefferson and George Washington. As for Jefferson, a small smile crept across his face. Peter took a moment to further survey the visitors' gallery until his eyes rested on Susannah. She was shaking her head, and Peter was a bit disheartened by that. He was drawing his own conclusions, and they were much different from what hers appeared to be. At that moment, as if hearing his thoughts, she looked toward the window where Peter was standing, and when her eyes met his, she couldn't help but smile demurely.

"Suffer not yourselves to be betrayed with a kiss. Ask yourselves how this gracious reception of our petition comports with those warlike preparations, which cover our water and darken our land," the young orator pleaded.

Henry was again moving around the room with arms waving, the tone of his voice imploring answers to his questions. Peter, too, was being swept up in the emotional pleadings. "Let us not deceive ourselves, sir. These are the implements of war and subjugation; the last arguments to which kings resort." Fatigued, Henry dropped his arms once again to his side. He looked as though he had been beaten, but he had not. For when he spoke again, his voice bellowed, reverberating off the interior of the church with persuading emphasis. "They are meant for us; they can be meant for no other. They are sent over to bind and rivet upon us those chains which the British ministry has been so long forging. And what do we have to oppose them?"

More of the delegates were nodding in agreement now, and Peter could sense his own head joining in unison. "Shall we resort to entreaty and humble supplication? Let us not, I beseech you, sir, deceive ourselves. Sir, we have done everything that could be done to avert the storm which is now coming on. We have petitioned; we have remonstrated; we have supplicated; we have

11

prostrated ourselves before the throne, and we have implored its interposition to arrest the tyrannical hands of the ministry and Parliament." Henry's voice grew louder, his gestures more exaggerated. "Our petitions have been slighted; our remonstrances have produced additional violence and insult; our supplications have been disregarded; and we have been spurned, with contempt, from the foot of the throne!"

Henry allowed himself a moment to turn completely around and cast his eyes across the sea of delegates. His eyes glanced out the window where Peter was standing, and the two men exchanged a brief look of acknowledgement. Henry began to speak more rapidly. "If we wish to be free—if we mean to preserve inviolate those inestimable privileges for which we have been so long contending, if we mean not basely to abandon the noble struggle in which we have been so long engaged, and which we have pledged ourselves never to abandon until the glorious object of our contest shall be obtained—we must fight! I repeat it, sir, we must fight." Henry grabbed a nearby banister that separated him from some of the delegates. He gazed at the men he knew to be in favor of appeasement and lowered his face to theirs, his eyes fierce with passion. "An appeal to arms and to the God of hosts is all that is left us!" Henry turned to face the rest of the body assembled there. "They tell us, sir, that we are weak, unable to cope with so formidable an adversary." Everyone knew that he was referring to those men he had just personally addressed. "But when shall we be stronger? Will it be the next week, or the next year? Will it be when we are totally disarmed, and when a British guard shall be stationed in every house?"

Some of the delegates began straining to hear every word of

the orator's now-moderated tone. Peter cocked his head further into the window as well, with the added benefit of being able to see Susannah more easily. "Shall we acquire the means of effectual resistance by lying supinely on our backs and hugging the delusive phantom of hope, until our enemies shall have bound us hand and foot?"

With a gradual rise in his voice, Henry further entreated his audience, "The battle, sir, is not to the strong alone; it is to the vigilant, the active, the brave. Besides, sir, we have no election. If we were base enough to desire it, it is now too late to retire from the contest. There is no retreat but in submission and slavery! Our chains are forged! Their clanking may be heard on the plains of Boston! The war is inevitable...and let it come! I repeat, sir, let it come!"

It was all Peter could do to contain himself. He so dearly wanted to cheer, yet he knew it was not his place to demonstrate in such a manner. Some shouts of affirmation issued from within the church. Other delegates yelled in the negative. Patrick Henry just stood silent, waiting for their voices to be still. When he spoke again, his voice was measured. "It is in vain, sir, to extenuate the matter. Gentlemen may cry, 'Peace, Peace,' but there is no peace. The war is actually begun!" His voice intensified. "The next gale that sweeps from the North will bring to our ears the clash of resounding arms." Continuing to scale, Henry's voice now reached a thunderous climax. "Our brethren are already in the field! Why stand we here idle? What is it that gentlemen wish? What would they have?"

Henry once again circled the room. "Is life so dear, or peace so sweet, as to be purchased at the price of chains and slavery?"

He returned to the center of the room, his eyes raised skyward. "Forbid it, Almighty God!"

With arms raised above his head, Patrick Henry made his final declaration. "I know not what course others may take; but as for me, give me liberty or give me death!" These last words were delivered as thunder, while he remained in his pose.

Many of the delegates were on their feet cheering and applauding, repeating Henry's words, among them, Washington, Jefferson and Judge Winston. Some shouted, with fists in the air, "Treason!" and "Traitor!" Others remained seated. Peter had never before been so swept away with emotion.

Out of the corner of his eye, he saw the Andersons rise and make their way to the front door. Peter pushed through the crowd of men gathered around him, pressing toward the window so that they, too, could hear. He ran around to the front of the church just in time for the Andersons to exit.

"Wasn't that speech compelling?" Peter exclaimed. "But do you not agree with it all?"

Susannah's father pushed past Peter brusquely, preferring not to engage in conversation. His daughter turned, and the eyes with which Peter had been so enchanted glared back at him. "If that foolishness is truly what you think, Peter Francisco, then you are also a fool—a fool on a fool's errand! So, go back to your foolish friends. But I warn you, this course will render nothing but heartache and despair. Good day."

"But what about freedom from slav—" Peter started to protest, but stopped abruptly when he saw a young man emerge from the crowd and help Susannah into the carriage with her father. The man said something to Susannah, which to Peter was inaudible. Looking him over, Peter could see that his charcoal suit had been tailored to fit and the cravat with lace at the ends appeared so tight around his neck that his large Adam's apple protruded out over the knot. His sandy blonde hair peeked through a tan tri-corn rim, just above his crooked nose that didn't really seem to fit his face. *He is tall,* Peter thought, *but he still looks at least eight or nine inches shorter than me, and he definitely needs to eat more.*

Susannah flashed him a coy grin. "Oh, George! You're such a gentleman," Susannah said deliberately, loud enough for Peter to hear. "We certainly need more men like you who know what the colonies need and how to treat a lady."

"George Carrington! Hello there, my boy! Good to see you!" Mr. Anderson said, tipping his hat in George's direction. "I do appreciate your chivalry. You'll make a fine husband one day. I certainly hope my Susannah will make a match with someone like you. Please give your parents my regards." Susannah's father barely took a breath before calling, "Let's get going, driver!"

As a cloud of dust kicked up behind the carriage wheels, Peter stood there feeling crushed, as though someone had just hit him in the chest with a twenty-pound blacksmith's hammer. While Peter watched George saunter away, he narrowed his eyes and glared at the back of his head until the crowd that still lingered outside the church swallowed his lanky figure. Out of the corner of his eye, Peter noticed Patrick Henry talking as he made his way through the large wooden doors at the front of the church. His inspiring speech began to drift back into Peter's thoughts. One word stood out more than any of the others. Freedom. Peter played that word over and over in his mind. What did it really mean? What would it mean for me? If I was free, could I come and go as I please? Could I own property one day? Could I marry a girl like Susannah Anderson?

Slumping down pensively on a nearby tree stump and propping his head up with his huge hands, a dejected Peter focused his eyes on the road ahead. Patrick Henry's words seemed to reverberate in his mind like waves crashing against a boat, their ebb and flow much like the emotional tide Peter was experiencing at this very moment. He looked down at the James River—the same river on which Portuguese pirates had abandoned him as a young boy at City Point nearly ten years ago. Where is my family now? He wondered. What are they doing? He had been just five years old, such an innocent age, when the precious gift of freedom had been stripped away from him. Peter thought about the long road behind him and the journey he had taken since that time when he was so young and so afraid.

Now putting fear aside and discounting how the Andersons had reacted, Peter knew—deep in his very soul—that freedom was well worth fighting for. More than that, he knew it was well worth dying for.

2.

LIFE IN THE AZORES

LIFE IN THE AZORES ISLANDS was nearly idyllic in 1765, especially for a five-year-old boy whose family was comparatively wealthy relative to many others on the island of Terceira. Little Pedro Francisco was a bundle of energy, and he loved exploring near the family home, a home that by the standards of the day and place would be considered a mansion.

Pedro could not recall all the details of his family's arrival from Portugal. He barely remembered the day when they set sail from the mainland to these islands, discovered by Portuguese explorers in the early 1400s. Located about nine hundred and fifty miles from Portugal, the island of Terceira, one of several making up the Azores, was originally known as the Island of Jesus Cristo and was later known as the Phantom Island of Brazil. But none of that mattered to Pedro.

The island, by any name, was the best place to live in the whole world, at least for this noble boy. Sometimes Pedro just stood in the front yard and watched the activity on the ocean. From there, on the hills overlooking the harbor of Porto Judeu, he could make out dolphins and whales cavorting in the ocean, including the mammoth sperm whale and distinctively marked orcas. Though very young, Pedro was saddened that whaling ships from all over the world could be seen harpooning these magnificent creatures, dragging them to shore and harvesting anything in the least bit worthwhile, then dragging the carcass back out to sea for an inglorious burial. However, that didn't dampen the boy's love for the ocean, and he imagined himself as a seafarer one day. At other times, he and his sister wandered down to the port itself. The harbor always seemed to be teeming with all types of ships and sloops, and there was a buzz of activity with these vessels offloading riches from the Americas and India, then taking on cargo of grain and woad, a local plant that yielded rich, deep dyes.

Terceira Island was actually the culmination of four overlapping stratovolcanoes, of which the combined mass was a mere one hundred and forty-eight square miles. The youngest of those volcanoes had erupted only a couple of years before the family had arrived, and since it was due west of Porto Judeu, and the winds seemed to prevail from that direction, the faint smell of sulphur, like rotten eggs, would occasionally waft over the coastal waters where Pedro roamed. On clear days, some smoke could still be seen billowing from the now-resting volcanic dome.

As with all tropically-influenced weather systems, the winds frequently interrupted a day of exploring by the sudden onset of a rain shower or thunderstorm. That didn't stop Pedro, and occasionally his sister, from exploring nearby grottos with their stalactites and stalagmites. From time to time, family and friends spent the day at Mata da Serreta, a forest on the volcano's slope that featured such lush vegetation that a soul could easily become lost in contemplation surrounded by such paradisiacal beauty.

Pedro was especially fond of watching the islands' variety of bird life, including all types of shearwaters and petrels. He was particularly taken by the Azorean buzzards, for which the group of islands had been named, as these birds were so tame that they would actually eat from the young boy's hand.

One evening Pedro's father, Machado Luiz, and his mother, Antonia Maria Francisco, were entertaining some guests. As always, Pedro, despite his youth, was allowed the run of the house, but he also knew to be quiet when the adults were deep in conversation.

"Father," said Antonia Maria, "it is time to eat. Will you say the blessing?"

"Aww—I wanted to say the prayer that you taught me, Mama," pleaded young Pedro in a sad voice.

"Alright, son. Are you sure that you won't be embarrassed to say it in front of our guests?"

"No, Mama!" replied Pedro. He then folded his hands, bowed his head and prayed.

> *Com Jesus me deito* (With Jesus I go to sleep),
> *Com Jesus me levanto* (With Jesus I awake),
> *Com a graça de Deus* (With the grace of God),
> *E do Espirito Santo* (and of the Holy Spirit),
> *Amen.*

After he finished praying, he sat down at the dinner table next to his papa and listened to him talk with a person who was held in high regard throughout the Azores.

"So, Machado, as a man of prominence in Portugal, what was it that brought you to our tropical paradise?" the man asked.

"Oh, well, I suppose the best answer is politics," Machado replied carefully.

"So, it would seem that you found yourself on the wrong side of the power struggle," the man replied knowingly.

"Actually, it wasn't so much that we were on the wrong side. No, we chose not to take sides. But when King Joseph decided to make the Marquis de Pombal the real ruler, everything began to fall apart. First it was the so-called conspiracy of nobles to murder the king and Pombal himself. Honestly, I don't know for certain if there was a conspiracy, but that was all that Pombal needed to begin his purge of anyone the least bit suspicious. Then, all the Jesuits were expelled, or worse, God forbid. Even though we had never aligned ourselves with any of those involved, a good friend with a connection to the power of the throne warned me that my noble family might be targeted. Really, we had no choice but to escape."

That conversation brought some clarity to Pedro. Even though he was very young, he did indeed remember living a royal life, residing in a castle with manicured grounds and servants who took care of every need. He then recalled the family loading up several carriages and wagons in the dark of night and boarding a ship that traveled for several days before making landfall here. He recalled asking his father where they were going, but there had been no reply.

What he didn't remember and had no way of knowing was that his father had secured the family's wealth and brought it with him. That was how his family could now live, even though Machado never had to work, and it was how his father could build such a magnificent home.

Although it had taken several months to construct, and the family had lived in somewhat less desirable quarters for a time, the home at the top of the hill was indeed breathtaking. The walls, soft brown and with quite a rough texture, were made of crushed shells and sand, which, when mixed with water and dried, were as solid as rock.

Inside, four rooms were dedicated as sleeping quarters. There were rooms for dining and food preparation and a gathering room where Pedro had overheard his father's conversation. Outside, an arbor had been constructed, where hydrangeas of every color were planted with great care. Off to one side was a courtyard where Pedro and his sister liked to play with an oversized ball. Because of the ruggedness of the surrounding terrain, a simple set of iron gates and minimal fencing was all that was needed to secure the property from those who might covet the family's apparent wealth.

This night, as the boy listened to his father conversing with guests, was a crisp evening in May, and the clouds had just cleared, making way for the sun's rays to light up the lush, green mountainside in Porto Judeu. Spring flowers on Terceira Island, with blooms in full color inviting bees in for nectar, drank from the seasonal showers. Pedro came running up the gravel hill and through the iron gates at his parents' home. He had just returned from evening church services on this holy day, although he could not remember the actual importance of this particular occasion. In fact, he was never especially fond of going to church in the first place. The problem was that he always had to get dressed up in clothes not entirely suitable for a young boy bursting with exuberance. Today he had worn a short jacket over a fancy blouse with ruffled cuffs and collar and pants like knickers. The only thing that didn't bother Pedro about this costume was his shoes. He loved his shoes. They had prominent buckles that bore the initials P and F on the right and left shoes, respectively. These had been forged from silver extracted from mines in Northern Spain.

Pedro was completely out of breath when the rest of the family finally caught up to him holding onto the gate. "Mama, do we really have to go to bed? The sun isn't even down past the mountain, and sister and I didn't get to play ball in the courtyard yet," Pedro whined.

"Tomorrow morning is going to come early, Pedro," said Maria, "and we are going to the market right after breakfast, so I want you to be well-rested."

"But, mama, you promised that we could play in the courtyard," Pedro insisted.

Maria turned to Machado. "Papa, what do you think?" she pressed on behalf of the children.

"All right, you have thirty minutes, but then you two are going straight to bed," replied Machado. He leaned down and kissed them both on the head and said, "I love you!" Giggling and skipping, Pedro and his sister ran off through the garden and into the south side of the courtyard where they liked to kick their ball back and forth. As the sky turned shades of azure and violet, Maria and Machado headed inside to settle in for the evening. Machado customarily took his shoes off and sat down in his favorite chair, one that he had brought from Portugal.

Playing in the corner of the courtyard around a makeshift net that his father had purchased from a fishing boat in the harbor, Pedro tried unsuccessfully to block the ball his sister had kicked past him. They had been playing for only a few minutes when they heard a noise across the courtyard outside the gate. The noise piqued the boy's curiosity because it sounded like one of the Azorean buzzards that he so liked to feed. After listening to the sound for a few seconds, Pedro ran off to find the tropical bird that he assumed was chirping.

"Come back here, Pedro!" yelled his sister as she hurried after him. "Mama and Papa will be angry." Either he couldn't hear his sister or he chose not to pay attention, the latter more likely. The lad never broke stride as he sought to catch at least a glimpse of one of his favorite island creatures. Curiosity fueled his purpose, a purpose that would ultimately change his life forever.

As he rounded the corner to the gate, he stopped dead in his tracks. His feet were frozen in the brown dirt, and his eyes grew wide. *I should be afraid,* he thought. But he wasn't, at least not yet. Standing before him were two men, sailors by the looks of them. Their pants were ragged at the bottoms and their well-worn shirts had been patched with a variety of colored fabric to cover where they had been torn. Bandanas covered both their heads, and both wore wide, brown, leather belts into which each of them had tucked a flintlock pistol and a fearsome dagger. Despite their ominous appearance, however, Pedro was transfixed by some sort of small sack carried by one of the men. He had stopped about ten feet in front of them, his sister nearly catching up to him.

Before he could utter a sound, one of the men looked the young boy in the eyes and smiled. "We just sailed in from Portugal, and your dad asked our captain to bring these sweets back as a gift. Now be a good boy and take these inside to your father," he said.

For a fleeting moment, Pedro thought, *maybe these were bad men like Mama and Papa had warned about so many times.* On the other hand, he had always had a sweet tooth, and the very thought of some candy—a scarcity on the island—was far too tempting for him to resist. As he started walking towards the men, his sister rounded the corner and saw the dingy-looking thugs enticing her brother.

"Pedro, stop!" she screamed.

When he turned to look at his sister running towards him, one of the men lunged forward throwing a burlap sack over his head. In a single motion, he flipped the sack onto his shoulder with Pedro in it. Pedro's sister let out a scream as shrill and as loud as she could muster. The other sailor ran toward her and tried to grab her, but he only caught the hem of her sweater, and that pulled right off. The man stood there clutching the sweater and looking at his comrade as if to say, "Now what do we do?" But they turned and hastily made their way down the hill toward Porto Judeu.

Meanwhile, Pedro's sister, still screaming in terror, was approaching the house. Hearing the commotion and instinctively recognizing the panic in her voice, Machado came running outside to see his daughter with a look of terror on her face, pointing toward the iron gate. She was mumbling something about Pedro and two mean-looking men. Machado, grasping the seriousness

24

of the situation, bolted past her. Unfortunately, the thugs, having had a significant head start, were well on their way down the path to the harbor. In the distance, Machado could see one of the men with a burlap bag slung over his shoulder, and he could faintly hear his son yelling, "Papa, Papa, help! Help me, Papa!" Machado immediately knew that he couldn't possibly catch up with the kidnappers if he followed the winding path—they had gained too much ground. But if he took a straight path through all the bush and bramble, maybe, just maybe, he could catch them.

Despite the fact that he was barefoot, without hesitation the father gave chase. He had run only about twenty paces before the bayonet palms and saw grass began to graze his upper body, cutting his arms and chest until they bled liberally. Still he pressed on. The soles of his feet were gashed by lava rock and pierced with sand spurs, whose little points could inflict an inordinate amount of pain. Still he continued. He felt no pain and worried none about the slashes and cuts. Adrenalin was driving him now, and he was gaining purchase. Machado could hear someone yelling, "Pedro! Don't worry, I'm coming for you!" Only later, would he realize that it was he, himself, who had been shouting.

Just then, Machado saw one of the men look back at him. He got near enough to just barely reach out and touch the man carrying Pedro on his back, but the kidnappers advanced. Machado tried to run faster, but he stumbled over a rock and began tumbling. Along the way, his wrist caught a tree root, and he heard a horrible snap—his wrist shattering. The pain should have been unbearable, yet he was oblivious. Eventually, the momentum of his tumbling enabled him to get upright, and he continued to run as fast as he possibly could.

Fear and rage are powerful motivators, and Machado was fully under their collective spell. His mind began to race with him. *Suppose I do catch up with them. What do I do then? There are two of them and only one of me. I must concentrate on the one with Pedro—perhaps I can free him, and he can escape. I will endure any beating they inflict to save my son!* At that moment, he saw the men with Pedro reach the dock. Seeing others on the wharf, he shouted for them to stop the sailors, but he was still too far away for them to hear. No one seemed to notice as the two men ran toward the end of the dock where a small skiff waited, with several other sailors manning the oars. The man carrying Pedro tossed the sack to one of those waiting in the small boat, and, even at this distance, Machado could see them stuff it under some planks. The two abductors jumped in, and the others pushed away from the dock and began to row toward a three-mast ship several hundred yards out in the harbor.

The race to save Pedro was over, and Machado had lost.

Though he walked slowly to the dock, his mind raced. *If they seek a ransom, I will pay anything they ask.* Stumbling onto the dock's weathered, wooden planks, he walked methodically to the end. Those working there looked in amazement at the man—a man of stature and gentility most of them knew—with his shirt soaked with blood, his wrist dangling limply at his side, and his feet leaving bloody footprints with every step. Torment pervaded his sweaty, dirt-caked face. Machado sat down at the very spot where the small boat had been moored and watched that boat arrive at the ship far off shore. As some of the men climbed netting onto the ship, a package was lifted up toward the deck.

That was the very last the desperate Machado would ever see

of his son, and deep inside he knew it. There would be no demand for ransom. His son was gone—forever. He held his head
in his hands and began to cry, his tears making rivulets through
the dirt on his cheeks and falling like raindrops into the ocean, to
be washed away with the undulate waves.

When he looked up once more, the ship had already set sail.
The other men on the dock crowded around, asking Machado
what was wrong. He couldn't hear them. He was oblivious to anything except the beating and breaking of his own heart.

3.

KIDNAPPED BY PIRATES

THE MOMENT THE BURLAP SACK dropped over little Pedro's head, his entire world literally turned dark and upside down, for, in that instant, the man who had approached him with the candy had turned from ally to menace. As if darkness wasn't enough, Pedro felt himself being picked up and flung over the man's shoulder, knocking the wind out of him. Just as suddenly, he felt himself being spun around. Apparently, the man was running, because Pedro could feel his ribs bouncing up and down, rising then dropping onto the man's shoulder as he bounded down the hill. The force was so intense that it took Pedro several moments to catch his breath. As loud as he could, he began to call for his papa to come and help him, and a few times he thought he heard his papa yelling that he was coming to rescue him. All the while, the pounding of his rib cage onto the man's shoulder never let up until the pain became excruciating.

After what seemed like an eternity, Pedro sensed something different. As he ran, the man's boots no longer pounded dirt but clacked against wood. *Where could they be taking me? Will they throw me into the water?* The thought terrified him, for he was not a strong swimmer.

Without warning, the man stopped running, and Pedro was airborne. In those fleeting seconds, he thought his life was about to end in a watery grave. He had already seen the bloated bodies of people who had drowned and washed ashore, and the thought of being like them was almost more than he could bear. Abruptly, he felt himself being snatched out of the air and slammed onto a hard surface, sending a shockwave of throbbing pain through every fiber of his small body. Now on his belly, he tried to rise, but something overhead prevented him from pushing to his knees. That barrier, which he would later recognize as the cross plank seating in a longboat, also kept Pedro from removing the sack that covered his head and shoulders. He could hear the men conversing, but even though they were speaking the same language he did, he couldn't quite understand what they were saying. Lying there wondering what would happen next, he sensed movement and heard oarsmen dipping their tools of the trade into the ocean. *I'm on a ship,* he thought with sudden comprehension.

Out of nowhere, two large hands wrenched him from the floor of the boat and in the process knocked his head on the seat plank. Pedro let out a scream and he heard someone say, "Easy there, the lad's not worth anything to us if he's dead." Once again, he was hoisted over someone's shoulder, but this time, instead of running, he seemed to be climbing. His ribs had taken a pounding, and the pain was becoming excruciating. Then he felt someone grab him under his armpits, lifting him the final distance to the deck of a much larger boat than the one that had brought him there. His shoes caught on a railing, causing one to slide halfway off his foot.

Oh, no! Pedro thought. *I can't lose my shoes. I love my shoes. What will Papa and Mama think if I lose my shoes?* As if salvaging the last vestige of home, he concentrated all of his strength into scrunching his toes to prevent losing the shoe adorned with the F-initialed buckle.

His efforts proved fruitless as someone stood the boy upright with enough force to push his shoe back solidly onto his foot. When the burlap sack was removed from his head, he felt a gust of salty sea air on his face. Looking westward into the sinking sun, he instinctively brought his hand up to shield his eyes, which, having been in total darkness for several minutes, hurt from the combined glare of sunshine and water.

When his eyes had adjusted, Pedro saw that he was surrounded by a large group of men, too many for him to count, all resembling the sailor who had enticed him and his sister with candy. Nearly every one wore tattered clothes and bandanas on their heads and had scruffy beards. Each was armed with guns and daggers or swords. *They look like pirates,* Pedro thought. One man in particular stood out, for he had no right leg. Instead, a cylindrical piece of wood protruded from his knee down, making a distinct thumping sound on the wood deck with each step he took toward Pedro.

"Alright, boy," the man said, "down you go below deck. We have a real nice place for you to stay." The sneer on the man's face

31

told Pedro the opposite. He spun Pedro around by the shoulders and hurried him toward a slightly raised area of the deck with a doorway half as tall as a fully-grown man.

Despite how quickly the man pushed him forward, Pedro was still able to get a glimpse around the schooner. She had two large sails suspended from spars reaching from the top of the huge masts and extending toward the back of the ship. Another mast stood at the bow of the ship. Rows of cannon flanked both sides, at least seven each, as well as he could count. The wood all around was old and weathered, and ropes were everywhere, neatly wound in concentric circles or tightly secured on the rails of the ship. Typical of schooners of the day, the ship had a very shallow draft, so she could be pulled as far inland as possible for a short longboat to make quick exchanges to and from shore.

The man behind Pedro barely had a grip on the boy. But as his eyes wandered toward the stern, past the raised structure that led to a second deck with a large wheel, little Pedro could see his island home fading in the distance. For a brief moment, pushing the fear of drowning to the recesses of his mind, he considered diving overboard. *What would be worse, drowning or dying at the hands of these pirates?* Jumping into the water was certain death. If he remained aboard this ship, he might at least have a chance, if only a small one, to live, he reasoned, not exactly sure where these ideas were coming from.

Pushing those thoughts from his mind, Pedro watched as a door beneath the stairs that led to the second deck suddenly flew open. From it emerged a man different from any of the crew Pedro had seen. This man seemed larger than the others, wearing a big blue coat that made his shoulders look broader than those of

32

the other pirates. He wore pants without patches and boots that rose over his calves almost to his knees. Two flintlock pistols were in his wide black belt, and a large sword hung from a leather sash in a most ornate scabbard.

As he approached Pedro, everything in this man's bearing brimmed with authority. *He must be a soldier*, Pedro guessed, recalling vague images of those he had seen as a youngster before they had moved to the island. But this was no member of the military. He was a pirate, and Pedro knew he was not to be trifled with.

As the man strode across the deck, he never once took his eyes off Pedro. If someone got in his way, he pushed them aside. If something was in his path, he kicked it away. In only a few moments, the fierce-looking man stood directly in front of the lad, staring down at him with coal black eyes and vile contempt. *Maybe*, Pedro gulped, *drowning would have been a better fate.* Taking his eyes off Pedro for the first time, the man glanced at the one-legged sailor behind him. "So this is the so-called treasure that you say is worth so much to us, the reason we've given up raiding other ships and islands?"

"Yes, Captain," the sailor replied, "he's the one I was told we should kidnap and take to Brazil. My contact in Lisbon was quite clear, and he's already paid us half a king's ransom to do his bidding. We'll get the rest of the gold when we deliver this package to our fellow Portuguese in the New World. Of course, it would have been better if we had grabbed up the girl, too, but the boy was always the real prize."

"So be it, then," the captain grunted. "But mind you this— even though I appointed you quartermaster, I'll not be sent on a fool's journey. We could have just kept the first payment and been about our business, so if we are to collect the rest, it'll be on your head to make sure we get 'im there alive. If we don't, or if they don't pay the rest of the gold, I'll have your head on the bowsprit for all to see."

"Yes, sir. I'll see to it."

As the captain walked past them, the quartermaster spun Pedro around again and bent down so that they were face-to-face, nose-to-nose. Pedro tilted his head slightly away from his foul-smelling breath. "Listen here, boy, for I'll only be sayin' this once," one-leg said. "For the life of me, I don't know why you're worth your weight in gold. In fact, I'll be thinkin' you might even be worth more than your weight. But this'll be no journey of pleasure. You'll do as you're told and make no fuss, or I'll make your life miserable. Do ya hear me, boy?"

Pedro, too scared and confused to respond, shivered in silence.

"Do ya hear me?" The last words were accompanied with spittle that struck Pedro on the cheek and forehead.

Pedro mumbled a weak, "Yes, sir."

"Then you'll be gettin' below, and you'll be good an' quiet."

With that, Pedro Francisco was shoved toward shallow stairs leading below deck. Forced into darkness again, he could barely see and began to stumble. He reached out to steady himself but caught his hand on one of the old beams. He yanked his hand away, full of splinters. Though, for the little boy, that was just a twinge compared to a day already punctured with pain. The quartermaster grabbed Pedro around the waist to steady him. "Wouldn't do to havin' you break your neck before we reach your final destination. Mind your step now."

In the bowel of the ship, Pedro's eyes began to focus again. This was obviously a cargo hold. Wooden crates of all sizes had been stacked along the sides of the hull. Pedro had no trouble standing, but the quartermaster had to stoop as he ushered his prisoner around a corner, revealing a pen outlined with bars. The sight of the pen was frightening enough, but the stench was overpowering, making the pirate's breath, so malodorous only a few moments earlier, seem like the sweetest island flower. The disgusting odor made the little boy gag instantly, causing him to vomit all over his favorite shoes.

"Aw, now look what you've gone and done. Never mind. You'll get used to the smell after a little while. Every one of our other guests has." With that, the quartermaster erupted into sinister laughter, opened the door to the pen, and shoved little Pedro inside. Then, spinning around on his good leg, he made his way back up the stairs. The boy listened with some relief to the cadence of the step-thump-step-thump going across the upper deck. Looking around at his surroundings, he suddenly realized he was alone, with the exception of a few mice that had made their home down there. Pedro's stomach pitched and rolled with the ship. His constant heaving finally turned dry. The darkness was as thick as the stench, but narrow streams of light gleamed through the cracks in the planks above his pen. The cage, about the same dimensions as his bed at home, was perhaps big enough for a fully-grown tiger. The wooden bottom of it was stained with urine and blood of others who had been imprisoned before him. Two small buckets had been placed in one corner. One was filled with water; the other was empty. Pedro scooped out some water with his hand, but immediately spit out the stagnant liquid. Exhausted, he curled up in the slimy straw left as bedding and cried himself to sleep, reciting over and over the prayer his mother had taught him. During the night, the sound of waves lapping against the side of the ship became his monotonous companion.

Too soon, Pedro was awakened by those distinct footsteps coming down the stairs again. His eyes, now accustomed to the dark, saw the quartermaster round the corner. Pedro pressed himself into the farthest crook of his cage.

"Now, now, boy," the pirate said, "not to be afraid. After all, you heard the cap'n. My survival depends on your survival. Here. Look what I brung for ya." The pirate held out his hand, and Pedro could see a small orange. "You'll be eatin' this or you'll be gettin' scurvy, and that wouldn't do. That wouldn't do at-all. I s'pose you found your water bucket. The other bucket is for doin' your business. I'll come and fetch it ev'ry couple days. Now, eat the orange. There's a good boy."

As the days wore on, this scene repeated itself over and over. On some days, the quartermaster presented Pedro with a bit of stale bread or some rancid meat that was frequently infested with maggots. Initially, Pedro would eat the meat and immediately throw up, but eventually his seasickness abated and the taste of maggots became tolerable.

Without the benefit of full sun to gauge the days, Pedro lost track of time. One night did come, however, when the quartermaster not only offered Pedro some food but the opportunity to spend some time on deck as well. Reaching the top of the stairs, the weak boy took a deep breath. He welcomed the fresh sea air into his lungs, which had experienced only stench for days. *Or was it longer?* He wondered. A hand in his back prodded him forward. Making his way out onto the deck, he looked up at a full moon playing its light along the soft swells of ocean as far as the eye could see, like a never-ending silver ribbon. Even the stars looked brighter than ever. Each one seemed to twinkle with a benevolence that belied Pedro's true situation. Regardless, he was thankful to finally be outside as he continued taking deep, uncontaminated breaths and felt the light zephyr on his face.

Near the stairs that led to the upper level deck was a small barrel latched to the side of the ship. The quartermaster motioned Pedro to sit there. The one-legged man, seeming genuinely kind toward the captive, sat on the third step from the bottom. "I know you're scared, boy. I know you're scared. I s'pose I'd be scared, too, if I was in your shoes." His words caused Pedro to look down at his silver buckles glint in the moonlight. "I don't know why, boy," the quartermaster continued, "but your papa must have made some bad enemies back in Portugal. We're gettin' paid a lot of gold to deliver you to Brazil. But I'm sure you'll be well-treated. Just doesn't make sense to pay all that much to do you harm, so...." After a long pause, he said, "Best be gettin' you back below deck, now. Wouldn't do for the captain to see you out here."

Days turned into weeks, and Pedro and the quartermaster developed a camaraderie of sorts, each relying on the other for his very life. Pedro was getting better food than he did initially, along with more frequent visits above deck.

One day, water started to drip through the cracks above Pedro's pen. The ship began to pitch and yaw, and Pedro's stomach, which had become accustomed to life at sea, began to churn as it had when he was first brought on board. As night approached, he could see flashes of lightning through the planks and could hear the wind howling above. He tried to stand but whenever he did, he was thrown down on the floor of his pen, so he gave up trying. Unknown to all aboard the ship, they were in the middle of one of the most powerful hurricanes the Atlantic Ocean had ever experienced, a storm born as a tropical wave just off the coast of Africa but turning into a monster storm as she made her way across warm ocean waters. There were times when the storm seemed to have ended, only to return a little while later in all its fury. Pedro longed for a visit from the quartermaster, but he never came. Finally, the storm seemed to have subsided, and all was calm again. Still, the boy's only human contact since being brought down to the bowel of the ship never arrived with any food or company.

That night Pedro could hear loud voices above him on deck. It sounded like a lot of arguing, and then a shot rang out. He tried to sleep but couldn't stop wondering what had happened and why his friend had not come to visit and bring him food. In fact, two whole days went by with nobody coming down the stairs to check on the little boy.

On the third day since the storm began, the first light of dawn filled the cracks above Pedro's pen. Suddenly, he heard the door from the deck open. *At last the one-legged man is coming to check on me*, he thought with relief. But as he listened to the steps, he could tell the footfalls were not those of his regular visitor. These steps were even. Pedro focused his eyes on the corner just as another pirate came into view.

"Get up, you brat," the man said. "Get up! Get up! Get up, now!"

Pedro had never known the name of the quartermaster, so he

asked, "Where is the one-leg man?"

"You'll not be worryin' about him," the pirate shot back. "You'd be best worryin' about yourself, you little curse." With that, the pirate opened the door, reached in, and snatched little Pedro by the front of his shirt. Then, he pulled the boy from his pen and marched him up the stairs, jabbing him in the back each step of the way. As they reached the doorway leading out to the deck, Pedro again clamped his hands over his eyes. He hadn't seen daylight in weeks, but a low fog had settled over the water, weakening its intensity and allowing his eyes to adjust quickly. Another sharp shove in the back caused him to stumble and fall face down on the deck, bloodying his nose. As he rolled over and looked up, the lad saw the body of the quartermaster hanging limply from a cross beam of one of the masts. On the front of his shirt was a large red stain, and sea gulls were pecking desperately at his body.

Without warning, Pedro felt himself being lifted up and held out over the rail where another pirate grabbed him and took him into the longboat below. Hoping that he was going back home, the little captive looked out across the water to see if he recognized his surroundings, but, because of the dense fog, he couldn't really make out the shore.

Fear began to set in and he yelled, "Papa! Papa!"

The pirate closest to Pedro grabbed him and covered his mouth with his filthy hands. "Say another word, and I'll slit your throat where you sit. God above must surely hate you, or us, to have sent that storm, but we'll be takin' no more chances. You already cost a good man his life. You'll not be takin' any others. If it was up to me, we'd feed you to the fish, but to his last breath, the quartermaster begged for your life, so do as you will with it and good riddance."

The little boat soon came within the sight of land, but Pedro recognized nothing. This was certainly not the port near his home or any other part of the island that Pedro could remember. His little heart sank.

The longboat quickly docked at the far end of a wharf in the misty morning. There was almost no activity. Quietly, one of the pirates directed Pedro to a small, makeshift ladder, and, as he clambered up onto the pier, the longboat turned around and disappeared into the haze.

4.

ALONE AND ABANDONED

As THE RIPPLED WAKE of the longboat faded away, Pedro Francisco began to fully comprehend what had happened. Only a few weeks ago, he had been a happy youngster with a warm and wonderful family. He had been whisked away from that idyllic life only to be tossed into what he could only describe as a seagoing dungeon. At least the one-legged man had befriended him, but now that man was dead, and here he sat on a dock in a strange place. Pedro looked down at the water and noticed a school of fish swimming freely in their never-ending hunt for food. At first, the little boy was too stunned to do anything but stare at the water, but, as he pondered his idyllic past and his uncertain future, tears began to well up in his eyes and stream softly down his face. Just as his father's tears had mixed with the rolling waves at the end of the dock in Porto Judeu, Pedro's did so here at the end of the wharf at City Point, Virginia. The culmination of recent events was too much for a five-year-old boy to deal with. His tears soon turned to sobs and then racking wails so strong his body trembled with each breath. He had never felt more alone in his life. He lay down on the dock, its old wood weathered to various shades of gray. Turning to one side, he pulled his knees up to his chin and buried his face in his hands. He had no way of knowing, but today was June 23, 1765.

Further up the wooden walk, longshoremen were just arriving for their early morning workday. The noise they heard at the end of the dock sounded like a wounded animal in the throes of death, and they each looked curiously at the small brown shape resting where the wharf ended and the James River began. Together, they set off toward Pedro, running the length of the wharf, their heavy boots raising a hollow racket as they pounded along the wooden planks. Even old Caleb, the dock's night watchman, who had just settled down in his cot to sleep, joined the procession. The first men to arrive just stood there staring in amazement at the boy still crying uncontrollably. All shared similar thoughts. *Where has he come from, and how long has he been here? A bit disheveled, but his clothes look finely made. His skin is dark. Too light to be African, though.* They also took in his eyes and hair, each as pitch black as the night itself.

Pedro looked up meekly at the sea of faces surrounding him. The little boy's mind was racing. *Who are they?* He thought. *Why are they staring at me? They don't look like pirates, but what will they do to me? What happened to their skin?*

Caleb, who thought of himself more as a dock master than a watchman, elbowed his way through the crowd of men to assume his self-appointed authority.

"Well, well, well, what have we here?" Caleb intoned. "A lost little boy? What's your name, son?"

Pedro knew the man was speaking to him, but it only sounded like gibberish. These were words he had never heard before, and that frightened him even more. The man's dress was different from the others, too. He had on dirty white pants that buckled below his knee, a white blouse and red waistcoat over which was a dark blue, long coat with gold trim around its edges. Most prominently, he wore a tri-cornered hat. Pedro had seen one of these before, atop the pirate captain's head.

Still not entirely sure of this unfamiliar crowd and their intentions, Pedro pushed himself closer to the edge of the dock. So far, he would have nearly fallen into the water had one of the men not grabbed him by the arm.

"Now, now," Caleb said in a gravelly voice. "There's nothing to be afraid of here."

Sensing that these men meant him no harm, Pedro's trembling began to subside a little. Still, he was wary. At that moment, another man appeared, wearing not work clothes but a suit that looked like one his father might wear. People stood aside to allow him access to what had captured their attention. Even Caleb snapped around upon the man's arrival.

"Mr. Durrell. What would you be doin' here so early in the day?" Caleb asked.

James Durrell, a noted merchant from Petersburg, surveyed the situation and looked down at Pedro. "I'm just here to check on a shipment of goods, and I couldn't help but notice all the commotion down here. What's going on?"

"Seems that we've come across a lost lad," Caleb replied. "Don't know who he is. Don't know where he came from. He was just sittin' here cryin' when the sun came up. I've been tryin' to talk to him, but so far he hasn't said a word. Maybe he's deaf and dumb."

"Well," said Durrell. "Let me try to make some sense of it." Durrell squatted low so that he could get a closer look at the youngster who looked so confused and afraid. "Now, then, laddie, tell me your name," Durrell inquired. In an instant, Pedro opened his mouth launched into a foreign language such as the men on the dock had never heard before. Durrell looked around at all the men who had gathered.

"Well, he's not deaf. Does anybody understand what he's saying?"

"Sounds a bit like Spanish," a voice from the back of the crowd said. "But I can't rightly say for sure."

Durrell turned his attention back to Pedro, reaching his hand out to the little boy and pulling him to his feet as he did. "Let's have a good look at you," Durrell said. "You look to be about seven or eight years old. Your clothes are filthy, but I can tell they were tailored from rich fabric—European, if my merchant's eye is correct." As a narrow stream of sun broke through the clouds, Durrell caught sight of the buckles on Pedro's shoes, glinting in the light. On the right shoe was the letter "P" and on the left shoe the letter "F." A thought occurred to Durrell. Pointing to the shoes, he asked the boy, "Is that part of your name? Are your initials P and F?"

"Pedro! Pedro Francisco!" the little boy shouted. He puffed his chest out, proud that he was finally communicating with these men. "Pedro Francisco," he repeated.

"Ah. Now we're getting somewhere," said Durrell. "Though I daresay that may be the most we get from him for awhile." Durrell signaled Caleb to follow him off to one side, and a couple of the other men joined the conversation, while the rest remained crowded around Pedro. "Does anybody know where he comes from, how he got here?" asked Durrell.

"No," Caleb piped up. "We just all heard this awful crying— wailin', it was—comin' from here. Don't nobody know how he got here."

"Well, the question now is what do we do with him?"

"I s'pose he kin stay with me in my wharf shack for the time bein', though I can't say as I have any idea of what to do with him," Caleb offered.

"I guess that'll do for now, but there are strict laws about runaways and waifs," Durrell responded. "If someone doesn't come to claim him in a couple of days, we'll have to inform the folks over at the poor house to come and get him."

The men turned their attention back to Pedro, and Caleb reached out to grab him by the arm. Immediately, Pedro drew away. Durrell knelt down again looking the little boy square in the eye. "It's all right. Old Caleb here won't hurt you. Nobody here wants to hurt you, Pedro. By the way, Pedro isn't a proper name here in the New World. From now on, we'll call you Peter. Peter Francisco." Durrell looked to see if the boy understood. Then he jabbed himself in the chest with his thumb. "James Durrell. James Durrell," he repeated. Then, he pointed his index finger at Pedro. "Peter Francisco. You are Peter Francisco."

Comprehension crept into the little boy's eyes. He poked his thumb to his own chest and mimicked, "Peter Francisco!"

Rather than grab Peter's arm, Caleb reached out his hand. It was rough, scarred, and calloused, and his fingers were gnarled from years of hard work on all sorts of jetties and seaports. That gesture proffered kindness that Peter gratefully accepted. He slid his much smaller hand into that of the night watchman while the dock crew parted, creating a path through which Caleb and the boy could walk back to the old man's shack.

Durrell knew what he had to do next for the boy called Peter, who looked as if he hadn't had a decent meal in weeks. He strode from the dock, turned left down the adjoining street and walked directly to the home of Edna Watkins.

Edna Watkins was well known in this area. Her husband was a tanner who made some of the finest leather goods in the territory. In fact, Durrell had bought some of his offerings from his own store. But food, not leather, was the order of the day, and Edna Watkins was recognized as one of the best cooks anywhere. Durrell walked up the three steps and onto a small, well-kept porch. He approached the whitewashed front door and knocked precisely four times.

"Why, Mister Durrell. What a fine surprise," said Edna as she opened the door. "But my husband's not here. You'll find him at the tannery."

"I've not come to see Albert," said Durrell. "It's you I'll be having business with today."

Edna came onto the porch, for inviting a married man into her home when her husband wasn't there would have been frowned upon by the neighbors.

Durrell began to relate what had taken place at the wharf

earlier.

"The youngster looks to be famished, and I can't really trust old Caleb to take care of his needs. Would you mind getting together some real home-cooked food for the lad and taking it down to the dock?"

"Why, of course, I will, of course. I'll see to it right away."

Durrell reached into his purse and produced eight shillings, coins of the realm, and offered them to Edna.

"Oh, no, Mister Durrell," Edna said. "There's no need for that."

"Edna," said Durrell, "I know how tough times are. Between all these new taxes and crop failures in the colony, things are tough for everybody. But I feel responsible for the boy, and I'll be thanking you to do this fine thing."

As Durrell turned to leave, Edna Watkins touched his arm. "God will be blessing you, sir."

A couple of hours later, Edna Watkins, laden with all sorts of food for the youngster, now known as Peter Francisco, headed toward the dock. She had roasted chicken, green beans, and some of the most delectable biscuits known to man. For dessert, she brought a warm apple pie. She arrived at Caleb's little shack and knocked on the doorframe, since the door was nothing more than an old blanket tacked across the top. Caleb pushed aside the makeshift door. Durrell had informed him of the arrangement, and he was expecting Edna's arrival.

"Oooooh, that smells good," he said, lifting the cloth Edna had used to cover the food and to keep it warm. Edna slapped his hand.

"That's for the boy, not for you, although from the looks of ya, you could use a decent meal, too. Whatever the boy doesn't eat, you can have the rest." Looking past Caleb, Edna rested her eyes upon the most pitiful looking youngster she had ever seen.

"Oh, you poor thing," she said as she crossed the few steps to the cot where Peter was sitting. "Everything is going to be alright by and by, you just wait and see." She offered Peter the food, and he tore into it ravenously. Caleb was left to wonder if there would be anything left for him, but Peter's stomach could hold only so much, and before long he stopped eating.

Edna reached over and ran her fingers through Peter's dirty, uncombed hair, then looked at his filthy face and hands. "My, my, my, you are a sight," she said. "Come along with me, and let's get you cleaned up." She reached out a hand, and this time Peter gladly placed his in hers. Hers were a bit softer than Caleb's, though they were considerably harder than his mother's hands. Along the way, Edna chattered relentlessly even though Durrell had told her that the boy didn't speak a word of English. It didn't really matter. She figured the boy wouldn't be so frightened if he heard some kind words, even if he didn't understand them.

The kind woman took Peter directly into the kitchen and brought in a wooden tub from the back porch. In it, she poured some cold water and then set about boiling more water in a big kettle over the fireplace. After she combined the hot water with the cold, she gently removed Peter's clothes, helped him into the tub, and began to scrub away weeks' worth of grime from his body. Peter, like most boys his age, wasn't especially fond of bathing, but this was more than that. This was someone showing him true kindness, and he was grateful for that. As she rubbed the washcloth over his arms, Edna noticed how well-defined his muscles were for a boy his age. "Goodness, aren't you going to be the strong one when you grow up. Yes sir, you will." After toweling Peter off, she went to a chest and found some clothes for him to wear. "These belonged to my precious departed son," she said. "He was only ten when the pox took him away, but I think they'll fit you just fine."

Peter didn't mind the new clothes. In fact, he was happy to get out of the ones he had been wearing. As soon as the dressing was complete, he jumped to put his shoes on. He wasn't about to give up his good shoes. Not now. Not ever. From that same chest, Edna dug out an old stuffed animal, although what it was supposed to be Peter could not imagine. Regardless, when she offered it to him, he plucked it out of her hands and hugged it close to his chest.

"My son always called this Pookie," Edna said.

Peter looked at the stuffed toy. *"Boneca de trapo,"* he declared. *"Boneca de trapo."* In English, that meant rag doll.

Later that afternoon, Edna Watkins delivered Peter back to the dock and to Caleb's shack. The tired, clean, and satisfied boy walked in, crossed the few steps to the cot, and lay down, still clutching his new best friend. Before Edna had the chance to say anything, he was asleep. She touched his cheek with the back of her hand. "Sleep well, young Peter Francisco, sleep well," she said.

For several days, the same scene was repeated. Edna showed up with some of the best food Peter had ever eaten, provoking and gaining his appetite. Poor Caleb had barely enough leftovers to feed a bird. Each day, she and the boy would go back to the Watkins' house. Some days, Edna would give Peter another bath, which was no different than back home. *Why did grown-ups insist that I take so many baths?* Peter wondered. On other days, Edna just sat in the kitchen and talked to him. He still didn't understand all that she had to say, but he was beginning to pick up some words here and there, words like food and water and sleep.

One early morning, Peter heard someone rapping on Caleb's doorframe. It was too early for Edna—Peter knew her name now—to arrive. Caleb, who had just settled down to sleep, rose and pulled the blanket door aside. There stood James Durrell.

"Caleb," he said, "your duties are over. I'll be taking young Peter with me."

"But why?" Caleb asked. In the back of his mind, the watchman knew there would be no more home-cooked meals once Peter left. "Ain't I been doin' a good job lookin' after the boy?"

"It's not that," said Durrell. "I've been talking with the authorities, and we all think it would be best for Peter to go to the Prince George County Poor House. They have an orphanage there, and Peter can play with kids and learn our ways and customs. Besides, this is no place for a boy his age to be brought up. You know that as well as I do."

"Well, of course. You know best, sir," said Caleb. "I was gettin' used to havin' the lad around, but you know best." He spent a few moments gathering up Peter's belongings, including the fine clothes he was wearing when he was kidnapped, along with a number of pants and shirts Edna Watkins had donated. And, of course, he couldn't forget boneca de trapo, even though Caleb couldn't figure out what it was supposed to be either.

Durrell took charge of Peter and led him off the wharf and straight up a hill toward one of the largest buildings Peter had ever seen, other than the family castle they lived in before moving to the island. Every once in a while, he looked up at James Durrell with a perplexed look on his face.

"I know it's not been easy, son," said Durrell, "but you're gonna like it here. They'll take real good care of you, and you'll have other kids to play with and everything. They'll even teach you to read and write. There's nothing to worry about. One day, who knows? Someone might just come along and claim you."

The building was two stories tall, all white, with a clapboard-like siding. To Peter, it seemed endless, and he thought for sure he'd get lost and never be able to find his way out again. From behind the house, Peter could hear the sounds of children playing and having fun. As they reached the steps leading up to the porch, much larger than the one at the Watkins' house, a woman opened the door to greet Durrell and young Peter.

"Peter, this is Miss Smyth, Miss Mary Smyth," Durrell said. "Miss Mary, this is Peter Francisco."

Peter looked up at the lady with wide eyes. She looked younger than Edna Watkins. *Would she be as kind?* Peter wondered.

"How do you do?" Miss Mary said.

"He doesn't speak much English," Durrell broke in. "In fact, we still haven't figured out what he does speak."

"That's all right," Miss Mary responded. "We'll take real good care of him, and we'll have him speaking the King's English in no time."

Durrell then patted Peter on the head, thanked Miss Mary for taking over his care, turned and walked back down the hill toward the wharf.

Miss Mary Smyth took Peter by the hand, a hand almost as soft as his mother's. She led him to a large room occupied with beds like Peter had never seen. They were stacked one on top of another and clearly made of scrap lumber. Peter counted four of these contraptions, making sleep space for eight. Other than that, and throughout the rest of the house for that matter, the furnishings were a mix of hodgepodge donations from the community. Mary showed the lad to a bed and told him to put his belongings in a small trunk at the foot of it. Peter pushed at the mattress. *It's so soft! Are those feathers inside? This is much better than the cot at the wharf! And there's a pillow, too!* It was so nice that, for once, Peter could hardly wait to go to bed, although there was still plenty of daylight left. Miss Mary signaled for him to follow her as she led him out the back door to the back yard, where more than a dozen children of all ages and sizes played. About half of them were boys. Peter had obviously received one of the last available beds.

"Boys and girls," Miss Mary spoke loudly to be heard. "I want you all to come here." As the children gathered around, she introduced Peter. "Peter doesn't speak much English yet, so you'll all have to be patient with him and help him for a while. Now everybody go back to playing, and take Peter with you." As the children ran back to playing their games, Miss Mary gently coaxed Peter in the same direction, then went back into the house. Once the door had closed, three of the boys came over to Peter.

"So. Peter Francisco, eh?" one of the boys said. "Well, let me tell you something. I run things around here. I've been here the longest, and I run things."

Peter looked at the boy quizzically. The boy was a good three or four inches taller than he was.

"Do you understand me!" the boy shouted. "I'm the boss around here!"

"Didn't you hear Miss Mary?" one of the other boys interrupted. "He doesn't understand English."

"Well, maybe he'll understand this," the first boy said as he took a glance at Peter's shoe buckles. Then he began to kick dirt all over Peter's shoes. Even though the boy was bigger than Peter and probably a few years older, Peter didn't hesitate. He launched himself at his mocker and knocked him flat on his back. Peter, not really knowing how to fight, jumped on top of him and pinned the boy to the ground. Although the boy from the Azores had arrived on these shores malnourished, even emaciated, the sustenance that he had been provided since then had restored his natural vitality and strength.

Just then the back door to the house flew open and out stomped Miss Mary. She rushed over to where Peter was holding the other boy down. "What in the world is going on here?" she yelled. "Who started this?"

"He did," accused the boy underneath Peter.

"No, he didn't," said one of the girls in a small voice. "I saw the whole thing, and Johnny was kicking dirt on the new boy's shoes."

"Peter, get off Johnny," Miss Mary said.

Peter looked around at Miss Mary. He had understood his name, his new name, but he hadn't comprehended the rest. Realizing this, Miss Mary reached down and touched Peter on the shoulder and motioned him to get up. He did.

"Johnny O'Neal, didn't you hear what I said? Didn't I tell you to be nice to Peter? Now shake hands and make friends," she demanded. Reluctantly, Johnny extended his hand. Peter didn't quite know what to make of the gesture, but he also held out his hand. Peace, at least for the time being, had been restored.

"Come now, children," Miss Mary said. "It's time for supper."

As the kids began to file into the house, one of the other boys came up from behind Peter and draped his arm around his shoulder. "Way to go. Way to put O'Neal in his rightful place."

That evening's meal was good, not as good as those from Edna Watkins, but still satisfying.

Weeks passed, and although Johnny O'Neal and Peter never became what anyone would call friends, the other children seemed to take the newcomer under their wings. They included him in their games and tried their best to help him with his lessons, although reading and writing were still too much for Peter to really grasp. However, he was picking up the language, and he could communicate in a rudimentary fashion.

A couple of months had gone by when a distinguished looking man came to visit. He told Miss Mary that he was looking for a young boy to come and work on his plantation, Hunting Tower. "I don't want an older boy," the man said. "I want a boy who can be trained in our ways. I don't want a boy who already thinks he knows it all. I have a certain way I want things done. A lad about eight or nine would do well."

Miss Mary lined the boys up in the back yard for the man to inspect. One by one, he grabbed the boys by the shoulders and gave them a shake to check their sturdiness. When he came to Peter, he guessed that the boy was seven or eight, but when he shook him, he could feel how solidly built he was.

"This one here," he said. "This one will do fine. I notice that his skin is really dark. Do you have any idea where he came from?"

"No, sir. They just said that they found him at the main dock in town. That's about all I know about young Peter," she said. "But he's one of the hardest working boys we've ever had at the orphanage. No chore seems to be too big for him."

"Well, that's what I'm looking for, and with his dark skin, he'll fit right in with my Negroes. My slave master will probably put him to work cleaning the horse stables or something like that. But, there are three thousand six hundred acres of chores, so we'll make sure that he stays busy. Will you take fifty pounds for him?"

"Well, first I think you should know that his name is Peter Francisco," Miss Mary said. "But he doesn't speak much English, and he can't read or write a lick."

"That's not a problem. He's got the makings of a fine farm hand, and that's exactly what I'm looking for. Again, I ask you, how much? Will you take fifty pounds for him?"

"With all due respect, that is how much I'm paid for the white children, but this boy has dark skin like a Negro, so I'm asking for two hundred pounds. That's the going rate for a slave his age," argued Miss Mary.

"Fine, fine, two hundred pounds it is. Get his things together. We've a bit of a journey before us, and I'd like to get home before dark."

As Miss Mary went in the house to put Peter's few belongings in a sack, the man bent down to look at him more closely. "My name is Judge Anthony Winston," the man said. Even though Miss Mary had told him the boy's name, he looked directly into Peter's black eyes and inquired, "What's yours?"

"Peter, Peter Francisco," the little boy said, and he stuck his chest out as proud as a peacock, as if somehow he knew a whole new chapter of his life was about to begin.

5.

SLAVERY NOT SCHOOL

WHEN MISS MARY HANDED Peter his sack of belongings, she looked at him and said, "I know this is all a bit unsettling, and I'm not even sure that you understand me all the time, but this is your lucky day. The judge here is a wise man, and he's a nice man, and he's well thought of hereabouts. Oh, my, I'm just going on and on. Just remember, life is going to be a lot better for you now. Now run along—best not to keep the good Judge Winston waiting."

As the two of them exited the front door, they saw Judge Winston standing next to a stylish landau. Peter's eyes grew wide. It was magnificent. With a luxurious deep brown color, it was so highly polished that sunlight danced off each delicate curve in the hand-hewn woodwork. Truly, it was a piece of art. A folded top could be raised in rainy weather, but because of the day's glorious sunshine, it was neatly compacted behind the passenger area, which had room for two or three people. Forward of the carriage body was a raised bench-seat, and there sat the blackest man Peter had ever seen. The sight of him startled Peter for just a moment, but that's when he saw the horses.

Two of them. Their beautiful coats looked as rich as creamed buttermilk, and beneath them peeked the pinkest skin, almost like that of Miss Mary. Pure, white manes and tails, long and lush, adorned both horses. One of them had distinctively beautiful eyes, a deep amber hue that matched the rich tone of the carriage. Both horses looked like they weighed two thousand pounds and stood so high, Peter could barely reach the harness. He couldn't take his eyes off these magnificent creatures; he was smitten.

Judge Winston followed Peter's gaze to the horses. "American Cream Drafts," he said, pointing at them, so Peter would understand. "Over here now, lad," said Judge Winston, motioning Peter into the carriage. "We've a ways to go before dark."

Peter, trailing his sack behind him, climbed in and settled into the farthest side of the seat. When Judge Winston sat down next to him, the leaf springs, crafted by Winston's own blacksmith and driver, sagged slightly, pushing back under his weight.

The black man in front tapped each of the horses on their rumps with a long stick and said, "Giddap." The horses made a perfect U-turn and began a slow trot down the path—the path to Hunting Tower Plantation and to a life that Peter Francisco could have never imagined.

Judge Winston began to make small talk, little of which Peter understood. Suddenly mindful of Peter's limited English, the judge fell silent. *Perhaps I've made a mistake.* He thought. *Perhaps it would be too hard to train this boy in the ways of the plantation. Then again, many of my slaves came to Hunting Tower with even less under-standing of spoken English, and they all worked out.*

Along the way, Peter marveled at the landscape. At home on the island, he had been accustomed to palm trees and tropical vegetation. But this was different. Their journey was taking them through forests of oak and maple, and with fall in the air, these trees were varying shades of red and gold. Scrub brush was plentiful, as though God had laid a green carpet on each side of the path on which they rode.

Even in the midst of this beauty, however, Peter couldn't stop glancing toward the front of the carriage where the two beautiful horses effortlessly pulled the three travelers to their final destination. As the sun faded away, Peter noticed that they had turned off the path and were now heading toward one of the most magnificent houses he had ever seen. Peeking out from among fuzzy trees and bright violet flowers, the beautiful two-story mansion reminded Peter of one of his sister's dollhouses. A large sitting porch welcomed guests with a wide set of steps that cascaded from the brick part of the house. *I could shoot marbles there,* Peter thought. On either side of the brick, two smaller wings were painted a deep yellow, like corn, with tall chimneys capping each end. There were so many windows, Peter couldn't even count them. Each was dressed neatly in black shutters. As they neared the main house, he could also see several out structures. Some resembled small houses, but most noticeably was an immense, white building with an angular roof and large doors that opened at the top of a loft.

Stepping down first, Judge Winston offered to help Peter, but the youngster literally leaped from the carriage in a single bound, still gazing at the house. Winston smiled at him. "Independent little guy, aren't you? Then again, aren't we all?"

Suddenly, the front door burst open and out rushed daughter Martha, the littlest Winston, followed by Alice, Anthony, Jr., and the eldest Sarah.

"Father, Father," Martha squealed. "What did you bring me for my birthday?"

"Now just hold up there, little lady," Judge Winston responded. "Your birthday isn't until tomorrow and if I ruin the surprise, your momma will have my hide." He did, however, motion toward the carriage boot just to let young Martha know that he hadn't forgotten.

Alice, the most timid of the three Winston girls, gave her father a hug and then simply stood to one side. By contrast, Anthony, Jr., the most gregarious, gave his father a bear hug and clapped him on the arm. "Father, we're so glad you're home."

Sarah, although not shy like Alice, was always the most reserved and rarely demonstrated much emotion. "I trust you had a good trip, Father," she said as she kissed his cheek.

"Yes, yes." the judge said. "It was a good trip, and I was able to negotiate a fine price for our hemp crop."

Even though Judge Winston had been gone for little more than four days, his family typically greeted him this way. Although most of the surrounding plantations produced tobacco as the chief crop, Judge Winston had wisely decided to diversify his 3,600-acre plantation, planting hemp on a substantial part of the acreage a few years ago. Now, while other plantation owners were weighed down by several years of failed tobacco crops, his hemp—commonly used to make rope, paper, and canvas—was filling in the gaps. It wasn't enough to entirely offset the poor tobacco yield, but the judge was never one to discuss the family finances, even with his wife Alice who had just appeared at the doorway.

"Anthony," she said. "It's good to have you home. I daresay the children missed you terribly. And what do we have here?" Her gaze had settled on Peter, who was taking in the whole scene from beside the carriage.

"This," said Judge Winston, "This is Peter Francisco. I just purchased him from the Prince George County Poor House so that we'll have plenty of help come harvest time."

"But, what is he?" she said, confused by Peter's appearance. "He's not white like us, but he isn't colored like our Negroes either. Is he a half-blood?"

"I don't think so, but nobody is really sure. They think he may come from Spain or Portugal or Italy or someplace like that." Judge Winston related Peter's story as well as he knew it from Mary Smyth. "I suppose the biggest problem is that he doesn't understand English real well yet, but we can get Petunia to help out with that."

The judge pulled Peter to stand in front of him, then pointed to each of his children, telling him their names as he went. Indicating his wife, he said, "Mrs. Winston, Mrs. Winston."

Immediately, Peter jabbed his thumb to his chest and said as proudly as he could, "Peter Francisco, Peter Francisco." Just as he did on the dock and at the orphanage, Peter stuck out his chest.

"Anthony," Mrs. Winston said in a quiet but agitated voice, "For the life of me, I don't know why you didn't get a white boy like we talked about. It would have been so much easier, and at least he would have spoken English. Sometimes I just don't—"

"He was by far the best of the lot," said Judge Winston, cutting her off, "and the decision has been made." Mrs. Winston was not too pleased to be admonished like that in front of the children, but family life in the New World was a true patriarchy, and the judge's word was always the last.

"Get Petunia out here," Judge Winston said. "I want her to meet Peter." As if on cue, Petunia, a house servant who lived in a lean-to off the back of the Winston home, was just coming around the corner.

"Oh, there you are," said the judge. "Come here, Petunia, there's someone I want you to meet." Peter's eyes almost popped out of his head. This little girl was even darker than the man who had driven the carriage.

"Petunia, this is Peter Francisco," said the judge. "You'll be in charge of him—except for his chores. The slave master will see to that. I want you to show him around and introduce him to the others; but most of all, I want you to help him to learn English so that he will speak it as well as you do and can understand what he is told. For the time being, he'll be staying with you in your quarters. I'll get a mattress brought in there in a little while."

Petunia eyed Peter up and down with some suspicion. She really didn't want to have to take this boy under her wing, and she surely didn't want to have to share her quarters with him. But Petunia had been a slave all her life. In fact, she had been born on this very plantation, and she knew that a slave didn't mouth the white master.

"Yes, suh, Mista' Judge," Petunia said. "I'll takes real good care of 'im." She immediately took Peter by the hand and guided him around to the back of the house. As they crossed the threshold into Petunia's small room, Peter glanced around. The furnishings were sparse, although Petunia had the luxury of a small bed that flanked one windowless wall. Alongside the bed was a little three-drawer, shaker-style chest that supported a metal washbasin.

As Peter surveyed his new home, he saw yet another black man, who entered carrying a straw mattress. He looked at Petunia, who motioned him to put it on the opposite wall under a window. Sam was her father and lived with Petunia's mother and two brothers in one of the outbuildings.

"Daddy," she said. "Mista' Judge say I gotta have this boy live with me, an' I don't like it, don't like it one bit."

"You knows the rules, Petunia," her father said. "What Mista' Judge say is what it will be. Ain't no use to gettin' all upset about it. Tha's just the way 'tis."

"I know, I know, but it ruins ev'rything. I always moves my bed by d' window on hot nights an' then ova' here on d' cold ones so's not to take a chill. Now what's I gonna do?"

"I 'spect we'll be havin' lots more cold nights than hot this time o' year, so don't you go worryin' on it so much," her father commented.

Sam took a look at Peter. "My, oh, my, my, my. You don't look like no Negro, but you don't look 'xactly white neitha'. What in d' world is you, boy?"

Understanding that he had been asked a question, Peter puffed himself up and jabbed his thumb to his chest. "Peter. Peter Francisco."

"He don't hardly speak no English, yet," Petunia said. "Tha's what Mista' Judge say I gotta do. I gots to teach him some English."

"Then you do as you been tol', girl. You do as you been tol'. You be only fourteen years, an' here you is sleepin' in d' main house, so you gots it pretty good if you be askin' me. Anyway, I gots t'git back to yo' momma now. She got supper waitin' on me."

Peter was trying his best to take in all this conversation, but the words didn't sound the same as when Miss Mary said them or Judge Winston. It had been a long day, and he was tired and hungry. *When will I get to eat?* He wondered.

Petunia looked at the boy and motioned him to put his sack of stuff at the foot of his bed. She may have to share her room with Peter, but she wasn't about to give up any of her dresser space.

Peter did as he was instructed, while Petunia resigned herself to this sudden disruption in her life, her demeanor softening. "You don't understan' much o' what we been sayin', do ya? Well, tha's alright. I'll be learnin' ya t' speak propa' in no time. Anyway, you hungry?"

Hungry was a word that Peter had come to know early on at the orphanage. "Hungry. Yes, hungry," he said.

"Well, I kin fix that. I'll jus' go into d' kitchen an' get us a couple o' plates. Livin' in d' main house means we gets t'eat what d'Winstons eat. You wait right here. I'll be back. Wait here."

Petunia then opened a door opposite the entrance to her bedroom. It led directly into the kitchen, where she spent each morning preparing the food for Mrs. Winston to cook: peeling potatoes, gathering eggs, measuring out biscuit flour, and setting out whatever meat they would be having that day. The slave girl never actually cooked; Mrs. Winston insisted that she and her daughters tend to that. When Petunia returned to her room with the food, Peter was already sound asleep. His straw mattress didn't compare to the feathered one at the orphanage, but it was comfortable enough for the tired little boy. Petunia set his plate next to his bed, and took her own plate to her bed, eating in silence. The sun was long gone now, and tomorrow was a big day.

The eastern sky was just coming to life when Petunia shook Peter awake. He hadn't even heard the insistent crowing of the plantation rooster, but sometime during the night he had awakened and eaten all his dinner. Today was a new day, one filled with promise on the plantation. Everyone usually took Sunday off, even the slaves. But today was also Martha Winston's birthday, and there would be a great celebration.

As the house servant, Petunia had plenty to do to prepare for the afternoon party, so she walked Peter down a short path past the big white building he had noticed on the way into Hunting Tower. He could hear horses whinnying from inside. He desperately wanted to go see them, but Petunia held tightly to his arm and guided him to a building that measured approximately fifteen square feet. Opening the door, Peter could see four straw beds on one side and four more on the other side. Some of these were stacked like the beds at the orphanage, but they were of better construction. Petunia's family lived in one side of the building and four male slaves occupied the other. The floor was packed dirt, but these were some of the best accommodations on the plantation. There was a fireplace on the back wall with pots and cooking utensils nearby.

Peter immediately recognized Petunia's father and smiled at

the man. Then Petunia introduced him to her mother Lizzy and her brothers Joseph, sixteen, and George, eighteen. They took to Peter immediately.

"I's s'posed t' show Peter 'round, but I gots to be fixin' d' stuff fo' Miss Martha's party. Will you do the showin' fo' me?" Petunia asked her brothers.

"Don't you worry 'bout nothin'," said George. "We'll shows d' place t' Peter." They spent the rest of the morning taking the boy around to the other slave quarters, the crop fields and vegetable garden, filled with rows of leafy plants bearing cherry-red tomatoes, thick cucumbers, long ears of corn, and wavy green beans now ripe for picking. The plot was well over an acre, and Peter had never seen so many vegetables in one place. Just beyond the garden was a vast pasture, enclosed by a split-rail fence and occupied by more than two dozen grazing cattle. Peter had not seen cattle like this before, and he thought them odd-looking creatures. Peter continued to shadow Joseph and George around the plantation, never once dropping his eyes in search of the one place he wanted to see most. At times, not minding his feet caused him to trip over small protuberances on the unfamiliar ground. As soon as Peter saw the white-painted wood, a wave of anticipation washed over him. *Yes! I'm finally going to see it up close!* He cheered to himself. When the whole building was within his sight, Peter saw the slave master, whom they called Alfred, emerge from one of the side doors.

"I was just coming to look for you," Alfred said, nodding toward Peter. "Mister Winston told me he had made a purchase at the orphanage."

Peter looked up at the man. He was not as tall as Judge Winston, but he seemed strong and there was something familiar about him. *He looks a lot like my father,* Peter thought.

"Come here to the barn tomorrow morning. I want you to report to Arthur. You met him yesterday. He drove the carriage, and he's in charge of the horses and everything else in the barn." Remarkably, Peter seemed to understand. There was something different about the way Alfred spoke compared to his charges, but Peter hardly noticed. *I will be working in my favorite spot on the plantation!* He thought, overjoyed. He nodded with enthusiasm. "Now you three run along," Alfred said. "Miss Martha's party will begin shortly. Joseph and George, I assume you'll be entertainin'."

"Oh, yes, suh," said George. "We'll be dancin' an' fiddlin' till d' cows come home."

"Fine, fine. Just be sure you save some of that energy for the harvest. We got a lot o' work to do tomorrow. Now run along."

The brothers took off in a trot, and Peter, with no place else to go, went into the barn to take a look around. Arthur was there cleaning some of his tools, and he looked up as Peter entered.

"Well, if it ain't my new helpa'. I'll be glad t' have a second set o' hands 'round here. Yes, indeed. These old bones are gettin' a bit too tired fo' muckin' out all these stalls." Although they spent several hours together on the carriage the previous day, both had yet to exchange a single word.

Arthur had been the first slave Judge Winston had bought and that made him the oldest, longest-serving slave at Hunting Tower. Arthur reckoned he was about seventy years old. Over those years, Arthur had served the judge as stable boy, carpenter, driver and blacksmith. Though not very tall, he was broad across the shoulders, with full biceps defined by his life's work. Because of his strength, he was also the judge's trusted bodyguard; although at his advanced age, it was unclear who was guarding whom.

At that moment, a loud bell rang, and Peter looked at the soft-spoken slave curiously.

"That there's the bell t' start Miss Martha's party," said Arthur. "Norm'ly, Sundays, we goes..." Arthur paused, looked around them quickly, then lowered his voice to a whisper, "we goes avisitin' with slaves from otha' parts. But today be special. We best be gettin' up to d'main house, now." As they left the barn and walked toward the main house, they caught a glimpse of all the other plantation slaves running in the same direction. Even though Peter had met most of them earlier in the day, it didn't prepare him for seeing them all together. There must have been at least twenty of them, and Peter was amazed how dark yet varied their skin tones were. Some were as dark as night, while others were lighter, like chocolate. *Where did they all come from?* Peter wondered.

As they reached the massive front porch of the main house, the Winston family members were seating themselves to watch the show that the slaves were about to present in Miss Martha's honor. One plucked a banjo; another drew a bow on a fiddle; and another beat with measured cadence on a homemade drum." The rhythm was intoxicating, sending many of the slaves to their feet in a raucous dance. Such a spectacle Peter had never seen. After a while, some of the female slaves set up a long table consisting of wooden planks and barrels brought out by the men. Before Peter knew it, tablecloths had been spread over the planks, and the ladies started a procession of food from behind the house. When they had finished, a veritable feast had been laid out on the makeshift table. Peter could not remember the last time he saw so much food: three turkeys, two hams, fried fish, varieties of vegetables, potatoes, and a large assortment of mouth-watering pastries. He could hardly contain himself.

Peter was about to rise from the bench where he and Arthur had been sitting when the old Negro touched his arm. "We waits 'til d' Winstons has their food. Then we gets t' eat. But this here birthday party sets me t' wonderin' jes' how ol' you is, Peter. Do you know?" Peter didn't understand the question, so Arthur tried again, using many different gestures. Finally he asked, "How many parties like 'is you had?"

Finally, it struck Peter what he was being asked. He didn't know the word, so he held up his hand displaying four fingers and his thumb.

"You is jes' five years ol'?" said Arthur astonished. "Good Laud, you is gonna t' be a big'n, you sho' is."

As was customary, after each of the Winston family members had filled their plates and retaken their seats, the slaves lined up to do the same. For them, this was an indulgence. Normally, the slaves would eat a breakfast of hominy, fried potatoes and onions, and some scrambled eggs. Dinner was usually a bit of beef or pork with biscuits, and supper generally consisted of a small amount of chicken plus biscuits and thin gravy. It was enough, but just barely. All things considered, the slaves at Hunting Tower deemed themselves fortunate, as they had heard about slaves at other plantations living in far worse conditions. Peter ate until his belly ached. He wanted to taste absolutely everything.

Well into the evening, Judge Winston produced a large box that had been hidden in the carriage boot just the day before.

He handed it to Martha, who tore at its ribbon and opened it to find inside a dress she had seen while on a shopping trip in town a few weeks ago. She had pointed it out to her father, and he had remembered how much she loved it.

"Mother, Father," she exclaimed. "How did you know this was the exact dress that I wanted? How did you know?"

"How indeed," responded Judge Winston, smiling at his daughter with a twinkle in his eye. "You haven't stopped talking about that dress since you saw it." As the birthday girl ran into the house to try it on, Judge Winston signaled that the party was over.

"Alright, everybody," said Alfred. "Back to your quarters with all of you. There's a lot to do tomorrow, and I don't want any laggards. Off with you now." Like clockwork, Alfred's charges removed the dishes and dismantled the table, after which the field slaves slowly made their way back to their respective shanties. Peter remained seated with Arthur, who hadn't made a move. Alfred may have held sway with the others, but Arthur, having been on the plantation the longest, held a special place in the judge's heart—at least as special as a slave could.

"Best you be gettin' along now, boy," Arthur said finally beginning to stir. "I've got lots t' show you t'morrow, so you bes' be awake; don't intend t' show you more than jes' one time."

Peter understood and made his way to the back of the house. Petunia hadn't arrived yet, so he crawled onto his mattress, pulled boneca de trapo to his chest and fell fast asleep.

The next morning, Petunia didn't have to rouse the lad. The rooster had positioned itself right under his window as the sun scaled the eastern sky. At the first crowing, Peter threw on his clothes and made his way to the barn. Along the way, he saw almost all of the slaves heading to the fields carrying pitchforks hoes and rakes and spades.

Breakfast would have to wait this day, because Peter's true desire was to see the horses, and Arthur as well. He liked Arthur. As he entered the barn, he saw the old man blowing air onto a fire over a large brick pit with a round tool Peter had never seen before. A few feet away sat a heavy anvil, black and shiny, sitting on the stub of a massive tree trunk. Next to the anvil was a bench with several large hammers and a mandrel that Peter would later learn was used for shaping the softened iron being taken from the pit, which Peter learned was called the forge. In his hand, Arthur held grabbers, a set of pincer-like tools. With these, the black-smith held a long, slender piece of iron from which he would make nails that day. He was just beginning to set the iron in the forge when he looked up and noticed Peter watching him.

"Ah, there you is, an' right on time," said Arthur. "We got lots t' do this fine day, so let's be gettin' you t' work." He crossed the barn and returned with a pitchfork. "Eva' work with one o' these?" he asked, holding out the implement. "This be a pitch-fork."

Peter took a step back. He had understood the word fork. He had learned it at the orphanage. But this thing—this massive thing must have been made for giants.

A smile came across old Arthur's face. "Come 'ere. Lemme show you." He led Peter over to a large pile of straw and drove the pitchfork deep into it. Then he lifted it, and a large quantity of hay followed. Arthur whirled about and took the straw over to one of the stables. Peter's eyes followed the direction of the large fork until they spotted what first drew him to the barn. The horses. He looked at them spellbound.

The two Cream Drafts that had pulled the carriage the day before were to one side, each occupying a single stall. Beside them, three larger stalls accommodated three Canadian horses. Originating in France, the breed had made its way to Quebec, and then slowly integrated onto farms in the colonies. They stood almost as tall as the Cream Drafts. *They're pretty*, Peter thought, *and fast, I bet, but nothing like the Drafts.*

The sound of George's voice over by the big doors startled Peter. "Mista' Alfred sent us t' fetch d' Canadians," said George. "We also gots t' get their hitchin' gear. I guess Mista' Alfred wants t' bring in a mess o' crops t'day, so we's s'posed t' hitch these horses t' d' carts."

Arthur pointed his thumb to a far wall. "There be d' hitchin' gear, an' here's d' horses. Don't be waitin' fer me t' do yo' jobs."

Joseph, who was with George, grabbed the horse collars and bridles while George dropped rope nooses over the necks of the animals. Together, the two of them led the horses out of the barn and on to a hard day's work. After the boys had gone, Arthur resumed showing Peter how he could use the pitchfork to clean out the stalls and replenish the hay. A short time later, just as Peter was getting the hang of his new duties, Alfred appeared.

"How's the young lad doin'?" he asked Arthur.

"He be doin' jes' fine, but he ain't as old as I think you think, Mista' Alfred."

"What do you mean?" challenged the slave master.

"Well, when we was sittin' at d' party yesterday, I asks him how ol' he is. It took a while t'get my point to 'im, but he finally tells me with his fingers that he be jes' five years ol'."

"Imagine that," said Alfred. "I figured him for at least eight or nine. Imagine that. Wait till I tell Judge Winston. Young Peter here is gonna be a big one."

"Tha's what I said." But the slave master didn't wait to hear the old Negro's last words. He was already heading for the main house to report what he had just learned. As he climbed the front porch steps, Judge Winston and his wife were coming out the front door. "Wait till you hear what I just found out about Peter," Alfred said.

"Oh, I just knew it," said Mrs. Winston, her voice plainly revealing her stress over this new information. "He's probably got some terrible disease, and he'll infect our crop of slaves. I just knew it."

"Hush, woman," rebuked the judge. "What is this about Peter?"

"You know how you said you thought he was seven or eight?"

"Yes."

"Well, he's not even close. That boy is only five years old."

"How on earth do you know that?"

"Arthur got it out of him."

"Well, I'll be."

"That's just great," Mrs. Winston interrupted. "He'll eat us out of house and home."

"Will you please hush," the judge snapped. "What he'll do is give us a whole lot more work than the average slave, that's what he'll do. Now go back inside and tend to... tend to something." Given the level of exasperation the judge exuded, Mrs. Winston knew when not to provoke her husband any further. She promptly retreated back inside the house.

Weeks passed. Trees shed the last leaves of the season, their bare branches all but inviting the blanket of winter. Because the days were getting shorter, the pace of work picked up in effort to beat the bitter cold.

Except for Sundays, each day was pretty much the same for Peter. He'd arise at the crack of dawn, chomp down a quick breakfast, and head off to the barn to do his chores. He'd work until dark, taking a few minutes for a midday meal, then trudge off to his room where Petunia would help him learn English as they ate supper together. He was a quick study. After eating and learning, Peter would curl up with boneca de trapo and, within moments, he was sound asleep, until the rooster's crow signaled the start of another day.

6.

FROM BOYHOOD
TO MANHOOD

Time moved forward at Hunting Tower Planta-
tion. Under Petunia's tutelage, Peter became fairly well-versed in
the Negroes' vernacular and could understand most of what he
heard. However, because he felt more akin to the Winston family,
he found himself naturally speaking more like them. He was also
growing in size. By his thirteenth year, he was well over six feet
tall and weighed more than two hundred pounds, mostly steeled
muscle. This brawn was largely the result of Arthur teaching him
the blacksmithing trade.

By now, Peter had his own living quarters, as Judge Winston
had deemed it inappropriate for him to continue sharing a room
with Petunia. Peter and Arthur had constructed another room adjacent to hers on the back of the house. Although it did not have
direct access into the main house, it was attached and reason-

ably well-furnished. An actual bed stood off the floor, and not one but two dressers held his clothing—most made by some of the plantation's female slaves—that he seemed to outgrow every few months. Occasionally, when Judge Winston went to town, he had Peter drive the carriage. While on these trips, the judge often took Peter into the general store for more durable clothing. In fact, one pair of his store-bought pants had been adorned with his salvaged silver-initialed buckles, since his feet had long since outgrown his favorite boyhood shoes. It was on one such trip when Peter first became personally acquainted with Susannah Anderson, whose family lived on a plantation near Hunting Tower.

It was a summer Saturday in 1773, and the judge wanted to go to town to make arrangements for shipping that year's hemp crop for processing in Richmond. He had asked Peter to drive the carriage, as Arthur was not feeling very well, which was happening more frequently. As Peter took his place on the driver's bench-seat in front of Judge Winston, the judge asked him to stop at the main house. At the last minute, he had decided to take his daughter Sarah on the trip as well. All of the Winston children relished the outing, and it had been a long time since Sarah had been off the plantation. As he approached the carriage with his pretty daughter, Peter jumped down from his seat, doffed his tri-cornered hat—a gift from the judge a few years earlier—and bent slowly at the waist.

"Good day, Miss Sarah. I trust that all is well with you today," the young man said.

Sarah Winston was astonished and even Judge Winston was taken aback. "Why, Peter," she said. "Where in the world did you learn such lovely manners?"

"Oh, I've been watching when we get guests here at the main house. I see and hear people do it all the time, so I thought it was the right thing to do. I didn't do anything wrong, did I?"

"Of course not, Peter," the judge cut in. "Of course not. You are learning our ways well."

Peter extended his hand to Sarah and assisted her into the carriage. Repositioning himself just behind the Creams, he gave them a soft-spoken "Giddyup," and the horses responded quickly, taking the happy party of three off to town.

Upon their arrival, the judge told Sarah to go across the street and pick out something nice for herself. He always did that when he took one of the children along, which was one of the reasons they always wanted to come. He told Peter to wait with the carriage and then entered an office right on the main street. Peter sat back on the hard rail that served as a backrest for the driver and was soon lost in thought.

His mind drifted to Arthur. *How many times had Arthur sat in this very position?* He wondered. Peter glanced down the street. *Is this how he sat waiting as the judge retrieved me that day eight years ago?* Peter slid his body forward on the bench-seat, tilted his head backward and closed his eyes, inhaling deeply. *It's so unlike Arthur to say he can't—or won't—do something. He must really be suffering. What if it isn't just temporary? Will the judge have to replace him? What would happen to Arthur?*

A commotion jostled Peter back to reality. A single-horse wagon was careening down the street in Peter's direction, and he immediately saw that no driver was aboard. People were running behind it yelling, "Stop that wagon! Stop that wagon!" Peter leaped from his seat with every intention of running out and grabbing the horse's collar.

Across the street, Susannah Anderson had just exited the same store in which Sarah was doing her shopping. Peter had seen Susannah several times when the Andersons had come to visit the Winstons, but they had never been formally introduced or even exchanged a word of conversation.

Susannah was carrying a heavy load of packages that blocked her view of the absconding wagon. Though she subconsciously heard the commotion, she was so lost in her own thoughts that she stepped into the street directly into the path of the driverless wagon. Seeing this, Peter dashed into the street and crossed its breadth in only a few steps. Just as the horse and wagon were ready to plow Susannah down, Peter swept the young woman off her feet in a single motion, tucked her safely behind himself, using his own body as a shield, and turned to face the onrushing horse and wagon. Fortunately, the horse recognized Peter as a rather formidable object in its path and swerved at the last second. Still, it walloped Peter with quite a force, and it was all he could do to maintain his balance and that of Susannah, whom he was able to protect successfully. Turning sharply to the left, the wagon overturned, spilling flour and other items into the street, and, thankfully, stopped the horse. As Peter loosened his grip on Susannah and turned around to check on her welfare, their eyes met. Susannah's packages were strewn about her feet. A small crowd began to congregate around them, but she couldn't take her eyes off the tall, swarthy young man who had just saved her life. Several moments passed before she could gather her composure.

"You're Peter—Peter Francisco, aren't you? You live at Hunting Tower, don't you?" Susannah asked, regaining her senses. She, too, had noticed Peter on her visits to the Winston Plantation, but it would have been unacceptable for her to initiate a conversation with him. This occasion, however, was quite different. "Do you know what you just did?"

"Yes, Miss…uh, no Miss…uh, I don't know, Miss," Peter stammered. He was flustered, but not because of a close brush with death. "Are you alright, Miss? I didn't hurt you, did I?"

"Am I alright? Am I alright?" she mindlessly repeated. "I am, but only because of you. You just saved my life. You do know that, don't you?"

"I—I guess so," replied Peter, still looking so intently into Susannah's eyes that forming sentences had become difficult. Peter and Susannah just stood there, staring at each other, interrupted only by Sarah, emerging from the store, and Judge Winston, exiting the office. Both had been drawn by all the activity and racket, and they were quick to notice Susannah and Peter in the middle of the street.

"Well, well, what do we have here?" said Sarah, noticing the locked gaze of the couple standing in the street, both surrounded by packages.

"Oh, my," said Susannah, finally breaking eye contact. "Why, your Peter, here, just saved my life from a runaway horse!"

"What do you mean? What in the world happened?" asked the judge, approaching the two girls and looking around not only at Susannah's packages but also at the overturned wagon, contents scattered about.

Susannah, still a bit shaken, pointed to the wreckage. "That wagon would have run me down if it weren't for Peter here."

"Do tell," the judge replied. Other townspeople began to

gather around as well.

"Did you see what he did?" questioned one man.

"Sure did," said another. "Never seen anything like it. That horse plowed right into this fella, and he never even flinched. Never seen anything like it. Never."

"Just exactly what did happen?" Judge Winston asked.

Everyone who had gathered around had his own version of the story, each slightly different from the other. After hearing everyone's account, Judge Winston had a pretty good idea of what had taken place.

"Seems like you are a bit of a hero," commended the judge, slapping Peter on the back approvingly. "I'm right proud of you, right proud. Now, let's help Miss Susannah gather up her things."

Peter was quick to that task, too, a bit embarrassed by all the attention. Soon enough, he was carrying all of Susannah's purchases to her carriage, which had just arrived on the opposite side of the street. He placed them in the carriage boot and offered his hand to Susannah to climb into the carriage. As their hands touched, she looked warmly into Peter's eyes and he into hers. They lingered for a moment before Susannah broke the silence.

"Thank you, Peter Francisco," she said sincerely. "Your bravery will not go unrewarded. I'm sure my father will want to have words with you when I tell him what happened today." Susannah sat down and told her driver to take her home, but as the carriage drove off, she turned in her seat to take one last look at her hero. Peter, not moving a single muscle, watched the carriage drive out of sight.

Judge Winston walked up behind Peter and slapped him on the back. "Well done, Peter, well done. But we must be getting back to Hunting Tower now, before the sun goes down much further."

"Yes, sir," Peter complied. They stowed Sarah's purchase in their own carriage boot, and Peter began the trip home, prodding the Creams on with just his voice.

In the passenger area, Sarah looked at her father. "Did you see how they were looking at each other?" she commented quietly so that Peter could not hear her.

"No, I didn't," replied the judge. "What do you mean?"

With callow wisdom, she answered, "I think Peter is in love, and I think Miss Anderson is, too."

"You don't say. I'm not sure if that's a good thing or not, given their different backgrounds. Besides, Mr. Anderson and I don't exactly share the same views on a lot of things. Still, I enjoy having the Andersons over for a lively debate now and again. I guess we'll just have to wait and see what happens."

Ever so softly, certain only her father could hear, Sarah began to chant, "Peter's got a girlfriend. Peter's got a girlfriend." The judge just smiled.

The next morning, the rooster, which had now taken to crowing outside Peter's new window, alerted him to the new day. He was quick to put on his work clothes and head off to the barn, anxious to see if old Arthur was feeling any better. Normally, he would work through Sunday or spend extra time with the horses while the slaves went off on their visitations, but today he thought about asking Arthur about going along.

As he was leaving his private dwelling to check on the old man, a thought struck him. His hearing was a lot better than the judge and Sarah had supposed, and once he had overheard the judge comment about Susannah and him being of different backgrounds. *What background do I belong to?* He wondered. His new accommodations had signified a certain standing among the rest of the plantation's residents. *I am not truly a slave, yet I still answer to the slave master,* he thought. He worked from sunup to sundown nearly every day, and he had been purchased from the orphanage. *I am not an indentured servant.* Indentured servants had contracts with their masters and at some point would be set free. He had no such arrangement with the judge. On the other hand, he had certain luxuries and privileges that the black slaves did not. *I have a private place to sleep. I eat better food, and the judge just treats me differently than the others.*

This was all too perplexing, and Peter tried his best to push the thoughts out of his mind. He really did want to see how Arthur was doing and see if he would be going to today's meeting. But there was something he couldn't stop thinking about—the look in Susannah's eyes yesterday and the way her hand felt in his. For the first time in his life, he had felt hands that were even softer than his mother's.

The feeling of her velvety hands was one of the most vivid memories he had from the short time with her. He could recall moments as a boy when he'd done something that made her proud, how she'd gently place one hand on his cheek and say, "Mi Pedro." Whenever they'd be walking somewhere—to the dock, to church or to a neighbor's house—she'd put out her hand, inviting him to take hold. Because he longed for the protective feel of it around his, tiny by comparison, it was the one thing he didn't balk at. When she'd tuck him into bed at night, particularly when he had been scared, she would caress his cheek lovingly with the back of her hand and softly hum a lullaby or recite a prayer.

He pushed open the huge double doors to the barn revealing Arthur putting some hard maple wood into the forge to fire it up. The old Negro turned to see who was entering.

"Ah, there you is, d' hero o' d' day," greeted Arthur.

"What do you mean?" responded Peter naively.

"You knows what I mean. D' way I hears it, you jes' 'bout flattened 'at runaway horse in town yesterday."

"Oh, that. That was nothing. I just did what was needed. Besides, you would have done the same. But how'd you hear about it?"

"I might o' tried t' do d' same thing, but these old bones prob'ly would o' stop me, an' you know how news like that travels fast on d' plantation. Jes' you remember this, Peter, you is big, bigger'n any otha' boy yo' age I eva' seen. You is strong. You is already stronger than anybody else at Hunting Tower an' you is gettin' stronger ev'ry day. An' you is smart. Lawdy, Lawdy, Lawdy, you is smarter'n jes' 'bout anybody I eva' met, 'cept d' judge an' some o' d' folks 'at come avisitin' d' main house."

"Ah, foolish talk," said Peter self-consciously, crossing over to the back wall of the barn to grab his smithy's apron from off the wooden peg. "Why are you in here working anyway? Shouldn't you be off on your weekly 'visitation?'" he asked while tying on the apron. Over the past year, Peter had been doing more and more of the blacksmithing as Arthur's advancing age slowed him down. It wasn't long before the sound of hammer on molten iron began to ring out across the plantation, and, once he got going, Peter could really make that hammer sing. Every time he slammed the ten-pounder down on the anvil, his biceps seemed to swell. Arthur was right. For a man of any age, Peter was one of the strongest on the plantation, in the county, maybe in all the colonies.

"I's still goin'," Arthur said with a knowing smile. "I jes' wanted t' see d' hero o' d' day 'fore I went."

"Well, what if the 'hero of the day' comes along with you today?" Peter ventured.

Arthur surveyed Peter for a moment, giving careful consideration to his request. Finally, he said, "Yes. I thinks you be ready. We gatha' down by d' pasture, then walks fo' few miles into d' woods."

As they walked with the other slaves, Arthur filled Peter in on why they assembled and why they were sometimes known as the underground church. Peter noticed how some of them had taken extra care with their appearance. Clothes as clean as they could get them. Hair neatly combed. *Maybe it's just me,* Peter thought. Most of them didn't change. They just went as they were. Bare feet and all.

A few times, Arthur had to stop and lean against a tree to catch his breath, causing them to fall to the back of the procession. Peter's brow furrowed. He was concerned for his friend's health, but he knew Arthur wouldn't want to discuss it. Arthur explained that because slaves were discouraged from worshiping openly like their masters, they had to meet in secret places. "Spot changes ev'ry time, so we's not found out. You been t' church 'fore, Peter?"

"Yes," Peter said, "I don't remember much about it, but my parents always took my sister and I to a small chapel on Sundays. Most of it was boring to me, but I do remember repeating a lot of things the priest said. Sometimes," Peter said, as if remembering it for the first time, "we had to eat bread. We sang a lot, too. The day I was kidnapped, in fact, I had just come back from Sunday mass. That is why I was wearing my silver shoe buckles when they found me."

A grunt escaped Arthur's throat. "We sing. We speak double. But our 'mass' be a bit diff'rent." That was the last thing Arthur said before they rejoined the others. By now, they had made their way to a large clearing, which was bathed in sunlight and blanketed with thick grass. In a routine clearly familiar to them, some of the slaves had started gathering fallen tree limbs to use as makeshift benches. In front of the branches, some folks squatted in the grass. Most remained standing. Peter followed Arthur to one of the natural seats down front, but lingered to the side, so he wouldn't block anyone's view with his leviathan-like frame.

Some of the men shouted greetings back and forth. Small children quickly found each other and began chasing each other in circles around the adults. Women laughed volubly and embraced each other. Among them, Peter could sense a burden had been lifted. They were easy and comfortable with each other, like they were one, big family. Peter suddenly realized this was the only time some of them saw their relatives, the ones who had been traded or sold to other plantation owners. A few of them seemed to recognize Peter and came over to welcome him.

Before long, the social buzz had quieted. No one seemed to be in a rush to keep things moving. No one checked the time. No one yawned. Peter waited for someone to come to the front as he thought customary. Instead, he heard someone from within the crowd start to pray. Peter couldn't locate the source, but he thought the man must have been shouting because it sounded like he was right beside him. Those nearest him had closed their eyes. Peter did the same so he wouldn't draw any more attention to himself than he already did.

"Almighty God, You is the Great Deliverer."

Someone near him said, "Yes, Lawd, thank you, Lawd."

"You has neva' failed yo' people. Bring us out these dark days." He stretched each sound, emphasizing the last with such force, it reminded Peter of a cracking whip. Clearly, it was a cue for the rest of them to react because nearly everyone responded with "hmm-mmm."

"Shine yo' light. Carry us home, Lawd. Amen."

When the man finished, Peter thought the praying was over, but it continued on like a chain of wildfire. Before long, everyone was uttering something toward the clouds until Peter could no longer make out any of the words.

Following the prayer, the entire throng of slaves erupted into spontaneous song, more like a chant. Peter didn't recognize any of the lyrics. No music accompanied them. As they sang, they moved closer together, sliding their arms around each other's waists and swaying back and forth in unison. Some stretched their arms upward, to the sky. They sang a while longer, until a man with the whitest hair Peter had ever seen stood up and faced the crowd. Peter didn't know who the man was, but he had an intelligent look about him.

The man stood silently before them. He didn't waste any time on announcements, the kind Peter vaguely recalled from his church back home. Instead, without the aid of any papers or books, he opened immediately by speaking of the political unrest.

Peter listened intently, conscious that worship wasn't the only reason for these gatherings. Having heard similar sentiments from those who had visited Hunting Tower, Peter let the man's words fade into the background and, for a moment, focused his attention on the people he knew around him.

Like most of the others, Arthur's head nodded in agreement to what the man said. Petunia sat next to a young man Peter had never met before. He noticed Tom standing with his arms folded, his fists clenched. When cheers erupted around him, Peter's attention was brought back to the man with the snow-capped head.

"…no doubt wond'rin', what'll their actions mean fo' us? Are we not still bound in servitude?" The mass of dark faces responded with cries of "Yes!"

The man really had Peter's attention now. *What in the world is he talking about?* Peter thought, not understanding.

The man lifted his hand to quiet them. "It's true that what the white folks 're plannin' will bring us a step closer to the home we seek. You know what I'm talkin' 'bout, now. An' they will need our help. Ain't no doubt. Listen now. It may be a while. We may not even live t'see that day, but I urge you, do not get so caught up in yo' current circumstances that you fail t'see the home that is yours now in Christ. Can I get an 'amen?'" The crowd emphatically nodded their heads and repeated his last word in unison.

The speaker had started pacing back and forth. The hot sun had caused sweat to build up on his forehead, now dripping down his face. He wiped it away with a handkerchief before continuing.

"I'm 'bout to preach y'all! Bible say, 'Stand fast therefore in the liberty wherewith Christ hath made us free, an' be not entangled again with the yoke o' bondage.' That bondage, my friends, is sin. But Christ, through His death on the cross, has made us all free. Did ya'll hear what I jes' said?" he asked, cupping his hear. "Lemme say it again," his voice rising, "He has made us *all* free! Anything else is lies! Bible say in Galatians, 'There is neither Jew nor Greek, there is neither bond nor free, there is neither male nor female: for ye are *all* one in Christ Jesus.'

As 'Hallelujahs' filled the air, Peter began to contemplate the man's words. *Did he say 'free?' Could this really be true?* Peter was beginning to wonder if anything made sense anymore.

"Do ya not freely think? Freely pray? Freely believe?" The man at the front urged on. Folks murmured and moaned in response. He lowered his voice to almost a whisper, pausing slightly between each word, "Watch 'is now. God yo' Father did not create you t' be slave t' sin. He created you t' be free in Him. Free, I say! He say in His Word, 'But now being made free from sin, an' become servants t' God, ye have your fruit unto holiness, an' the end everlasting life.'

"Yo' body may be bound to this earth an' t' yo' master, but yo' spirit be free," he said beating his chest with his hand. The man's posture and the tone of his voice didn't change, but Peter knew his next words were directed to God. He prayed that anyone who didn't know God would receive Him. Peter thought he heard the man say something about the balm of Gilead, but he wasn't sure what that meant either.

When the man concluded, he motioned with his arms for the people to gather around. A few of them beat on drums made from cowhide and played well-worn fiddles. Men, women and children arranged themselves in a large circle and started clapping. Not knowing what to do, Peter joined them. They rocked back and forth, using their hips, slowly at first. They chanted and sang the phrase "Holy Spirit, revive my soul; Holy Spirit, revive my hope; Holy Spirit, revive my heart" over and over. The repetition fascinated Peter, but it continued for so long, Peter began to wonder if it would ever end. Peter was moved by their expression of worship and soon found himself dancing with them. Their voices continued to rise. Their rhythmic steps had gone from tapping to sweeping thrusts of the knee. Some of the women shouted and hurled themselves on the ground. This startled Peter. At first, he thought they had succumbed to exhaustion from the heat, but after seeing so many of them do the same thing, he realized it was all part of the ritual.

The ring dance gave Peter a chance to think about what the white-haired man had said. If this was freedom, he wanted nothing more. But his mind was filled with questions. *Does background really not matter to God? How is God my Father? How can I know this freedom? The man said it was only through Christ. Could it really be as simple as asking?*

When the circle broke up, Peter had to scan the heads around him for Arthur. He didn't see how the old man could have survived that when he he'd had a hard enough time just walking here. But Peter should have known that he himself would be the easier one to spot. Petunia bounded up to him and said excitedly, "Peter, what'd'ya think?"

"I think I have a lot of questions," Peter replied with a chuckle.

"Oh, I's sho' Mista' Arthur will answer 'em fo' ya. See ya back home!" she exclaimed and ran off, Peter gathered, to bid a temporary farewell to her new sweetheart.

Arthur appeared shortly after. On the long walk back, Arthur answered Peter's questions as best he could. He spoke of God sending His Son to die on the cross and how that was payment for all sin. Borrowing some of the words from their speaker, Arthur reminded Peter that Christ made that sacrifice for everyone. "God sees all folks equal. We's all His children," Arthur said, sensing what Peter was after. "All's we have t' do is invite Him into our hearts."

So, there, in the middle of the woods, trees their only witnesses, Peter asked Arthur to guide him in prayer until he had asked Christ to release him from the heavy burden of sin and to come live in his heart. When he lifted his head, copious tears fell from his eyes. Something unspeakable had been lifted from him. For the first time in his life, Peter felt peace in his heart. No matter what the future held for him on earth, his place in heaven was secure. That much he knew for sure.

Following his experience at the slaves' clandestine meeting, Peter's relationship with Arthur continued to develop. The two were almost inseparable. They spent nearly every day together, working from sunrise to sunset, and they often spent evenings in deep conversation. Arthur had recounted joyful memories of being married with a family prior to being a slave, and the trauma of being separated when they were sold to different owners on the auction block. Even though it was many decades ago, he still shed a tear when recalling the ordeal and admitted that he still dreamed of being reunited with them one day. A special bond began to form between them, as Peter commiserated with Arthur while he reminisced about Mama, Papa and Sissy, followed by the horrific memories of being kidnapped from his homeland, just like Peter. Without even realizing it, their relationship had slowly evolved into the father and son they had both longed for.

During one of their after-dinner talks in Arthur's cabin, which he shared with several other male slaves, Tom and Richard, two of his roommates, came in arguing. They didn't noticed Peter and Arthur in the dark corner. "So what reason we got to stay here on the plantation? Give me one reason," Tom's voice was agitated and adamant. "All we ever do is picks tobacco an' hemp an' plant an' works all day." His voice was excited.

"Yeah, I knows," said Richard. "Believe me, I knows, but where ya gonna go tha's any better? And s'pose you get catched? You know what they do t' runaways. If'n they don't shoot ya, they hang ya, an' if'n they bring ya back here, you know Mista' Alfred would nearly whip d' hide off'n ya."

It was true that Judge Winston treated his slaves better than those owners on a lot of other plantations, but he gave Alfred his lead to maintain discipline in whatever way he thought necessary. Peter could only remember one time—his first year on the plantation—when one of the slaves had mouthed the master. Alfred promptly had that man strapped to a tree. Twenty bullwhip lashes later, the slave's back had been laid open raw. It was a sight that had turned Peter's stomach and one he would never forget. The next day, that slave was gone, never to be seen or heard of again.

"It don' matter. I jes' gots t' get away from here. I gots t' be free," Tom insisted.

"You listen t' me," said Richard. "No matta' where you goes, you ain't never gonna be free. Free is fo' white folk, an' you ain't no white folk."

Arthur had heard enough and cleared his throat to make his presence known. From his dark corner where he and Peter had been talking, he crossed the room. The fireplace light played on his features.

"You best be listenin' to Richard, Tom. He be dead right. You two was born slaves, you is slaves t'day, you be slaves t'morrow, an' on d' day you dies, you still be slaves," Arthur told them. "Besides 'at, you got one o' d' bes' masta's 'round. Bes' you rememba' 'at." Arthur turned to Peter, "And bes' you be gettin' some sleep. We gots a long day t'morrow."

Peter rose, walked across the room and strode out into the cool night air. What he had just heard was making his mind run in all sorts of directions. Other than his first five years of life with his family, a time that was quickly becoming a fading memory, Peter had never been physically free. *First, I was a prisoner of pirates, and then I was a ward at the orphanage, followed by my life here at Hunting Tower Plantation.* Now that he was approaching manhood, he wondered, *could I really be free again?* Peter didn't know. He didn't even know who to ask. But he was determined to find out. That night, alone in his bed, he couldn't get the idea of being free out of his mind, and he slept restlessly.

The next day was one that Peter would never forget. He and Arthur were working in the barn when Alfred entered. Motioning toward Peter he said, "Judge Winston would like to see you up at the main house."

Peter wondered what he might have done wrong. As he approached the house, he saw the same carriage that had whisked Susannah Anderson homeward on the day he had rescued her from certain death. He also noticed that an older gentleman accompanied Susannah, and the idea made his hands grow clammy, his breathing grow shallow. Before he could reach the carriage, Susannah and the man were already standing, and Judge Winston was greeting them.

The judge turned toward Peter. "Ah, here he is. Peter, come over here. I have someone who would like to meet you."

Peter's mind raced. *I've already met Susannah, so the judge must want me to meet the man, but whatever for?*

"Peter," said the judge, "this is Mr. Anderson, Susannah's father, and he would like to have words with you."

"Peter," the man broke in, "I wanted to come here today to thank you for your gallantry and bravery in saving my little girl's life a few weeks ago. I would have liked to do this sooner, but things at our plantation have been so busy. I hope you'll forgive me for not coming directly."

Peter stood there a bit dumbfounded by all this attention. "I'm just glad I was there," said Peter.

"Well, we're glad you were there, too," repeated Mr. Anderson, "and as a small token of our appreciation, I've brought you something I hope you can use." Mr. Anderson reached into the carriage and produced a package wrapped in brown paper. "Peter, this is for you. Wear it well."

Peter accepted the gift and looked at Susannah. "Open it, Peter, please do," she said.

He looked at the judge as if seeking permission. "By all means, Peter. Open it," he insisted.

Peter tore at the paper and produced a magnificent, dark blue tri-cornered hat with silver trim. For a moment, he just looked at it. His own hat was well worn and dirty, covered in sawdust. This—this was a real gentleman's hat. Peter didn't know what to say.

The judge piped in to rescue him from the awkward moment. "I think Peter would do well to say 'thank you,' but I see that your fine gift renders him speechless."

"Thank you, sir, thank you," Peter said. "I...I...," his voice trailed off. Peter had turned his attention back to the most beautiful creature in the world, Susannah Anderson.

"Do try it on, Peter," she said.

The reluctant hero removed his own work hat and placed the new one on his head. It fit like a saddle on a horse, much to everyone's approval. For the second time, Peter was actually embarrassed by all the attention.

The silence became a bit uncomfortable before the judge spoke again. "Where are my manners? Please, come into the house, you and Miss Susannah. I'm sure we have some refreshments at hand." Turning to Peter he said, "That will be all. You can return to your chores now." As the three of them went into the house, Susannah turned again to look at Peter. She silently mouthed a thank you, and Peter could feel the blood rushing to his cheeks.

When the door closed, he set out for the barn as instructed, but not before he had taken his new hat to his room, where he placed it on top of the dresser. He wanted to see it as soon as he entered the room later that day and every day.

★

The radiant hues of autumn's leaves soon gave way to sparse branches, a stark contrast to the bustle on the plantation. Each day, Peter and Arthur worked side-by-side in the barn as they crafted farm implements out of iron and wood. By this time, Peter was also becoming well-schooled in carpentry, and he could wield an auger and a gimlet with agility. He especially liked using the wide variety of chisels and gauges, drawknives and spoke shaves, all of which he used to transform wood into useful shapes. The pride he took in his work always showed in the finished product as if he were liberating its purpose.

Peter was still trying to grasp the whole idea of freedom. He watched the slave children as they played in the evenings, rolling hoops, walking on stilts that Peter himself had made, or engaging in a game of ninepins. He thought of Arthur and the rest of the slaves. *Even the food they eat isn't as good as the Winstons'.* Corn meal was a main staple, while the Winstons, Petunia and even Peter feasted on fish muddle, Welsh rabbit and, Peter's favorite, shepherd's pie. Indeed, there was a difference between freedom and slavery, but the line of separation was becoming more and more apparent in Peter's mind, and it was a line that he didn't much care for.

★

As the long winter finally gave way to the spring of 1774, the activity in the main house increased with frequent visitors. Always wanting to put on a show for his guests, Judge Winston asked Peter to act as a doorman for those who visited Hunting Tower. As they arrived, Peter greeted them, led them to the front door, and announced their names as they entered the main house. These growing gatherings kept him busy.

On one particular occasion, a gentleman of obvious stature arrived in one of the most magnificent carriages Peter had ever seen. He had noticed this man several times from afar, but this time when the servant held open the door to the carriage, the man stepped down and extended his hand to Peter. "You must be Peter Francisco. My uncle, the Judge, has told me a lot about you. My name is Patrick Henry."

Peter shook his hand and replied courteously, "How do you do, sir." He always wore his new hat for this assignment, sweeping it from his head while giving a slight bow, evidencing his refined manners. Peter was quite impressed by Patrick Henry's bearing and by his height. This man, although a few inches shorter than Peter, was a good six feet tall, a half-head taller than most men of the day. When Peter announced Patrick Henry's name upon opening the front door of the main house, he did so with a flourish reserved only for guests he knew to be particularly important.

On this same night, the Anderson family—with Susannah and her brothers Thomas and James, Jr. included—was also in attendance. Once again, Peter found himself somewhat weak-kneed when their carriage arrived. Whenever the Andersons visited, Peter felt as though his heart was about ready to jump right out of his chest. He was always eager for their visits, for it gave him a reason to be near Susannah, to hold her hand as he helped her from the carriage and to look into her eyes as she thanked him.

When all the guests had arrived, and the judge told Peter that his services would no longer be needed, he retired to his room.

Since it adjoined the main house parlor, Peter could easily hear the conversation.

"What you speak of is tyranny," said one of the voices. "Tyranny, I say." The voice sounded like Mr. Anderson's.

"Tyranny! Tyranny! I'll tell you what tyranny is." This voice was unmistakably that of Judge Winston. "Tyranny is all these taxes, taxes that we're having to pay because the King had to fight the French. He should have kept that war in Europe where it belonged. Tyranny was the Stamp Act!"

"But that was repealed," rebutted the first voice. Peter knew it was Anderson speaking now.

"Then how about the Townshend Act? The king wanted to tax everything of value coming to the Americas," said the Judge.

"That, too, was repealed," retorted Anderson.

"Yes, it was repealed, but not until the king's men shot down several peaceful people at that square in Boston. Shooting your own people, now that's tyranny." This voice belonged to the man who had introduced himself earlier in the day—Patrick Henry. "And what of the Proclamation of 1763? The colonies can't even expand to the West because of this cowardly act to protect the very Indians who would have had our scalps only a few years earlier. And the Sugar Act, and…oh, I could go on and on. Gentlemen, I say that those of us in the colonies know best how to govern our interests. We are taxed and we are told what to do and when to do it, yet we have no voice, no say in the matter. Such talk of rebellion is not tyranny. No, it is the reason that so many sacrificed so much to settle in this new land. It is the talk of freedom, and it is freedom we must have."

There it was again, Peter thought. *Freedom.* Slowly, he was beginning to understand. *Freedom is something people are willing to fight and sacrifice and die for it.* Still, Peter was confused. *Mr. Anderson has been so nice to me, and he is deeply devoted to Susannah, yet he is arguing against freedom.* Peter knew deep in his heart freedom was the right thing. *This makes no sense.*

The arguing back and forth went well into the night, but Peter, exhausted from a long day's work, could no longer fight sleep. The voices faded, and Peter found himself dreaming. Dreaming of Susannah Anderson. Dreaming of freedom. Dreaming of the freedom to make Susannah his wife. *Would that, could that possibly ever happen?*

★

In the spring of 1775, Judge Winston came to a decision that had been in the making the past few years. One Friday morning, he felt the time had come to put his decision into action.

Peter and Arthur were hard at work in the barn when an early morning shadow cast itself upon the wide double-door opening. They looked up to see Judge Winston standing inside the frame—truly unusual, since the judge most often sent Alfred to relay any messages or information he might have for them.

"Peter," said the judge, "I would like to speak with you."

Arthur, sensing that this was to be a private conversation, was the first to respond. "Yes, suh, Judge Winston, I'll jes' go out here an' check on some otha' things."

"No, Arthur, I want you to stay as this concerns you, too," replied the judge.

"Peter," the judge repeated. "You've been with me for about

ten years now. You've certainly grown as a man. Just look at the size of you. You're as strong as—no, stronger than—any I've ever seen. You're also smarter than most, even though you don't read or write. Now, Arthur, here, has been as loyal to me as anyone. I've depended on him for a lot of things over the years. He's been my driver, my bodyguard; and he's been my faithful companion." There was a long pause, as the judge seemed to be looking for just the right words to say. "Arthur, I think you'd be the first to admit that time has caught up with you, with both of us, for that matter. I know that riding around the countryside has become a painful experience, though you never complained, not even once. I also know that if the situation arose, you would gladly lay down your own life for my safety."

Arthur interrupted, something he seldom did when the judge was speaking, "Yes, suh, Judge Winston, I sho'ly would."

"Yes, Arthur, I know you would. But the times are different now. These are perilous times for us all. I feel that the time is rapidly approaching when the views of those of us in the colonies and those of the King of England shall be in total opposition. Certain people will be considered enemies of the crown, and danger, perhaps even bloodshed, is coming to the land. Arthur, if ever a white man and a Negro could love each other, we share that kind of love. But from this day forward, I will be having young Peter here as my driver and bodyguard. Peter," continued the judge as he looked at the massive young man, "you have earned this privilege. If you can assume these duties and perform them even half as well as old Arthur here, I will be forever grateful."

Peter, who hadn't spoken a word, cleared his throat. "Of course, I will. Yes, sir, and I'll be honored to."

"Good then," said the judge. "It's all settled. In a couple of weeks we have a journey to make to Richmond. My nephew, Patrick Henry, will also be there along with some other very important people. Good day then."

As Judge Winston left the barn, Arthur looked at Peter with the eyes of a father to a son. "I hates admittin' that I's gettin' old, but I's real proud o' you, Peter Francisco. I's powerful proud."

7.

A CALL TO ARMS,
MARCH 1775

THE MOUNTAINS STOOD at the mouth of the James River like sentinels in the distance. Rays from the warm morning sun reached out over the sweet scent of budding blossoms like maternal arms and swept gently across the calm water and upward along the grassy hummock to St. John's Church. Nearby, still perched on the remains of a once-majestic tree, Peter remained restless. Hunched forward, he let his head rest on his clasped hands, revealing his thick, black locks, which were gathered at the nape of his neck and flowed in long swirls down his spine. Although he was content with his new post as Judge Winston's carriage driver and bodyguard, Peter couldn't help pondering the words he had just heard both inside and outside the church. Inside, Patrick Henry had created a frenzy of shouts with his stirring speech. Even now, the bedlam that ensued continued as delegates shouted at one another. Outside, Susannah Anderson's father had rebuked Peter for siding with those calling for freedom from England's tyranny. And the young lady herself—the woman who had so easily won Peter's heart—had called him a fool.

Regardless, he yearned to attain this freedom, fully believing that it was something no one should live without. *How could the Andersons not see this? How could they possibly be so wrong?* While he continued struggling with his thoughts and emotions, Peter felt a tap on his shoulder. He looked up, eyes squinting in the mid-morning sun, to see Judge Winston. "Peter, my boy," the judge said, "Did you hear what my nephew had to say? Did you understand what he meant?"

"Yes, sir," replied Peter, standing up to show proper respect for the judge. "I heard Mr. Henry speak. I didn't understand everything. Some of his words I never heard before, but I think I understood enough—enough to know that everyone wants to be free, but some don't understand what real freedom is or how to get it. It just seems that some folks don't want things to change."

"Very good, Peter. I think you probably understood more than you think."

"But what about those who don't think like you and Mr. Henry? What about those people? When they left, Mr. Anderson wouldn't even speak to me, and Susannah called us both fools!"

"Peter, you have to understand that not everyone wants to possibly risk all that they have, perhaps their very lives, for something they don't fully understand. They are pretty happy with the way things are. What they fail to see is that, if we were to allow things to go on that way, the King of England will strip us of all that we have tried to acquire for the sake of families and our-selves. Many of our ancestors came to this new world to escape the very tyranny which we now face."

"Does that mean that the Andersons are wrong? Or that someday they may agree with us?"

"That's hard to say, Peter. I do know that young Susannah has won your heart," the judge said, raising his eyebrows with a knowing glare. "I've seen the way you look at her when they visit. But Mr. Anderson is pretty set in his ways. We call him a loyalist, and I'm not too sure that he will ever see things our way. Peter," he hesitated, "I say this to you as though you were my son. I think that any further thoughts of Susannah should be put to rest. There will be plenty of other young ladies that will capture your attention. Besides, there's still considerable work for you to do at Hunting Tower. I'm going to be relying on you even more in the future. I'd better be getting back inside now. The day's business still is not done." The judge turned and disappeared inside the church as other delegates filed in with him.

Peter looked solemnly out at the road in the direction which Susannah and her father had disappeared in a cloud of dust. The judge's words rang in his head. *Will I ever see her again? Will the future I imagined for us never come to be? Is the judge right? Should I just forget about her?* He was so confused. Peter strolled over to the horses he loved so much. He could always depend on them.

With the approach of evening, the delegates—Judge Winston, Patrick Henry, George Washington and Thomas Jefferson—be-gan to exit the church. Some walked in quiet reflection; others spoke in animated tones. As the judge and Patrick Henry drew near the carriage, Peter held the door open for them.

"Peter," the judge directed, "my nephew and I will be dining together this evening, so he will be riding back to the inn with us."

"Very well, sir," Peter said. Nodding toward Patrick Henry, he added, "I liked your speech today, sir."

"You don't sound all that enthusiastic," replied Henry.

"Oh, no, sir, those were some of the best words I ever heard in my life."

"Patrick," the judge interrupted, "you have to understand that the boy is having some mixed feelings right now. I suspect young Peter liked what you said just fine, but the young lady he had his cap set for seems to disagree. You know her, Susannah Anderson, James Anderson's daughter."

"Ah, yes," Henry recalled. "Her father and I have had many a lively debate. But I'm sure you'll find some other winsome lass to take your breath away again."

"That's exactly what I told him," the judge chimed in. "Now let's be off, before the dining room at the inn gets too crowded."

Peter closed the carriage door behind the judge and Patrick Henry, took his place in the driver's position, and guided the Creams out onto the street. Most of the other delegates had the same idea, and dozens of carriages were trying to exit the church grounds at the same time. But the sheer size of Peter and the Creams caused other horses and drivers to make way for the Winston carriage.

Peter dropped Judge Winston and Patrick Henry off in front of the inn. Then, he drove down the street to the livery stable, where he unhitched and corralled the magnificent animals. After pulling the carriage behind the building, he returned to rub down and feed his horses. He took his time with each of them, allowing his mind to drift back over the day's events. He knew that he would always embrace the idea of freedom and wholeheartedly supported what Patrick Henry had said that day. On the other hand, he wasn't about to give up so easily on Susannah Anderson, no matter what the judge and his nephew had said. *There just has to be a way,* he thought, shoving his hands into his pockets.

Feeling something, Peter discovered the biscuits the innkeeper's wife had made for him the previous night. The day's events had been so unsettling that he had forgotten to eat them. Since he still had no appetite, he offered the biscuits to the horses, which greedily gobbled them down.

The next day played out similarly to the three preceding it. Peter arose early, prepared the wagon and drove Judge Winston to St. John's Church for more meetings of the Second Virginia Convention. Ultimately, Patrick Henry introduced a resolution calling for the establishment of militias throughout the Virginia Colony. Although the delegation was quite divided on the proposed action, everyone knew there would be ramifications, and they dispersed on the final day with full knowledge that, like it or not, war with England was imminent.

On the journey back to Hunting Tower, Peter contemplated the role he might play in the upcoming conflict. After about an hour of driving in silence, the judge addressed his driver from inside the enclosed carriage. "Peter? Peter, can you hear me?

"Yes, sir, Judge Winston," was the reply.

"Peter, I think you understand there's going to be a war."

"Yes, sir, I think I do."

"Do you know what that means, Peter?"

"Men are going to fight, and men are going to die, and in the end, if we win, we will all be free."

"Well, not exactly. But our country will be free. Free from the oppression of England. Free from the king. Free to determine our own destiny as a country. Do you understand what I'm saying?"

"Yes, sir. I think so, and I've been thinking that I should join the army, too."

"Well, Peter, while I admire your noble thoughts, I think there are a few things we must consider. First, you are simply too young to go off fighting in a war. After all, you're barely fifteen years old, even though you're bigger than most fully-grown men I know. The other problem is that there's no real army to join yet. Right now, it looks like we're just going to have some local militias to protect our interests here in Virginia. But what's most important is the work right at Hunting Tower, and that includes you, Peter. I'm planning to convert most of our cropland to growing more hemp. That way, when the time comes, we'll be able to produce more rope. Rope is going to be a vital commodity for our troops and especially our sailors. We will all have a role to play as the conflict begins, and that includes all of us at Hunting Tower. With Arthur's health such a concern, I need you more than ever before."

"Yes, sir," Peter replied with resignation.

Not another word was spoken as each man contemplated his own thoughts during the rest of the sixteen-hour trip.

Upon returning to Hunting Tower, Peter discovered that Arthur's health was indeed rapidly declining. More often than not, the old Negro arrived at the barn no earlier than midday, if at all. Thus, Peter found himself doubly busy caring for all the horses and doing all the daily blacksmith and carpentry work that the plantation required.

In early May, a rider galloped up to the main house, dismounting before his horse came to a complete stop. He bounded up the steps to the porch and pounded on the front door. When the judge opened it, he and the rider exchanged a few animated words. Then the man left just as quickly as he had arrived. Responding to the racket, Peter went to stand in the double door opening to the barn. As the judge walked briskly toward the barn, he said soberly, "Peter, it would appear that the fight has just begun."

"What? Where?" asked Peter, shaking his head in consternation.

"In Massachusetts. Some places called Lexington and Concord. The local militias there exchanged gunfire with the English."

"But isn't that far away?"

"Indeed, it is, but there has also been some trouble right here in Virginia in Williamsburg, and it involves my nephew."

"Mr. Henry?"

"Yes, Peter, my nephew Patrick. It seems that when Governor Dunmore heard about the conflict up north, he decided to move fifteen half-barrels of gunpowder out of Williamsburg to make sure nobody could get their hands on it. Well, Patrick and a bunch of others heard about it, and they rode to Williamsburg to stop the transfer. The governor sent his family away and then threatened to set fire to the whole city. From what the messenger just told me, they spent several days in a standoff before the matter was settled."

"Is Mr. Henry alright?" questioned Peter.

"Yes, yes, he's fine, though your concern is deeply appreciated. However, Dunmore issued a proclamation against Patrick and others accusing them of treason, so I fear that this will all begin to press forward to all-out war very soon. In fact, the Second Continental Congress is set to convene in just a couple of days, and Virginia's representative, a fellow named Richard Henry Lee, has been instructed to propose that the colonies declare themselves as free and independent."

"What does all that mean, sir?" asked Peter.

"It means that we are pressing ever closer to war."

"So, what should I do?"

"I know what you're thinking, Peter, but remember what I told you on the way back from Richmond. You are still too young to fight, and there's plenty for us to do here to help the war. Now, please go back to your chores."

"Yes, sir." Peter knew when not to contradict the judge's wishes, even though, deep inside, he was sure that it was his destiny to fight—fight for the freedom of his country, and fight for his own freedom.

That evening when Peter went to his quarters, he rummaged through one of the dresser drawers until he found his best pair of breeches. Just below the knee were the silver buckles with P and F that had once adorned his shoes.

Peter sat down on his bed, looking at the buckles. They were the only remnants of his childhood at the beautiful home on the ocean, where he had once been free. Fingering the worn buckles, he thought. *I'm not sure how, but one day I will be free again.* Even though the judge had been kind to him, he had always known his place at Hunting Tower. If the judge told him he couldn't go off to war, then so be it. But Peter knew—he just knew—that the day would come when he would fight in war and, through that struggle, he would one day be free.

He thought of Susannah and her father. *What is she doing right now? Are they finally seeing the truth? Do they understand that fighting the English is the right thing to do? Is there any chance I will see her again?* As Peter lay back on his bed, clutching the silver buckles, he pictured Susannah in his mind and slowly drifted off to sleep.

The next morning, Peter slept a bit later than usual. Even the faithful rooster had no effect on his slumber. When he entered the barn, he was pleasantly surprised to see Arthur already hard at work. Nearly a week had passed since the elderly man had felt strong enough to work, although Peter had made it a point to visit with him each evening.

"My, my, my," Arthur said looking up from the forge. "Look who couldn't get up out of bed today."

Peter just stood there looking sheepish.

"Well, snap to it, boy. We gots lots o' work to do 'round here, an' it ain't gettin' done with you jes' standin' there."

"Do you remember the night when we heard Tom and Richard talking about running away? Do you remember what you told them?" asked Peter.

"O' course, I does. I may be gettin' feeble in d' body, but I remembers everythin'. Why's you askin?"

"It's just that whole thing about freedom and being free."

"Peter, why you keep goin' on 'bout all this, I jes' don' know. It's 'bout all you talk since you be comin' back from Richmond. Peter, you needs t' get yo' mind right. You may not be nearly as black as me an' the otha' slaves, but the judge pay good money fo' you, an' you'll be doin' as he pleases, no matta' what. 'Sides, the judge, he treats you better'n jes' 'bout anybody else 'round here, 'cept his own family. He even treats you better'n that old slave masta' Alfred."

"I know, Arthur, I know." Peter said as he began to gather up his blacksmithing tools. "But doesn't it bother you wondering what it would be like to be free?"

"Peter, maybe I'm jes' too old t' rememba' a time when I be free, but I do know this—I's lived a pretty good life here at Hunting Tower, an' I 'spect this is where I been endin' my days. An' I understan' what a young buck like you might be thinkin'. But you need to be puttin' them kind o' thoughts outta' yo' mind. Now let's not be talkin' no more 'bout it. We gots alotta o' work t' do, an' it don't get done talkin'."

Peter was a bit confused by Arthur's curt way of ending the conversation. Arthur had always been his sounding board, but today it seemed as though the old Negro didn't want to discuss the matter anymore. Peter tried his best to forget about the whole thing, and soon he had anvil, hammer and hot iron singing in a perfect, three-part harmony. Still, the idea of being free haunted his every thought and dream. But after his conversation with Arthur, he stopped talking about it with anyone.

★

As the days became hot and the air humid at Hunting Tower, riders arrived almost daily bringing Judge Winston the latest news. Peter eventually heard what was happening either directly from the judge or sometimes from the riders themselves, when he tended to their horses.

In early June, fearing for his life, Governor Dunmore had left Williamsburg, certain that the rebels would do him harm if he stayed. Initially he fled to Porto Bello, his hunting lodge in York County. Later, he and his family took refuge on the British warship Fowey, which was anchored in the York River at the time.

But, to Peter, the announcement that on June 14 the Continental Army had been established was more significant. At least now one of the judge's objections to Peter's going to war had been eliminated. Now there was an actual army to join. The very next day, the tall gentleman that Peter had seen in Richmond was appointed as the army's chief commander. Peter tried his best to remember his name. *What was it? George. George something. George... George... Washington! That's it!* Peter could not have been happier. Even though he had not spoken with the man, he could just tell that he was a leader of men.

Unfortunately, news arrived only a couple of days later that was not nearly as uplifting. The American forces had suffered a dramatic defeat at the hands of the British at a place called Bunker Hill. From what Peter could gather, the Americans had fought with intrepidity and inflicted heavy losses on the English but were forced to retreat.

That very evening, Judge Winston knocked on the door of Peter's quarters and entered without waiting for an answer. Peter could not recall the last time the judge had actually paid him a visit. The sole kerosene lamp barely lit the room, even with the wick fully extended. The judge's shadow played languidly across the wall of wooden planks.

"Peter, I would like to speak with you," the judge said gravely.

"I know you've been hearing all the news about the war, and I know you would love to join the army. But before you get that notion back in your head, I want to put an end to it right here and right now. The truth is that you are just too valuable to me here at Hunting Tower. Alfred has just informed me that he is planning on leaving to join the Continental Army in New Jersey. I have to admit that I never thought a great deal about him as a slave master, but he's kept things running around here for a good many years. I'm going to ask Anthony, Jr. to assume that role, but he's not had much experience, so I'm going to rely on you to help him as much as you can. You seem to get along with all the slaves, and Lord knows you and Arthur seem to have a special bond. I think everyone will listen to you. The reason I'm telling you all this is that, while you might be thinking the time is right for you to go off and fight, now is just not the time, and I'll hear no talk of it. I need you here. My decision has been made." Without waiting for Peter to respond, Judge Winston left, closing the door behind him.

Peter just sat there in silence. Indeed he had thought of going to the judge with another request to join the army, but now that seemed out of the question, at least for the foreseeable future.

★

Another summer passed on Hunting Tower. That season's hemp harvest was by far the largest ever produced on the plantation, and the judge was especially pleased. Rather than take it all to market, he decided to store a significant portion in the barn until the time was right to send it to be processed for the war.

Anthony, Jr., with a great deal of help from Peter, successfully took over as slave master, and the little farming community seemed as productive as ever with stocking the root cellar and preparing the fields for winter wheat. Peter's influence was significant. The slaves looked at him as one of their own, even though he had always been treated better. In no small measure, Peter's relationships with Petunia and Arthur had also helped.

Meanwhile, news from the war itself was not good. Although the Americans were inflicting great casualties on the British troops, the redcoats always seemed to have the advantage. They had better-trained soldiers, more equipment—especially artillery—and what seemed like an almost endless store of basic resources.

As winter settled over Virginia and Hunting Tower, Judge Winston was particularly anxious about how the war was being waged. He had gambled a great deal in supporting the drive toward independence. If that gamble failed, surely the king would take retribution, and the judge and his family would probably be forced into poverty or worse. He had also gambled by switching to an even more highly concentrated crop of hemp, and the risk was doubled by not having sent a part of the previous harvest to market. However, the burning of Falmouth in the northern campaign was instrumental in the decision of the Continental Congress in establishing a navy, which would increase the demand for hemp, and that did set the judge's mind at ease a little.

The judge was also concerned with the well-being of his nephew, Patrick Henry. Patrick had been one of the most outspoken of patriots, and the royal crown would stop at almost nothing to secure his capture, trial and, presumably, quick hanging. The mere fact that they were related caused the judge to fear for his own life and that of his family. But there was little he could do about it, for these were also difficult times financially, and the Winston family had to refrain from frivolous spending. In fact, at one point, the judge had offered a portion of Hunting Tower for sale, though no deal was ever consummated. Patrick Henry visited his uncle less frequently as he had in the past, fearing that their association might cause even more problems.

In December, some good news reached the plantation. The colonialists had won a decisive victory in the Battle of Great Bridge, an important shipping point to the port city of Norfolk. As a result, on New Year's Day, 1776, Lord Dunmore began a bombardment of Norfolk that would eventually leave a majority of the city in ashes. His action was less of an attempt to win territory than it was revenge, as British rule in Virginia had essentially come to an end.

The balance of spring and early summer passed without significant news, and life at Hunting Tower settled back into a familiar routine. Crops were planted and cultivated. Peter and Arthur worked hard to keep the farm stocked with flails, spoke dogs, gimlets, hay hooks and other tools in addition to tending the horses.

Although the Continental Army had been established more than a year earlier, the time-consuming task of recruiting and training troops continued. On August 27, 1776, those troops were finally ready to do battle with their British counterparts at the Battle of Long Island. According to reports that filtered back to Hunting Tower, this was truly the first major battle of the war, and it didn't go well. Under the command of General Washington himself, the Americans were forced to withdraw. A few weeks later, Patrick Henry ignoring his self-imposed banishment, rode to Hunting Tower to confer with his uncle. Working in the barn, Peter saw Patrick arrive and emerged to see what urgency could have caused him to ignore danger and visit the plantation.

As Patrick dismounted, he saw the giant youth approaching. "Peter," he said, "would you look after my horse and then join me and my uncle in the main house? I have news of the war, and I think you may be interested in what I have to tell him."

"Yes, sir, Mr. Henry," Peter replied. "I'll see to it right away." Peter led the horse to the trough outside the barn, where the animal could quench its thirst. Walking toward the open doors, he caught Arthur's attention and asked him to take care of the horse once he had finished drinking. It was unlike Peter to let anyone complete a task to which he had been assigned, but he was eager to hear what Patrick Henry had to say. He walked briskly toward the main house, his legs hastening to an involuntary jog, and tentatively knocked on the door. After waiting a few seconds with no response, Peter lifted his arm to rap on the door again when it opened.

Judge Winston drew his head back in surprise. "Peter, what do you need?" the judge inquired.

"Mr. Henry told me to come to the house for news on the war."

"Well, for the life of me, I don't know what it is that would concern you, but come in, my boy, come in." Peter followed the judge to the parlor. In a stately wing-backed chair, covered in a plain-woven, avocado-colored linen fringed at the seams, sat Patrick Henry, drinking tea. Anthony, Jr. stood near the fireplace.

Patrick looked up and said, "Good, good. I'm glad you could join us, Peter, because what I've got to say concerns you, too."

115

Addressing the men in the room, he continued, "As you probably know, the war has truly begun. General Washington has done the best he can, although he is quite constrained with limitations in troops and materials. Unfortunately, after the Battle of Long Island, he was forced to withdraw from the field. He led his troops, some nine thousand strong, to Kip's Bay, and although the retreat was orderly, some of the troops took to looting and deserting, and morale disintegrated rather rapidly.

"I was told that the remaining troops did manage to dig in, but the English sent their navy and bombarded with such a barrage as even the most seasoned soldiers had never seen. Then the British conducted an amphibious landing, and some say that our boys were buried with so much dirt from the cannon fire that they couldn't even return fire. From what I hear, General Washington was absolutely furious as our troops began a somewhat disorderly retreat. I've even heard tales that the Hessians were bayoneting Americans who were trying to surrender.

"Most of the remaining troops were able to make it to Harlem Heights, but the next day—I think it was September 16—the British came after us intent on crushing our army on the Island of Manhattan. We were down to about two thousand troops, and the good general was determined to keep what remained of our forces intact, so they were again in retreat.

"That's when the English made a rather formidable mistake. They sounded the foxhunt bugle call and, rather than intimidating our lads, insulted them, and they turned back to fight. According to reports, our boys faced five thousand British troops, and, even though they were outnumbered more than two to one, they pushed the English back into retreat. We were able to win our first major battle.

"However, unless we can recruit some reinforcements, I fear we shall not prevail in our worthy cause. That's what I've been doing for the past several days, and it's why I'm here now."

"What do you mean?" asked Judge Winston.

"In this room, uncle, we have two strong lads who would most certainly do us both proud if you would let them join the conflict. I know this is a difficult thing for you to consider, but consider it you must, for we are desperate for able-bodied men. I truly believe that Anthony, Jr., with the proper training and with his breeding, could well be promoted to an officer's position within a short period of time. As for Peter, he will make a fine soldier and will be an imposing figure on any battlefield."

The judge's face went pale as he contemplated what he had just been asked. Allowing Peter to go off to war was one thing. After all, Peter had been pestering him to go to fight ever since the convention in Richmond. But the thought of sending his only son off to battle was a notion the judge was simply not willing to entertain. "I'm afraid you ask too much, Patrick," responded the judge, speaking as though neither subject was in the room. "Sending Peter off to war is one thing, though I fear that our productivity at Hunting Tower shall suffer the consequences. But to send both Peter and Anthony would cause great harm to our abilities to function and fulfill our obligation to provide hemp to the war effort. I will agree to let Peter go, but as for Anthony, I must decline your request."

There was a long, awkward silence in the room. Secretly, Anthony, Jr. was breathing a sigh of relief. Peter, meanwhile, was so elated he could barely contain himself. This was what he had wanted all along, a chance to be free, and a chance to fight for freedom for his adopted country.

Finally, Patrick Henry broke the silence. "I understand," he said to his uncle. "Of course, you need young Anthony to run things here at the plantation, and your efforts have not gone unnoticed."

"I appreciate your understanding," replied the judge in a formal acknowledgment. Then he looked directly at Peter. "If I didn't know any better, I'd say you conspired with my nephew. But I know how you feel, and I release you from any further obligation to me and to Hunting Tower so that you may join the army. I would only ask that you take a couple of weeks to help train someone else to assist Arthur."

"Yes, sir," replied Peter. "I wouldn't think of leaving until all was in order. Thank you, sir." Immediately, he said goodbye to Patrick and left the room. He didn't want to show too much emotion, especially in light of how the judge had treated him over the past ten years, but deep inside he felt elated. *This is one of the best days of my life,* he thought, only vaguely recalling happy days with his family on the island. Those memories now lived in the furthest recesses of his mind.

Peter stood on the porch surveying the place he had called home for almost a decade and thought of Susannah Anderson. *I must see her before I leave. But how? When?* Still contemplating this, he descended the steps of the porch and crossed the short distance to the barn where Arthur was still at work.

"Arthur, I have the most wonderful news," Peter said. "I'm to be allowed to join the army."

Arthur looked up from where he was repairing a moldboard

118

on one of the wheeled plows. Arthur stopped swinging the hammer, but remained silent for several moments. When he finally spoke, he did not turn his head. "I knows how much this means t' you, Peter. I really does, but I's goin' t' miss you a powerful lot. You's been more like family t' me than anyone else I can remember. You's been like a son, and I fears that the day you leaves, I's never gonna see you 'gain. But I's happy fo' you, Peter. I's happy fo' you."

Peter walked the few paces that separated the two men. Arthur still wouldn't look at him, not wanting Peter see the tears welling up in his eyes. The young man took Arthur's face in his hands, lifted his head and looked directly at him.

"Know this, and know it well," Peter said. "I love you, and I always will. You have been the father I needed desperately after losing my family so long ago. I will always remember the time you spent teaching me everything you know about blacksmithing and carpentry, about family, about being a man and..." Peter's voice broke, emotion welling up in his throat. "...and about God and freedom of the heart." Peter could tell Arthur was fighting back tears.

The two men embraced. Arthur said nothing. When they parted, he reached into his satchel and pulled out a small, worn book. The plain paper cover was creased and torn in some places. Arthur held it in his hands for a moment, then handed it to Peter.

"What's this?" Peter asked, still unable to put the puzzling letters together in his mind.

"It's a Bible," Arthur said, "Ol' an' New Testament. Not somethin' folk like me even thinks o' gettin'. I's saved my Christmas shillings t' get it. Taught myself its words. Go on now, take it."

"You're giving this to me?" Peter asked, while Arthur nodded. "But I can't read."

"You will," he said with certainty. Peter threw his arms around the old Negro again.

"Thank you. Don't worry," Peter said in his ear, "nothing's going to happen to me, and I'll see you sooner than you can blink an eye."

It wasn't Peter's safety that Arthur was concerned about. He had been feeling poorly, and his body was failing him in more ways than he had let on. He was certain that his days would soon to come to an end.

8.

PREPARING TO LEAVE

THE NEXT FEW DAYS were a flurry of activity for Peter as he prepared for what he thought to be his certain destiny—to gain and fight for freedom. At Hunting Tower, he set about teaching his replacement, Richard, how best to assist Arthur in the barn. They covered care and feeding of the horses. He also showed Richard various carpentry tools and their uses. Most difficult was attempting to teach Richard the tricks of the blacksmithing trade.

Richard quickly grasped the function of each tool and how to use them. He was quite intelligent, and soon understood his responsibilities. Performing those tasks presented a problem. Richard had always been assigned to fieldwork, where he had developed sinewy muscles best suited to flexibility and endurance. But work as a blacksmith required pure power and the kind of massive muscles that Peter had acquired naturally. Peter was by far one of the largest men in all the colonies. Had a formal accounting of size been conducted, he may have been ruled the largest. Richard was no match for Peter's brute power, but he was slowly adapting, and Arthur, despite his failing health, would continue the training long after Peter had left.

Peter also had to decide what he was going to take with him. His precious silver-initialed buckles would go with him wherever his travels might lead, as would the Bible he'd just received from Arthur. He would also be taking the tri-corner hat that Judge Winston had purchased for him many years before, but the hat given to him by Susannah's father, James Anderson, would be staying here at Hunting Tower, since the judge had assured Peter that the plantation would always be his home. He had meager clothing. Peter had not received any new clothes in some time, and most of his shirts and trousers were well worn from hard labor. In addition, Peter had filled out to a massive 260 pounds, and many of his clothes simply didn't fit.

Sitting on the bed in his room while sorting through his paltry wardrobe, he heard a knock on his door. Judge Winston walked right in, such a rarity that Peter was again a bit startled.

"I see you're packing, Peter," intoned the judge, clearing his throat. "You know, you'll be sorely missed here at Hunting Tower. You've become as much family as anyone could possibly be, save my very own flesh and blood."

"Yes, sir," replied Peter, "except for Mrs. Winston. I don't think she really likes me."

"Well, Peter, Mrs. Winston is quite set in her ways. She's not much for a change in routine, and when I showed up with you

some ten years ago, she was not too pleased, I'll admit. She's become used to you, though, and I hasten to say that she'll probably
miss you, though I doubt that she'll ever admit to it. How is the
packing coming along? Do you have everything you need?"

"Yes, sir, I think so."

"Let me see."

Peter held up a couple of shirts, the best he could find in his
small collection.

"No, no, no," said the judge. "Those won't do at all. You're
going to be representing Hunting Tower and Buckingham County, I daresay, and you need to look better than that. What about
your trousers?" Again, Peter showed the judge what he was planning to take. After a few moments of studying Peter's selections,
Judge Winston was not too pleased. "Peter," he said. "I believe a
shopping trip is in order. We need to procure some more suitable
clothes for you."

"Yes, sir," Peter agreed, thrilled by the prospect of having new
clothes that fit. "I'll go hitch a team to the carriage. Which one
would you like to take?"

"No need for that. You'll be going by yourself. After all, in a
couple of days, you'll be on your own to join the army. You don't
need me to go with you to town. Just go to the mercantile, select
a couple pair of britches and a couple of shirts ... oh, and a jacket
to keep the chill off during the cold northern evenings. Just have
them put your selections on my bill at the store.

"By the way, when you decide which horse to ride into town,
choose wisely. That horse is my gift to you. Any horse except one
of the Creams, that is."

Peter hardly knew what to say. He stammered a couple of

unintelligible syllables before the judge walked over to where he was standing beside his chest of drawers. Judge Winston opened his arms and, considering Peter's size, gave him as big a hug as he could muster. At first, the giant young man just stood there with his arms at his side, trying to decide what to do. After several seconds that actually seemed like minutes, he raised his burly arms and returned the judge's embrace. When they broke away, Peter could see tears welling in Judge Winston's eyes. This was the second time in recent days that a man more mature than himself had exhibited such emotion. Although Peter wasn't quite sure how to react, there was an unfamiliar but welcome feeling in his heart. It wasn't quite the same as with Susannah Anderson, but it was genuinely warm and sincere.

The judge held up his index finger. "No words, Peter, no words. Just know that I love you almost like a son, that I shall miss you, and I shall pray for your well-being and safety every day." As with his previous visit, the judge did not want nor did he wait for a reply. Rather, he turned on one foot and exited the room, leaving Peter to muse deeply.

Peter didn't quite know what to make of the exchange. *First Arthur, now the Judge,* he thought. A blend of unfamiliar feelings swirled inside Peter. He ran a finger over his silver shoe buckles, which rested just inside his haversack. Picking them up again, he turned them over and over in his hands, his mind flashing to the kidnappers' ship and his desperate attempt to rescue his falling shoe, the only remnant of home he had kept with him all these years at Hunting Tower. *Is this what it would have been like?* He wondered. As a grown man, he had never known a father's love, but now, in the same day no less, two of his mentors had demonstrated fatherly-like affection. For a fleeting moment, their words gave him pause, and he briefly considered staying. After a few seconds, he carefully tucked the shoe buckles back into his haversack, determination set on his face. *Freedom is worth any cost*, he thought, resolute.

Peter did as instructed. That very afternoon, he chose a Canadian horse named Isabel. He grabbed one of the saddles from the stall railing inside the barn and slung it over her back. Securing his satchel just behind the saddle, he reached into it and pulled out his silver shoe buckles. With his deft hands, he quickly adjusted the cinch strap to temporarily accommodate the buckles, which now rested neatly near the skirt on either side of the saddle that he and Arthur had worked on together. Peter thought it fitting that he would be carrying a memento from each of the paternal figures in his life. Satisfied with the result, he hoisted himself on her broad back, grabbed the reins and trotted her out of the barn. He had usually driven a team of horses from a carriage or wagon, so mounting his own horse was a fairly new experience. His innate relationship with horses served him well, though, and he was soon comfortable astride the filly.

On the trip to town, his thoughts turned back to the day when Judge Winston had purchased him from the orphanage. As then, the season was now turning the leaves on the trees hues of red and gold, and there was a crispness and freshness in the air. Peter inhaled deeply, savoring the moment. *I am a free man!* He rejoiced inwardly. *Free!* The result of that glorious thought made the trees seem more vibrant. Their leaves were almost sanguine, spilling like blood onto brilliant gold. The scent in the air was unmistakably that of freedom. He opened his lungs to take it in.

125

Feeling happier than he could ever remember, Peter arrived in town, hitching Isabel to the post in front of the store and striding in with confidence in his step. Looking around, he saw several bolts of material for bedding and curtains and various accoutrements that went into the making of fine furnishings. He spotted countless leather goods. *Crafted by Edna Watkins' husband?* He wondered. Fleetingly, he recalled how kind Edna had been to him while he had lived in old Caleb's shack on the wharf at City Point. Then, remembering his purpose for visiting the store, he surveyed the layout and recalled that shirts were kept in the back left-hand corner. On his way, Peter glanced momentarily to the right side of the store. What he saw made him halt abruptly, forgetting all intention.

About halfway toward the back of the store, giving thoughtful consideration to the new shipment of straight-lined dresses, stood Susannah Anderson. A combination of anxiety and glee flooded Peter's chest. His heart thumped wildly, and he felt a discernible weakness in his knees. He wanted to speak to her. He wanted to sweep her into his arms. He wanted to hold her tight to his chest and never let her go.

But Peter couldn't move. Just the sight of her heightened his nerves. His body went limber, making him lose all sense of coordination.

In a trance, he gazed at this beautiful young woman, unable to avert his eyes from her petite, slender frame. His cheeks burned as he noted the shape of her dress. *She looks so fragile. So tiny. Did I hurt her that day on the street?* Peter wondered, instinctively protective. *She would disappear in my arms.* As she moved, her narrow nose cast a moving shadow on her rose-pink cheek, ending in a small point just above her round lips. *How would they taste?* He wondered.

She pulled her lip inward with her teeth in concentration, looking doubtfully at her selections. Sensing her dilemma, a clerk made his way over to Susannah. When she looked up, Peter could see her wide, bright eyes. *Green,* he recalled immediately from their prior encounter on the street. *If I was only close enough to look into them again for just a moment.* She grinned in response to something the clerk said. Peter was within earshot, but failed to hear. He took in little else but Susannah. On her right cheek, he noticed a small dimple that deepened when she smiled. He imagined how it would feel to place his finger there, then to those lips. His spine tingled with excitement.

Another female customer passed by, remarking to Susannah that she would look lovely in anything, even those awful frocks. Susannah shook her head and giggled in response, which unexpectedly warmed Peter's heart. As she did, she raised one of her delicate hands to cover her mouth. He could see the swell of small veins in the back of her hand, no doubt visible from many hours of household chores. He recalled the countless times he was fortunate enough to hold that soft hand in his. He imagined now how it would feel resting on his chest and her fingers against his lips.

As she made her way to the counter, Susannah reached back with her hand to check the arrangement of her flaxen hair, its light, sundry tones pulled back from her round face and fastened in the back, dangling a mass of curls. Peter couldn't fathom what held it all in place, but it looked to him loose enough to fall at the slightest bump. He pictured those long locks cascading freely around her face, over her shoulders and back. *How would they smell?* He wondered. He felt his voice rising from his throat as he was about to call out to her, the loveliest young girl in the county. Wondering suddenly if anyone else had caught him ogling Susannah, his eyes darted around the store.

A loud crash erupted behind him. A large stand bearing an array of men's suspenders had fallen to the floor. Realizing he had caused the spill when he backed up and soon everyone in the store would know it, he quickly ducked behind a tall cabinet. After a few moments, the patrons returned to their business, and a clerk walked over to pick up the mess, frowning in his direction. Thankfully, Susannah was at the front of the store and had not seen him.

She probably would have scoffed at me, Peter thought, renewing the memory of her reproach in Richmond following Patrick Henry's speech in which she had called him—and those who thought like him—fools. He quelled the urge to call out to her. In fact, he thought it best to avoid any contact whatsoever, so he turned on one foot toward the opposite side of the store and cautiously ducked down as best he could behind a few displays of men's clothing to conceal his frame. The detour took him to the trousers rather than the shirts. He selected two pairs of tan breeches, determining that the waist would fit him well. He wasn't concerned about the length, since his habit was to simply roll the legs up just below the knee and buckle them. Besides, he knew not a single pair would have been long enough for anyone as tall as he.

Peter cast a furtive glance over his shoulder. Susannah still hadn't noticed him as she made her choices. *So far, so good,* Peter thought, making his way back to the shirts. He selected two, brown and tan to match the breeches he had previously chosen. He again glanced in Susannah's direction, but she was gone. Immediately, he felt conflicted. *Probably just as well that she left before she saw me,* Peter reasoned. But his heart battled his mind. *What if I never see her again?* He wondered with dejection.

Remembering what Judge Winston had told him, Peter made his way to the center of the store where outerwear was prominently displayed in anticipation of winter's onset. As he rounded the corner, paying careful mind to the shelves and racks around him lest he knock them over, too, a female customer, balancing a tower of parcels that obscured her face, crashed right into Peter's chest. "Oh my, pardon me," she said, packages tumbling to the floor.

Realizing the girl was Susannah, Peter once again felt that familiar tightness gripping him from throat to waist. *Why does she have to look that way?*

Never lifting her eyes, she bent over to gather up her purchases. Just as he did before in the middle of the dusty road, Peter immediately bent down to help her, and her eyes locked on his. An awkward silence seemed to linger before Peter finally spoke.

"It was entirely my fault," he apologized. "I should have seen you coming and gotten out of your way. Although I must say, you need to have someone help you with your things so you don't have to pile them up so high. Thank goodness there are no wild horses in here," he teased.

Susannah just looked at him for a moment and then threw her head back in laughter, again flooding Peter's heart with warmth. "Why, Peter Francisco, you've just made a joke. I didn't think you had it in you."

"Yes, I guess I did, but please don't think it was at your expense."

"Well, of course, it's at my expense, and I deserve it. Oh, Peter, how have you been, and what are you doing here?"

"I've been well, Susannah. But I don't think you want to know why I'm here."

"Why in the world not?"

"I'm buying things to take with me to sign up for the Continental Army."

"Oh, I see." Susannah seemed to be gathering her thoughts for a moment. "Peter, can you ever forgive my rudeness when last we spoke? My words were quite harsh, and the times have found Father thinking differently than when we last met in Richmond."

"How is that?"

"We've been following the events very closely. England's rule has become almost unbearable. We have family in Boston, and they have convinced us that our path is undeniable. We must claim the colonies for ourselves or suffer the consequences. In fact, Father has accepted a commission to establish a militia here in the south. He is to be a captain."

"Susannah," Peter said, overjoyed at this unexpected revelation, "what surprisingly good news! Does this mean we can be friends again?"

"Of course. Yes, of course. I just hope you can forgive my words. I simply cannot apologize enough."

Peter took her hand and they both stood up, oblivious to Susannah's packages still strewn on the floor.

"Forgive you? How could I not forgive you?" Peter said. Without thinking, perhaps emboldened by his newfound independence, he added with unwavering self-assurance, "How could I not forgive the woman I love?"

"You…you love me?" Susannah breathed in disbelief. "Oh, my dear Peter, I love you, too," Susannah confessed quietly, so no one in the shop would overhear. "I have ever since the day you saved me from the horses on this very street," she whispered, moving toward the storefront.

A fiery passion lit within him, stirring him to the core. The euphoria was intoxicating, unlike anything he had ever felt before. Then, a disheartening thought occurred to him. "Do you realize that we've spent this last year and a half in silence? Do you realize how much time we have wasted?"

"Yes, Peter, I do. But we have our whole lives ahead of us."

"But first I must go to fight in the north. I must! It's the reason that Judge Winston has granted my freedom, and it's that very freedom that gives me the courage to ask if you'll wait for my return."

Susannah hesitated for a moment. Then looking up at him, she spoke without restrain, "I don't want you to go, but I do understand why you feel you must. Of course, I will wait for you. I will wait the rest of my life if that is what it takes."

Peter reached out slowly and gently touched the soft back of her hand. Her hand seemed like a child's next to his. With his fingers, he traced the maze of violet-colored veins. Taking her hand in both of his, he raised it to his mouth and planted soft kisses on the top and along her delicate wrist, then pressed it against his chest. In a swift, impulsive motion, he wrapped one arm gently around her small waist and enveloped her, drawing her close. His powerful arm lifted her slightly off her feet so her face pointed upward, directly into his. They were oblivious to the curious patrons congregating around them, now straining to see Susannah, who had all but disappeared inside Peter's massive frame. Peter could feel her tremble in his arms. *Or is that me?* He thought for a fleeting moment. Pausing slightly in anticipation, he buried his face in her cascading curls and inhaled deeply memorizing their pomade scent.

At that moment, one of the men in the store, who had witnessed Susannah's rescue at the hands of the giant, raised his fist in the air. "To Peter and Susannah, huzzah, huzzah, huzzah! May Peter return home safely and may they have many offspring." The small crowd began to applaud and shout their approvals. Though Peter had not proffered a formal marriage proposal—that would have to wait until he could ask Susannah's father—the nature of their relationship was evident and witnessed by many.

As if just remembering they were with company, they looked around, a bit embarrassed by all the attention. The two set to the task of gathering up all the dropped packages. Peter stopped at the counter, requested that his items be placed on the judge's account and carried both his and Susannah's items to her carriage.

As Peter assisted Susannah into the landau, she turned and looked at him. "Promise me that you'll stop by our farm before you go off to the army. Please promise."

"I will be there tomorrow afternoon," Peter replied. "I promise."

Susannah's hand lingered in Peter's until the driver began to pull away. As the carriage made its way out of town, Peter saw her lean her head out of the window, looking back at him. As he watched the dust flying from the wheels of the carriage, he thought, *This is a far better parting than the one at Richmond.*

Peter barely needed Isabel to transport him back to Hunting Tower, the only real home he had known for the past ten years. He felt like he was drifting. Every once in a while, he could hear someone yelling "Huzzah, huzzah!" After a time, he realized that he was the one hollering.

The autumn dusk was just settling when he arrived home, and Judge Winston was stepping out onto the front porch. "Peter, my boy. I was wondering what had happened to you. You were gone a long time. How much of a bill did you rack up?"

Peter looked at the judge thinking he might be in trouble, but then the judge started to laugh.

"Come and show me what you bought for yourself. I hope you made your selections as wisely as you did in choosing Isabel for your horse."

Peter walked up the steps to the porch, and the two men sat on chairs while he showed the judge his trousers and shirts.

"But what of the winter jacket I told you to get?" the judge inquired.

"I was on my way to get it, but ... I got distracted," said Peter somewhat sheepishly, and he related the story of his encounter with Susannah.

When he had finished telling his story, the judge looked at him and said, "Well, that's fine, Peter. But remember what I told you. You always have a home here, and I hope you'll come back to us someday."

"Thank you, sir," Peter said. "I'll never forget that." He rose and shook the judge's hand, then went to find Arthur. There was no one he wanted to spend time with more than the old slave who had taken him under his wing and taught him so much. Their final hours together passed much too quickly before they bade goodbye and shared one last father-son embrace.

With his mind continuing to think about everything that lay ahead of him, Peter slept but a single fitful hour. He had said all his farewells the night before, and he wanted to get an early start. So, well before the faithful rooster could announce the dawn of another day, he finished packing his few possessions in a satchel, slung it over his shoulder, saddled Isabel, and rode away from Hunting Tower for what could be the last time.

There was one more stop he wanted to make before setting out on the long ride that would destine him for the army. He directed Isabel toward the Anderson farm. He would arrive well before the afternoon hour he had promised Susannah, but he was certain she wouldn't mind.

9.

OFF TO WAR

THE RIDE TO THE MANSION, the Andersons' 1,600-acre plantation, normally took about an hour, but Peter was so excited at the thought of seeing Susannah again that he had Isabel at a near full gallop, and he covered the distance in about half the time. He rode up to the main house, dismounted and knocked on the door. James Anderson answered. Peter's mind was so preoccupied with recent developments, he didn't even think about how Susannah's father would react to his visit.

"Peter," he said, extending his hand, "it's good to see you."

"Th—Thank you, sir," Peter said tentatively, hesitating to take his hand. He was a little surprised by the warm greeting. "It's good to see you, too, sir."

Sensing Peter's uneasiness, James Anderson tried to make amends. "Peter, I'd like to apologize for my conduct in Richmond.

It was I who acted the fool, and, for that, I am sincerely sorry."

"No need to apologize, sir. We each have our different views."

"That's just it, Peter," he said, stepping out onto the porch with Peter, "We are no longer on opposing sides. We have changed our thinking, and I am to be commissioned as an officer in the militia."

"That's great news, sir," Peter said, genuinely pleased. "I guess we'll be fighting in the war together, even though we may be hundreds of miles apart. If you don't mind me asking, what changed your mind?"

"Well, there are many reasons, but, primarily, we believe that since we are part of the Church of England, it is our duty to remain loyal to the King because he is recognized as the head of the church. Admittedly, many of us have feared loss of land and general lack of support that would result from severing ties with the Crown.

"I've since realized," he continued, "that our ancestors didn't risk everything, including their lives, to venture to a New World just to perpetuate their future generations with the same merciless oppression and obligatory acquiescence. They wanted something better. To ignore that would betray their sacrifice. I see that now."

James Anderson put his hand on Peter's shoulder before he said, "I know this might sound a bit strange coming from me, especially in light of our last encounter, but Susannah told me about your plans to join the Army, and I think what you are doing is commendable.

"But enough of this talk. I know you've come to bid farewell to Susannah, not talk to me. Besides, she'd have my head if she lost any of the precious little time you two have remaining. Let me go and find her while you make yourself comfortable here on the porch."

Peter sat down on a two-person swing suspended by chains from the veranda ceiling, and it wasn't long before Susannah came around the corner wearing a working dress like the ones he remembered seeing her examine in the store. "Peter," she said with surprise, "I didn't expect you until later in the day."

"Yes, I know, but I couldn't wait to see you again."

"Well, I must look a sight. I was picking the last of the tomatoes, but since you have arrived early, I don't look my best."

"I suppose I could get back on my horse and circle the plantation for a while," Peter said dryly.

"There you go again, making another joke," she smiled. "Anyway, will you wait here for just a bit while I go make myself more presentable?"

"You look just fine to me," replied Peter approvingly.

"Well, wait here anyway." Susannah disappeared into the house, returning shortly in one of her finest dresses and bearing a pitcher of cold tea. After pouring a glass for each of them, she took a seat next to Peter on the swing. This was exactly what he had hoped for—the chance to sit close to the girl who had captured his heart. They spoke of things to come, but their conversation wasn't nearly as important as the chance to just sit and enjoy each other's company. Though it hardly seemed like it, three hours disappeared as quickly as the morning mist on a warm summer's day.

Susannah's father soon appeared. "I realize you two have a lot of catching up to do, and I know how difficult it is, knowing you'll be apart for some time, but if young Peter is going to make any headway on his trip, he should be getting on his way."

"Of course, sir. You're absolutely right," Peter agreed. Turning toward Susannah, he continued, "Your father is right. I do have a long journey ahead of me. I can't be certain where it will lead. But know this deep inside you," he said, looking intently into her green eyes, trying to make her understand, "I will return. No matter how far away I go, no matter how long it takes, I will return."

"Peter," responded Susannah, "that's all I need to know. And when you return, I will be here waiting." She then pulled a dainty handkerchief from the sleeve of her dress. "I want you to have this. I want you to keep it with you at all times. Take it out and think of me whenever you get lonely, knowing I will be with you."

Peter took the handkerchief and held it to his nose, smelling the sweet scent of Susannah. "Thank you," he said, smiling at her. "I will carry it close to my heart."

They both looked around and were surprised to find that Susannah's father had withdrawn to give them a last few moments of privacy. Glancing back at each other, their faces drew closer and closer, and soon they felt the warmth of each other's lips. They lingered in that kiss for several moments before Peter pulled away.

"Forgive my boldness, Susannah," Peter said. "Perhaps I shouldn't have done that."

"If you hadn't," Susannah interrupted, "I would have. My lips and my heart are yours to keep, Peter Francisco, and don't ever forget that. Will you write to me to tell me how you are?"

"I don't know how to read or write," he said regretfully, "but I will enlist the aid of someone more educated than I am. So, yes,

I will write to you."

Peter rose from the swing, offering his hand to assist Susannah to her feet as well.

"Where are you headed when you leave here?" she inquired.

"To western Virginia to join up with the 10th Virginia Regiment. Those were the arrangements that Patrick Henry made for me."

"Then your journey is indeed a long one, so I'll not keep you. Just remember," she said, lowering her voice to a whisper, "that I love you. I'll always love you."

As natural as breathing, their hands connected as they descended the porch steps. Halfway down, he turned back. Susannah's hand was still in his. He released it and with both arms encircled her waist, lifting her effortlessly into the air, swathing her in his arms. Her balance slightly offset by the sudden feeling of weightlessness, Susannah placed both hands onto Peter's arms to brace herself. They lingered like that for several minutes, the novel proximity of their gaze stopping the world. Finally, Peter returned her gently to the stairs. He kissed her again, and they embraced one last time.

Peter walked down the last few steps, and then reached into his satchel. When he removed his hand, he was holding boneca de trapo. He walked back to the steps and held out the cherished rag doll to Susannah. "This is one of my only childhood possessions, and I want you to keep it for me until I return." After mounting his horse, he looked at Susannah from atop Isabel and said, "I love you with all my heart. Wait for my return."

"I love you, too, Peter Francisco. Keep safe, my love," Susannah breathed, just as her father emerged onto the porch.

The young soldier-to-be wheeled his horse around and headed off the Anderson plantation. As he reached the main road, he couldn't resist turning around and waving the fragrant handkerchief.

"He is going to war," her father stated evenly from behind her. "He may not return."

Hearing those words, Susannah could no longer suppress the wrenching knot of emotion that had been building in her throat. Though her eyes brimmed with tears, she fixed her smile. "He will return," she replied, her lip quivering slightly. She exaggerated her wave, not wanting Peter to sense anything had changed.

"You are pledged to George, Susannah. Do not forget that."

Susannah answered his warning with silence and continued to wave at Peter.

Peter watched her as he tugged at the reins and headed down the road—a road that would lead to celebrations and misery, to victories and defeats, but Peter knew none of this. *Someday, somehow,* he thought, *I will return on this road and claim Susannah Anderson as my wife.*

As Susannah and The Mansion disappeared out of view, the cool December air hit his face and his hard body gave with the rhythm of Isabel's charge. Peter pushed Isabel harder and faster, spurred by both a desire to explore and a new sense of purpose. Peter began to think about his journey. He felt certain he was exactly where God wanted him to be. He didn't regret the years he'd spent working at Hunting Tower and serving Judge Winston. He realized that the past decade had prepared him for this moment in ways he could have never imagined. He knew God had used each circumstance in his life to shape him—his mind, his heart, and even his body—for the fight ahead. Though it still often disturbed him that he knew nothing of his roots, where he had come from or what made him who he was, he did know where he was going. And he'd be going as a free man. He imagined being on the front lines, running alongside cavalrymen and officers, sword drawn, bellowing the battle cry as he cut into the enemy in the name of love and liberty. He could almost hear the pounding of horses' hooves on the ground as they retreated in victory.

★

The galloping sound, he realized, seemed so vivid because it was directly behind him, and closing fast. Before he knew it, a rider had overtaken him and stopped just ahead, blocking the path and forcing Peter to stop. *Did something happen back at the Andersons?* Peter wondered with a twinge of panic, pulling tightly on the reigns. As Isabel slowed, Peter tried to decipher who the gentleman rider was, but branches from a nearby maple tree hanging low over the trail cast a dark shadow on his face.

"State the nature of your business," Peter demanded.

"I saw you back there with Susannah," the eclipsed rider said, accusingly. "Who do you think you are?"

"What are you talking about?" Peter asked, realizing with a bit of relief that this intruder was not about to rob him.

Neither man dismounted his horse.

"I'm not blind. Now that you're a free man, do you think

the world is yours for the taking? Including Susannah? You have no business being with her. You have nothing! You are nothing! Heh, you don't even know who your parents are," he heckled, contempt in his voice. Peter felt a rush of blood and a roar in his head as the cutting words sank in. The rider's horse clopped forward into the sunlight shimmering through the Virginia pines, his narrowed, glaring eyes and furrowed brow now visible.

Peter recognized his nemesis immediately. He had the same crooked nose and sandy-colored hair Peter remembered from that day back at St. John's Church. His mind began to race as he quickly contemplated his potential actions and their consequences. Though he wanted nothing more than to beat this nuisance into a bloody pulp with his steely arms, Peter remained calm knowing full well, if given the chance to fight, his strength could kill his adversary which would permanently estrange him from the Anderson family and ruin any hope of one day marrying Susannah.

"Well, if it isn't George Carrington!" Peter said evenly. "Did you track me down just to taunt me or are you going to get off your horse and fight like a man? We both know that your scrawny little frame wouldn't last one blow from my fist." Suddenly, George jumped off his horse and threw his fists up in the air. "I'll take you on any day, Peter. You don't scare me."

Peter looked down at George and began to chuckle to himself. The mere notion of them fighting seemed humorous, particularly at the sight of George's hands, which were slender and appeared soft and unbroken from a subdued life of aristocracy. *He's probably never been in a fight in his life,* Peter thought to himself as he leaned down to consult Isabel. "What do you think, girl? Should I teach him a lesson now or wait until his muscles have matured a little more?"

"Get off the horse, slave!" George yelled as he yanked at Peter's leg, his foot still in the stirrup. "It's time you learn who is serving whom and why you will never marry Susannah." As George kept tugging at Peter's leg with one hand, he used the other to loosen his saddle, which caused Peter to slowly twist towards the ground.

Having no other recourse, Peter made to jump off his horse and shouted, "You asked for it, and now you're gonna get it."

George had located and picked up a thick tree branch off the ground as Peter was dismounting and swung it as hard as he could at Peter. The log, nearly as round as a cannonball, hit Peter squarely in the back of the head, knocking his tri-corn hat to the ground. As Peter's feet hit the earth, he stood straight up barely flinching at the large piece of timber that had just struck his skull.

George swallowed deeply when he realized that his makeshift club didn't seem to faze his enemy.

"Did you just hit me with that little stick?" Peter teased. "I don't think you really know who you're dealing with, George."

Peter swung his fist, but George blocked the punch by holding up the log with both hands. They both heard a loud crack as the branch split in two. George's eyes widened at the two pieces of wood now left in each of his hands. Within seconds, George was doubled over on the ground as Peter's second swing caught him in the middle of his gut.

Standing over George, Peter cocked his fist to deliver another punch when he realized that George was grunting and gasping for air. *Great! Now I've damaged something. I knew this was a bad idea.*

Peter leaned down and whispered in George's ear, "I could take you right now. I could beat you to a pulp and no one would know it. You want me to do that?" George shook his head as vehemently. "I didn't think so. It's your lucky day, because I'm not going to. You know why?" Peter asked rhetorically. "Because I know that is not the way to win Susannah's heart."

"Come on. Get up!" Peter shouted. "You're the one that tried to pull me off my horse, remember?" Peter grabbed the back of his pants in one hand and the collar of his shirt in another. He tossed George back up onto his horse with his head and arms hanging over on one side and his legs dangling down the other.

"Don't say I didn't warn you, ol' Georgy," Peter sneered as he slapped the backside of George's horse. The horse jumped and began to gallop while Peter yelled, "I'll talk with Susannah any time I want and don't you forget it."

★

Heading northwest toward the mountains of western Virginia and the Shenandoah Valley, Peter maintained a steady pace throughout the rest of the day. Sometimes he found traveled paths on which to journey, but, as Peter progressed toward the setting sun, he found himself riding deeper and deeper into dense forests and places where no man had preceded him. Pine trees and other conifers dominated the landscape, and their piquant scent filled his nostrils and ignited his senses. Abundant deer and squirrels curiously watched the lone traveler as they foraged for food. Peter had never been in such a land, a land almost devoid of the living, unpolluted by human endeavors. The topography—gently rolling hills and majestic forests—was unlike any he had seen. *This was truly a land worth fighting for*, he thought, and he felt as one with the earth. The only sounds to be heard were those of Isabel's hoofs rising and falling in the lush forest blanket and those of the birds chirping from the highest boughs of the trees.

A mix of magnificent colors painted the far horizon as the sun gradually dropped out of sight, and Peter began looking for a clearing where he could camp for the night. Eventually he found a spot thick with pine straw, which he thought might make a comfortable mattress. Though he had ridden for many hours, fatigue was not great. Time had passed quickly with his thoughts constantly drawn back to the image of Susannah waving goodbye from the porch of her family's house.

So soft and delicate, he mused wistfully, closing his eyes and envisioning her again in his arms, an image he would turn to again and again over the coming months. *Her beautiful green eyes.* They revealed so many things unspoken. *Her sweet lips.* The memory of them sent his heart into a tailspin. *'My lips and my heart are yours to keep, Peter,'* he thought, replaying her words in his mind. He had never felt so content. Everything he had dreamed for so long was coming true at last.

Dismounting Isabel, he unsaddled the horse, removed her bridle, and hobbled her. Then he searched for some kindling with which to build a small fire to take the chill off the night. After clearing a large circle to avoid setting the forest itself on fire, he opened a second satchel containing dried beef and pork and biscuits, a going-away present of sorts from Petunia. As he ate, his mind contemplated what the future might hold, but he could never have imagined what was in store. Soon the day's events left him too weary to fight off slumber any longer. Using the saddle as a pillow, his silver buckles close by and Susannah's handkerchief in hand, Peter Francisco fell into a sound and dreamless sleep.

The next morning, there was no rooster to rouse Peter from his bed, only the light of the new day streaming through the trees. As he adjusted his eyes to the morning sun, he sensed that he was being watched. *Maybe if I keep still for a few minutes, whoever it is will go on his merry way.* A distinct odor filled his nostrils. *What is that smell?* The air reeked of tilled weeds and musk. *Could that be George, back for more? Could it be someone else?* His heart beat faster. Hearing a rustling in the leaves, Peter slowly reached under his belt for the small knife he had forged with a chestnut pistol-grip handle back at Hunting Tower. He rolled over quickly, arm raised, ready to defend himself against any marauder. His body stiffened at what he saw. He stopped the blade mid-air just before it came down. An inquisitive raccoon stared back at him. Peter breathed an immense sigh of relief. Startled by the creature's coal-black eyes, which mirrored his own, Peter lashed out with his hand, but the raccoon was too fast and bounded off into the underbrush. Chuckling to himself, he grabbed his water jug, slaked his morning thirst, and used the remainder to fully extinguish the dying embers of his fire. After eating a couple more biscuits, he saddled Isabel, then refilled his water jug from a nearby brook, and continued his journey. When Peter reached the edge of the Shenandoah Valley, he noticed the terrain had begun to change. To the west stood mountains like none he had seen before. They rose majestically skyward, jutting into the middle of the azure skies. Patrick Henry had told Peter that the sight of these would indicate he was to head in a more northerly direction, up the heart of the valley that bordered the mountains.

He spent a second night much like the first, and on the third day, about mid-afternoon, Peter cleared a small ridge and came upon an encampment near what would one day be Waynesboro, named for General Anthony Wayne, who would become one of George Washington's most important leaders in the Northern campaign. The center of the clearing was populated by all sorts, shapes and sizes of canvas tents clustered around campfires with steaming kettles suspended over them. Around the edge of the clearing were lean-tos, somewhat less accommodating structures. These had been built by the mountain men of western Virginia. Peter was surprised to notice the number of women and children also inhabiting the camp. *Surely,* he thought, *they are only here to bid their men folk farewell.* Something else also stood out—the wide variety of clothing worn by the camp's occupants. Some of the men wore clothing much like Peter's, while others appeared to be going off to a formal tea rather than a war. Most startling were the clothes of the mountain men. These were obviously the skins of animals that they had killed. Some of the skins were fairly plain. Others were adorned with colorful beading, and fringe hung from many of their shirt sleeves. Even their footwear was of animal skins. As Peter rode Isabel slowly into camp, people repeatedly stopped whatever they were doing and stared at the huge man joining their legion. There was only one word to describe someone of his stature—giant.

One tent in the center of the camp stood out from the others. It was considerably larger and whiter than the rest. What gave it prominence were the men in front of it, dressed in uniform. *This is probably Captain Hughes Woodson's tent,* Peter reasoned, though not entirely certain. Peter dismounted as one of the two men standing on either side of the tent flap approached.

"Good day," said the soldier. "What business have you here?"

"My name is Peter Francisco from Buckingham County. I was told to find Captain Woodson when I arrived and ... I've just arrived," he said with a sly grin.

"Well, well," mused the soldier looking up at Peter. "Aren't you the big one? Well, you've come to the right place. I'll tell the captain you're here." Retreating into the tent, the man soon reappeared followed by a young officer who carried an air of importance as he strode out to meet Peter.

"Oh, my goodness," Captain Woodson said, with eyebrows raised while, extending his hand. "Aren't you the big one?"

"So I've heard," replied Peter. "I was told to report to you so that I can join the army."

"I must say, it's nice to be getting two men for the price of one." Although Peter had developed a dry sense of humor over the years, he wasn't quite sure what the captain meant. "Alright then," the captain continued. "Come with me to sign your papers."

As they entered the tent, Captain Woodson indicated a small folding stool on which Peter was to sit. However, because of his size, the newcomer chose a solid wooden stool to the right of a makeshift table, which was just some planks spanning a couple of barrels, similar to those used during plantation feasts back at Hunting Tower.

The captain handed some papers to Peter, who looked at the two sheets for just a moment and then back at Woodson. "I don't know what these say," he told the captain.

148

"I'm sorry. Rest assured, you're not the first one unable to read or write, and I daresay you'll not be the last. Let me explain. By signing these papers, you are agreeing to serve in the Continental Army for a period of three years. In return, you'll receive one hundred acres of land, the sum of six dollars and sixty-seven cents each month, and a fine uniform. The uniforms have not been delivered as yet, although it might not be so easy to find one for your size. Do you understand?"

"Yes, sir, I think I do."

"Very well, then," Woodson said as he turned to the second sheet of paper. "Just make your mark there," he said, pointing to an area at the bottom of the page."

"Mark?" inquired Peter, tilting his head slightly to one side.

"Yes, your mark. Most men just make an X."

Peter did his best to make a perfect X and handed the paper back to Woodson.

"Congratulations, Peter Francisco, and welcome to the army. You are now officially a member of the 10th Virginia Regiment, Company 9. By the way, we are also called the Prince Edward Musketeers, since muskets will be our primary weapon." The captain then summoned the soldier who had greeted Peter outside the tent. Addressing him, Woodson ordered, "Show our newest recruit around, assign him to a tent and issue him a musket."

The soldier stepped out of the tent just behind Peter, who took another look around. What had appeared to be a crazy quilt of scattered tents was actually a group of fairly neat rows. Every group centered around a common fire. The soldier motioned Peter to follow, so the new musketeer took the reins of Isabel and fell in behind the young man. At the outer edge of the clearing, just a few paces in front of the lean-tos, the man came to a stop and pointed to a tent. "You'll be staying here for the time being, and you have three other tent mates, although I don't know where they are at the moment."

"Thank you," said Peter. "I'll meet them later. Where should I take my horse?"

"Up there," said the soldier, indicating the edge of the forest. "We have a makeshift corral set up, but I suggest you keep your saddle and bridle here with you."

He did meet his tent mates that evening, though none was especially distinguishable. Of course, each commented on the newcomer's size, and Peter was beginning to become a bit self-conscious about it all.

After a welcomed hot evening meal prepared by some of the camp women, Peter made his way to where the mountain men had staked their claim to temporary land. They were gathered around a campfire where they prepared and ate their own meals without the help of any females, and one of them was playing a harmonica. Since these men generally stayed to themselves and weren't much attuned to social skills, they looked up at Peter as he entered their area, none of them saying a word. Those who knew each other spoke among themselves. In a few minutes, Peter began to recognize the repetitiveness of the harmonica's tune, and he started to hum along with it in a marvelous tenor voice. All conversation stopped as he began to harmonize with the music, and when it was over, several of the mountain men voiced their appreciation and introduced themselves to him. That night, inside the tent, he was comforted by the thought that, for the first time, he had made friends with his peers. Before he lay down, there was just one more thing he had to do. Reaching over to his saddle, he slid his silver buckles off the cinch strap with care and wrapped them gently in Susannah's handkerchief, which was in his satchel. He drifted quietly into a deep sleep. His dreams, however, were not of new friends but of the young lady he had left behind.

We are on Susannah's porch. She is in my arms. She feels so warm. Our lips gently come together. My eyes close. My heart beats so fast, I think it will explode from the pressure. When I open my eyes, Susannah and I are alone on the deck of a schooner. It's like the one I remember. Boneca de trapo rests limply against the handle of a tangled mop on a cross plank. The topsails are taut from the wind, but the briny air around us remains still. Where are we sailing? I look down at Susannah. We are dressed in wedding clothes. She is radiant. You look beautiful, Susannah. I hear myself say. A familiar dock soon becomes visible. As we get closer, I see two figures watching as we approach. One of them is barefoot. The other wears what looks like a crimson cloak. Who are they? I cannot see their faces but hear them frantically yelling my name. Anxious, I pull Susannah into me. As I strain to identify them, the vessel lurches slightly, releasing our embrace and splashing us with surf. Spotty sections of my clothes cling to me.

A wet sensation awakened Peter. One of his tent mates had doused him with water to stir him.

"Hey, Goliath, stop your chattering," scoffed his neighbor, while the rest of them sniggered.

Peter smiled. "Sorry," he apologized, slightly embarrassed. *I didn't realize I talked in my sleep. What must I have said?* He thought, bemused.

He needn't wonder long. Soon, the entire tent broke out in a discordant rendition of the fife tune "The Girl I Left Behind Me." Amused by this revelation, Peter started laughing, then joined them in chorus until cantankerous shouts erupted from surrounding tents, silencing them back to slumber.

Since the regiment was not yet at full strength, the next several mornings Peter spent becoming familiar with army life, including taking and delivering orders, understanding lines of authority, and learning the basics of marching as a unit. This was not especially to his liking. After all, he was here to fight. That's what he wanted to learn most, and that's why he liked the afternoons the best, because that's when the enlistees were trained on how to use their weapons.

Each man had been issued a musket, a bayonet and a fighting sword. The men were taught how to load their nine-pound, five-foot long muskets using a cartridge of powder and ball. First, they were to tear the cartridge open with their teeth, prime the pan or frizzen, load the barrel with the balance of powder and the ball, and ram it all home with a rod. They were also shown that they could substitute the ball with pellets or even use a combination of pellets and ball. Once the weapon was loaded, rammed, and primed, the soldiers were to cock the musket, aim and fire. According to the Continental Army manual, this was actually a thirteen-step process, and each soldier was expected to complete the steps in about twenty seconds.

Peter had a fairly good aim, although he couldn't quite get the hang of reloading his musket as quickly as most of the others. On the other hand, his height, and especially the length of his arms, made him quite proficient in the use of his bayonet, which, when attached to the end of the musket, made quite a formidable weapon for close-range fighting. But that same size also made Peter uncomfortable in wielding his sword, and he often found himself swinging the blade too high, completely missing his intended target. This led to some lively discussions around the campfire with the mountain men, but Peter, naturally good-humored, usually took the kidding in stride.

John Allen, one of the men in the group, commented that he had heard that Benjamin Franklin thought the troops might be better equipped with bows and arrows, since that weapon could be fired six times compared to just once for a musket.

"Heck," said Allen, "if we was countin' the Virginia Giant, the bow and arrow could be fired a *dozen* times for ev'ry shot Peter got off." Laughter rang out from the others. "Now, I'll be first to admit that it takes a bit longer to get off a shot with our long guns, but I kin hit a squirrel at better'n a hunerd yards, and them muskets can barely hit a cow at fifty yards."

"I'm not looking to shoot a cow," Peter shot back. "That is unless the cow's wearing a red coat." The other men at the campfire broke out in cackles and horselaughs, but John Allen began to think that their joking was at his expense. As with most of the men in the group, Allen carried a tomahawk in his belt, and he withdrew it just as the laughter reached a crescendo.

"I kin hit any target same as you with your musket. Alls I need is my tomahawk. Go ahead. Pick a target, any target, and I jes' betcha I kin hit it."

Peter pointed to a tall pine tree and indicated a target area about ten feet up. "There you go, John Allen, see if you can hit that split in the branches."

Allen stood up, drew back with his weapon and let her fly. And

153

he stuck his tomahawk right where Peter had pointed. "There, you see," Allen boasted. "I put 'er right where you pointed."

"Well," said Peter, trying to hide a smirk. "I guess I'll not be starting a tomahawk war with the likes of you, John Allen. Just tell me one thing. How are you going to get that tomahawk down from that tree?"

This time the laughter of the others was uncontrollable, and this time John knew it was indeed at his expense. "I ain't much used to bein' laughed at," he growled, and at the same time, his hand reached behind him where he kept his skinning knife.

Peter's eyes narrowed, and for a moment he thought he might have a fight on his hands. Then he thought the better of it. "John, I'm sorry if I offended you. Come here and I'll help you get your tomahawk." The two men walked over to the pine tree, and Peter held his hand out palm up. "Sit on my hand," Peter said.

"What, are you daft, man?" retorted Allen.

"Just sit down," ordered Peter impatiently.

Allen did as instructed, and Peter calmly lifted the mountain man's entire weight up and over his head until Allen could easily reach the embedded tomahawk. Then he gently set him back on the ground. Allen looked at Peter and said, "I'll be startin' no kinda war with you, Peter Francisco." The two men shook hands and everyone had one final laugh before calling it a night.

Friends are often more kin than family, Peter concluded, content with his newfound comrades and silently thanking God for them. In his tent, before he lay down to sleep, Peter pulled out the Bible Arthur had given him. He ran his fingers gingerly over the soft paper cover and fanned its pages gently forward and backward. He was filled with a profound longing to read and understand

154

what God had to say to him. *I'm going to learn,* Peter thought, *even if it's the very last thing on earth I do.*

"Just wanna make sure no tomahawks had come t'find ya in here," John Allen said, poking his head inside the tent, interrupting Peter's thoughts.

Peter chuckled. "Nah, I'm good."

"Whatcha readin'?" John asked, tipping his head at the book in Peter's lap.

"Hoping to learn how to read it is more like it," Peter said quietly so he didn't disturb his tent-mates. He had already disturbed their slumber enough with his sleep-talking. "It's a copy of the Holy Bible."

"Bible? What's 'at?" John asked with sincere honesty.

"Well, God is new to me," Peter started, realizing with sudden clarity that, as a man from the wilds, John had probably never even seen a Bible much less heard of God. He explained it the simplest way he knew how. "From what I do know and understand, this book is somehow God's instruction manual to us—His wisdom about life written by people who knew Him best."

"Don't need none o' that," John said, holding up his hand. "But I kin respect your wantin' t'learn." John didn't give Peter much chance to respond before saying, "'Night, Peter."

Peter smiled and replied "'Night, John," even though he was sure John was already out of earshot. Inwardly, Peter knew that God had brought them together for a purpose, and he bowed his head and prayed that God would give him more opportunities to talk with John.

★

For weeks, the men continued to drill and become proficient with all of their weapons, and new men continued to filter into the camp. Almost a month after Peter's arrival, Colonel Edward Stevens was commissioned to be in charge of the regiment. More and more men came to sign up, and on December 15, 1776, the 10th Virginia Regiment finally met her quota of just over 700 men and was officially accepted into the Continental Army.

In the early months of 1777, the regiment received orders to join the main army, under the overall command of General George Washington, telling them to report to New Jersey to help defend Pennsylvania's capital, Philadelphia. Uniforms had finally arrived, but none was of suitable size for Peter, which was just fine with him. He had struck a kinship of sorts with the mountain men who were not issued any uniforms, and Peter found himself among them during their march north. *Interesting,* Peter thought, noticing that the women and children continued to tag along.

Is it really safe out here for them? He wondered. He couldn't even think of Susannah being out here. The very thought made his muscles tense. They quickly relaxed, though, when he let his imagination consider life as Susannah's husband. *What would it be like to see her every day? To make a home and a family with her?* He speculated. The reverie made him forget, for a moment, that he was marching to war.

10.

A BATTLE AND
A FRIEND FOR LIFE

In MAY, PETER AND THE REST of the regiment arrived at Middle Brook, New Jersey, where the main body of the Continental Army was assembling for battle. This army and its militia were a rag tag group, but Washington was pleased to count as many as 10,000 men under his command, especially since he'd had only about 1,000 just a few months earlier. The problem was that many of the men—especially the militia—were volunteers who felt no obligation to a long-term commitment. Frequently, men stayed only for several weeks or months before leaving to attend to their farms and businesses. This group seemed a bit more stable, though, and was swelling by the day, so Washington felt that the time was ripe to make a stand against the Redcoats as they threatened Philadelphia.

In July, British General Sir William Howe set sail from Sandy

Hook, New Jersey, with the intent of sailing up the Delaware River to make his assault against the colonial capital, Philadelphia. Wanting to reassure the residents of the city that their welfare was not in peril, Washington decided to parade his troops through the city. Thus, on a muggy Sunday morning, August 24, the entire Continental Army, save a few, marched for two hours through the city streets.

Because so many of the troops, for a variety of reasons, had not been uniformed, they were all ordered to wear green sprigs in their hats. They were also commanded to polish their weapons to the highest sheen possible. To both of these orders, the men responded quite favorably. To one other order, many of the men were not nearly so inclined. It was rumored that some 40,000 people would line the streets to watch the parade, and many of the spectators were said to be extremely pretty girls. Some of the troops saw this as an opportunity, but Washington, in an attempt to show dignity and respect, notified his officers that any man who left the ranks during parade would be subject to thirty-nine lashes as punishment.

Each regiment and division was led by its respective cavalry, followed by foot soldiers and artillery marching twelve abreast. Fife and drum corps interspersed throughout the parade route. Standing head and shoulders above his comrades, Peter Francisco was not happy about becoming a spectacle, for he had left Hunting Tower and the love of his life not to be gawked at in a parade but to fight the British. In well over a half year, he had yet to see battle, but that long wait was about to come to an end.

★

A dense fog lay heavily on the main streets of Kennett. Only the dim outline of a burning oil lamp was visible from an upstairs window at Unicorn Tavern, beside which Howe's troops now gathered awaiting his orders. Despondent, some of the soldiers looked at the misty air and wondered if this is how heaven might greet them later that day. Somewhere across the street, behind Green's mercantile, an agitated dog barked at intrusions it sensed but couldn't see.

Taking advantage of the natural cover, at four o'clock in the morning, on September 11, 1777, General Howe marched his troops east toward Philadelphia, bent on destroying the colonials and ending this rebellion quickly and savagely. Relying on what would turn out to be faulty intelligence, General Washington had stationed the majority of his troops near Brandywine Creek at Chadds Ford. This was where he expected the primary thrust of General Howe's troops to attempt to break through the American lines. Peter and the 10th Virginia were among those in this battle group.

Standing among his fellow soldiers, Peter could see Washington riding up and down the lines encouraging the troops through the early morning fog. Peter reached inside his satchel and pulled out his silver buckles and Arthur's Bible that he kept carefully wrapped in Susannah Anderson's handkerchief. As he held them in his hand, he suddenly remembered a Portuguese prayer he had recited as a child. Bowing his head, he murmured softly, as if directing an invocation.

> *Com Jesus me deito* (With Jesus I go to Sleep),
> *Com Jesus me levanto* (With Jesus I awake),

Com a graça de Deus (With the grace of God),
E do Espirto Santo (and of the Holy Spirit),
Eu vou para a batalha (I go into battle).

Only now, he added the last phrase to his childhood litany.
Peter kissed the talismans just as the sound of English cannon fire
broke out.

Most of their volleys fell harmlessly. American artillery answered the call, but their aim at an unseen target was just as in-
effective. As the sun began to climb the eastern sky, some musket
fire could be heard from time to time, but this, too, caused few
casualties. Looking across the Brandywine Creek, Peter could see
Redcoats taking cover but not attempting to advance any further.
They were not truly attacking there at Chadds Ford. Instead, unknown to even Washington himself, this was simply a diversion,
while the main body of Howe's forces planned to attack a few
miles north. By early afternoon, cannon and gunfire could be
heard from just north of their location, so Washington ordered
a number of his troops to quickly head in that direction to reinforce the troops there. Peter Francisco's unit was among those so
ordered.

As they approached the now full-blown battle, the reinforcing
troops, Peter among them, could barely believe their eyes. The
colonials were in complete disarray. Many of them were running
away. Peter saw one man who was bleeding profusely from his
nose, mouth, ears and eyes. *I've never seen someone so badly injured,*
he thought. Some men might have been tempted to join the others who had simply thrown down their weapons and run away,
but not Peter. Onward the 10th Virginia pressed into an open

field where the battle was at full rage. Meanwhile, Peter could see General Washington riding throughout the troops, unconcerned for his own well-being and trying to rally the troops to stand and fight. With him was another officer who was frantically waving his saber to encourage the colonials onward into the fray.

"Spread out and stand your ground," screamed Captain Woodson. "Hold them off, boys."

About two hundred miles away and facing Woodson's men was a contingent of British troops, marching in formation with fixed bayonets gleaming in the afternoon sun. They were still too far away for the colonials' muskets to be of any use, but there was no cover in this barren field. *This is mad*, Peter realized. *We're just leaving ourselves exposed.* Spotting a medium-sized fallen oak near the edge of the field, he ran over to it, wrapped his massive arms around it, and with sheer brute force dragged it to the center of the field so his fellow soldiers could take cover. Woodson saw what Peter had done and ordered the mountain men with their long rifles to take up positions there. Even George Washington took note of Peter's feat and spoke of it with his junior officer. "I've seen that man before. He was at Richmond if I recall correctly."

"Ah, but of course, you would remember him," said the other officer. "Who could forget such a large man?"

The order came to fix bayonets, but the mountain men could not fit the weapons with them, so they just waited behind the tree for the British to come into range. As the English advanced to about one hundred yards, John Allen looked to Captain Woodson for the order to fire. Woodson didn't have to say a word. Allen could read his eyes.

Snuggling his long rifle tight against his shoulder, Allen took careful aim and fired. A British officer near the front of the line dropped where he stood. Other mountain men began to fire, too, and with each distinctive crack of a long rifle, another Redcoat was laid to rest. Still, the English refused to break ranks but rather just kept advancing.

Soon the British were within range of the regular infantry muskets, and the order to fire when ready came down the lines. Peter had loaded his weapon with both ball and pellets, and when he fired his weapon, another English trooper went down. The air all around Peter filled with musket balls, and he heard several as they whizzed by his head. Kneeling now, Peter did his best to reload in the twenty seconds allowed by the manual, but when he fired again, he could not be sure that his aim had been true, for the air was so filled with smoke that it became difficult to even see his target. The smoke comingled with the sulfur scent of many weapons being fired simultaneously, wafting around, filling their nostrils with the smell of rotten eggs.

Enemies and friends were falling all around Peter. Directly to his left, he heard the sound of a musket ball as it penetrated human flesh. He spun around to see one of his tent mates from the Shenandoah Valley with a dazed look on his face, clutching his chest. When he withdrew his hand, a red stain on his chest spread out all over the man's blouse. The soldier then fell to his knees and dropped face first on the field.

Just then, Peter felt a sensation like none he had ever known. Every muscle in his large body tightened as if turning to the molten lead he had forged so well as a blacksmith at Hunting Tower. He could hear a roar in his head, but it was not that of gun or cannon fire. His very skin tingled. Enraged, Peter stood and fired his musket, bayonet affixed to the muzzle. "Kill them, boys," he shouted. "Kill them. Kill them all."

He pressed forward toward the tree he had dragged onto the field of battle. There he found John Allen flailing with his tomahawk taking down British troops with almost every swing. Soon Peter and Allen were back to back. Redcoats surrounded them, but each man was dealing out death and destruction with his weapon. In the midst of it all, Peter felt a sharp pain in his left leg, but he ignored it to take down the remaining British around them. Then, without warning, there was an eerie silence. Cannon had not fired for some time since the confrontation had become hand-to-hand. But now, even the muskets fell silent, and the British had resumed positions at the far edges of the field. John Allen and Peter looked at each other in amazement, perhaps stunned to see that they were alive.

"Remind me next time, big fella," said John Allen, "whenever we go into battle, I want you close by."

"I'll remember," said Peter grinning ear to ear.

Allen looked down and noticed blood staining Peter's britches from his thigh down to his knee high socks. "Peter, sit down," he said. "You've been wounded."

Peter did as John told him, but his adrenalin had been strong enough to dull any pain. He straightened his left leg as John cut through his trousers to more carefully inspect the wound.

"Yes, sir," said John. "Looks like you took a musket ball to your leg. You're lucky on this day, though, because it seems 'at ball went right through your leg and out the other side."

"Is that good?" Peter asked.

"You bet your life 'at's good. At least this way, you don't have to have anyone fishin' around in your leg lookin' for the ball. But I reckon it may be a few days 'fore you kin walk on it."

Although Peter and the 10th Virginia had stood their ground, and the British had vacated the field, the Battle of Brandywine would go down as a British victory, for while the majority of Washington's troops had defended the right flank, General Howe had re-concentrated his forces back to Chadds Ford and pushed the Americans into an orderly but necessary retreat. Howe's troops, however, were exhausted from the early morning march and battle, and declined to pursue the Americans. The colonials would live to fight another day.

As for Peter, he was evacuated to the home of a Moravian farmer to receive medical attention. There, he met a man who would become a lifelong friend. He arrived in the evening and was taken into a back bedroom dimly lit by two oil lamps. Another figure lay on a wooden framed bed, and Peter could see considerable blood on the lower half of the sheet that covered the man. As Peter was assisted to the bed on the opposite wall, the man lifted himself up and looked over at his new roommate.

"Well, look who 'as arrived to keep me company," the man said, with a grin. "If it isn't ze giant who fights like...a giant." This was the same man whom Peter had seen riding with General Washington as one of his junior officers. "Allow me to introduce myself," the man continued. "I am ze Marquis de Lafayette, but please just call me Lafayette. And what is your name, or should I just call you Giant?"

"My name is Peter, Peter Francisco, but you can call me Peter rather than Giant."

"Peter it is, zen. It is much more, how do you say, dignified zan Giant anyway." They both laughed at the thought.

"So, what brings you 'ere to zis farm?" Lafayette inquired.

Peter lifted his left leg as well as he could, and for the first time Lafayette could see the blood stain on his britches.

"*Magnifique,*" said Lafayette. "We suffer wounds in ze same place."

"Well, you might think it's 'magnifique'," Peter bumbled, "but I'm not so sure." Their voices brought a doctor into the room to check on Lafayette.

"What's going on in here?" the doctor queried. "I thought I told you to stay calm, General, to lessen the loss of blood."

"But of course, doctor, and I would be doing as you told me except for zis big fellow 'ere who keeps me from my slumber."

Peter looked at the Marquis, who gave him a wink.

"Zis is a good friend of mine and a brave warrior. I know zat General Washington personally sent you to take care of my needs, but what I need most of all is for you to take care of my friend."

"Of course, General Lafayette." And the doctor set about tending to Peter's wound. As he cleaned and dressed Peter's leg, Lafayette fell back on his bed in pain and fell into exhausted sleep. Neither did Peter have the energy to stay awake while the doctor fixed his leg. He, too, drifted into exhausted but fitful sleep. For several days thereafter, the two recuperating young soldiers exchanged stories from their past. Peter learned that Lafayette had come from a wealthy family, that he was just nineteen years old, and that he had come to America to learn all he could about war and tactics, because he had never actually seen combat.

As for Peter, he remembered being kidnapped about twelve

years earlier, so that made him seventeen. He remembered being abandoned and then purchased by Judge Winston, but he
couldn't recall anything about where his own family came from.

"Perhaps I can 'elp," said Lafayette. "Do you remember any
words from when 'you were little?'"

Peter recited the prayer he had said just before going into
battle.

"But, of course," said Lafayette when Peter had finished. "If
I'm not mistaken, zat language is Portuguese. You are from Portugal, mon ami."

"Portugal? Hmm." Memories Peter hadn't been able to recall
in years came flooding back to him. He remembered his father
talking about Portugal, but, as a child, it had sounded to him like
"portoogull," and he thought his father was talking about some
type of bird not their homeland.

"I think you could be right. My father mentioned that often in
our house on the island.

"An island, you say?" Lafayette asked, curiously. "Was zere
much water traffic to ze island from ozer countries?"

"All the time," Peter said, nodding in amazement as much
at Lafayette's vast knowledge as his own recollections. "We lived
close to one of the main ports. Ships from all over would dock
there. My sister and I would watch the men moving large sacks
and crates back and forth between hulls." Peter's expression was
vacant, fixed intently on another time and place. The images
were so vivid. "Sometimes the ships even carried people."

"Zat is what I zought," Lafayette said, smiling at Peter. "Ze
island is probably part of ze cluster called ze Azores. Ze ship zat
carried me 'ere from France stopped at São Miguel. I do not

know which of ze islands was your 'ome, but I am confident one of zem is." Lafayette proceeded to tell Peter everything he knew about the islands.

"I'm Pedro Francisco," Peter said, emphatically, when Lafayette concluded. "I'm Pedro Francisco, and I'm from Portugal." Peter dropped down on the bed trying to process this revelation and what it meant. He didn't have any doubt that Lafayette's words were true. He seemed delighted to have finally solved the mystery. He felt a renewed sense of identity, like someone unconscious, waking and seeing something familiar again for the first time.

The fuzzy images of his parents and sister also filled his heart with lament. *Where is my family now? My sister is almost a grown woman. Maybe even married. Would she remember me?* Peter buried his face in his hands, the full emotion of his loss spilling forth. One thought led to another until Peter bolted upright and looked straight into Lafayette's eyes, clarity filling his face.

"I wasn't just a slave," Peter declared with resolute self-belief. "I know who I am. I know who my parents are. I know where I'm from." In that moment, he not only felt he was fighting for his future but also his past.

While Peter was having an introspective moment, Lafayette was staring at Peter but it was as if he were looking for Orion's belt. There was an awkward silence as they were both staring at each other and then he blurted, "Lusitania!"

"What?" Peter said in bewilderment.

"Zat iz what Portugal was called many centuries ago." Lafayette stated emphatically. "Lusitania. I was trying to remember from my history classes at Collège du Plessis in Paris."

167

"Does that mean something? Was my family part of something bigger than Portugal?" inquired Peter with excitement.

"No, no, no." replied Lafayette. "You are a full blooded, Portuguese giant all right. Centuries ago kings and queens would have named you, Luso, to strike fear in the hearts of their enemies." He started to chuckle, "Someone warn King George. Don't make us send Luso over zere…because we will!"

They were laughing so hard that Peter fell backwards out of his chair onto the floor, which made them laugh even harder. When they finally gained their composure, Lafayette stopped, lifted his chin, and began sniffing an aroma that was coming from outside.

"I think I smell some food cooking over the fire. Come on, Luso, it's time for dinner." They couldn't help but burst out into laughter again.

★

After a few days of bed rest, Lafayette asked the doctor if they could stretch their legs and go into town. Although the doctor wasn't entirely happy with the idea, he also knew better than to keep young men such as these lying down for too long, lest they become so restless that they do something foolish. So, Peter and Lafayette headed to a tavern, sharing a couple of grogs at an old wooden table, carrying on a quiet conversation. One of the patrons of the tavern noticed that Peter still had the green sprig in his hat and, having had more than his share of the local brew, approached the two men, undeterred by Peter's obvious stature.

"I'll be supposin' that you two are revolutionaries, aren't you?

I saw you fellas with your green sprigs in Philadelphia a few weeks back. Now why don't you just turn in your guns and such and just go home where you belong?"

Lafayette looked at the man for a moment. "Perhaps it is just me, but I zink you show poor manners. Luso and I are 'ere to relax and enjoy ourselves. You, on ze ozer 'and, appear to be what ze English call a sot, so why don't *you* just go 'ome and sleep it off. In a barn, if I guess correctly."

Actually, the man was well beyond intoxication, because the first punch he threw was aimed directly at Peter, who was much larger than Lafayette. His first swing missed. His first would also be his last as Peter rose from his chair and landed a blacksmith's right hook squarely on the man's jaw. The man teetered across the room before collapsing at a table where his friends were also drinking too much. The ensuing brawl wasn't really a fair fight, even though Peter and Lafayette were outnumbered by more than three to one. But when it was over, seven Tories lay flat out on the floor, and Peter and Lafayette stood in the middle of the room with satisfied looks on their faces.

Lafayette looked at Peter and said, "I don't zink General Washington fully understands what kind of Luso 'e 'as in 'is army, but I promise you 'e soon will."

When they arrived back at the Moravian farm, new orders had come for Lafayette. He was to report to another area farm that could better provide for his comfort. He immediately asked if Peter could be transferred there, too, but it was obvious to everyone that Peter's wound had been less serious, and he was ready to report back to the 10th Virginians.

Besides his orders to report, something else was waiting for

Peter. A letter from Susannah Anderson. After several months, it had finally caught up with Peter. He opened it and looked blankly at the page.

"What does it say? What does it say? Is it not from your sweetheart?" Lafayette inquired.

"Yes, it is from Susannah. But…I don't know what it says," Peter confessed, looking longingly at the ink that had absorbed into the pages.

"Why in ze world not?"

"Because I don't know how to read. I never learned." Peter could recognize some of the letters, but strung together, he had no idea what they meant. Apart from the Bible, Susannah's letters had given him another important reason to learn.

"But why did you not tell me?"

Peter didn't answer.

"My friend, zis is nothing to be ashamed of. Many fine men never learned 'ow to read or write. Please, may I read it for you?"

"Would you? Would you, please?"

"Of course. But of course, I will." Lafayette took the letter from Peter and began to read.

> *My dearest Peter,*
>
> *I am distressed to begin my first letter to you with bad news, but I knew you would want to know. Your friend Arthur has passed away at Hunting Tower. Judge Winston visited us a couple of weeks ago and said that Arthur had passed peacefully in his sleep. I hope you find some small comfort that your friend didn't suffer. I wish I could be there to console you.*
>
> *I think of you day and night. I wonder where you might*

be and if you can hear my thoughts. I long for you to return. When you left that day, I stood and watched you ride off until you were out of sight, then I went straight to my room and cried for three days. Holding boneca de trapo was my only comfort. My father finally insisted that I come out.

I miss you so much and shall cherish our last moments together. Some days, I sit out on the porch and imagine you are still here. I replay the events of that afternoon over and over in my mind. Please know that my heart aches for you. You are my hero and my love, and I miss you so much.

It would seem that the British are gathering troops for war here in the south, and my father is preparing to take command of his militia. Word is that they may be sent to South Carolina, but we can't be certain of that as yet.

I must go now, my love, as I want to get this letter posted today. I pray God will keep you safe each and every day. Take care of yourself and know that my heart is yours to keep forever.
Love,
Susannah

"I am sorry for your loss, Luso," Lafayette offered, as he finished reading.

"He was like a father to me," Peter revealed, downcast.

"Susannah must be a lovely lady," said Lafayette attempting to lighten the mood.

"She truly is," replied Peter. "She truly is. Can I ask you a favor? If I tell you the words, will you write a letter to her for me?"

"I would be 'onored." Lafayette secured some paper, and Peter began to recite his reply.

Dear Susannah,

It pains me to hear about my dear friend Arthur. Truly, he was the closest thing I ever had for a father, and I shall miss him deeply.

Your letter has found me recovering from a slight leg wound, but I have made a new friend, and it is he who is writing this letter to you. He is the Marquis de Lafayette, and he comes from France. He was also wounded in battle, but he is recuperating well. As for me, I am healed enough to rejoin my friends in the army, and I shall do so in just a few days.

In the midst of the chaos of battle, I didn't realize that I had been wounded. Afterwards, I couldn't help but think of you and what we would have lost had that musket had a deadly aim.

I, too, think often of our afternoon on your porch, and that memory is one that I shall carry for the rest of my days. I wish we had had more time together, but what I do now is for the great cause. Along with the memory of your beauty, I carry your handkerchief in my satchel wrapped around my silver shoe buckles. Even though you can't be here with me, I think of you often.

Please know that it is my love for you that keeps me fighting for freedom.

Peter

"Is zere anyzing else I can do for you?" asked Lafayette.

"Actually, there is," said Peter, with a sly grin. "When you tell General Washington about what a great warrior I am, ask him to send me a bigger sword—a sword about five feet long—that I could make sing as it cuts down those lobster-backs."

"Indeed, Luso. Indeed. A giant man needs a giant sword, and you shall 'ave it. I promise, you shall 'ave it."

II.

NEW BATTLES AND
A WINTER OF DISTRESS

AFTER BRANDYWINE and the Battle of Paoli, British General Lord Cornwallis had successfully seized the colonial capital of Philadelphia. Then, General Howe, for some reason, decided to split his forces, leaving about one-third of his men to defend the capital and marching the balance north to Germantown to seek out and destroy the colonials.

Just a few weeks after being wounded at Brandywine, Peter rejoined his fellow troops just north of Germantown where, despite their recent defeats, General Washington and his officers were emboldened by the ability of their men to hold their own against the British professional soldiers. It was with that confidence that Washington conceived a plan that he felt could rout the British.

At dusk on October 3, the American army, including Peter's 10th Virginia, set out marching toward the hamlet of Germantown. The plan was to arrive shortly before dawn and attack from four directions. Each of the four columns would converge in a pincer-like movement, eventually crushing the British defenders. The plan was bold and called for silently taking out British sentries before launching the full attack. It might have worked, but Almighty God had a different plan in mind.

Throughout the night, a heavy fog settled on and around Germantown. As a result, communications between the four columns became almost impossible, and coordinating the attack—a crucial part of the plan's success—was no longer possible. Under the command of General George Weedon, Peter and the rest of the Virginians, having marched an extra four miles, were a bit late in arriving at their position. As Peter and his comrades took their positions, they set about placing torn pieces of white paper on their hats as previously instructed in order to distinguish themselves from the enemy amid the thick, miserable fog. Again, Peter reached inside his satchel, removed the buckles that were wrapped inside Susannah's handkerchief and recited his Portuguese prayer:

> *Com Jesus me deito* (With Jesus I go to Sleep),
> *Com Jesus me levanto* (With Jesus I awake),
> *Com a graça de Deus* (With the grace of God),
> *E do Espirto Santo* (and of the Holy Spirit),
> *Eu vou para a batalha* (I go into battle).

Almost as soon as he had returned them to his satchel, the Virginia regiment could hear an outbreak of gunfire to their right, and Peter could feel that familiar sensation that had overtaken him during Brandywine return. His skin tingled, his breathing became labored and the fury in his head returned. John Allen stood next to him, sensing that his friend may be losing control in his deep-rooted desire to kill more Redcoats. He reached over and rested his hand on Peter's arm. Just to their left, a single flair illuminated the early dawn. One of the British sentries had been able to fire the sparkler just before being bayoneted to death by one of the scouting colonials. The element of surprise had been lost.

"Easy, big fella, easy," John said. "You'll get your chance to kill the lobster backs soon enough."

Peter restrained himself and stood his ground, waiting for the signal to advance. Without warning, the air shook violently with the sound of cannon fire. Although the aim was inaccurate because of the early hour and the increasingly dense fog, it made a deafening roar. Almost immediately, musket fire broke out. The shots resulted in few casualties, for no one firing could possibly see where he was aiming. However, because the smoke added to the nearly impossible visibility, there was a definite effect.

All hell broke loose. The order finally came for the Virginians to advance, and they came within sight of the British. This time, rather than standing in defensive positions as they had at Brandywine, the Americans took the fight to the enemy. At one hundred yards, the mountain men again used their long rifles precisely, dropping several British soldiers.

As before, the balance of the troops had been ordered not to fire until they were within fifty yards of their targets, and Peter, whose urge was to charge full speed into the mass of red standing in front of him kept himself in check. He customarily loaded his musket with a combination of ball and pellets and, arriving at the correct distance, brought his musket to his shoulder, took careful aim and fired. A British soldier went down. Since the Redcoats were just holding their ground, Peter found the time to reload and fire four more rounds; each time, another enemy fell to the ground.

Meanwhile the fog and smoke comingled, further obscuring the lines, until the soldiers could see no more than thirty yards in front of them. Off to one side, some of the Americans became befuddled. Thinking that the British had launched a counterattack, they fired in the presumed direction of the enemy. But they were firing on their own troops.

Cries of "We're trapped! Retreat!" could be heard, and many men threw down their weapons in withdrawal and ran from the field. Washington's plan was deteriorating rapidly. Peter's Virginians stood their ground, fighting valiantly while at the same time allowing the retreating troops through the lines. Just as at Brandywine, General Washington had tried in vain to rally his soldiers. The British troops surged back at the Americans, and Washington's men were compelled to give up the field. Once again, the battle itself had been lost.

However, Washington and his general staff came to a very important conclusion. It was now obvious to them that they could hold their own against the British military and drive them back. This was a good omen.

Soon thereafter, the Americans were further encouraged by the outcome of the Battle of Red Bank. The colonials had built two forts on opposite sides of the Delaware River, which were to cut off the British supply line into the city of Philadelphia.

If Washington could not physically defeat the British there, he would starve them out.

The Redcoats' next move was to send a large contingent of Hessians—their German allies—to root out the considerably smaller American force defending fort Mercer, positioned on the left bank of the Delaware. In fact, Colonel Karl von Donop was so sure of victory that he declared the fort would either soon be named after him or he would be dead. Three days after the attack on October 22, von Donop died of injuries sustained when the Americans inflicted heavy casualties on the German forces.

Prior to that victory, the colonials had withstood a bombardment of the sister Fort Mifflin, also known as Mud Island. The second and far more intense attack would serve notice that the Americans still had a long way to go before they could have any real hope of defeating their enemy.

November 10, 1777, was a cold, dreary day. Fort Mifflin, to which Francisco had been assigned, had been under occasional bombardment for almost a month now. The cannon fire had taken its toll on the partially completed fortifications, but the impact of war inside the fort was far greater. The men were cold. They were wet. They were hungry. And nearly thirty days of cannon fire had left them sleepless. For Peter, this was not the war he anticipated. Here there was no musket fire. No hand-to-hand combat. There was only the constant pounding of the British cannon in rhythm with a headache inside Peter's head. He crouched down behind a bunker on the north side of the fort alongside his friend, John Allen.

"Do you think this will ever stop?" asked Peter of the mountain man.

"'Course, I do," replied John. "After all, they's got to run outta cannonballs sooner or later," he remarked dryly.

The two friends shared a hearty but brief laugh that came to an abrupt halt when the British forcefully opened up with cannon fire. Even the fort's stone walls on the south and east sides were soon reduced to little more than rubble.

The withering fire continued throughout the day. At one point, one of Peter's friends stood to run for a more protected spot, but a three-pound cannon ball caught him squarely in the chest. His arms and legs were literally blown from his body, spraying a mist of blood onto Peter and John. Other Americans were blown to shreds or suffered horrific injuries, but with most of their artillery destroyed, the colonials could do nothing to return fire.

For the first time since Peter had been kidnapped, he was afraid. *What if I die without being able to put up a fight? What if I'm lying under a pile of rubble, Susannah never knowing my fate? What if I never get to have the life with her that I've been dreaming about?* More than anything else, these thoughts angered him.

In the midst of a bombardment that later was reported to include one thousand cannonballs raining down every twenty minutes, Peter stood up, aimed his musket at a British ship two or three hundred yards away, and fired.

"Peter," said John. "What in the world are you doin'? You can't possibly hit anything but river fish at this distance, and probably not even the fish."

"I don't care," snapped Peter, enraged. "I've got to do something."

"Well, just stop it. Besides, you're too big a target, and if they aim at you, they'll probably kill me, too."

While Peter was reloading his musket, a cannonball ripped into their embankment, spewing mud and dirt on the two friends and causing Peter's rage to dissolve into amusement. He broke out laughing.

"Just what do you find so funny about this?" asked John incredulously.

"You, John Allen. With that mud on your face, you look just like one of the slaves back at Hunting Tower," Peter shot back.

"Well, you don't look much better. Your skin is a whole shade darker now."

Up and down the ranks, others heard the laughter and looked at the two friends who couldn't contain themselves. Although not a word was spoken, most of them concluded that Peter Francisco and John Allen had momentarily lost touch with reality.

The brutal pounding upon Fort Mifflin continued for five straight days. By day, the walls and embankments were destroyed. By night, the remaining American defenders reconstructed them, discouraging any attempt by the British to land troops on the island and overrun its defenders. But by October 15, more than half the men in the fort had been killed, and the order came down to set fire to anything that would burn. After having done so, the survivors, including Peter and John Allen, made their way by the cover of night to the wharf where three boats facilitated their escape to Fort Mercer.

Having been unable to conquer it less than a month before, the British sought to seize the advantage and turned their attentions back to Fort Mercer. After five more days of sustained cannon fire, the Continental forces were forced to abandon this last barricade to Philadelphia. Peter Francisco found himself retreating with his comrades once again, and he didn't like it all.

After several small skirmishes with British and Hessian troops, Peter and the rest of the 10th Virginia Regiment were compelled to follow the whole of the Continental Army from Whitemarsh, New Jersey to Valley Forge, Pennsylvania, where they would camp for the winter. As he, John Allen, and the rest of the Virginians marched, they noticed bloody footprints left by the shoeless. Without even much of their clothing left, they wrapped themselves in blankets in the twenty- to thirty-degree temperatures. Crossing the Schuylkill River near Gulph, they encountered a snowstorm of such fury that they had to make temporary camp for several days. Conditions were absolutely miserable, but the worst was yet to come. Finally, on December 19, 1777, the troops arrived at Valley Forge. They had marched only thirteen miles, but it had taken eight days. Upon arrival, Peter and John Allen looked around at what would be their home for the next several months—a fort sitting on a high plateau with the river protecting one side and two small creeks providing natural barriers against an enemy attack.

"Looks like we've at least got a place where we can defend ourselves," Peter commented.

"From what I hear tell," said John, "these armies take the winter off, so I don't think we'll have to do much defendin'."

"Good, then. At least we can rest up a bit. I just hope we can make it through the winter snow and ice."

One of the first priorities in the new location was securing food. The first few days the men existed on nothing more than fire cakes, a mixture of flour and water that resulted in a tasteless, sooty sort of biscuit. Peter, eating his daily ration, longed for some of the biscuits that were served in great quantity at Hunting Tower. John Allen sat down next to him on a log fronting one of the many campfires. After biting into the fire cake, he spat it out on the ground. "Enough is enough," he declared. "I can't exist on this." With that he grabbed his long rifle. "With all these woods around here, there's got to be some critters we can hunt." Several of the other Virginia mountain men grabbed their weapons too.

"Mind if I go, too?" Peter inquired.

"Come ahead if you want to," was John's response. "Just don't try shootin' anything. These ain't Redcoats, and you ain't that good a shot anyway. This here is serious work, I tell you." Peter was taken aback by his friend's rebuke, but he joined the hunting party anyway. Most of the animals knew instinctively that the winter would be a hard one, and they were safely tucked inside their burrows. After four hours on the hunt, the party returned to camp with just one raccoon and a few squirrels to show for the effort.

Meanwhile, General Washington had issued an order to build huts to ward off the winter elements. Each sixteen-by-fourteen hut was to house twelve men. The walls would be six-and-one-half feet high. *I'll barely be able to stand up in there,* Peter thought. A fireplace made of wood and covered with clay was also to be constructed. Although a twelve-dollar reward was offered to the first squad in each regiment that successfully built a hut, Peter and the mountain men were far behind on the task because they had spent so much time hunting. However, Peter was adept at wielding an axe, and his group narrowly missed out on the reward. But it didn't matter. They were all just glad for the shelter. Unfortunately, the huts were quite drafty with nothing more than a straw floor and a blanket for a door and a fireplace that belched an overwhelming amount of smoke because of the green wood they had to use. *Just like at old Caleb's,* Peter thought, recalling his first days in America on the wharf.

Food was the major problem. Supplies were available but getting them to the encampment was thorny at best. They observed Christmas with a brief service in the gathering tent and a dinner composed of the same bland fire cakes and cold water. The roads and trails to the camp were just about impassable, so even when supplies could be secured, it was impossible for them to reach the soldiers. Although the quartermaster, a fellow by the name of Thomas Mifflin, had been a merchant in Philadelphia, he hated his job and ignored it for the most part.

During the first six weeks at Valley Forge, there were thirteen days of icy rain or snow, causing the morale of the men to rapidly deteriorate. One afternoon, Peter was on the outskirts of camp to get fresh water from one of the small streams when he happened on a shirtless sentry wrapped in a blanket, standing on his hat. This was the only way he could avoid standing barefoot in the four inches of snow.

"You aren't comfortable," Peter stated evenly.

The soldier looked at Peter. He was shivering so much, his teeth were chattering audibly. "I've never been so cold in all my life," he said. "I come from Virginia, and we don't often get winter like this."

"I thought I recognized you," said Peter. "I come from Virginia, too, and right now, I wish I was back there. But listen here, I have a proposal for you. I could just pick you up and hold your feet off the snow while you stand guard, or I could take your place, and you can go back to your hut and get warm by the fireplace."

The sentry looked at the huge man, almost speechless. "You would do that for me?" he questioned, hoping it wasn't some sort of twisted joke.

"Well, now if you mean holding you up in the air, I could do it, but I think it would serve no purpose for us both to be cold."

The soldier looked at Peter for a moment, then spontaneously reached up and threw an arm around one shoulder. When he let go, he said to the man, "I don't know where our paths may lead, but I owe you a great debt of gratitude that I will endeavor to repay some day." With that, the man trudged back to the lines of huts. Just like on the march to Valley Forge, Peter watched him leave bloody footprints in the snow. *How much more could these men endure?* The Portuguese soldier wondered.

Later that evening, as Peter sat in his hut trying to warm himself by the pluming fire, a man pulled back the canvas door. With a blanket wrapped around his torso and up to his eyes, Peter squinted to make out who had entered. Much to his surprise, it was Lafayette.

Peter jumped to his feet and rushed to greet his friend. "Lafayette! It's so good to see you again." The two men exchanged a bone-crushing embrace after which Lafayette kissed Peter on one cheek and then the other, surprising him by this outward show of affection.

"Do not be offended, Luso," said Lafayette. "Zis is a greeting between friends in my country. I zought I 'ad told you zat when last we were togezer."

"Well, that's fine with me. After all, we wouldn't want to insult the French, now, would we?" Peter said with a glint in his eye and a smirk on his face. Just then, he started to cough but not from all the smoke in the hut. The hacking cough was relentless, and Peter was soon doubled over with the heaving until spittle and phlegm dripped from his mouth.

"Luso—my friend. You are not well."

"It's just all this cold and wet and snow. I don't know how people live in a place like this. We had snow back at Hunting Tower, but never like this. I haven't felt good for days, and ever since I got back from standing guard duty, I can't stop coughing and wheezing."

"Well, tonight, you shall share my quarters. Zey are considerably more comfortable zan 'ere. And we shall inquire of ze services of a doctor. I'm sure General Washington would agree zat we can ill afford to lose soldiers like you."

Peter tightly pulled his blanket around himself and followed the Frenchman back to his officer's quarters in the falling snow. He was thankful for the respite in Lafayette's hut, but the two men talked well into the night until Peter could stay awake no longer and fell swiftly into a fitful, cough-broken sleep. As he slipped in and out of slumber, his mind conjured visions of Arthur and Susannah.

I am alone in the barn, cleaning Isabel's old stall. I can see Arthur's empty chair. I hear a banging noise coming from outside and exit into the cold night. A wraithlike Arthur is balancing my silver shoe buckles on an anvil, striking them feverishly with a mandrel. Why is he doing that? Sensing me, Arthur slowly lifts his head, halting the mandrel's trajectory mid-swing. He gathers up the buckles and walks steadily toward me. His mouth is moving but I cannot hear the words. His breath is invisible in the air. When Arthur nears, I reach instinctively for the buckles, but Arthur brushes past me and heads for the barn. Baffled, I follow. A bright light emanates from inside the barn, blinding me briefly when I enter. Arthur is gone. Sitting in Arthur's chair is Susannah. She is a seraph. In her hands are my cherished buckles. Engraved on them are the letters "P" and "J."

Peter woke the next morning puzzled by the vivid dream.

Lafayette was nowhere in sight. He tried his best to get up, but he was so weak he could barely raise his head. A few minutes later, Lafayette returned, bringing one of the camp doctors. After examining Peter for a short time, the doctor turned to Lafayette.

"He is quite ill but to provide the proper care, he needs to be transferred to our hospital in Yellow Springs. In any event, this man is not to report for any kind of duty."

"Of course," said Lafayette. "I will see to it immediately."

Yellow Springs was the first true military hospital, and Lafayette arranged for Peter to be taken there that very day. As Peter was loaded onto the back of a wagon for the ten-mile trip, Lafayette placed his hand on Peter's arm.

"Do not be concerned, Luso. Zey will take very good care of you at ze 'ospital." Lafayette was looking at the doctor who was to accompany Peter and several others on this journey. "Zey will take very good care of you or zey will feel ze wrath of a very unhappy Frenchman." With that, Lafayette winked at his friend.

Peter, in a voice weakened by his condition, murmured, "Thank you, my friend. Thank you. I don't know how I can ever repay you."

"You need not worry about repaying me. Razzer, take down a few more lobster backs when you return to ze battlefield. Get well, my giant friend, for ze British wish zey 'ad seen ze last of you." As the wagon left the encampment, Peter managed to raise his head a little to see Lafayette wave goodbye.

I2.

HEALING AND
A HELPING HAND

WHEN THE WAGON PULLED UP to the hospital, the patient felt some of his strength return and was able to slide out unassisted. Standing in the snow, he savored the sight of the size-able three-story building with its nine-foot-high porches and gabled roof that looked as if it could accommodate several hundred men at a time. After months of war and camp life, he imagined sinking his head into a down pillow, slurping warm soup, and giving in to the impulsive need for sleep. *It will feel so good,* he mused, indulging the thought.

As he made his way to the entrance, a hospital worker emerged carrying a black object about three feet long. Peter recognized it as a leg that had just been amputated from one of the soldiers. The worker made his way to a two-wheeled cart off to one side and lifted a tarp. Underneath was an array of similarly colored body parts—feet, arms, hands, and even ears. Peter looked away, covering his nose with his hand to block the nauseating smell. The doctor nudged his arm. "This way," he said, leading him into the hospital.

Once inside, Peter was aghast by what he saw and by the smell that permeated the whole first floor. Rows and rows of makeshift beds lined the walls and filled the center of a large room. Some of the men, recovering from amputations, lay groaning beneath bloody sheets. The collective din rivaled that of some artillery barrages. Others lay in wait for amputations, with their limbs and extremities as black as those Peter had seen outside. The smell of rotting flesh hung in the air, as gangrene was a chronic malady. The odor made Peter gag in reflex.

Peter was taken upstairs to the second floor where men with his condition were treated. He still heard moans and groans but not nearly as desperate as those from the amputees downstairs. The stench, however, still assaulted his nostrils. Buckets had been placed beside the beds so the men could vomit, but frequently, the ill soldiers missed their target. The indoor outhouse was attached to the rear of the building on the first floor, but most of the sick couldn't get out of bed at all, much less stumble their way down-stairs. Those who tried didn't quite make it. As a result, the smell of feces and urine was nearly unbearable, despite the best efforts of several women assigned to clean up.

Peter was escorted to a bed about halfway down one row. "Lie down there, and Doctor Bodo will take a look at you in a while," the camp doctor told him. Doctor Bodo was an older German fellow. He and his two sons, also doctors, were running the hospital, as Peter would later learn. He did as instructed and quickly dozed off. A finger in his side soon roused him, and he opened his eyes to see an elderly man with a shock of white hair in a bloodstained white coat bending over him. Looking at a piece of paper that had been pinned to Peter's sheet by the camp doctor, the physician seemed to be pondering the information provided. "It says here dat you haf bad cough, high fever and trouble breathing, ja?" the doctor inquired.

"Yes, sir," Peter said in a raspy, weak voice.

"Well, it is likely you haf pneumonia. Do not vorry. Ve vill take good care of you and send you back to duty in no time. Consider yourself lucky. Most of dese men haf come down vif dysentery and typhus. For da life of me, I don't know vy da men insist on reliefing demselves upstream rather dan downstream from da camp. I hear dat da general has issued orders about proper sanitation, but looking around here, I would say dat is a horse dat's already escaped da barn. Anyvay, I am sure you do not vant to hear about dat. You just rest easy and someone vill be along vif some hot soup. Dat vill make you feel better." Peter lay there, his mind spinning. *The stream is where I got my drinking water,* he realized, his stomach churning at the thought. He dozed intermittently waiting for the soup.

A while later a woman came by with some clear broth of animal stock with a few pieces of turnips, onions and carrots. As she held a spoonful to Peter's mouth, he noticed her face was blotchy, like she had been crying. *It doesn't taste too bad,* he thought, *and it's hot.* The woman continued to feed him, but never lifted her eyes to his. Instead, she kept them fixed on the spoon. Her hand shook slightly with each bite. The warmth spread throughout his chest as he swallowed the first of it, and that felt good. Ravenous, he quickly consumed the entire bowl, and the woman daubed at Peter's chin with her apron, this time willing her gaze on his mouth.

"Thank you," Peter said emphatically, leaning slightly in her direction. Somehow, he guessed this woman wasn't a nurse. *She must be volunteering her time,* he thought. *No, devoting her time,* he quickly amended.

A few moments passed in silence.

"What is your name?" Peter asked, unable to stifle his curiosity.

"My name is Christina Hench," she said quietly, reaching for the paper tacked to his sheet. "I'll be looking after you under the doctor's orders."

Reading the patient's record, she said, "It says here that you're Peter Francisco." In attempt to avoid his scrutiny, she cocked her head to the side and curved one side of her mouth into a playful half-smile. "Well, Peter, I wish this bed was another six inches longer because then you might just fit."

Peter grinned but still wasn't distracted from her sad eyes. *There's something about her,* he thought.

"It says here that you are to get soup four times a day and extra blankets," Christina said, again avoiding his intent gaze. "I'll see to that right away." Not waiting for a response, she scurried off toward the far end of the room. By the time she returned, Peter was sound asleep. From the hospital stores she had retrieved a fairly thick blanket, which she gently laid across her patient and ever so carefully pulled up to his neck, touching his cheek as she did so. Now that his eyes were unable see hers, she could look at him. His upper body was taut and muscular. He was built so massively, there was virtually no distinction between his neck and shoulders. She wondered how many of the enemy he might have killed. His bronze skin was unlike that of any other patient she'd seen. His smile and gentle manner flooded her mind with memories of her sons.

The last day she saw them the morning sky over their 300-acre farm was clear and promising. The chickens, having escaped the coop for the third time that week, were squawking and running amok. As she went around the back of the house to take the laundry off the line, Christina chuckled and thought to herself, *I'll just grant them freedom and save myself the hassle of rounding them up, at least until dinner.*

Her mind had shielded her often that day, she realized, filling itself with countless inconsequential things and causing her hands to fidget so her feelings weren't able to run wild like the chickens.

While she was folding the last of Johann's and Peter's clothes, Christina saw her neighbor Maria approaching from across the road. Since she and Christian first bought the farm a few years back, Maria normally stopped over around this time for a visit or to help with chores, but today she had different reasons. Just the sight of her sent Christina's hand to her stomach, which felt so heavy it was like she had swallowed a small boulder instead of breakfast.

When Maria reached the clothes line, she stood facing her friend, shirts and trousers hanging between them like military colors in salute, and searched her eyes for what she knew lay beneath. Without a word, she began folding the remaining items alongside Christina and took them inside. Later, Christina would need her comforting shoulder and fervent prayer, but, for now, the silence between them continued inside as the two women prepared what would become the final lunch at the farm for two of her sons.

"How many places should I set?" Maria asked, reaching for the bowls.

It was a simple question, yet thinking about it only reminded Christina that soon it would change. "Five," she said tersely, then turned back to the stew, stirring it with a bit more ferocity than was necessary.

Johann was the first one in the door. "Father's readying the horses," he said. "Should be a good day for traveling." Before he sat down in his usual spot at the table he'd built with his own hands, he added, "Smells good."

"How long will it take you to reach the dock?" Maria asked, attempting to spare Christina some distress.

"On a day like this, two, maybe three hours," Johann replied, just as Peter entered with their father.

"I'm starved," Peter said. "I sure hope the food on the ship is as good as Ma's."

As if on cue, Christina turned, her lower eyelashes cradling fresh drops of escaped tears, and said in a slightly scolding tone, "You'll eat whatever they plum well give you. You'll need nourishment." She raised the basket she was carrying and added lovingly, "I made your favorite biscuits."

Christina didn't remember how that meal tasted. She spent the entire hour pushing stew around the bowl with her spoon and stared across the table at her handsome, grown-up boys, memorizing their faces. She tried willing them to stay, but knew it was no use.

"Well, no sense in putting off the inevitable," Christian said, trying to break the tension. "Boys, you'd best be heading out if you are going to make it to the dock on time."

Christina held each of her sons and silently prayed for them. The only thing she could think to say without losing her composure was, "Remember to write to George."

"We'll be back, Ma," they had promised, and she had believed them. It was difficult for her now not to think of what became of them after they were captured, seeing the soldiers here at the hospital. Their mothers wouldn't recognize some of them.

"Such brave lads must suffer so much," she murmured, as a tear fell freely down one cheek. She knelt beside Peter's bed watching him for a few minutes until the weeping subsided.

Then she noticed that in pulling the blanket up to Peter's chin, she had exposed his feet, so she went to the foot of the bed and gave a gentle tug to cover his feet; when she did, Peter's chest was bare. After several useless attempts to get the coverage just right, she fetched another blanket.

Several days passed and Peter went through the same regimen of eating and sleeping. In a few weeks, the magic elixir of soup and rest in a warm bed had done its job, and Peter was allowed to report back to camp.

By mid-February he arrived back at Valley Forge and immediately began searching for the hut that had belonged to his friend Lafayette. He knew he must be in the general area but had been so ill the night of his only visit that he couldn't determine exactly which it was. And he didn't want to disturb any of the other officers. In his confusion, he noticed a tall man rounding the corner. *It's General George Washington!* Peter realized. Peter snapped to attention as he had been taught to do when in the presence of an officer.

195

"You're Peter Francisco, aren't you?" acknowledged Washington, in the muted tone he had become known for.

"Yes, sir," Peter said with the appropriate decorum, which quickly broke. "How did you know?"

"Patrick Henry pointed you out to me in Richmond. Besides, at your size, you're a bit unmistakable. I've seen you on the battlefield, too. You're quite the warrior. Would that I had a thousand just like you—I could kick the infernal British in their collective backsides all the way back to England." Peter almost laughed at the thought but caught himself as he remembered he was in the presence of the most important man alive. Seeing Peter's distress, the general asked, "Who are you looking for, young fellow?"

"I was hoping to find Major General Lafayette, but I can't remember which hut is his."

"You're standing right in front of it, my boy, but he's not here right now. He and several of my officers are meeting with Barron von Steuben. He's telling them about our new training for the soldiers. That meeting should be ending soon. I'm sure the Marquis wouldn't mind if you waited in his hut. In fact, he's told me that the two of you have become comrades and, if my memory serves, that you have inquired about a larger sword."

"Yes, sir. I would be grateful for a larger sword. With my God-given stature and strength, I know I could swing a five foot blade just fine," Peter said enthusiastically.

"Now, I can't make any promises. It's hard enough to get almost any supplies right now, but I will look into it. I must admit that sometimes I, too, find my saber a bit on the small side, and you appear to be a good four or five inches taller than I am. Just wait inside this hut right here. I'm sure that the Marquis will be along forthwith."

Peter further stiffened his back and snapped a salute to the general. Washington offered a more relaxed salute, turned and walked away. The young soldier stood there trying to grasp the moment. The thought crossed his mind, *General George Washington knows who I am. He thinks I'm a great fighter. He may even get me my sword. Wait till Susannah hears about this!*

Though General Washington himself told him he could wait inside Lafayette's hut, Peter thought that might look a bit too presumptuous, so he waited outside for his friend. The weather wasn't as severe as before, and the snow had melted. Besides, after so much time spent in that stench-riddled hospital, Peter was thankful for the fresh air that filled his healing lungs.

Presently General Lafayette approached. When he spotted Peter, he hurried to greet him in the traditional French way with a hug and two kisses, one on each cheek. "Peter, 'ow great it is to see you. 'ow are you? Are you feeling better? Come inside and let us talk." Words came in a torrent as the Frenchman opened the door to his hut. "What was it like at the 'ospital? Did zey treat you well? Tell me, for if zey did not, I'll have zeir 'eads on a spike."

"Well, I'm here, aren't I?" said Peter in jest. "I guess they must have done something right, so I suppose their heads are safe for now," he chided.

Lafayette tilted his head back in laughter. "Peter, it is so good to see you. Zat day zey took you to ze 'ospital, I feared zat it might be ze last I saw of you." Lafayette's mood quickly turned solemn. "What was it like zere? We 'ave 'eard many stories about ze conditions. Did you know zat we've lost nearly three thousand men since zis camp was established?"

"I'm not surprised," Peter said as he went on to describe what he had seen at the hospital. "They do the best they can under the conditions. Our casualties would be far greater if it weren't for Doctor Bodo and his sons."

"I'm sure zat's true. Perhaps General Nazanael Green, Washington's new quartermaster, will 'elp, also. 'e's only been at 'is post for a short time, but already supplies and food 'ave begun to arrive. I have ozer good news as well. Word 'as come zat my country and yours have signed an alliance. It still needs to be ratified by your—'ow do you say?—your Congress, zat's it. But it is a mere formality. We are now officially in zis war togezer, Luso. Is zat not good news?"

"Well, if you ask me, we've been in this war together for some time now. At least that's what I thought when those lobster backs were trying to shoot us both."

For the second time in the past few minutes, Lafayette broke out in laughter. "But I almost forgot. I 'ave even better news. I just came from a meeting wiz Baron von Steuben, who was an officer in ze Prussian-German Army, and 'e 'as volunteered to conduct ze training of our troops. Believe me when I tell you zis, Luso, I 'ave seen ze Germans in battle and I 'ave 'eard of zeir exploits. Zeir training sets zem apart from almost any army in ze world. Just look at ze Hessians. You 'ave seen 'ow well zey make war. We are indeed fortunate to 'ave 'im on our side. Wiz 'is guidance, I truly believe zat we can win zis war."

"Well, that's a good thing," Peter piped in. "When do we begin to train?"

"Tomorrow. Ze Barron wants to start immediately so zat we can all train before breaking camp in ze spring."

After talking for a while longer, during which he related his encounter with Washington, Peter excused himself to go back to his own hut to see how his mountain men friends were doing. When he entered, John Allen looked up and greeted him enthusiastically. "Look who's here. The Virginia giant's finally come home. It's good to have you back, Peter. We was worried about you, especially for the first coupla days when we didn't know where you was."

"So how did you find out that I was sick in the hospital?" asked Peter.

"Oh, that was easy. They started posting duty rosters every day, and your name showed up on it as being sick. I guess they want us to be a real army, what with the new rules and regulations and duty rosters."

"You don't even know the whole story," Peter said with a certain glee, knowing something that John Allen didn't.

"So tell us, or do we all have to sit here and guess?"

"No, no. I'll tell you," and Peter recounted to the group what he had just heard from Lafayette. Some of the mountain men just shook their heads. They weren't used to having someone direct their every movement and every moment. Most of them were pretty independent fellows. But John Allen spoke up. "Fellas, the sooner we win this war, the sooner we get to go back to the mountains. Now, I don't know about any of you others, but I'm for anything that gets us back home quick as possible. I'll train, Peter. I don't mind a bit."

"Well, that's good, because I didn't get the idea that any of us have a choice in the matter."Despite some groans from some of the mountain men, Peter was certain they'd all join, even if they weren't exactly in favor of it.

What von Steuben found was an army in total disarray, if it could even be called an army. Until recently, there had been no regular roll calls. Even the size of fighting units varied considerably, and many orders went totally ignored. Frequently, soldiers just left camp, never to return. Knowing that he couldn't train thousands of men at one time, he broke it down to a select group of about a hundred men. These men would be taught correct military bearing, attire and skills that would make a proper soldier out of a civilian. The first group of one hundred, still under von Steuben's guidance, would then train other groups of soldiers.

The fact that von Steuben spoke very little English posed a problem. He had to enlist the aid of people like Lafayette to interpret. At times, this was almost comical, as von Steuben was a man with little patience and used much profanity. Translating his cursing and swearing became a joke among the soldiers throughout the spring. However, the troops began to see the value of his training and their cooperation, and they appreciated that von Steuben often participated in their drills, demanding that junior officers do so, as well. As a result, most of the men became fond of their drillmaster, without realizing that many of their own lives would be saved by this man's manual of training. Before long, there was an obvious change in the morale and spirit of the men.

Meanwhile, the alliance with France had been ratified, and French-made uniforms and armaments began to arrive. Food became more plentiful, especially shad spawning in the Schuylkill River. Even a German baker from Philadelphia had arrived with about seventy employees. They began baking all sorts of goods, winning the soldiers with the camp favorite, gingerbread. Additional rations of rum were distributed, as well as the reward of an extra month's pay.

When the middle of June arrived, it was time to go back to war. The troops, under von Steuben, had been well-trained. Under the new quartermaster, supplies had increased. The agreement with France produced, among other things, a navy capable of going against the British fleet. Only a few days before camp was to break, Lafayette sought out Peter at his hut. "Peter, I 'ave just been given a letter meant for you. It is from your sweet'eart, Susannah. Please, come to my 'ut, for I mistakenly left it zere." Lafayette hadn't really made a mistake. He remembered that Peter couldn't read or write, that he was quite self-conscious about it, and that he didn't want the others in the hut to know. As Lafayette walked toward his personal quarters, Peter raced ahead.

"Come on. Come on," Peter called back. "What's the matter, Lafayette? Has all this training tired you out?"

"Ah, ze energy and zest of new love," muttered Lafayette, as he picked up his own pace to catch up with his friend. Handing the letter to Peter, Lafayette watched him tear open the envelope quickly and carefully unfold the letter. Then he stared at it for a few moments.

"What's zis? asked Lafayette. "'Ave you learned to read during our stay 'ere?'"

"No," replied Peter. "But I like looking at her writing."

Lafayette sighed. "Like I said, ze zest of new love. Give it to me and let me read it to you."

Peter handed over the letter, and Lafayette began to read aloud:

My Dearest Sweetheart, Peter,

I hope this letter finds you well. Word has come to us about the horrible conditions that all of you endured at Valley Forge. I was hoping you might return for the winter, but I guess that was out of the question.

My heart aches for you, Peter. I long to be in your arms. Your words are a feast to my soul. I think that Father has guessed well the nature of our relationship. He's caught me more than once in a dreamy trance. He says I pine for you too much, but then he laughs and says he understands. I am not sure that's true, though. He had made arrangements for me to marry another even before you left for the army. I did not speak of this to you before now because it means nothing to me. I know to whom my heart belongs. Father has not spoken another word of it since you left, either. He has spoken of you frequently and how he would not be at all opposed should you return to our farm rather than Hunting Tower. I believe he has begun to accept that, if it be the will of God, you and I shall spend our lives together. I do know that is my wish. I hope it is yours, too.

Word from Hunting Tower is that they have done quite well with their hemp crop, and things are much better for Judge Winston. Late last summer he advertised some of his plantation for sale, but there was no buyer. That would appear to be just as well, considering how well they prosper now.

The British have begun to invade Georgia and South Carolina, so Father is to leave today for his first command. I fear for him as I do for you, but I know that it is something we must all bear in our separate ways. I pray for you every day.

With that, I must close, my darling. Father is going to post

this letter in Richmond tomorrow when he reports there for
duty. Always remember that I love you with all my heart, and I
remain here awaiting your safe return.
My love always,
Susannah

"Luso," said Lafayette. "You are truly a happy man to 'ave a woman like zat waiting for you. It makes me envy you and your future."

"Thank you, my friend. But why would you envy me? You have a wonderful family and much wealth to return to one day."

"Oui, but sadly, all zat I possess cannot possibly purchase what you already 'ave found."

"Will you write my reply?"

"You need not 'ave asked," replied Lafayette, reaching for a paper and quill pen. "I 'ad already made ze arrangements to take your dictation."

Peter wasn't entirely sure what the last word meant, but he knew that his friend would write the letter:

My Dearest Susannah,

It is so good to hear from you. I cannot even begin to tell you
how much your letters mean to me. Your love for me sustains me
through the most difficult times.

I must say that the past few months have been some of the
most difficult of my life and of everyone else's who spent the
winter here at Valley Forge. For a time I was quite ill, but they
took good care of me at the army hospital, and I am now fully
recovered. Others, I'm afraid, have not fared so well.

The spring, however, has brought a renewed spirit and confidence that we can endure and succeed in this war. Supplies have begun to arrive, although the uniforms are all still too small for me. We have also had plentiful food. A German officer has taken over our training. His teaching has been very good, and we shall approach upcoming battles with the ability to defeat the British.

I suppose that you have heard of our treaty with France. I am told that this will give us an advantage in rescuing the capital of Philadelphia. It is everyone's hope that this will lead to a much quicker end to the war.

I met General Washington in person. You might recall that he was at the church in Richmond. He even knew my name and called me a good fighter. He has said that he will try to get me a larger sword.

Your father's offer gives me comfort in pondering our future. Although I feel a great gratitude toward Judge Winston, I fight this war for the freedom of this country as well as for myself. I will be free to choose my own destiny, which includes my very reason for living—you, my dear Susannah.

Without the comfort of knowing you are waiting for me, I should have given up the struggle. My heart longs for your smile, your touch and your embrace, and these thoughts sustain me until I return again.

I shall also pray for the safety of your father and those under his command.

I remain forever yours,

Love,

Peter

13.

ANOTHER BATTLE, ANOTHER MUSKETBALL

THE ALLIANCE WITH FRANCE and the arrival of their navy to form a blockade on the Delaware River did indeed have a large impact on the progression of the war. As a result, the British determined that their best course of action would be to abandon Philadelphia and move to New York. General Henry Clinton had relieved General Howe as commander of the British troops, and he began to evacuate Philadelphia on June 18, 1778. Having sent approximately 3,000 troops by ship to Florida, Clinton was left with 11,000 soldiers, about 1,000 loyalists, and a baggage and supply train that stretched nearly twelve miles long and could travel only forty miles a day.

This was exactly the opportunity General Washington was hoping for. With no fortifications behind which to hide, and with their column stretched thinly, the British should be easy to attack and destroy by a few small elements at a time. Preparing to take the fight to the Redcoats, approximately 13,000 men broke camp at Valley Forge.

As for Peter, the training inspired by von Steuben had revealed a goliath man surprisingly nimble and light on his feet. Toward the end of training, he was chosen to become a member of an elite force of skirmishers that would serve as an advanced scouting group and the spearhead of future attacks. Peter relished the task, but it also meant that he was to be separated from his mountain-born comrades. Although Peter and John Allen would participate in some of the same battles, their days of fighting side-by-side had come to an end.

While the British headed toward New York through New Jersey, Washington appointed General Charles Lee to shadow, harass and provide any obstacle possible to Clinton's force. Serving directly under the command of Colonel Daniel Morgan, Peter was among the troops assigned to this task. Unfortunately, General Lee was not nearly as enthusiastic about the plan as Washington, thus his halfhearted efforts were not as effective as they might have been otherwise. As a result, General Washington called a meeting of his staff for the morning of June 24, during which General Lee argued convincingly for prudence.

"Gentlemen," Lee said. "We must proceed with caution. Our troops have not the experience to defeat the British under these circumstances. Were we to launch an all-out attack and be defeated, surely it would mark the end of our efforts to win our freedom." Despite all the advanced training provided by von Steuben, Lee still felt that the Americans were no match for the professional soldiers the British put on the field. Several of the staff officers also agreed with Lee.

Washington, however, remained convinced that this action against the British rear guard had a great chance for success. Although he relented and held the main body of colonial troops in reserve, he ordered Lee to take command of 1,500 troops and attack the rear flank of the British column. Then he turned to General Marquis de Lafayette.

"General, do you think you could circle behind the British rear guard and coordinate an attack on the other flank with the same measure of force as General Lee's?" Washington inquired.

"Yes, General," said Major General Lafayette. "And I believe zat our troops shall prevail in such an action."

"Then it's settled. General Lee, you will attack from one side and Lafayette will attack from the other. Meanwhile, I will keep the main column in reserve to intercept Clinton at Monmouth. Are we all agreed?" Washington didn't wait for a response to his rhetorical question, instead standing, as did the others. As the men filed out of the command tent, Lafayette approached General Washington.

"General," he said, "I 'ave but one request."

"Yes, what is it?"

"I would like for Peter Francisco to be assigned personally to me. I prefer a personal assistant zat I can trust to carry out my commands and relay information to my ozer officers on ze battlefield."

"So be it. The Virginia Giant is yours."

"Merci, General," said the grateful officer, quickly taking leave.

Lafayette hastily sought out Peter to give him the news. "And so it is zat we shall be fighting togezer, at last," Lafayette concluded.

"It will be an honor and a privilege to serve with you, General," Peter responded. *How many soldiers would get this kind of opportunity?* He wondered, his mind reeling. He recalled when Judge Winston appointed him as his bodyguard after only a few years of working on the plantation. *This is no coincidence.* He began to see how God had brought these things to pass in precisely His time. *What else could He have in store?*

Lafayette interrupted his mild speculation. "Luso, please let us not be so formal. Let us go togezer and kill as many British as we possibly can. Zen you can go back 'ome to Susannah," he said wryly. "You will invite me to ze wedding, will you not?"

"I suppose I have to. It wouldn't be right if Susannah never met the man who wrote all my letters, would it?"

With that, the two men laughed and swiftly prepared to march.

As the scorching summer sun rose in the sky, Peter, Lafayette and the balance of troops under Lafayette's command left to make a sweeping arc south of the British, after which they would circle back north and take up positions. Peter, as Lafayette's personal assistant, was issued a horse and rode alongside his friend. Having a new horse made him wonder, *whatever happened to Isabel?* He had been told that she would be used to pull field artillery into action, but he soon lost track of her whereabouts. *She was a good horse and a good companion*, Peter thought. *Especially during the ride to Shenandoah.* He hoped that she had fared well.

With Peter at his side, Lafayette and his men maneuvered into position and awaited orders. Peter, astride his horse next to the commander, remembered his precious battle ritual. He reached for the handkerchief-wrapped buckles and Bible from his satchel, knelt down on one knee, and again recited the Portuguese prayer.

> *Com Jesus me deito* (With Jesus I go to Sleep),
> *Com Jesus me levanto* (With Jesus I awake),
> *Com a graça de Deus* (With the grace of God),
> *E do Espirto Santo* (and of the Holy Spirit),
> *Eu vou para a batalha* (I go into battle).

Lafayette watched this spectacle with intrigue. When he saw that Peter was finished, he indulged his curiosity. "Is zat prayer from ze Bible?" he asked.

"I honestly don't know," Peter replied genuinely, while reaching for his satchel. "I learned it when I was a kid, but I can't read this," he said, pulling out the worn Bible. "I guess it could be."

"Why do you recite it?" Lafayette pressed.

"Just before Brandywine, it entered my mind out of nowhere. The last time I remembered reciting it, I was a little boy, awake and afraid," Peter explained. "It comforted me then. The only thing I can think of is that maybe I was having nightmares at the time."

"So, you were 'aving similar feelings before your first battle, and zat is why it entered your mind," Lafayette concluded.

"Yes," Peter confirmed. "But not only that. It reminds me that God is in control, and He knows the outcome, good or bad. And, no matter what, at the end of the day, the battle for my soul is already won."

A smile began to play at the corners of Lafayette's lips. "Luso," he said, hands outstretched in front of him. "I knew I made ze right decision, choosing you to assist me. It sounds to me like you understand zat good book more zan ze most literate among us."

"I still have much to learn," Peter replied humbly. "That is another reason I am grateful to you for giving me this position."

Placing one hand firmly on Peter's shoulder, Lafayette deflected, "Luso, ze zanks is—'ow do you say—all mine."

★

While his contingent prepared to execute his battle plan, Washington had decided to add an additional 2,000 troops to the action against the British rear guard. Since these troops were a late addition to the plan, they were placed under Lee's command. Having more troops under his command than those of Lafayette, Lee requested that he be appointed as overall commander of the action.

"I shall grant your request," said Washington, "under the condition that if Lafayette has already engaged the enemy upon your arrival, you will not interfere with any orders the Marquis has already given." Lee agreed and set off with his force more than twice the size of Lafayette's.

However, unknown to Lee, on June 27, Washington had become so convinced that attacking the rear guard would ultimately lead to an overwhelming victory that he wheeled his column to support Lee and Lafayette at Englishtown. He sent orders to Lee to commence the attack as soon as possible.

On the morning of June 28, the British were just breaking camp as Lee's battle group neared them a few miles north of

Monmouth Court House. While Lee's main body slowly approached without a specific plan of action in place, the British were alerted, and sporadic gunfire broke out.

Thinking theirs was to be a coordinated effort, the young Frenchman gave orders for a rapid advance.

The fire of muskets broke out, and colonial artillery sent a barrage of cannon fire into the British camp, inflicting heavy casualties. Lafayette turned to Peter and shouted, "We 'ave caught zem by surprise. The victory is ours for ze taking!"

Peter nodded in impassioned agreement. Not used to sitting so far back from the action, he wanted nothing more than to dismount and join the battle taking place about two hundred yards in front of them.

Without warning, Lafayette gave his horse a kick and sprinted off to the right to speak to one of his captains. Unaccustomed to having a personal assistant, the general had forgotten that was why Peter was there, to deliver messages. Just as the commander dismounted, Peter caught up with him and took the reins of both horses. When Lafayette finished the conversation with his subordinate officer, he turned to see Peter in control of both their animals.

"I thought this was my job," said Peter.

"You are correct. It is your job," Lafayette replied, "and you 'ave performed your duty well." He had barely completed his sentence when British cannon fire landed near the two men—the enemy had swung around. The ground shook and spooked the horses, and Peter strained to grip their reins. Trees splintered all around them as the British began their counterattack. The crackle of musket fire grew louder and closer.

Sensing danger, Peter looked directly at Lafayette. "I'm not so worried for my own safety as for yours. General Washington would be hard pressed to replace an officer like you. We should move to safety."

Noticing some of the Americans beginning to retreat, Lafayette would have none of that. Taking his horse back from Peter, the shrewd young general spoke, "Luso, ze time to withdraw to safety 'as passed. We must rally ze troops. I shall stay 'ere to encourage ze men. You go to ze left and do ze same."

Peter remounted his steed and drew his saber from its scabbard, waving it over his head as he had seen Lafayette do on more than one occasion. He yanked the reins to the left, jabbed his feet into the horse's ribs, and yelled at the retreating soldiers, "Turn and fight, men! Turn and fight! The British are not invincible. Turn and fight for your lives and for your freedom!" Most of the soldiers did turn around and reload their muskets to face the British advance. A few did not. But Peter, maneuvering his horse and brandishing his sword, tried to block their way, screaming, "Turn and fight, or I swear to cut you down myself!" Luckily, he didn't have to make good on that threat. The remaining men turned around.

As the British troops moved closer, Peter rode directly toward the hand-to-hand combat. He leaped from his mount, grabbed his musket, took aim and fired once, eliminating a British officer from the battle. With no time to reload, Peter affixed his bayonet and pushed forward. One Redcoat lunged at him with his own bayonet, but Peter deftly parried the thrust, swung the butt of his weapon at the soldier's face, and took him to the ground. With his bayonet at the man's chest, he ended his enemy's life. It was cruel, but it was war. Some of the soldiers around Peter saw that he was on the ground fighting with them. His action inspired them even more than his words, and, though weary from the heat, they fought with everything they had.

Meanwhile, Lee's lack of planning was beginning to turn the tide in favor of the British. He was getting conflicting reports of what the British were doing. One said the British were in full retreat; another said they were attacking. Still wary of the colonial soldiers' fighting ability, Lee was unsure what to do. Finally, he issued orders for several units to move both to the left and to the right, with the intent to encircle about 2,000 British troops and force them to surrender. But he had not clearly informed his subordinate officers of the plan, and once in position, they were unsure how to proceed.

British General Clinton realized that he was being attacked from behind, and he ordered his troops to turn back and support the rear guard. Simultaneously, British artillery was ordered to wheel about and provide cannon cover. Assessing his position to no longer be viable, Lee ordered a full retreat, including Lafayette's contingent.

Back at Lafayette's command, the colonial troops were more than holding their own—they were driving the British back. Remembering that his assignment was to be Lafayette's personal aid, Peter realized that he was unintentionally ignoring orders. When he turned his back on the battlefield to locate his horse, he made a mistake that would haunt and inflict him for the rest of his life. Just as he was about to hoist himself into the saddle, a musket ball tore into the highest point of his left thigh. *Not again!* Peter thought, grabbing his leg. With his foot already in the stirrup, his shoe caught and he tumbled to the ground. The horse bolted and, for a few moments, painfully dragged him along the ground. *This is it,* Peter thought, praying silently for death to take him quickly. Mercifully, the stirrup released Peter's foot and dumped him face up on the forest floor. When he opened his eyes, the sun blinded him through the trees, and for a split second he thought that he was in heaven.

Though he had been shot in the same thigh before, this was far worse. This ball had not gone completely through the other side of his leg, and the pain was searing.

Without warning, Peter felt himself being hoisted by his shoulders. A retreating soldier, struggling mightily under Peter's bulk, was able to help him back onto his retrieved horse. But the pain of putting that left foot back in the stirrup and the pressure on it as he swung his right leg over the mount elicited an agonized "Holy hellfire!" from the Virginia giant.

Finally in the saddle, he glanced down at the face of the soldier who had come to his aid. Peter recognized him as the sentry he had relieved of guard duty at Valley Forge, the man who had been standing barefoot on his hat. *He had said he'd repay the favor one day,* Peter recalled. Peter was about to thank him when a British musket ball ripped into the back of the soldier's head, lodging itself in Peter's saddle.

Time seemed to stand still as the growing circle of blood on the man's forehead began to trickle down his face. He looked up at Peter with a blank expression. He had been steadying Peter with a hand on his arm, but it slipped away as he fell backward. The soldier had repaid his debt of a small sacrifice with the sacrifice of his own life. *I didn't even know his name,* Peter thought with remorse.

Instinctively, he bent his head into his hand. Musket balls whizzed around him, thwacking into trees, but completely missed Peter, who was oblivious yet remained inexplicably unharmed. Overcome with reverence and gratitude, he prayed aloud, "Heavenly Father, bless this brave soldier's life. I do not know him, but you made him with Your hands for Your purpose. His selfless acts have spared my life. Receive his soul into heaven. Amen."

Slightly regaining his senses, he yanked on the reins and joined in the retreat, although with every bounce and every step his horse took, the burning in his leg turned to throbbing pain. His heart thudded in his chest. He could feel himself passing out. Fighting the urge to relinquish consciousness, he forced his mind to remain alert by focusing on his surroundings and thinking deliberately. Thick, humid air mixing with ribbons of smoke. *Breathe. In. Out. Look at the ground.* Grass. *So green here compared to the field.* Horses' hooves gaining purchase ahead. *Must keep riding. Follow them.* Fervent shouts to fall back from other cavalrymen. *Follow their sound.* Musket fire growing faint. *I must survive. For myself. For Susannah. For the soldier who just sacrificed his life for me.*

A cloud of unconsciousness enveloped him. Vaguely he heard someone shouting his name and felt something grab his arm. When he opened his eyes from the near-blackout, he saw Major General Lafayette.

"Peter, we must ride quickly to escape," he urged frantically. Grabbing the reins of Peter's horse, he drove both animals as fast as he could to the rapidly deteriorating lines.

On the other flank, Washington had arrived to find that General Lee had ordered a hasty retreat, which infuriated the commanding General. After a heated exchange, Washington removed Lee from command and sent him to the rear line. With his reinforcements, Washington was able to rally most of Lee's troops and resume the offensive, but by mid-day, unseasonably high temperatures reached in excess of one hundred degrees, along with unbearable humidity, taking its toll. Both sides ceased organized attacks. That day more soldiers succumbed to heat exhaustion than combat.

Relentlessly, Washington set about the task of reorganizing his forces and prepared for British General Clinton's next move, but nothing happened. Night began to fall, preventing an attack. After a few hours of rest, Clinton ordered his column to rejoin the baggage train, and the British escaped into the darkness.

Meanwhile, the French patriot successfully guided his friend to a temporary hospital overflowing with wounded soldiers. Recalling his own leg wound from the battle at Brandywine, Lafayette carefully helped Peter from his horse and sat him down with his back against a large maple tree. With his leg throbbing terribly, Peter was grateful for the small respite from the intensity of pain.

Lafayette went in search of a doctor. "My friend 'as taken a musket ball in ze leg. He needs immediate attention," he pleaded.

The doctor, obviously harried by all that surrounded him, looked at the general in disbelief. "Don't you have eyes, man? Don't you see what's going on here? We can only take wounded men in the order that they arrive, and right now there are about twenty others ahead of your friend."

Lafayette's eyes narrowed to slits. His hand rested on a dagger that was always at his side, and the doctor took notice of this action.

"Go ahead and slit my throat," he said defiantly. "At least then I'll not have to witness any more death. I'll not have to cut off another man's limbs. I'll not see any more misery. Go ahead!"

With slumped shoulders but a compassionate heart, Lafayette returned to sit with his friend outside until morning, listening throughout the night to the shrill cries of dying and mutilated men.

When the morning light shone early in the eastern sky, the very doctor Lafayette had threatened appeared at the opening to the hospital tent and signaled that he would look at Francisco next. Lafayette roused Peter from a fitful sleep and helped him into the tent.

As the doctor examined the musket wound, the officer kept poking his face in to glimpse the progress of treatment. "It would be easier if I could see the wound rather than the back of your head," the doctor complained to Lafayette. He proceeded to clean the dried blood and wound where the ball had entered Peter's leg as well as he could. Then he sewed the wound closed, while the oversized soldier winced and grasped the side of the table on which he rested, squeezing so hard, the veins in his hands bulged.

"Doctor," Lafayette yelled. "What are you doing? Don't you see ze ball is still in zis man's leg?"

"I'm doing the only thing I can do," replied the doctor curtly. "I don't have anything to properly go digging into his leg to find that ball, and if I did, he'd probably lose the leg anyway. This is the best I can do for him under the circumstances."

Almost apologetically, Lafayette glanced at Peter. "It's all right," said the wounded man. "Let's just get it over with."

The general nodded at Peter, then looked at the doctor. "Proceed."

14.

THE HERCULES
OF THE REVOLUTION

THE MORNING AFTER THE PROCEDURE closing
the wound on Peter's thigh, Lafayette came to visit at one of several recovery tents that had been set up for the injured. As the
Frenchman entered the tent, Peter looked up at him from his cot.

"You are looking much better zan when last I saw you," commented the young general.

"I may look better, but my leg sure is sore," Peter complained.

"I am sure zat it is, and it will likely remain so for some time
to come. Zat is why I 'ave made arrangements for you to recuper-
ate at a private farm'ouse called White Plains. It is somewhere in
New York. I spoke personally to General Washington about you,
and 'e is making sure zat you get ze proper care needed to recover
and rejoin ze struggle as soon as possible."

"I don't know what to say. You are a good friend."

"You need not say anyzing. It is what friends do for each ozer. But now, I must leave you. Ze general 'as given me a new assignment, and I leave wizin ze 'our. Rest well, recover quickly, and remain safe, Luso." He leaned over and gave Peter a kiss on the left cheek and then the right.

"I'm not quite sure I'll ever get used to that," commented Peter. "Can't we just shake hands?"

"I shake 'ands wiz zose I don't care about. I kiss my brozer, and you are my brozer. I look forward to kissing you again when next we meet."

With his friend's departure, Peter was left to contemplate Lafayette's words. Although they did not share the same parents or even the same country, truly he and Lafayette were brothers.

Later that day a wagon arrived, and Peter was taken to the White Plains home of William Dickenson. The man with his stout frame and trim beard reminded Peter a little of Judge Winston when he greeted him. Peter noticed a tobacco pipe in his hand. As Peter climbed down from the wagon using a makeshift crutch to steady his weakened left leg, William motioned to a dark man beside him to offer Peter his assistance. *A slave,* Peter presumed. *What I used to be,* he reflected. The man couldn't be much more than five feet tall because his head reached just above Peter's waist, making it quite a challenge for him to really support Peter.

"Come in, young man," William said with genuine hospitality. There was a slight pause between each of his words, like he was a father giving due consideration to Peter as a would-be suitor for one of his daughters. "We've been expecting you. My wife has been overseeing Letty's preparations in the kitchen. Some nourishing food will help you regain your strength."

Upon entering the house, Peter was greeted with a faint savory smell, the kind that would sometimes settle into the mainhouse room he shared with Petunia at Hunting Tower. Peter was eager to locate its source, but, ignoring it at least for the moment, he took in his surroundings. *Wow!* Peter thought, awestruck as he hobbled through a set of double doors that opened into the parlor. For once, he didn't have to duck his head under the doorframe. *This is even nicer than the Winston home at Hunting Tower!* Mr. Dickenson was obviously a man of great prominence.

The first thing Peter noticed was the size of the room. Even a step stool wouldn't have put the ceiling within his arm's reach. Everything from the draperies and pillows to the seats bore the same deep blue fabric, criss-crossed with a gold design. In fact, the whole room seemed inlaid with gold. *It's like a treasure chest!* Peter thought. He was afraid to move, for fear he'd knock something over with his large frame. The tables and fireplace were kissed with the whitest marble Peter had ever seen. The mahogany chair backs and table legs had been carved with an elaborate pattern. *I wonder if I could craft something like that,* Peter thought. A tall mirror with a hefty-looking frame rested against the wall between two windows that stretched from floor to ceiling. Something in its reflection caught Peter's eye, and he located its position in the room. Hanging from the wall next to the fireplace was a painting depicting a taut, bareback Cream Draft, standing in a large fenced-in field amid auburn-colored trees. The horse's mane was out of sight. Peter could almost sense this animal's longing to be free and untamed.

"Like that painting, do you?" said Mr. Dickenson, rousing a mesmerized Peter as he lighted the bowl of his pipe and puffed several times to get the tobacco burning. Peter had been so entranced by the painting, he realized he had somehow found his way across the room. "It's a George Stubbs. He's out of Liverpool. Paints animals. Equines, mostly."

Mrs. Dickenson appeared in the other entrance to the room. "I see our house guest has finally arrived. We're happy to have you here," she said, welcoming their tall visitor. Peter beamed in response to her warm welcome.

"My name is Peter Francisco," he said.

"Why, of course. Now, you sit there for just a minute," she said, gesturing toward the settee opposite the fireplace. Reflexively, he checked himself for dust and dirt before lowering himself onto its lavish seat.

Looking at Mr. Dickenson, she tilted her head slightly and continued talking, in almost a whisper. "They didn't tell us he was so big. You'll need to have Zechariah put a bench at the bottom of the bed so the dear man's feet don't stick out."

"Yes, love." William responded, setting his pipe on the mantel. "I already figured that out. After all, I did witness Zachariah helping this giant up the steps. You, my darling, should probably tell Letty to prepare some more food. I'll bet it takes a lot to fill up this big fellow."

The Dickensons exited the room in opposite directions, leaving Peter to ponder their exchange, among other things. *How odd,* he thought to himself. *They spoke like I wasn't even in the room and so formally. Still, they seem nice.* The couple was gone long enough for Peter's thoughts to wander. Soon, he found himself imagining a home for him and Susannah. *It wouldn't be anything like this,* he thought. *But I will build it myself. It will be practical but comfortable.*

And warm. Because Susannah will be there to share it with me.

When William returned, he was accompanied by Zechariah, who carried a rugged-looking bench. The wood was stretched and split in some places, weathered from the sun and rain. But it looked to Peter like it would be just the right size. "Let us get this set up for you, and then I'll show you to your room," William said. He walked toward the back of the house with Zechariah and returned a few minutes later. "Come with me, and let's get you settled into bed. I'm sure you're tired after a long journey. Let me take your things."

The old man grabbed Peter's satchel, his musket and his sword and guided him by the elbow down a softly-lit hallway. Peter was able to manage on his crutch unassisted. The aroma that filled his nostrils when he first arrived suddenly became stronger. Soon, he knew why. Mrs. Dickenson was at the end of the hall where her kitchen was in full preparation for the next meal. The large table contained an endless bounty of earthenware, baskets, bowls and pie plates filled with carved roast beef, vegetable stew, puddings, tarts, cheese, nuts, pickles, and pies. As they passed by, Peter caught a whiff of something sweet like cinnamon and had to will himself to continue following his gracious host down the hallway. His body moved forward but his face turned in the direction of the kitchen until it disappeared from view.

To his right, a door led to the main bedroom. William extended his arm, directing Peter into that room and invited him to sit on the bed. "Normally, this is where Mrs. Dickenson and I sleep, but we want you to sleep here. Mrs. Dickenson and I will be right upstairs."

Peter didn't move. The bed was unlike anything he had ever

seen much less slept in. It was like a self-contained chamber complete with a wooden top supported by four posts that looked like long stair spindles and curtains that clearly drew closed around the perimeter. "But... I couldn't... I don't want to put you out of your own bedroom," Peter stammered, incredulously.

"Nonsense. You'll be more comfortable here. Besides, with that wound of yours, it wouldn't do to have you lumbering up and down the stairs. Why, George would be sorely disappointed if anything bad happened to you. He must be quite fond of you. Anyway, you just lie back and rest now. There's a nightgown right behind you. I think you'll rest more comfortably in that. A bit later, Letty will bring you some food."

How much later? Peter wondered fleetingly, certain he felt his stomach rumble, but couldn't be sure if it was really hunger or just a intense craving. The thought of a little rest was comforting, though, and Peter reclined as Mr. Dickenson left the room and closed the door. He looked sideways at the nightgown, and reluctantly put it on. He was silently grateful for the extension that proved necessary; his feet would have been hanging over the end of the bed by a good eight inches but for the bench that had been piled high with extra quilts.

After only a few hours of sleep, Peter was awakened by the creak of the door. Mrs. Dickenson entered the room followed by her husband and another gentleman.

"This is Dr. Dodge," William announced. "We've arranged for him to take a look at your wound and make sure it's healing properly."

"Good day, sir," greeted the doctor as he set a black leather bag on the side of the bed.

"Good day to you, too, sir," Peter replied.

The doctor started to lift the sheets, but he was on the wrong side of the bed. "It's the other leg," Peter said.

The doctor looked slightly embarrassed, though he couldn't have known which leg carried the musket ball. He walked around to the other side and lifted the sheet. The nightgown made it easier for the doctor to access Peter's leg.

"We'll need to change this dressing," the doctor said as he carefully removed the bandage congealed with dried blood. "Now, let me take a closer look. Hmm. All things considered, this was sewn rather well. In a few days, we'll take the stitches out and see how well you're healing."

Turning to Mrs. Dickenson, the doctor continued, "You'll need to change the dressing twice a day to prevent infection. Other than that, just keep him comfortable, quiet and well-fed."

Why do they keep talking about me as if I'm not in the room? Peter wondered. He kept this recurring thought to himself. He didn't want them to think he was ungrateful. It was clear these folks genuinely cared about him and that their involvement had been arranged by General Washington.

After applying a new bandage, the doctor left, but it wasn't long before Letty appeared with a bowl of soup and square of brown bread. "Docta say start you on this, but t'night you be eatin' on meats'n vegetables we been makin' all day." The soup was delicious, far better than what he'd had at Yellow Springs. Later in the evening, Peter enjoyed some hearty meat pudding before settling back into the most luxurious bed he'd ever slept in.

This routine continued for the next few days. Mrs. Dickenson dutifully changed Peter's dressing twice a day, and Letty fed him so much food that he almost felt like he was a pig being fattened for slaughter. The doctor returned later in the week, removed the stitches and pronounced the wound "healing as well as could be expected." Two months later, Peter was well enough to rejoin the army. His orders, having arrived a few weeks before, were to transfer to the 6th Virginia Regiment. The Dickensons had treated him well, and he had regained almost all of his strength. He no longer needed his crutch, although his leg did twinge now and again, and he walked with a noticeable limp.

His good friend, Major General Lafayette, arranged for a horse to be delivered, and as Peter and the Dickensons stood on their front porch, Peter couldn't resist the urge to kiss Mrs. Dickenson on both cheeks. She accepted politely that display of appreciation, but Mr. Dickenson was startled when Peter extended the same gesture toward him. Seeing William Dickenson's bewildered expression, Peter said with a knowing grin, "Ask a Frenchman." Descending the steps, he added, "And thank you for all that you have done for me." As he mounted the horse, his left leg sent a pang up his side when he hoisted himself up in the saddle. Tugging at the reins, Peter rode down the lane, bidding White Plains farewell.

★

Peter aimed south toward New Jersey. Even though he would miss the friends he had made in his original unit, Peter was happy to be getting back to the action.

When Peter reported to Middlebrook in October 1778, he was immediately selected for special training. Even though he had

226

already been assigned to the skirmishers, a select few of those soldiers were chosen for even more training as a reconnoitering and advanced party in missions that required a completely different style of combat. From fall to spring, Peter was exposed to all sorts of techniques that could be used to surprise the enemy in sneak attacks. In addition, these troops were shown methods to be used in night fighting, which was quite uncommon among organized militaries that preferred to fight by day in traditional confrontations and on typical battlefields.

During the fall training, Peter's leg was becoming stronger by the day. Again, his officers were completely surprised that a man of such size would be so quick and light on his feet. However, during the winter months, his left leg was often quite painful, especially on cold and damp days. This resulted in a walk that produced a noticeable limp as well as a few clumsy spills. Even when others inquired, Peter never once complained and never missed any drills or training exercises.

One day, as his troop was returning from the day's drills, Peter's leg buckled, and he went sprawling onto the ground with a thud. A few of the men around him sniggered, among them French nobleman Lt. Col. Francois de Fleury.

Recognizing Peter instantly, Fleury jested with some of the other men, "Lafayette is right. Zis giant is quite intimidating." His comment caused another outbreak of laughter at Peter's expense.

Not one to miss out on a good joke, Peter played along. "Ha! Very funny. You'd fall too if your feet were as big as mine," Peter said, pushing himself to his feet. Fleury extended his hand to assist Peter.

"I am 'onored to meet you, Monsieur Francisco," Fleury said, shaking Peter's hand before letting it go. "Major General Lafayette speaks very 'ighly of you. I am Lieutenant Colonel Francois de Fleury."

"It's an honor to meet you, sir," said Peter at attention, remembering his rank.

"Nonsense," Fleury said. "Call me Fleury. Lafayette 'as spoken very 'ighly of you. Says you are like a 'erd of wild 'orses on ze battlefield. I look forward to serving alongside you."

He is just like Lafayette, Peter thought. *He even smells like a Frenchman.* "Likewise," he said.

"We just 'ave to figure out a way to keep you on your feet first," Fleury taunted.

Smiling at that, Peter amended his thought, *Maybe with one exception. Fleury didn't mind a little friendly competition.*

★

Spring was much kinder to the soldiers as temperatures and the overall climate began to moderate. Peter especially liked training for night fighting. Wearing dark clothing, the soldiers were taught to smudge their faces with dirt, secure all their weapons so that they didn't make any noise, walk quietly through any terrain, and use hand signals and animal sounds to communicate with fellow soldiers. Peter, though tall and large, took special pride in being able to sneak up on just about anybody undetected.

On May 1, 1779, most of the men who had been training at Middlebrook were assigned to West Point, where General Washington's army had spent the winter. This was certainly an improvement over the previous year's encampment at Valley Forge.

In the meantime, the British, in effort to cut off Washington's supply line along the Hudson River, had set about establishing fortifications slightly south of West Point on both sides of the river. One particular location, known as Stony Point, had become of keen interest to General Washington, and he observed its construction through a telescope from atop Buckberg Mountain.

In a further attempt to gain intelligence about the fort, its armaments and garrison strength, Washington had enlisted a number of civilians to visit the fort on the pretense of conducting business there and to report on what they had seen. Those reports indicated that the so-called fort was manned by approximately 625 British soldiers under the command of Lt. Colonel Henry Johnson. Not entirely satisfied with nor trusting of the intelligence gathered, Washington sought out a volunteer for a dangerous mission to gain further knowledge about Stony Point. To that end, militia Captain Allen McClane stepped forward.

Two weeks later, near the first of July, McClane disguised himself as a local female farmer. As such, "she" told the British guards that she was there to visit her sons who were loyalists staying at the fort. Once inside, McClane was able to determine that the fort wasn't really a fort in the traditional sense. Neither stone walls nor defensive walls of any type had been constructed. Instead, the British were relying on an extremely defensible terrain.

The land at Stony Point jutted about a half mile into the Hudson itself, the three sides being well-protected by nearby British vessels and land-bound cannon. Outside the fort, immediately in front of the isthmus that connected this small peninsula to the mainland, was an area of marsh and swamp. To further deter any attack from that direction, the British had constructed rows and rows of abatis, which were sharpened sticks and logs positioned to point directly toward any advancing army. They looked like a bundle of large, sharpened leads. These barriers, coupled with artillery and guns placed in two semi-circular lines, formed a seemingly impregnable position.

Against the odds, Washington and General Anthony Wayne came up with a plan to take the fort and ease the Hudson River blockade. It called for a three-pronged attack that included a diversion toward the center of the fort and a flanking movement by two other units to breach the well-manned embankments fronted by the wooden abatis. The plan was aided by short-sighted British engineers as well as the hand of Almighty God Himself. Although their use of the natural fortification had initially appeared ingenious, the engineers had failed to realize that at low tide, soldiers could approach the ends to that particular fortification, chop through a minimal amount of the spears, and allow following troops to flood in.

Thus, General Wayne's plan called for launching the attack on July 15–16, 1779 at midnight, when a low tide would occur. In addition, during the days leading up to the attack, any stray dogs within two miles of the area were to be rounded up and killed so as not to raise alarm when the troops approached the fort in the dead of night.

After marching since Noon that day, at 8 o'clock on the night of the 15th, General Wayne gathered his troops at the Springsteel Farm. "Okay, men, listen up. Major Hardy Murfree will lead the smallest force, which will provide diversion by approaching the center of the fort just outside the wooden defenses. When Murfree gives the order, they will begin firing on the British in the fort. Colonel Richard Butler will command a larger force that will attempt to breach the British defenses on the north. I will lead the largest group of about seven hundred in the assault on the south side of the fort."

Each of the north and south assault forces was further broken down into specialized groups. Each unit of this advanced group, called the Forlorn Hope, consisted of only twenty men. The next to attack were one hundred and fifty riflemen. The balance of the troops would then overwhelm the remaining British and capture the fort.

As Wayne prepared the three groups to depart in separate columns, he issued some final orders. "All muskets, with the exception of those used in the center diversionary assault, are to be unloaded. An accidental discharge might warn the British of the impending flanking attacks. In addition, if a column should encounter any civilians during the march to their positions, take them immediately into custody in case they are British sympathizers who might sound the alarm."

Wayne paused, bowed his head momentarily as he contemplated his next words. "Men, I'm aware of the risks in this mission. If we expose ourselves, it could be devastating. But I know we will succeed. I'm surrounded by some of the best in the Continental Army. For your effort, I'm offering something extra to motivate you on behalf of General Washington." Murmurs spread throughout the ranks as they wondered what it could be.

"Washington is offering five hundred dollars to the first man who breaches the British defenses," Wayne said. This announcement sparked a wave of cheers among the soldiers. "That's not all," Wayne continued, holding up his hand to quiet them. "The second man into the fort will earn a sum of four hundred dollars; the third man, three hundred dollars; the fourth, two hundred dollars; and the fifth, one hundred dollars."

At these words, some of the soldiers thrust their axes into the air in enthusiasm. Others mouthed their excitement with subdued shouts.

Peter, having distinguished himself as a night fighter during training at Middlebrook, was assigned to the Forlorn Hope contingent in front of the northern assault group. He was especially pleased to have been given the task, and he could hardly contain himself during the night march. Advancing alongside him, Fleury sensed Peter's impatience.

"What do you say, Francisco?" Fleury whispered. "Zink you'll beat me over zat line?"

"Sure," Peter said, picking up on Fleury's playful tone. "It'll be easy after I use you as a stepping stool."

"Oh, you zink so?" Fleury said, taking Peter's punch in stride, then returned fire. "Zose British will spot your gangly frame and mistake you for a grizzly bear before you even see ze fort."

"Ok, Frenchie," Peter said. "Care to make a wager?"

Fleury pursed his lips and directed his eyes upward into the night sky, contemplating the challenge for a moment, said, "First one to penetrate ze defenses gets ze ozer's bounty, also."

"Deal," Peter said, without the slightest hesitation and reached out to shake his comrade's hand.

As Peter thought about the task that lay ahead, it wasn't the bounty on his mind. He knew what his reward would be. *You're my incentive, Susannah.* He said, directing his thoughts to her. *I am fighting for you, to have a life with you. How it eases my heart, knowing*

I have you waiting for me back in Virginia.

God's timing was perfect, as a thick cover of clouds shrouded the moon, limiting visibility over the swamp and marshland through which the Americans would make their way. He also provided just enough wind so that the British ships protecting the watersides of the fort were forced to seek a more sheltered area of the Hudson. That also meant that they could not provide any covering fire for their fellow soldiers in the fort.

By midnight, all of the American forces had taken their positions. Wayne was to the south, Murfree was positioned in the center, and Butler's troops, including Peter Francisco's group of Forlorn Hope, were staring at the northern slope. Peter put his hand in the satchel and removed his ever present shoe buckles and Arthur's Bible, still wrapped in Susannah Anderson's handkerchief. So as not to make a sound, he silently recited his Portuguese prayer and carefully returned the buckles to his satchel.

Murfree's troops began firing at the center of the fortification. Their goal was not so much to hit any of the British troops as it was to draw attention to that particular area. It was also the signal for the two Forlorn Hope groups to begin their silent assault.

Peter and his nineteen comrades began to trudge across the last bit of swamp and marshland. Even though it was low tide, the earth remained sodden, and the muck clung to their boots. Every time Peter tried to take another step, there was a sucking sound as he removed first one foot, then another, from the soaked dirt. It was especially difficult for him to move his left leg, and he winced as the pain reminded him that he was carrying a British musket ball high in his thigh. *Will it always feel this way?* He wondered with each exertion.

The plan had called for the Forlorn Hope to use axes to cut through the abatis. The hope was that the diversionary fire and the British response would cover up any noise from the axes. But when Peter arrived first at the obstruction, he threw his axe away, lowered his shoulder, dug in his heels, and with all of his might and power pushed the pointed spears and logs out of the way. It took quite the effort but before long, Peter had cleared a path about ten feet wide.

Immediately, Peter and the others in his advanced group began making their way up an exposed abatis point. Yanking a little too hard to extract his foot from the sodden earth, Peter nicked his maimed thigh against one of the sharp limbs. On impulse, he hollered, attempting to muffle the sound with his hand, but it was enough noise to alert the British troops above them. Withering musket fire rained down on them, and several of the men accompanying Peter fell. He took hold of his musket strapped across his back with its bayonet already attached as per instructions.

As the regiment reached the first perimeter of defense, one of the British soldiers had just finished reloading. Swinging the muzzle in Peter's direction, he failed to notice that the Portuguese, with his long legs, covered the last few paces more quickly than the soldier had anticipated. Peter stood above him and ruthlessly drove his bayonet completely though the man's neck. The soldier dropped his weapon and clutched at his throat, and his eyes grew wide. At the pace of his own racing heart, blood spurted from the wound that had severed his carotid artery. He lived only moments longer.

The hand-to-hand combat became even fiercer, and Peter waded in among the British soldiers wielding his sharp-pointed weapon, dealing death and ungodly wounds with every step he took.

Having eliminated most of the defenders of the first ring of British defense, Peter and the remainder of his commandoes continued to charge up toward the second embankment. Again, a fusillade of musket balls filled the air with deadly lead. More comrades fell all around Peter, but even though he was at the front of the attack, it was as if a guardian angel protected him from the deadly fire.

Peter and Fleury were rapidly approaching the British upper works of the fort. Now the two of them were racing for Washington's cash prize.

As they reached the second line of defense, three soldiers jumped up and leveled their guns at Peter, Fleury and another man who was with them. Their effort wasn't very well-coordinated, as all three musket balls cut down the third man in their advancing party. *His reward will have to be collected in heaven,* Peter thought.

Fleury chose the grenadier on the right and drove his bayonet deep into the man's chest. Peter had to contend with the remaining two soldiers. The first was dispatched with a bayonet thrust to the stomach. As Peter tried to remove his weapon, the blade ripped a gaping hole in the soldier and his entrails spilled to the ground. The other soldier turned his weapon toward Peter. Like the earlier British trooper, he had fired his weapon but had no time to reload. However, his bayonet was ready. As he swung his weapon in a sweeping arc, the bayonet fell haphazardly to the ground, for in his haste the soldier had not attached it properly.

The two men, Peter and the soldier, were momentarily

stunned, though it seemed like an eternity to both of them. Just before the grenadier could react, Peter brought the butt end of his musket around and caught his combatant square on the jaw. As the soldier's head spun by the force of the blow, Peter noticed small white objects spew from the grenadier's mouth, presumably teeth. The man crumpled to the ground writhing in pain, and then he lay still.

The extra time Peter had taken fighting the second Redcoat had cost him one hundred dollars in reward money, as Fleury had already scaled the last embankment. Yet the money had never been Peter's primary incentive. In all the battles in which he had fought, Peter had always wanted to capture a British Union Jack.

Fleury was now engaged with another British trooper when Francisco spotted the British flagpole. His eyes drifted upwards in the night sky. He couldn't make out the flag in the darkness, but he could hear the distinctive sound of it flapping in the breeze as the howling winds picked up even more.

A lone sentry guarding the pole was looking in the other direction, while Wayne's men were now entering the fort from the opposite side. The sentry must have sensed Peter's advance, because at the last moment he turned and slashed at Peter with his bayonet. Unlike earlier, this bayonet was firmly attached and it caught Peter across the midsection, opening a nine-inch gash. Peter clutched at the wound for just a moment, then, being too close to use his own weapon, he dropped his musket, grabbed the man in a death-squeeze until he suffocated. Still ignoring his wound, he grabbed at the rope to which the flag was attached and lowered it from the pole. Once within his reach, he grabbed the flag and held it to his stomach, now bleeding profusely. Woozy, he then dropped to his knees still clutching the flag. He could hear shouts of "The fort's our own!" a signal that was to indicate the success of the Americans.

As he lay there holding onto his prize, only one word escaped Peter's lips before passing out, "Susannah!"

Two days later, he regained consciousness in the hospital ward of West Point. His friend, Lafayette, was standing next to his bed holding Peter's massive hand in his own. Behind him was General George Washington. There was a doctor on the opposite side of the bed examining the wound that he had treated when Peter was first taken there.

"Luso, you are truly a happy man. You and Fleury were ze only two from your group to make it out of Stony Point alive. I am starting to wonder just 'ow many of God's angels are watching over you! Rest well. Just like wiz all your ozer injuries, you'll be better soon, I am sure."

Washington then addressed the doctor. "Make sure he gets the best of care. This man is the Hercules of the Revolution, and we can ill afford to lose such a great soldier."

Peter drifted back to sleep with Washington's words subtly ringing in his ears, *This man is the Hercules of the Revolution.* The Union Jack, with his own blood dried on the intersection of the crosses, laid over the foot of his bed.

15.

A RETURN TO VIRGINIA

AFTER A FEW WEEKS of bed rest at West Point, Peter was sent to Fishkill, New York, to finish recuperating. When he was able to rejoin the Army, he participated in a number of small battles throughout New York and New Jersey, but the Battle at Stony Point had brought an end to the war in the North, and in December of 1779, Peter had completed his three-year enlistment.

Peter had served with honor and distinction. He had become recognized as one of the best soldiers in the entire Continental Army. He had suffered and survived that horrible winter at Valley Forge, had witnessed friends die brutally, and had been wounded three times, still carrying a British musket ball in his left thigh as a reminder. Having fulfilled his duty, he decided that it was now the time for others to do the fighting. He longed for Virginia, and he ached for the sight and the touch of his beloved Susannah.

At his last posting in Morristown, Peter happened upon his old mountain friend John Allen. He had also completed his enlistment, and had arrived at the same decision as Peter. Now he was headed home, not to the sweeping valleys and rolling hills of eastern Virginia, but to the never-ending expanse of the Shenandoahs. Despite their different destinations, however, the two determined to travel together down the coast before John headed in a more westerly direction.

Before his departure, Peter also came across another old friend, the Marquis de Lafayette. Just one day before he and Allen were scheduled to leave, Peter was exiting his hut when he saw Lafayette riding toward him.

"Luso," Lafayette shouted. "I was afraid you would leave before I could see you again. You are going 'ome to Virginia, is zat not right?"

"Yes, my friend," replied Peter. "I'm going home. It's been three years, and my wounds, they——"

Lafayette cut Peter off. "You need not explain anyzing to me. I shall miss you—ze army shall miss you—but you 'ave done your duty, and you need not apologize to me nor to any man." A long pause followed and when Lafayette spoke again, his voice cracked slightly. "I shall always be proud to call you my friend. In fact, more zan zat, you are my brozer."

"I feel the same about you, General, and thank you. I knew you would understand. I just feel guilty that the fighting is not finished."

"Of course, you do, but who among us can predict when zat day will come? Next year? Ze year after? Who knows? But it is time for you to go 'ome. Go 'ome to lovely Susannah, and take 'er for your own. Just do not forget, you are to invite me to your wedding. Tell me when ze glorious occasion will take place and even if I am in pitch battle wiz ze lobster backs, I shall break off ze attack and rush to your side, Luso."

"As soon as I know, you'll know," replied Peter. "Now, let's find a tavern, drink a coupla beers and relive our adventures."

The two men laughed as they walked into town and, while snow fell softly to the ground, they spent the evening regaling each other with one tall story after another. By the time they had finished, dawn was breaking, and they had both killed about twice as many British soldiers than had even been sent to the continent.

Enough snow had fallen to produce a fresh layer on the ground. On impulse, Lafayette bent down, gathered up a quantity in his hand and formed a snowball that he immediately unleashed on an unsuspecting Peter, who, with his large frame, was a rather easy target. Surprised by his action but not to be outdone, Peter carefully packed snow in his hands and glared wily at Lafayette until the ball was solid and hard. Faking his toss at first to throw off his agile friend, he then released it into the air, nailing Lafayette squarely in the chest. Soon, the Frenchman and the Portuguese, who had been joined by a common conflict in a new world, were in an all-out snowball fight, allowing them to shed the burden of their enormous responsibility and, for just a moment, laugh as young men should.

With arms slung over each other's shoulders, the two strode into camp to find John Allen waiting for Peter. He had two horses saddled and ready to go. The army, in honor of all men completing their enlistment, gave each a horse for their respective journeys home. Peter's meager belongings were secured to the saddle.

Acknowledging Lafayette, John said, "It's good to see you 'gain, General. You might not 'member me. Name's John Allen."

To which Lafayette replied, "Ah, oui. Likewise, Mr. Allen. I do remember you from Valley Forge. You were Peter's tent mate, no?"

With a confirming nod to Lafayette, John turned his attention back to Peter, "You look awful."

"I probably feel worse than I look," Peter said.

"Well, the road is long, so we best be getting' on," said John, mounting his horse.

Peter turned to Lafayette. "I can't be sure when our paths will cross again, but know that I look forward to that day." He then grasped the Frenchman by both arms and planted a kiss on each cheek.

Stunned by his friend's action, Lafayette stood speechless as Peter climbed aboard his mount. Peter looked down and said with a weak French accent, "Au revoir, mon ami. I shall miss you."

"Goodbye, Peter. I feel in my 'eart zat we shall be togezer again sooner zan you zink."

Peter and John yanked the reins of their horses and set off on a southerly course. After they had ridden only thirty yards, John looked over at his companion. "What in the world was that all about?"

"What do you mean?" said Peter, feigning innocence.

"Well, unless my eyes h'gone bad, you just up'n kissed a general back there."

"Oh, did I? I guess you'd have to be French to understand."

Both men broke out laughing, something Peter had done a lot

over the past several hours, so much that the area around the scar on his stomach began to ache—but in a good way.

During the rest of the trip, John and Peter shared stories about their respective battles both won and lost. The December weather was miserable, and it brought back memories of Valley Forge for both of them. As they skirted west of Baltimore, a fierce snowstorm caught them, and they had to make camp for a couple of days before pushing on. As they crossed into Virginia, it became apparent that the time had come for the two men to part ways.

"Peter Francisco," John said, "it's been an honor to serve wit' you. You are truly the Virginia Giant. I'll always be grateful fer knowin' ya."

"The honor has been all mine. Be well, my friend. Keep safe, and stay away from those Redcoats. But if you do see any, shoot them down like the cur dogs they are!"

"You know I will. Goodbye, Peter."

"Goodbye, John … and good hunting in your mountains."

Peter sat astride his horse as he watched the first friend he had ever made in the army head west—west to a country of mountains and streams, but a country that was still yet theirs.

★

The next couple of weeks couldn't pass quickly enough for Peter as he arrived closer to home. *Should I stop at Hunting Tower first?* He wondered. *That would be the right thing to do, I guess.* His heart was telling him to head directly to the Anderson farm. Like most young people in love, his heart won the battle. Around

243

mid-morning, Peter arrived at the front of the main house of the Anderson plantation and found himself alone; not a soul was in sight. He dismounted, walked up the steps where he and Susannah had last embraced and knocked on the door. Nobody answered. He went around to the back of the house where Susannah had been tending the garden on the day they last saw each other. Still, Peter could see no one. To his immediate left, he heard a faint noise coming from the barn. He walked toward the open door, and saw her, tending to the horses. *She looks even more beautiful than I remember,* Peter thought. Susannah appeared to be giving them a ration of oats, and her attention was completely on her task. Peter narrowed his eyes and smiled deviously, an idea forming in his mind. Making use of the stealth training he had acquired as an elite Forlorn Hope soldier, Peter walked up silently behind her. As she turned to refill the bucket, she bumped right into a tall figure. Upon seeing the man's broad chest, her breath caught in her throat. She hoped against hope that what she saw wasn't just a trick of her mind. Slowly looking up, she was filled with a rush of emotion, and she started to shriek, "Pet—"

He didn't wait for her to finish. He gathered her in his strong arms and swung her around in circles like a child would a favorite toy. Both couldn't believe that their long-awaited reunion was finally happening. All of the feelings came flooding back to him even more intense than before, and, suddenly grateful for the solitude, Peter pulled Susannah closer, then leaned down to meet her lips. The last time they had kissed, he had been tentative and gentle. This time, his kiss was hard and convincing. Susannah returned his kiss with equal passion. Her scent was even sweeter than Peter remembered, and he imbibed it like a natural remedy for his suffering. Peter could feel her heart beating against his chest. *Can she feel that, too?* He wondered. Peter couldn't get close enough to her. It was like they were trying to fit three years' of lost moments into this one embrace. The world around them no longer existed. They were alone with each other.

When they could no longer sustain the kiss, they pulled slightly apart but continued to embrace each other. In his arms, Susannah felt safe. A wave of relief washed over her, and she knew everything would be all right.

"Peter, how I've longed for you to come," Susannah whispered, burying her face in his chest. Then she stepped back to look up at him. "Why didn't you write that you were coming home?" she scolded. Before he could answer, she glanced down at herself and continued without drawing a breath, "I must look a sight. You always seem to catch me at my worst." In a feeble attempt to tidy herself, she brushed dirt from her apron and smoothed wrinkles from her blue dress, but Peter stopped her hand with his.

"And you're always wrong about that," he responded, pushing an escaped lock of her golden hair away from her flushed cheek. He noticed the way the coarse shawl wrapped loosely around her petite shoulders. "You're the most beautiful thing I've seen in three years."

"Oh, Peter, I've missed you so much. You have no idea what it's been like here without you. But what am I saying? You've endured much worse." Her words were spilling out so fast that he thought he was listening to a female version of Lafayette. "I have missed you too, sweetheart. Truly I have. You cannot possibly know how much I've thought of you, longed to touch you, to kiss you, to hold you in my arms. If there's anything right in this world, I will never have to leave your side again."

Suddenly remembering something, Susannah drew in a short, quick breath, and changed the subject. "Come inside with me, Peter. I'm sure Father will want to see you. He's in the house."

"He is? I knocked on the door but no one came to answer. Is it possible that he didn't hear me?"

"No," she said slowly. "I'm sure he heard you. He has only recently returned from the fighting in Georgia, but he's changed... so much. He was wounded in the leg, which I know causes him considerable pain; now he walks with a limp. But I fear that is not the worst of it. He won't talk about it, but I know he has seen things that no man should have to witness, just as I am sure you have. How the poor man suffers. There are nights when he actually screams until he wakes himself."

"What of your brothers? Where are they?"

"Thomas went with Father to fight in Georgia, and he remains there to this day. James, Jr. joined him when Father returned. The idea was that one of them would always remain here at the plantation to keep the things running, but when James, Jr. left, Father seemed to sink deeper and deeper into himself. Look around. Our lovely farm has fallen into such disrepair...." Susannah's voice trailed off.

Peter glanced around him. When he had first arrived, he was so excited to see Susannah that he hadn't noticed the farm's rundown condition. The fields had been poorly kept and were covered with wild growth. A wagon adjacent to the barn leaned into the ground because of its two broken wheels. Boards had fallen from the sides of the barn and the village tavern yellow paint had begun chipping off the exterior of the main house.

"And what about your mother? Where is she?" Peter inquired.

"She's visiting the Morgan farm just up the road. A number of our slaves have run off to fight in the war, and the Morgans have more than they need. She's hoping to rent some for the spring planting season—that is, if she can negotiate a reasonable price. I'm sure she'll be home directly."

Peter and Susannah began to walk toward the main house. He looked down to find that she had slipped her small, delicate hand into his rough, oversized one. *Just the way it should be,* he thought contentedly.

When the two of them entered the house and scanned the parlor, James Anderson was nowhere in sight.

"Father," Susannah said in a loud voice. "Father, where are you?" There was no answer. "He must be in the kitchen," she suggested. "He spends a lot of time there."

Susannah led Peter to the back of the house where, as she had predicted, they found James Anderson was sitting at the kitchen table drinking some tea. He stared out the window in a cataleptic state, appearing to survey his property.

"Father, look who is here. Look who has come home."

The elderly gentleman turned his head. His eyes looked vacant and listless, but when he got a good look at Peter, some life seemed to return. He rose unsteadily to his feet, holding onto the back of the chair. "Peter. Peter, my boy. You've come home. It's great to see you. You're a sight for sore eyes. We've heard a lot about your exploits in the Northern army on behalf of our cause. I surely wish I had had someone like you in Georgia."

Peter walked over to Susannah's father and extended his hand. "It's good to see you, too, sir. Susannah says you have not been feeling well."

"Oh, it's nothing, nothing at all. I just need to rest a bit." It was the same excuse that James Anderson had been giving ever since returning home several months ago. "Peter, I would like to talk more with you about the war, but for now, I think I need to lie down. You two go and enjoy each other's company."

As her father shuffled across the room, Susannah took Peter through the back door and with her hand in his, gave him a guided tour of the plantation, revealing even more evidence of the ruin that now plagued the once-thriving farm. Peter saw a small group of cattle wandering aimlessly as they searched for a grassy spot to graze. The fence surrounding the fallow pasture was clearly in need of mending. Some of the rails had been knocked out of their holes and many of the posts were askew. The roof had caved in on the chicken coop, still charred by soot and smoke from a fire that wasn't discovered in time. A plow, one of its handles split, was stuck in the middle of what used to be the vegetable garden.

"It's just been so hard. We only have a handful of the slaves that we did when the war began. Things are just falling apart here," Susannah lamented, looking up into Peter's eyes.

"Let me ask you something," Peter broke in. "Is your father's offer still good? Would he still want me to stay here rather than go back to Hunting Tower?"

"Oh, yes, Peter. Yes, I'm sure he would be most grateful."

"Then that's what I'll do. I'll go and inform Judge Winston immediately."

"Peter, must you leave so soon? Please stay the night. Mother would never forgive me if I were to let you leave before she saw you again and gave you something to eat. You look a sight. Why,

I'll bet you haven't had a decent meal in weeks. And you and Father can talk tomorrow. I'm certain he'd be so appreciative having a man to talk to. Please say that you will stay. Please."

It wasn't hard to convince him. The home-cooked meal sounded inviting, but what he couldn't turn down was a chance to be near Susannah. "I would be honored."

When Mrs. Anderson arrived, she was delighted to see Peter and rising on her toes, planted a motherly kiss on his cheek. "Peter, we are so happy you have returned to us safely. Susannah, show Peter where he can sit and relax, then come help me in the kitchen. Tonight, we shall dine properly."

Susannah directed Peter back to the parlor, where he selected a traditional-looking armchair covered in a pink floral fabric. He sank into the cushioned seat and lifted his feet onto the matching footstool, truly able to relax. Within moments he was fast asleep. Looking around to make sure they were still alone, Susannah bent forward and gazed into his peaceful face for a few moments before closing her eyes. *Dear God, thank you so much for protecting Peter during the war and for bringing him back at this precise moment,* Susannah prayed with grateful fervor. *Please give him strength in dealing with all that he has been through. If it is Your will that we should be together, please help me to be patient and comforting.* When she opened her eyes, a faint smile playing at her lips, Susannah leaned into Peter and kissed him gently on the forehead. "I love you, Peter Francisco," she whispered before returning to the kitchen.

Before long, winter's early darkness had enveloped the plantation and softly blanketed the house. Peter probably would have slept right through the night if a nudging on the arm hadn't startled him. Waking with a start, he instinctually reached for a weapon, but when his eyes adjusted to the twilight, he saw Susannah leaning over him, smiling.

"Dinner is ready, love. Wait till you see. Mother has prepared quite a feast in honor of your homecoming. And Father seems... well, refreshed. I told him that you would be staying with us, and that appears to have lifted his spirits."

Together, they walked into the dining room where Peter took in the sugary aroma of sweet potato pie and the airy flavor of salt-cured ham. Mr. Anderson, seated at the head of the table, smiled when the couple entered the room. "Come and join us, Peter. I daresay that my wife is the best cook in all of Cumberland County. Let's pray and eat. Then, you and I have much to talk about."

Grasping hands, Mr. Anderson led them in prayer. "Heavenly Father, as Your servants, we humbly thank you for Your many blessings. We are grateful for Peter's safe return and thank you for the Army's success. Thank you for the bounty before us and for the hands that made it. May it sustain us to continue doing Your work. Amen."

As they feasted, the head of the household continually prompted his guest to tell them stories of his adventures with the Northern army. Peter did so willingly, though because of Mr. Anderson's delicate condition and because he wasn't ready to relive it, he was hesitant to talk about any of his personal actions and left out entirely some of the more harrowing moments.

After dinner, the two men retired to the parlor for a few puffs of tobacco. The elder gentleman preferred a pipe while Peter settled for a hand-rolled Virginia cigar. During his three year enlistment, he had learned to enjoy the smooth, earthy taste of a spicy oak-flavored cigar while unwinding around the campfire with the other soldiers at night. Although he wanted to spend more time with Susannah, Peter knew that there would be time enough for that. For now, he sensed that the family patriarch needed to confide in someone who understood what he had been through. They talked for hours, well past the Andersons' typical bedtime. The conversation seemed to breathe new life into Mr. Anderson's spirit. By the end of their dialogue, they found themselves talking about all the things that they could do to restore the plantation to her pre-war glory.

While Mr. Anderson continued to make plans, his back to the entryway, Peter saw a bleary-eyed Susannah peak her head into the room. *I'd much rather be talking to her, but I am so tired.* Peter was grateful to see her, for his short nap had not been enough to relieve the weariness of his long journey home.

"Father," she said, coming to Peter's rescue, "Peter has traveled a long way in the past few weeks. I'm sure he'd like some rest."

"Yes, yes. Of course," he concurred. "I've kept you up far too long. You go now and get some rest."

Peter stood up from his chair, but uncertain where he was to go, he looked at Susannah curiously.

"Mother says you are to sleep in my brothers' room." Carrying an oil lamp, she led Peter up the stairs to the second floor, stopping in front of a closed door. "I'm sure you'll be comfortable in here."

Peter looked into Susannah's revealing green eyes, sparkling like emeralds over the glimmer of the lamp, bent down, and was just about to kiss her when they both heard her father's awk-

ward gait on the stairs. The sound sent a momentary jolt of panic through Peter's body, which lodged in his throat. The sound
transported him back to the long nights in the hull of the ship,
when the hours of quiet would be interrupted by the sound of the
one-legged pirate's wooden leg coming below deck. The trepida-
tion he experienced now was of a father's protective wrath, but
the terror he had felt from those lonely, sleepless nights, triggered
by the sound on the stairs, still lingered in the periphery of his
mind. They pulled away from each other as James reached the
top of the stairs. He tugged at Susannah's sleeve. "Now you let
Peter get some rest, young lady. You'll have plenty of time to talk
tomorrow."

Susannah followed her father on down the hall while Peter
opened the door to Thomas' and James' room. It was enveloped
in darkness except for the faint glow of moonlight around the one
window on the opposite wall, but as his eyes adjusted quickly, he
could see the outline of twin beds. He flopped down on the one
closest to him, so spent he didn't have the energy to even take off
even his boots. His last fleeting thought before falling fast into a
dreamless sleep was of Susannah, *I am sleeping so close to her.*

The next morning, Peter awoke to the near-blinding sun
breaking through the sheer curtains. At first he was momentarily
disoriented, while he opened and closed his eyes until they could
finally tolerate the intense light. *Is this the Dickenson farm?* Shaking his head, Peter recalled his surroundings. Memories of the
conversations he'd had with Susannah and her father just the day
before drifted back into his mind, and he knew instinctively that
his decision to live with the Andersons was the right one.

As he walked downstairs, Peter guessed he was probably

the first one up, but he was quite surprised when he entered the kitchen to find Susannah and her mother preparing breakfast. A white, oval-shaped teapot whistled softly as the smell of buttermilk scones filled his nose. Ham and eggs sizzled on a pan atop the wood burning stove. *The eggs are probably fresh,* Peter thought, wondering how either woman was able to retrieve them from the dilapidated chicken coop. Peter noticed that James sat in a different chair this morning, but his posture was still indicative of the same broken man Peter had encountered the day before.

Susannah was the first to notice Peter standing in the doorway. "Good morning, love," she said, suddenly realizing that she had used a term of endearment toward Peter in front of her parents. She hoped they hadn't noticed. "Ah...good morning, Peter," she repeated, trying to sound platonic. "I trust you slept well."

"I did indeed. It's been three years since I've slept as well," Peter said, shooting a telltale glance at Susannah.

Mr. Anderson looked at Peter as he sat down. "Good morning, Peter. I know I kept you up rather late last night, but I trust you remember our conversation?" He asked, not giving Peter a chance to respond. "It's a new dawn for us and the plantation. We have much to talk about and plans to make."

"Yes, sir, I know, and I'm eager to discuss them. But today I must go to Hunting Tower and address Judge Winston. He treated me well, and granted me freedom, and he said I would always have a home at Hunting Tower. If I am to decline his offer, I must do it face-to-face, and the sooner, the better."

"I understand, Peter. Though we've had our differences in the past, Judge Winston is a good man and a good friend. After we have eaten, go to Hunting Tower and make your plans known.

We can speak later about your decision."

After consuming the delicious breakfast, Peter went outside to saddle his horse. Susannah followed him. As he cinched the saddle, he turned toward her. "Do you really think your father understands about … us …" Peter ventured, recalling Susannah's retraction in the kitchen.

"I don't know for sure. I think he understands we have strong feelings for each other. Yet, I believe that he still clings to the notion that I will marry George Carrington; that's the man I wrote you about. Our families have known each other for a long time, and I've known George since I was a little girl. He's a cavalry officer, you know."

"Do you love him?"

"No," Susannah said emphatically. "Father just wants me to marry him because he comes from a wealthy family, but I don't want to marry him …" Susannah said diffidently, looking down at her hands. She knew what was in her heart, but in revealing it she also knew she would risk rejection. Lifting her eyes to Peter, she took both of his hands in hers, then, erasing any doubt, added boldly, "I want to marry you, Peter."

"Then I will return and make my case to your father for your hand in marriage."

Her face filled with concern. "Father will not be easy to convince."

Peter swung himself onto his horse with his uninjured leg and eased down on the saddle. "Don't worry," he assured her. "I have fought bigger battles." Then he tugged at the reins and headed his horse toward Buckingham County and Hunting Tower. He wasn't sure how the Judge would react to his decision, so he took his time, letting his horse dictate the pace, which gave him time to ponder the situation.

Will the Judge be happy to see me? Will he be grateful? Will he think I am returning home? Will he be angry when he hears about my decision? No matter what, at least I have Susannah.

When he arrived at Hunting Tower, Peter felt anxious as he anticipated his reunion with the Judge. *Things look about the same,* he mused, reflecting on its appearance. He examined the barn, where he had spent so many hours with Arthur, and noticed Alfred coming through the doors. He had returned from the war and resumed his position as slave master. *Perhaps that is why everything looks so normal.*

Alfred walked over to Peter and offered him a hearty handshake as his returning friend dismounted. "Peter Francisco. You've come home," he greeted with a sincere smile. "The Judge will be happy to see you. We've all heard so much about you." *That's what James Anderson said, too. That makes the second time someone has said that,* Peter thought, surprised. He didn't realize how well-known he had become throughout the area.

At that moment, Petunia, the trusted house servant who had taught him to speak and understand English, walked around the corner, the same corner she rounded when she had first laid eyes on Peter. *She looks so grown-up,* Peter thought. She broke into a run and flung herself at the Virginia Giant, landing in his arms with her feet dangling several inches off the ground. "Peter, Peter, Peter! You's back! You's back! Mista Judge, he sho' be happy to see you 'gain."

"The Judge is in town attending to some business, but I 'spect he'll be home soon," Alfred broke in.

"I s'pose you heard 'bout Arthur?" Petunia inquired.

"Yes. Yes, I did," replied Peter softly. "Where did they bury him?"

"He be ova yonda back behind d' hemp fields. C'mon. I'll take you. He sho' loved you, Peter Francisco. When you left, near broke his heart."

Peter followed Petunia as they walked through the now-fallow field awaiting next season's round of hemp planting. After several minutes, they arrived at a patch of grass crowned with a solitary rock. Inscribed on the rock were the words, "Faithful slave and friend." Peter looked at Petunia.

"Mista Judge had Richard carve dem words." Petunia assumed that Peter still hadn't learned to read, so she recited the words aloud.

Turning to Petunia, Peter asked, "Would you wait here for just a minute."

"Sho', Peter, sho'. What's you gonna do?"

"This rock isn't finished." He walked back to the barn and returned with a hammer and chisel. Slowly, and with Petunia dictating each letter, he set about carving on the rock. When they finished, it read, "Faithful slave and friend and father." Setting his tools aside, he again bent down, extending his hand as he did to touch the rock, and, resting his elbow on his knee, he bowed his head. *Heavenly Father, thank you for leading me to Arthur and for allowing him to be a part of my life. Thank you for shaping him into the man he was and for his influence. I know he is with You now. Please rest his soul. Amen.* A single tear fell from his eye and splashed directly onto the word "father." When Peter had finished paying his respects to his great mentor, he and Petunia walked back to the barn in silence.

Not long after that, Judge Winston's carriage rolled up the pea-gravel drive. Peter walked out to open the door just as he had done on so many prior occasions. When the judge looked out the door, he was stunned.

"Peter. Peter Francisco?" said the Judge, as if trying to recall Peter from his memory. When it had finally sunk in, he exclaimed, "Peter! When did you get here?" The Judge was almost ecstatic. "Good Lord, boy, it's good to see you. How are you? Did you have a good trip? What was it like in the war?" *Why doesn't anyone wait for my answers?* Peter thought, chuckling to himself. "Come into the house," the Judge continued. "It's too cold to stand out here and talk."

Together the two men walked up the steps and entered the house. *Strange,* Peter thought. *I spent ten years of my life on this plantation but only been inside this house a few times. Yet, I've only been to the Anderson home twice and actually slept in the main house. Where I wouldn't have been welcome before, now, it seems, I am welcome with open arms.* As they settled themselves in the parlor, Peter found himself in the same chair once-occupied by Patrick Henry. Trying his best to recall all the questions Judge Winston had asked outside, Peter began, "I arrived at the Anderson home yesterday and stayed with them last night," he volunteered.

The Judge's eyes became wary and suspicion took hold in his mind. *Were the Andersons, using their daughter as bait, trying to lure one of the best workers Hunting Tower had ever seen away from me?* Trying not to divulge his misgivings, the Judge interjected, "I'm sure you were tired by that time, so you needed a rest before coming home. But you're home now, and that's all that matters." The Judge's voice was resolute and his posture rigid. He looked out the window toward the barn as if by doing so, he could somehow will Peter out there.

Peter went on to tell the judge about the war. He told him about training in the Shenandoahs, fighting at Brandywine, Germantown, surviving Valley Forge, and everything else he could remember. Again, because the memories of his friends' deaths were still so fresh in his mind, he declined to discuss his own heroics or provide some of the more gruesome details.

Finally, he could no longer avoid the subject that he sensed was going to upset the judge. "I know that when I went off to war, sir, you said I would always have a home here at Hunting Tower. I want you to know how much I appreciate that. But," he ventured, "the Andersons need me even more than you do. The two Anderson boys are off fighting in Georgia. Mr. Anderson is not well. Most of their slaves have run off, and the whole place is just falling apart. For these reasons, I've decided to return to the Anderson plantation to help them in any way I can."

The Judge could no longer contain his frustration. "What? You can't be serious. This is your home. Hunting Tower is your home," said the judge, raising his voice. "I'll hear nothing of it." Then, regaining control of his temper, he added more calmly, "And if it's that Anderson girl who has you thinking about this, I can tell you right now that James Anderson has already made plans for her. She's to marry the Carrington boy. Now, let's stop all this foolish talk. Hunting Tower is your home, and here is where you'll stay. That's final!"

"No, sir. That's not your decision to make. When I left, you granted me my freedom. I just spent the last three years fighting for freedom, both yours and mine. The decision is mine to make and as grateful as I am for all your kindness, I'll be moving to the Andersons."

The Judge slammed his hand on the table. "Then get out. Get out! Get off this plantation and don't come back. You ingrate! After all I've done for you! I took you into my home. I treated you like a son. I never want to see you again. Get out, and take your belongings with you. Get out now, or I'll have Alfred escort you off the property!"

Peter felt the mingling of hurt and anger over this unexpected rejection rising from deep inside him. He wanted to dispute that the Judge had taken him into his home. He had slept in a shack. And he surely was never treated like the Judge's sons. But when Peter spoke, his voice was even, "I'm sorry you feel that way, Judge Winston. But this is something I must do."

Peter stood up, walked out the front door and behind the main house into the room that he and Arthur had built together for him so long ago. Looking around, it was exactly as he had left it, sparsely furnished with just a bed and dresser. Atop the dresser was the tri-corner hat that Mr. Anderson had given him for his act of gallantry. He rummaged through the dresser drawers. There were only a couple of shirts worth taking. Gathering those up along with his hat, Peter walked around to the front of the main house. His horse still stood there saddled, since his visit had been short.

Alfred came out of the barn and walked over to where Peter was just about to climb onto the animal. "The Judge says I'm to throw you off the plantation," he said in a flat tone, "though I don't know how in the world I'd do it." He paused, looked into

259

Peter's deep eyes, so brown they were almost black, and added, "I'll miss you. I was looking forward to having you back. Good luck to you." Extending his hand, he offered Peter a farewell handshake.

"Thank you. I'm sorry the Judge feels the way he does," Peter said, looking down at the ground. Then, returning Alfred's handshake, he uttered a simple, "Good bye."

He rode away from the plantation with mixed emotions. All he had wanted was to return home from three years of fighting and hear his father say, "I'm so proud of you, son!" But that moment in time had been ripped from him by the pirates some fourteen years earlier. At the very least, he hoped that Judge Winston would have been proud of his efforts toward freedom for the colonists. *I thought he would understand that I want to be free to make my own life and my own decisions.* Instead, he had walked into a hornet's nest.

Although he anticipated the prospect of becoming a part of the Anderson family, he was upset by the Judge's reaction to his news. Part of him had anticipated it, but not to that extreme. This had been his home for the majority of his life, and he would miss everything about it. Even though the Judge had stung him, Peter would still miss him.

16.

PETER AND SUSANNAH

AS PETER DIRECTED HIS HORSE back toward the
Anderson plantation, snow began to descend lightly to the ground.
At first, it fell in flurries, then more heavily until the thick speckles
of white no longer melted when they hit the ground, gradually
covering the mossy forest floor with a protective blanket. Within
a few more miles, Peter could barely make out the trail. He un-
consciously pulled his coat tighter—the coat that Lafayette had
purchased for him during his recuperation at Yellow Springs in
Valley Forge. He was also thankful that Susannah had given him
one of Thomas' scarves, and he wound it tightly around his neck.
The day had begun with unusually moderate temperatures, but
the cold had come back with a vengeance, and, with it, one of the
most powerful snowstorms of the winter.

Though he was still miles away from the Anderson plantation, Peter could scarcely see the mane of the horse he was riding. The snow surrounded him like a dense cloud of fog. Regretfully, he realized he could go no further. When he finally found a clearing, he had no hobbles for his horse, so he unsaddled her and wrapped her reins under a large, fallen tree limb. He cleared away a patch of snow until he reached a bed of pine needles. Using the saddle again as a pillow, he covered himself as well as he could with the needles, a rather poor attempt at insulation but it would have to suffice.

As he lay awake shivering, the cold going right to his bones, he thought for a few moments of that bitter winter at Valley Forge. *Drafty huts. Insufficient clothing. Rampant illness. Scarce rations. Miraculous any of us survived at all. I certainly didn't make it through all of that just to die out here in the middle of the forest.* As he prayed God would keep him warm through the night, his mind began conjuring images of Susannah and all that had happened over the past two days. Recalling how soft she felt in his arms, her honey-sweet lips, and how her sea-like eyes filled with longing and promise, lighting his mind and body afire, he knew now without a doubt that Susannah loved him.

Susannah's father was another matter altogether. Judge Winston's reaction to Peter's news caused him deep distress, more than he anticipated. He hoped that someday the Judge would reconsider. When sleep finally came, snow had almost completely covered the giant who lay on the forest floor.

By early morning, Peter could barely lift himself beneath the weight of the fresh, wet snow. For a moment, he stopped to appreciate the tranquil silence that often followed a winter storm. Closing his eyes, he silently praised God. *Thank you, Lord, for spar-*

ing my life yet again. The forest was so deafeningly quiet that the rumblings of his empty stomach seemed to echo off the trees. Since he had brought no provisions, he simply readied his horse for the trip and was soon on his way again. The path had disappeared under the thick layer of white. *At least the snow has stopped,* Peter thought. Soon, he was able to discern a faint outline of the trail. Around noon, he finally arrived at the Andersons. Before he even had a chance to bring his horse to a halt, Susannah was rushing out the door.

"Peter, Peter," she cried. "We were so worried about you. I stayed up all night waiting for you to return!"

As Peter climbed down, stiff from the long night on the cold ground, Susannah continued on. "I was so afraid that Judge Winston had convinced you to stay on at Hunting Tower. Then, when it began to snow, I thought you might have gotten lost and frozen to death."

"Calm down, Susannah," Peter said soothingly, seeing the distress in her eyes. "I told you I would be coming back, and here I am. The Judge did expect me to stay, and he was furious when I told him of my decision to return here. In fact, he threw me off the plantation and said he never wanted to see me again."

"Oh, Peter. I'm so sorry. I know you feel genuine appreciation and respect for the Judge and love Hunting Tower. I'm just so sorry it ended like that."

Attempting to divert her comments, Peter reassured her, "As for me getting lost and freezing to death, I found my way home from the war, didn't I? And I survived nights a lot colder at Valley Forge than the one last night."

Susannah sensed his lassitude, no doubt from the combination of cold and hunger, and said, "Never mind all that. I'm just glad that you're back. Have you had anything to eat?"

"I ate yesterday. You remember … at breakfast." A smile flashed across his face.

"Then you must be half-starved. Come on, I'll get you something nice and hot." After taking his horse to the barn and tending to her care and feeding, Peter and Susannah headed for the main house. Quietly, he slipped his arm around her waist.

At the end of that day, Peter and the Andersons retired early, none of them having slept very well the previous night, least of all Peter. Peter and Susannah again found themselves in front of the door to his bedroom. With her father already in bed and out of earshot, Susannah turned her face up to Peter, the lantern light making her eyes shine.

This time, Peter did not hesitate. Leaning forward, he wrapped his long, defined arms around her slight frame and drew her close. His right hand spanned the small of her back, the size of it curving slightly around her waist. He pressed his lips into hers with a new sense of urgency, like she was finally his. A small sigh escaped Susannah's throat, as their mouths parted slightly. With the fingers on his left hand, Peter stroked the bare skin at the nape of her neck, sending a tingling sensation down her back. Susannah's tender lips tasted like nectar and secretly Peter didn't want the moment to end. He had to fight the urge to carry her into his room. Susannah wanted to stay lost in Peter's protective arms forever. When they drew back at last, they lingered in each other's arms, transfixed, certain they knew what the other was thinking. Finally, Susannah broke the silence and whispered, "Sleep well, Peter, my love."

"A kiss like that will find me dreaming the dreams of angels. Good night, sweetheart."

The next morning, Susannah woke early, but not early enough. Peering out the window, she could see the barn already illuminated with a lantern and two shadows bouncing around its glow. Wrapping herself in a large overcoat, she crunched her way through the snow to the barn and peaked inside. Peter and her father were talking. Mr. Anderson also appeared to be writing on a small piece of paper. When Susannah entered, both men looked up.

She cocked her head slightly pretending to be angry. "And just what is it that the two of you are plotting out here in the near dead of night?" She tapped her foot on the dirt floor of the barn for emphasis.

"Susannah," her father said. "What do you mean? Peter and I are making a list of materials we need. He says we need an anvil, and hammers and all sorts of things so that he can begin to make repairs around the place."

"Good morning, Susannah." Peter broke in.

"Good morning, Peter," she replied, her tone suddenly pleasant. "Alright, both of you. Finish your list and then come into the house. Mother and I will have breakfast for you shortly."

Of course, both men became fully engrossed in what they were doing and when breakfast had been prepared, Susannah had to summon the men from the back door. As she watched her father and Peter walk toward the house, she noticed something for the first time. Both men walked with a limp. Her father, she could tell, had a slight bounce in his step that wasn't there before. Looking at Peter, Susannah realized he, too, limped, favoring his left leg. *I'll have to ask him about that later,* she thought.

As the four of them ate, James and Peter talked eagerly about plans for effecting repairs on the plantation. Later that day, the two men hitched up the one operable wagon and set off for town. If Susannah hadn't known better, she might have become jealous that her father had usurped all of Peter's time. Deep inside, she knew it was for the best. The closer her father and Peter became, the easier it would be for James to accept Peter as the one she wanted to marry.

Throughout the rest of the month, Peter was a man on a mission, rising well before dawn and working well past sunset. As had been the case at Hunting Tower, Peter was making fine music with his hammer and anvil, but something felt different. As he swung the hammer, he realized for the first time that quite possibly he was working for his own future. *A future that would include Susannah,* he thought. This epiphany ignited something within him, and he worked with intense vigor. He repaired the broken wagon wheels and re-rimmed all of the carriage and wagon wheels. As he prepared to set one of the tires, Peter daydreamed about hitching horses to the wagon and riding into town with Susannah one day. *She'd sit next to me, not behind me,* he imagined. *She'd laugh at something I said, revealing that irresistible dimple of hers.*

Something shifted to Peter's right, interrupting his thoughts. When he looked over to see what it was, he could see a tiny foot hooked around the corner of the barn and the side of a small, dark face peeking out from behind. Peter smiled, amused. The slave boy had been following him around the plantation the last few weeks like a shadow, but had always darted away whenever Peter tried to speak to him. Peter knew from conversations he'd had with Eli's mother, that his father had left the plantation to fight in the war several years ago, but still hadn't returned. Peter placed the boy at roughly five years old, the same age he was when he first arrived at Hunting Tower. Peter realized with chagrin that Eli probably had little to no recollection of his father. Something he could certainly relate to.

In attempt to draw him in, Peter leaned in Eli's direction and projected loudly, "I sure could use some help marking these tires."

Eli had moved so that his entire body was now in full view of Peter, but still didn't speak.

"You want to?" Peter asked, raising the chisel toward Eli.

Eli took a few tentative steps forward and grasped the chisel with wide eyes. He watched as Peter showed him how to cut a mark in the tire and listened as he explained that the marks were important in order to set the tire on the axle of the wagon exactly where it was originally.

When they were finished, Eli looked at Peter, his eyes filled with wonder, and said in a mousy voice, "Tank you."

"You can come help me anytime, Eli," Peter said, swallowing the boy's pint-sized shoulder with his large hand.

Eli took Peter at his word and from then on only left his side when it was time for him to do his own chores or when his mother called him back for a meal. He tripped and stumbled along behind Peter, keeping up as best he could. He did whatever he could to help Peter and hung on his every word. His favorite thing to do was work the bellows. He loved watching the flames in the forge flare and skip among the cinders. As Peter watched the reflection of the blaze in Eli's eager eyes, he reminisced about his time with Arthur. *Is this how I looked to him?* He wondered.

With the onset of Advent, a traditional time of spiritual reflection a few weeks before Christmas, which Peter observed along with the Andersons, he found himself thinking a lot about the past and what seemed to be a promising future. As he continued to make repairs around the plantation, he imagined performing the similar tasks on his own farm one day and what that would feel like.

He started on the fence around one of the outlying pastures alongside the remaining slaves, who were receptive to his instructions. Eli stayed beside Peter and placed his unsullied hands on the rails, attempting to assist the men. More than once, Peter spotted him straining to lift a hammer off the ground. Whenever Peter instructed Eli, he'd reply with an enthusiastic, "Yes, Mista Petuh, suh." Peter had never been addressed by other slaves in this manner before. As they discussed plans, he wondered. *Could I own a plantation like this? Would it be this one?* Together, he and the slaves tore down the old chicken coop and built a bigger one in its place. He mended the damaged plow. He stripped and repainted the main house the same village tavern yellow, and even made time to fix up the slave quarters, having harbored the belief that the more comfortable they were, the harder they would work when required.

Peter's final task was to replace missing boards on the barn. He stood at the entrance of the cavernous structure admiring his work for several minutes, wiping beads of sweat from his face that had formed above his dark eyebrows. For a brief moment, he recalled the excitement he felt upon seeing the barn when he first arrived at Hunting Tower as a boy. He thought the anticipation he was feeling had resurfaced with the memory. Then, he realized with sudden clarity, a new hope pervaded his spirit. *I ... will have ... a barn ... of my own. And it will contain* my *tools and shelter* my *horses.*

Looking up towards the sky, Peter noticed a single, endless cloud, like the underbelly of a frozen lake. The air was crisper than he ever remembered this time of year. The weathervane he had forged into the shape of a horse the week before perched motionless atop the barn. Peter and Mr. Anderson, along with the remaining slaves, had all worked tirelessly to ensure all of the repairs were made before the full onset of winter. *A good thing, too,* Peter thought, as he turned to survey the once-overgrown field, now cleared and ready for tilling come spring. He was disappointed they didn't finish mending the fence around the far pasture in the last few weeks, but they would make quick work of it when the weather broke. *That may not be as soon as we think. The way it feels now, seems like the Almanac's snowfall prediction will be just about right.* He could hardly believe Christmas was now only two days away. As he imagined the festivities, only one thought occupied his mind. *My first Christmas with Susannah.*

After much turmoil and hardship, the Anderson family, along with Peter, welcomed the respite of the Christmas season. Though most Northern colonies didn't formally observe the holiday, Virginians wholeheartedly embraced its revelry and reflection. Susannah and Elizabeth rose early and began making preparations for the celebration meal. Because the farm had remained uncultivated for so long, they wouldn't be celebrating as lavishly in years' past, but they were thankful to be together and safe.

This morning, Peter shot out of bed to the sounds of gunfire all around the house. He searched frantically for his musket, and then realized his mistake. The pop and echo was a common signal that Christmas—and invariably the fox hunts—had officially commenced, but Peter's time in battle had conditioned him to react defensively.

Downstairs, he found Susannah and her mother already hard at work. With the slaves off today, that left them to prepare the day's feast. A bittersweet aroma nearly sedated him as he approached the entryway to the kitchen. *Is that gingerbread?* He wondered, hopefully. He could see Susannah laboriously kneading dough. A light strand of her hair had come loose and must have been tickling her face because she stuck her lower lip out several times, blowing a stream of air in its direction.

The room was as lively as any other day, but today a tacit tranquility had settled upon the house. After contemplating the feeling for several minutes, Peter concluded that it must be the peace and joy of knowing God. Looking around at their preparations, he was suddenly awash in self-revelation. *This will be the first Christmas I'll spend at home as a free man. That alone is reason enough to celebrate!* he thought in wonderment. At Hunting Tower, he was always able to enjoy Christmas Day off and attend services like the other slaves, but never the fortnight of salubrious merry-making. He did not want to miss one detail.

On the center table, he spotted the plump goose he had wrangled the day before, now plucked and ready for roasting. Hanging by the open fire was a heavy-looking kettle that bubbled and mulled with sundry spirits. Bobbing on its surface were small roasted apples and oranges studded with cloves.

"My mouth is watering already!" Peter exclaimed, not sure he would have patience enough to wait. *Anything would be better than what we had in the army,* he recalled, wrinkling his nose. *If I never see that again, it will be too soon.*

"Merry Christmas, Peter," Susannah said, looking up with a cheerful smile.

"Merry Christmas to you, too! Can I help you ladies with anything?" Peter asked. He was unaccustomed to his hands being idle.

"After breakfast, my brothers and I usually decorate the house," she said eagerly. Then the joy immediately drained from her face. Susannah's hands relaxed, the kneading slowing to a stop, as if she only just realized that neither sibling would be spending Christmas at home this year. Peter thought she wouldn't be able to continue, but she collected herself. "Father is on a fox hunt, and mother will be continuing with the meal preparations. This is her favorite time of year to cook. Will you decorate with me?"

"I would do anything with you," he said with deep conviction. "Besides, I am eager to see what your plans are for all the things you asked me to collect outside."

They ate a light breakfast of tea and scones, then set quickly to work. Susannah had already laced together several needle-leaved boughs into garland and instructed Peter to drape them around the porch and over the entrance. She had fashioned a wreath out of pine cones and boxwood sprigs for the front door and coniferous swags ornamented with forced blossoms for each of the windows on the lower level. Peter marveled at Susannah's ability to weave remnants of God's natural beauty into exquisite pieces of art. *Some things,* Peter reasoned, *even neglect and abandonment couldn't destroy. A gentle reminder of God's constant presence and un-*

failing love.

While a fire blazed and crackled beneath the antique wood-carved mantel, the young couple brought the already-cozy parlor to life. On the chairs, Susannah arranged small pillows that had been hand-embroidered with ivy and holly from years' past. Peter placed candles on each of the four window sills. While Susannah stood on a small stool, Peter handed her holly stems, which she attempted to tuck between the glass and the white wooden muntins around the perimeter of the windows.

Peter stopped to watch her for a moment as she tried to work each stem into the narrow space. She moved her tongue around her lips in intense concentration, reminding him briefly of last evening when they had similarly decorated the inside of the church together. The sticking of the church, he recalled Susannah saying.

Along with other parishioners, they had hung every sort of greenery imaginable, particularly mountain laurel, from the galleries and pews. At one point, when he was standing at the altar, carefully draping holly and ivy around the pulpit, he turned around and saw Susannah walking down the aisle scattering herbs along the floor, her tongue hooked around her lip just like it was now. In that moment, Peter froze. There would be only one other occasion when he would see Susannah walking toward him down the aisle. As if she had sensed him watching her, she looked up and flashed him a beautiful smile, creasing her cheek with that sweet dimple.

Peter imagined many Christmases to come with Susannah as his wife, decorating their own house, her belly round with child. The images came so easily to him. *Why does this have to be so hard?*

He questioned to himself, contemplating how he would approach James Anderson. Behind him, the oak-laid grandfather clock chimed, pulling Peter out of his reverie.

He didn't notice Susannah crying softly, her hands covering her face. "What's wrong, Susannah?" he asked, putting his arm around her.

"It's just that … I can't figure out how to get these blasted stems into the window!" she said, her voice muffled through her hands. "James and Thomas know exactly how to do it."

"Have you heard from your brothers?" Peter asked gently, knowing that the holly stems wasn't what troubled her.

"Not in a while. Father keeps saying it's because they just don't have time to write, but …" she trailed off, not wanting to articulate what she was thinking.

With a pang, Peter realized just how unbearable her anguish must have been when they were all away.

"I'm sure they're just fine, Susannah. God is watching over them. Do you want to pray for them now?"

She nodded and slipped her hand into his. Facing the window, they knelt down. Peter pulled her hand to his chest, then began, "Heavenly Father, Your wisdom is infinite and You orchestrate all, using each of us for Your greater purpose. You've promised to protect Your children. Please under Your watchful eye, spare Thomas and James. Lead them where You have called them and bring them home safely to us. Amen."

When they finished, Peter turned to Susannah and lifted her chin until her moist eyes were even with his. "Feel better?" he asked. She gave him a weak smile. "Good. Now, why don't you let me see about putting the holly stems in the windows?"

"Okay," she said, her voice a bit croaky.

"I say, we start with this one," he said, raising his arm above their heads to reveal a large cluster of mistletoe.

Susannah couldn't help but notice the impish grin that had usurped his face. She giggled and pretended to object, but after craning her neck to make sure her mother wasn't anywhere nearby, she leaned into Peter and let him softly touch her lips with his. She wanted to prolong the kiss, but knew that would be risky. When she pulled away, Peter said, raising his thick eyebrows, "I think ... *I'll* select a spot for this."

Susannah shook her head and waved a hand at him in mock protest, but inwardly she couldn't wait until they found themselves captivated beneath its spell again.

The house felt festive and warm. The Andersons gathered around the dining room table enjoying the wonderful spread Susannah and her mother had been preparing the last few days. They laughed heartily and marveled again at the farm's transformation.

At the end of the meal, Elizabeth served coffee from an ornate silver pot with a dark, wooden handle that resembled the curvature of a cane. As she made her rounds, she asked, "Peter, will you be attending services with us tomorrow?"

"Yes, ma'am, I certainly will if you'd like me to. With all the repair work, I haven't had time for much else up till now."

"Wonderful," said Mr. Anderson, clasping his hands together. "Well, with that, I think it's about time for gifts."

"Father!" Susannah exclaimed. "You shouldn't have done that."

"Nonsense," he said, waving her comment off with his hand.

"I know times are tough, but what's Christmas without a little something extra?" He disappeared momentarily, then reemerged with a small object wrapped in cloth and secured with a bit of twine. This, he presented to Peter.

Astonished, Peter looked at Mrs. Anderson then at Susannah as if trying to identify the true recipient. "For me?" he asked, dubiously, pointing to himself.

"Peter, my boy, if not for you, this plantation would still lay in ruin. Your arrival and hard work has been nothing short of miraculous. This is the least we could do."

Peter recalled with fondness the last gift he had received from James Anderson—his tri-corn hat—which he was rewarded with for saving Susannah's life. Eager to see what it was, he tore into the package, revealing a bundle of hand-rolled cigars.

"Rolled them myself," he said. "Same as the one you smoked the day you returned."

"Thank you, sir," Peter said, touched by his gesture. "I am truly grateful."

"The thanks is all mine," he said. Then turning to Susannah, "Now, for my sweet daughter. Come with me."

Susannah followed him into the kitchen. Seeing that he was heading out the back door, she grabbed her shawl that was hanging from a hook on the wall. When they were both outside, he pointed to a small oak chest that had been intricately carved, stained and fitted with iron hinges and a lock.

Susannah gasped, her breath visible in the cold air. "Father, it's beautiful!" She threw her arms around him and planted a kiss on his cheek. "When did you ever find time to make this?"

"Don't worry about that," he said dismissively. "Your mother said it was time you had one, so you can begin making things for the new home you will soon have."

She bristled slightly at his words. She knew he meant with George Carrington. Still, she didn't want to seem ungrateful.

"Thank you so much, Father. I'll begin sewing this winter." *For Peter and me,* she clarified silently.

"Very well," he said, "when you go back inside, would you ask Peter to come join me?"

When Peter emerged, James Anderson instructed him to visit the slaves in their quarters to distribute a ration of rum, a traditional token of holiday cheer from masters to servants. Before proceeding to the small outbuilding, Peter stopped in the barn to check on the horses.

As he walked, he felt the hardness of the ground under his feet. *Snow would stick fast to this,* he thought. He patted his pocket with his hand to make sure the small item he had placed there earlier was still in its spot. He could hear the merriment from inside before he was even at the door. Even with their repairs, the loose log structure of the house looked more like an extension of the split-rail fence than a separate building. He rapped hard once. In a few moments, the door opened and Eli stood before him.

"Mista, Petuh, suh!" Eli turned and looked expectantly at his mother, who invited Peter inside. He noticed the food Susannah and her mother had brought to them was still spread out on the table. The rudimentary beds were covered with what looked like half-finished quilts, mostly red. Peter guessed they were holding a quilting bee or making them to sell.

"Merry Christmas!" he said in a booming voice, presenting a crate containing a half dozen bottles filled to the brim with tipple.

"Mr. Anderson asked me to give this to you as thanks for all of your hard work."

"Why, thank you, Petuh," said Naomi, Eli's mother, as her eldest son Isaiah took the crate and set it on the only table in the room.

Peter cleared his throat. "I...uh...also have something for Eli, if it's okay."

Eli perked up. "Fo' me? Momma, ken I has it, oh please, please, please!" He begged.

His mother obliged. "Thas' mighty nice o' you, Petuh."

Peter pulled a familiar object from his pocket, though much smaller than the normal size. It looked like a toy in Peter's hand. "I made this for you," he said. "I thought you could use it when you're helping me around the plantation."

"A hammer!" he exclaimed, his eyes growing wide. He turned it over and over in his hands. Impulsively, he hugged Peter's leg. Peter took a few giant steps with Eli still attached to his leg. Eli squealed with delight. Peter visited with them a while longer, then showed Eli how to use the hammer.

Before he left, Peter said with a wink, "Now, remember, that's just for fixing things!"

Inside the main house, Susannah and her mother had finished cleaning up from supper, and they had all retired to the parlor where they had gathered to sing songs. Susannah occupied the bench near the fireplace, moving her fingers swiftly over the strings on a harpsichord to the familiar tune of "Joy to the World," while Mr. Anderson accompanied her on the fiddle. Peter listened to the Andersons harmonizing in chorus. Mrs. Anderson motioned for Peter to sing with them, and he joined at the reprise.

Upon hearing his voice, Susannah bowed her head slightly in approval. Peter surprised even himself with the power and range of his baritone voice. The sound was deep and pure with a pleasant, unwavering tone. They continued the impromptu cantata well into nightfall. The candlelight in the windows seemed to swing in gentle cadence to the music, bathing their faces in light as it warmed their hearts. To round out the day, Mr. Anderson read a portion of the story of Christ's birth from the second chapter of the book of Luke.

Both having had a long day, Mr. and Mrs. Anderson took leave and retired upstairs, leaving Peter and Susannah alone. Both had been eager to have a few moments of solitude together.

"You have a superior singing voice," Susannah said, as she busied her hands with storing the harpsichord. "Where ever did you learn?"

"Some things come naturally," he replied evenly.

Susannah wasn't sure he meant singing.

Peter stopped her fidgeting, delicately extricating her hands from around the instrument and set it down on the bench. Taking her hands in both of his, he led her over to the settee opposite the fireplace, where they sat side by side. She could feel his dark eyes on her.

He paused for a moment, trying to collect his thoughts. Finally, he began, "Susannah ... I wish I had more to give you—"

She placed her finger on his lips to silence him. "I know what you are going to say. And it's simply not true."

He removed her hand from his mouth and let out a deep sigh before continuing. "Susannah, I know my hands are empty. I have nothing. Not even roots. I can't even read," he lamented. "But, as soon as I get the land the army has promised me, I plan to change all of that. I will get an education and establish a home...for us."

"Peter, you are the bravest, most industrious man I've ever known. I wouldn't change a thing about you. I love you just the way you are. Your strength. Your humor. Your ingenuity. Your kindness and sincerity. Your love is the greatest gift I could ever hope to receive."

Peter opened his hand before her, revealing a small, iron key, its long handle ending in the shape of a heart. "Susannah, you and you alone hold the key to my heart. One day, I will forge a lock to match it, and together, we will open the door to our new home, to our future together. It belongs to you and no one else," he said, placing it in her hands.

"Oh, Peter. It's perfect," Susannah breathed, turning it over several times in admiration. She reached up and locked her arms around Peter's neck.

"My promise to you is true," he whispered in her ear, certain that by next Christmas, he would be able to make that promise a reality.

17.

EPIPHANY

THAT CHRISTMAS SERVICE, all heard the same message of Jesus' humble birth and all who come bearing gifts with different backgrounds and different means, a message that certainly resonated with both Peter and Eli.

Just as they arrived home, snow began to fall, lightly at first, and then turned to thick, heavy flakes within a few short hours. Eli, unaware of how severe the storm would become, wandered off, thinking he could finish the fence for Peter with his new hammer. Peter intent on running some rope from the main house to the barn, in preparation for the worst, didn't notice Eli sneak past. By the time he'd finished, the snow became so thick, it seemed like they were all trapped inside a dense cloud. None knew how long the storm would last or how severe it would become.

Out in the far pasture, snow accumulating quickly around

him, Eli tried hoisting one of the long fence rails the way he had seen Peter lift them. He heaved and pulled and eventually managed to push it into the air, but he couldn't make it budge. The weight of the rail soon became too much for him and it toppled down toward him, sending him tumbling backward directly into one of the empty postholes nearby. The force of his fall had lodged him snuggly into the hole up to his chest. His legs were free, but he couldn't get a footing. He tried to paw his way out of the hole, but the slippery snow prevented him from gripping the ground around him. His energy was quickly spent. No one was close enough to hear his desperate cries for help. He frantically searched around for his hammer. Unable to see or feel it, he began to give up hope, as tears streamed down his face. He had felt alone and frightened before, but losing the most cherished gift he had ever received twisted his heart in a painful, unfamiliar way.

When Eli didn't return that evening, his mother Naomi ran toward the main house, yelling for Peter. "Petuh, he gone! He gone!"

Peter was already outside trying to keep a path clear from the main house to the barn, so they could tend to the horses. When he saw her emerge from the pallid haze, he dropped the shovel and ran to her. He tried to calm her down, while barraging her with questions, "Where do you think he went? What was he wearing? Did he have anything with him?"

"When we's all come back from service, he walk right off in 'at there direction," Naomi said, raising her arm and extending one finger.

"I thought he's jus' goin' t' d' barn. He was clutchin' that hammuh you give 'im. Hadn't let that thing outta his sight, not fo' one minute, no, suh."

Peter had a slight hunch where Eli might be. Without a second thought, he grabbed a few things from the barn. Amid protests, he instructed, "Mr. Anderson, shoot your rifle in the air once every thirty minutes if I haven't returned." The women fretted with worry.

Peter trudged through the snow over the hill. His mind flashed to the weeks at Valley Forge, the shivering, ill-clad men, their bloody footprints in the snow, and emaciated bodies. Without realizing it, he had stepped directly into a sink hole obscured by the snow drift. Immediately, he felt a searing pain in his leg and dropped to the ground. "Bloody hell!" he yelled, clutching his leg. Snow fell around him the way it did that night he returned from Hunting Tower, accumulating quickly and creating a massive whiteout. Determined to find the little boy, Peter ignored his pain and slogged on toward the far pastures. In some ways, his search for the little boy became a search for himself. *I don't have much time*, he thought, knowing what a fiend the freezing temperatures could be.

Susannah paced around The Mansion. Needing something to do, she went to her room to pray alone. "Father God, please surround Eli and Peter. Protect them with your all-knowing hand and bring them back here safely to—"

The sound of her father's rifle interrupted her supplication. Looking out the window, she thought she could see the faint outline of something moving through the snow, but her mind had played tricks on her before. The outline soon became more defined. Then she knew.

Her father and a couple of the other slave men ran toward the looming figure. By now, they could tell he cradled a small, limp body in his arms. Naomi gasped and fell into the snow, burying her face in her hands. She assumed Peter wasn't able to get to him in time. She couldn't hear anything over her heaving, unrelenting sobs. She didn't even know it when Peter reached her.

A small, weak voice stammered, "M—Momma." Naomi thought she was hearing things, but when she looked up and opened her eyes, Peter held Eli toward her, and his eyes, though weary from his ordeal, were filled with the same usual eagerness.

"Warm him up," Peter instructed. Naomi nodded and thanked him profusely, while some of the other slave women wrapped Eli in a blanket and carried him back to their quarters.

Peter was weak from trudging through the snow, and his leg, where the musket ball remained lodged, throbbed in rhythm with his racing heart. He didn't realize how cold he was until Mr. Anderson had helped him inside the house by the fire. Mrs. Anderson prepared some warm broth while Susannah wrapped him in blankets. She wanted to give him what-for for scaring her like that, but seeing how exhausted he was, thought better of it. Instead, she just leaned down and murmured softly into his ear, "You are a hero, Peter Francisco."

By late evening, the snow had stopped, but the wind had left drifts in some places up to twelve feet. With Peter still recovering, they began to think they might miss this year's Twelfth Night Ball.

★

Susannah rarely left Peter's side during his recuperation. He protested, but James and Elizabeth insisted on sending for a doctor to examine Peter. The doctor arrived two days later and entered Thomas' bedroom. After getting a thorough history and description of current maladies, the doctor asked Peter to recount what happened in order to ascertain his coherence. He listened to Peter's heart, felt his forehead and counted his pulse. Every so often, the doctor would purse his lips and an audible "hmmm" would bubble up his throat. He placed the index and middle finger of each of his hands directly under Peter's ears and pressed lightly inward.

Perched on a wooden chair in the corner, Susannah fidgeted. She folded and unfolded her hands, pulled on her thumbs and gnawed impatiently on the inside of her mouth. Her parents stood in the doorway. Lastly, the doctor tested Peter's dexterity by having him open and close his hands on command. At times, there was a bit of delay in his response. Finally, the doctor spoke.

"I'm concerned Peter might have a mild case of hypothermia," he said, returning his stethoscope to his medical bag. "He is pale, but no longer blue, which is a good sign, but his reflexes aren't as responsive as I'd like. His body temperature could still be improved. He needs plenty of rest, warmth—blankets, hot water bottles, hot liquids—and his muscles require periodic stimulation."

Susannah emitted a quiet sigh of relief. "Thank you, doctor," she said. Then without thinking, she blurted, "Do you think Peter will be well enough to attend the Twelfth Night Ball?"

"Absolutely not," her father cut in.

"But, father," Susannah pleaded, shooting a glance at Peter, "Peter needs to have the chance to meet eligible ladies, too! And he has done so much to help us."

Peter curled one side of his mouth into a half-smile, slightly amused.

Trying not to eavesdrop on their conversation as he gathered up his things, the doctor responded to Susannah's question, "If he continues to get adequate rest, I don't see why not." Then, as he reached the doorway, addressing Peter directly, he amended, "And that means rest *off* your feet, sir."

After much petition from Susannah, James Anderson finally acquiesced and invited Peter. His only stipulations were that he must not arrive with the Andersons, since Susannah would be formally presented for potential suitors, and it wouldn't look right otherwise. And he must agree not to ask Susannah to dance during the entire ball. Peter agreed without hesitation. He would never turn down an opportunity to spend time with Susannah, especially in public.

"Peter, we ..." Anderson added, speaking slowly in attempt to suppress any feeling. "... are grateful for what you've done. For everything you've done," he amended, wanting Peter to understand that his gratitude extended well beyond his sacrifice on the plantation.

"Yes," Susannah agreed. "Naomi has been asking after you every day. She is desperate to repay you for saving Eli's life."

When Mr. Anderson and the doctor had both taken their leave, Peter asked, "And what, exactly, is the Twelfth Night Ball?"

"Oh! I assumed you knew since the Winstons have been attending for years," Susannah said, somewhat surprised. Walking over to the window, she gazed out in the direction of the apple orchard, the uncloaked branches bending stiffly against the wind. The heat from the room had caused a thin layer of condensation to form on the window panes. She traced her finger in it, making a long straight line, then doodled absentmindedly as she explained, "We look forward to it every year. Especially we girls." She dipped her head in Peter's direction when she said that. "Traditionally, it's held on or around the twelfth day of Christmas, otherwise known as Epiphany, the day we recognize when the Magi arrive to see the Christ child."

"I see," Peter said, nodding his head. "But, why especially do girls look forward to it?"

She hesitated for a moment, searching for the right words. She gestured outwardly with her hand, as if that would somehow extract the thoughts from her mind. "As girls, we dream about the year it will be our turn. Since we live in such a small town, we don't have many opportunities to attend formal social events, so it is also one of the only times when, as father alluded to, young ladies, who are of age, are presented to potential suitors." Ordinarily, Susannah might have stated this wistfully, but in her voice was melancholy.

"Every potential suitor but me, that is," Peter said with chagrin.

"It's just a formality. I wish I didn't have to go through with it. But father is the host this year. That is why he was able to extend you an invitation and why he wishes to present me this year. Each year, during the cake ceremony, the king and queen of the ball are determined. The king hosts the ball the following year, while the queen bakes the cake." Susannah shook her head in disbelief before saying, "You really don't know any of this?"

"Not at all," Peter said. "I can recall the Winstons dressing for formal events, but I had no knowledge of the details. They never spoke of it, and, given my...position, I never asked."

"I almost forgot this part. The morning of the ball, we wassail the apple trees," Susannah said, her face lighting up.

"Do what to the trees?" Peter asked, not sure he heard her correctly.

"You'll see," Susannah replied with a smirk.

"Well, I guess if I'm going to attend these events, I need to get well. And to get well, I need to stay warm," he said deviously. "Come sit by me and hold my hand." Susannah did more than hold his hand. For the next several days, she changed his water bottles, kept him well-covered with blankets, and fed him piping hot broth. One afternoon, as she lifted the spoon to his mouth, Peter's mind flashed momentarily to the nurse back at Yellow Springs Hospital. *Does she still have those sad eyes?* He wondered. The memory prompted Peter to say, "Susannah, if you're ever distressed about anything, anything at all, promise you'll tell me."

His impromptu words surprised her. She didn't press him for anything more. She simply responded, "I promise."

★

Early on the morning of the ball, James Anderson readied himself and briefly inspected his team of horses for the morning journey to Prince Edward Tavern in Buckingham Square. He was obligated to travel ahead of his family to prepare the venue and welcome early-arriving guests. Peter watched him climb into the carriage from the parlor window, outlined with frost, while sipping on a cup of hot cider he had found bubbling over the fire in the kitchen. His breath formed an oval of moisture on the glass then quickly evaporated. The sun appeared deceivingly warm.

As he ogled Susannah's father, his eyes narrowed slightly. *How can I convince him?* Peter wondered. *I thought he had been warming to the idea of me. Especially after all I've done.* But it was evident to Peter—and Susannah—that the restrictions he had issued the week before clearly indicated otherwise. Peter had already proven he could operate a plantation and manage hands, even revive it from desolation. Once he had the seed money the Army had promised, the rest would be easy.

There must be something else, he thought. As the carriage door closed behind James Anderson, Peter's eyes rested on the Anderson family coat of arms that had been etched into the grain. A knight's helmet was capped with an oak tree over a braided wreath. Above that, on an unfurled scroll was the simple phrase "stand sure." *Could it really boil down to pedigree like Carrington said?* Peter wondered, shaking his head slightly in disbelief. He knew the Anderson roots ran deep, but did they run so deep, he'd sacrifice his daughter's happiness even in this time of uncertainty? Whatever it was, Peter wouldn't rest until he uncovered the answer. The question he had left to ask himself was: *are you prepared to act should the reasons be made clear?*

At that moment, Susannah bounded into the parlor and, interrupting his thoughts, exclaimed, "There you are! Are you ready?" He was startled by her words, as if she had plucked them directly from his head. "How is the cider?" she asked, indicating his cup.

"Good," he said, still trying to emerge from his thoughts. "Warm," he said, smiling at her with his eyes.

"We'll take some with us," she said, "but there will be some there, too, over a fire. Before we go, I just want to make sure mother really doesn't need any help with the cake."

Elizabeth Anderson had been hard at work in the kitchen all morning, barely stopping for breakfast. They found her covered in a fine mist of flour powder. Susannah sighed. "Mother, won't you please let me help you?" she pleaded. Her mother waved her off. "Nonsense," she said. "It's my duty, and I won't be satisfied unless I do it myself."

"I know, Mother, but you've been in here so long. I insist you take a break and let me bake the next layer."

While the two women argued back and forth, Peter spotted the large round fruitcake cooling on the table. Just to see if they were paying attention, he extended one arm in the cake's direction feigning to snitch a tiny piece. Mrs. Anderson saw him out of the corner of her eye. "Peter Francisco, don't you dare!" she shrieked and swatted away his hand with hers.

He laughed heartily. "Oh, the look on your face was worth it, Mrs. Anderson! I never would have taken a piece. What is the cake for anyway?" Beside a mixing bowl of batter sat a small jar covered with brown paper and twine. Contained inside was a small black bean. Picking it up and turning it around in his hand, he commented, "Odd ingredient for a cake."

"Well, tradition dictates that both a King and a Queen are chosen each year at the ball, determined by the bean and the pea. Each hardened vegetable is baked into the cake. The gentleman who finds the bean is King and the lady who finds the pea is Queen. If a lady finds the bean, she may choose the King. If a gentleman finds the pea, he may choose the Queen. The King hosts the ball the following year, while the Queen bakes the cake.

Mrs. Anderson explains significance."

"Really? So, anyone can be King or Queen?" Peter asked with genuine interest.

"Yes," Elizabeth said. "James found the bean last year, but no one found the pea, so, naturally, he selected me as Queen." She laughed, recalling the memory. "I'll never forget how James whirled me around on the dance floor after that, with everyone watching. It was like we were a young couple courting again."

Still holding the small jar with the bean, Peter said, "There's only a bean in here. Where's the pea?"

Elizabeth looked at him, her eyes giving nothing away. "I guess you will have to wait and see at the ball, Mr. Francisco."

"Very well. I look forward to the festivities."

"Okay, Peter, let's go!" Susannah said, tugging at his arm.

When they were out of earshot of Mrs. Anderson, Peter asked, half-jokingly, "Does your father plan to prevent me from eating cake, too?"

"Nonsense," was her one-word reply.

Peter followed Susannah into Mr. Anderson's study or the cigar room as he liked to call it. He had never spent any significant amount of time in here. Susannah stopped and looked at him expectantly. Peter shrugged. "What?" He asked. She gestured toward the far wall. "You are going to need a gun," she said, as though that could have been the only reason to come in here.

"I think I'd rather have a cigar," he said, looking dubiously at the row of hunting rifles suspended over the fireplace.

"It's part of the celebration," she said. Then asked pointedly, "Won't it be a nice change to shoot simply for recreation?" Peter couldn't argue with this, though he wondered with some apprehension what images the sounds might call to mind.

They joined other neighbors and friends out in the orchard. Along the way, Susannah grabbed his hand and beamed at him while humming a song. Something told him he'd be hearing it again very soon, but her beautiful smile chased away every thought he had. The bare branches shifted and swayed as if welcoming their company, grateful for the mid-winter purpose. A fire crackled in the center as they arrived. Some were already singing and dancing around the trees like they would a maypole.

As he looked around, Peter realized he didn't recognize a single person. Doubt crept in his mind. He began to wonder how he would be able to build a life for himself and Susannah with no foundation. *Maybe Carrington wasn't all wrong*, Peter thought, feeling somewhat insecure.

Peter watched as the fire breathed with life. As he stared intently at the pyre, an icy chill swept over his body. He wasn't sure it was from the cold. He felt a goblet being placed in his hand.

"Cider," said a melodic voice. Peter looked up to find a young woman about Susannah's age standing before him. Her auburn hair was pulled smoothly back from her elegant face. When her directive didn't seem to register with Peter, she added, "You drink it."

Susannah laughed at her comment, then said, "Peter, I'd like you to meet my best friend Catherine Brooke. We grew up together in Richmond when our fathers worked there together."

Catherine already seemed to know of him, so he was thankful there was no need to explain his presence. In fact, she made him feel immediately at ease. "Peter, so nice to finally meet you," she said, tilting her head slightly in graceful acknowledgement. "I see why Susannah has gone on about you. She has told me of your heroics. We're certainly fortunate to have a leader such as your-self among us."

Her words were enough to squelch any feelings of inadequa-cy he might have had when they first arrived. In a gentleman-ly manner, he took Catherine's hand, kissing it gently, and said warmly, "Any friend of Susannah's is a friend of mine."

"I'm so glad the two of you have finally met," Susannah said, as they made their way to the trees. Along the way, Susannah whispered to Peter, "We all pour cider together, but someone sticks a piece of dried fruit on the bottom of one goblet. The person who receives it is the King or Queen whom everyone else lifts into the limbs of the tree. That person must place a piece of cider-soaked toast in the tree." She made a dismissive gesture with her free hand, and added, "This is supposed to ward off evil spirits or something."

Shortly after, the chant began. All around them goblets were raised. Steam from the hot liquid ascended briefly before being enveloped by the cold. Peter lifted his goblet among them. He in-tentionally didn't extend his arm fully to keep people from staring.

> Here's to thee, old apple tree,
> That blooms well, bears well.
> Hats full, caps full,
> Three bushel bags full,
> An' all under one tree.
> Hurrah! Hurrah!

After that, they raised their goblets higher into the air and toasted the new year. Peter followed suit.

293

"Look!" shouted a young man, whom Peter had never met. "That tall bloke has got the fruit!"

Peter, unable to deflect this accusation, peaked under his goblet. Sure enough, there was a bright red piece of dried fruit. Knowing what this meant, Peter chuckled, as he said, "Well, surely I don't expect you all to lift me up into the tree!" No one laughed with him. In fact, they all stared at him incredulously with scheming eyes and devious grins.

"Come on. You can't be serious," he said, his hands raised as if at gunpoint. He backed up in a feeble attempt to make an escape. But there was nothing around him but trees and soon he had nowhere else to go. He looked at Susannah, begging her with his eyes to please put a stop to this.

He had never felt so many hands on his large frame. It took several tries, but with the help of each and every person, Peter was airborne. He tried desperately not to let all of his weight fall onto any one person. He started to feel spatially disoriented. *Where is Susannah? Do I still even have the goblet?* He thought, trying in vain to locate his hands. An answer came from somewhere beneath him in the form of a rotund cup that looked more like a bowl. Its appearance was simple and looked to be carved out of maple wood. Peter eyed its massive size. *This just seems too appropriate,* he joked to himself.

As he was being heaved over to the largest and oldest tree in the orchard, the revelers chanted.

> Apple tree, apple tree, we all come to wassail thee,
> Bear this year and next year to bloom and to blow,
> Hat fulls, cap fulls, three cornered sack fills,

Hip, Hip, Hip, hurrah,
Holler biys, holler hurrah!

Peter was now level with the top of the tree trunk. *Is there no end to this ritual?* He wondered, longing to place his feet back on the frozen ground. They instructed Peter to remove the soggy cider-soaked toast and nestle it in the crevice, then douse it with the remaining cider. When the oversized goblet had been emptied, the crowd fumbled with Peter's long limbs. There was no setting him down gently.

"Just let go of me," Peter said. They did as he instructed, and he found the ground with his feet, righting himself. He immediately located Susannah who handed him the hunting rifle. They exchanged a brief glance. She could see the worry in his eyes. "It will be quick," she said. She grabbed a pot as they all once again began to sing. Soon everyone was banging on drums, pots or pans. When they had concluded, the men, including Peter, stood in a line, aimed their weapons skyward and shot off one round.

Peter was momentarily transported back to his final moments of consciousness inside the fort at Stony Point when, clutching the Union Jack to his chest, sticky with blood, all he could hear were muffled shouts and the faint, erratic volley of guns. In those moments, when he thought he had breathed his last, he was filled with anxious fear. Not for what was to come, but for what never would be. The sounds still haunted him, and when the smattering of gun fire in the orchard ceased, he could feel his heart pumping fast and the blood coursing in his veins.

When the ceremony had ended, the group prepared to move onto the next orchard, but Susannah and Peter stole away and walked among the expanse of bare branches. The revelry had warmed them up, making the cold air bearable.

"You were such a good sport," she said while hooking her arm around his. She let her gloved hand rest on his forearm. "I daresay many today will not forget the sight of you being carried like that."

"I would only do something that humiliating for you," he said, as he covered her hand with his and watched it disappear from view. This image planted an idea in Peter's mind. "Fortunately, though, I don't need a crowd to do the same to you." As he spoke, he tucked his arms behind Susannah's legs and scooped her off the ground. Susannah squealed and tightened her arms around Peter's neck. He spun her around a few times before coming to a stop.

Their breath, visible in the cold, swirled together before dissipating. There was no sound around them but a hallow wind and a few fading voices cheering and singing in the distance. He looked directly into her eyes and said with heartfelt conviction, "How I cherish moments like this with you." He opened his mouth as if to continue, but something held him back.

"What is it, Peter?" Susannah asked. "Please tell me."

"I just want other people to see us this way. Your family. Friends. The world. Then, they would know what is between us."

"I know, Peter," she said, her smile fading. Her eyes began to fill with tears. "It's not fair." She placed her hand on his cheek and gingerly let her finger run along his jaw line. "I so long to change the way things are."

A wave of fleeting anxiety flooded his heart. *Would this be one of their last moments in solitude?* Determined not to let anything rob them of this joyful moment, Peter pushed the thought from his mind and said, "Well, if I can't dance with you at the ball, I'll just have to do it out here," Peter said, returning her to the ground. "May I have this dance, Lady Anderson?" he asked in a formal tone.

Susannah smiled and curtsied slightly. Peter took Susannah in his arms and sailing with her around the trees. Susannah felt weightless and warm in his arms. She laughed as they twirled and waltzed.

"Peter Francisco," Susannah said in surprise when they came to a stop. "Wherever did you learn to do that?"

"Fighting isn't the only thing I learned to do in the army," he said. With one arm, he lifted her to him until her face was nearly even with his. "And you're the only one I ever imagined practicing with." Peter brushed her forehead with his nose. "George might be able to dance with you at the ball, but can he do this?" He asked as more of a statement than a question and did not wait for a reply. With his free arm, he placed his index finger under her chin, gently tipping her head upward, and kissed her softly under the high sun.

Susannah and her mother took what seemed like the rest of the day to ready themselves for the ball. As he waited patiently in the parlor, Peter began to wonder if they were even still alive upstairs. He had yet to dress himself. He had only one modest suit that Lafayette had given him to wear when he served as his personal aide. The cut of the waistcoat was a little small, and the color an abysmal gray. It wasn't what most would consider formal attire. He wanted to wait until the last possible moment to put it on. *One day,* he vowed to himself, *I will have a wardrobe of tailored suits.*

Finally, Peter heard Susannah descending the steps. He went directly to meet her at the bottom.

Never had a more radiant beauty stood before him. It was like the sun had risen a second time that morning just for him. She was perfection. He drank her in. Her golden curls had been done up in a high, elaborate fashion, and easily added at least three inches to her height. Resting neatly atop her hair was a white muffin-shaped cap adorned at the base with a wide, wavy swath of satin fabric that to Peter looked the color of salmon. It tied neatly under her chin with a thin black ribbon. Susannah's face had been painted to match that of a porcelain doll. Her skin looked so pale and delicate. *If I touch her face, will it crack?* Peter wondered. She wore rouge on her cheeks, a similar but lighter shade than the ribbon. A dark beauty mark had been pasted just to the left of her chin. Her lips were full of color. He longed to kiss them, but he dared not, lest he ruin those long hours of preparation.

The bodice of her dress hugged her tightly and narrowed at the waist, emphasizing her figure. He hardly noticed its color, but later, after she left, he thought he remembered it having a little of the salmon color and maybe a muted sort of green, but the sight of her had weakened his acumen. He was momentarily transported him back to his dream when they were together on the ship, sailing toward the dock, dressed in wedding clothes. It was as if she had been plucked straight from that dream and placed in

298

this room. *That moment will be real one day,* Peter thought, certain now more than ever of their future.

"You are a glowing beauty," he said, taking the sateen pelisse that she cradled in her arms and draping it around her shoulders as she turned around. Then, he leaned down and whispered in her ear, "My glowing beauty." He noted her smile. Her scent was exquisite, and he lingered there for a moment and committed it to memory just as he did on that fateful day in the mercantile when they first learned their feelings were mutual.

"If I'm glowing," she said, "it's only because you are near." Susannah placed her hands inside her muff and looked at Peter. It was only then that she noticed he was not dressed. Then she wondered with pang of regret if he even had any dress clothes.

"Peter! You're not dressed. What will you wear?" she asked. "It didn't even occur to me that you might not have anything suitable."

He shrugged. "Lafayette gave me a modified suit to wear when he first appointed me his personal aide following Valley Forge. It will do," he said, escorting her to the front door and out onto the porch. "I would say, save a dance for me but…"

"I will be dancing with no one tonight, only stepping around a stage someone else has built for me," she said, trying to make him believe with her eyes.

His eyes never left her as she made her way to the carriage. He extended his hand to provide support as she stepped up into the covered landau. When she was settled, he leaned in and said, "I *will* see you tonight." He emphasized the word as if to remind her that regardless of circumstance he would still be hers.

He noticed little else until Mrs. Anderson gently cleared her throat, and he watched her directing two of their house servants as they navigated the layered cake, carefully packed and secured in a basket, down the steps and into the back of the carriage.

"We'll be sure to save some cake for you, Peter," she said with a bright smile.

Peter waited the appropriate amount of time, as he and Mr. Anderson had discussed. He reluctantly dressed himself in the ill-fitted suit. *George won't have to look hard for something to taunt me about tonight,* he thought as he examined himself in the mirror. His mind wandered to the events over the last weeks and the time he and Susannah were able to spend together, particularly their intimate moments and conversations. *After tonight, will all of that change?* Peter wondered. A mix of fear and pain filled his throat at the thought of watching Susannah with George Carrington or anyone else.

Outside, he aimed for the barn to hitch up one of the functional carriages and instead found that some of his slave friends had already done that for him. They had mended and re-installed the simple cover to shield him from the elements. All the wheels appeared perfectly aligned. The horses had been bridled and at the end of the reigns sitting atop the driver's bench waiting to take him to his destination was Isaiah.

On the porch, Peter froze.

Naomi approached him and presented a package. Peter looked at her with curiosity. "What..." he began but couldn't find the words, unable to fathom what could possibly be inside the careful wrapping. She finished his thought for him. "I think you be needin' this t'night," she said simply. He carefully untied the package. Inside was a beautifully tailored suit—coat, waistcoat and breeches—that she had clearly sewn herself. The fabric had been dyed a deep indigo like the night sky.

"Mrs. Anderson, she give us d' fabric an' stuffs afta we tol' her we's wantin' t' do something fo' ya so's we could thank ya proper fo' what ya done."

Peter didn't know what to say. *Why would Mrs. Anderson do such a thing?* He wondered. *Unless…*

"Well, what you waitin' fo' Masta Petuh? Time's awastin'!"

She was right. There was no time to change now. He decided to wait until he got to the tavern, and wrapped the suit back up as best he could, placing it inside the carriage. He picked up Naomi and swung her around until she giggled. When he set her down, he looked around and said, "Thank you all." Then, he climbed up into the carriage. For the first time, as a passenger.

As they pulled out on the main road that ran along the plantation, a cold, light drizzle began to descend from the twilit sky. Peter was so used to working the reigns, he wasn't quite sure what to do with his hands. Beside him on the seat rested the package containing the suit. He pulled a piece of the wrapping back and ran his fingers over the rich fabric. Again, he marveled at Mrs. Anderson's unexpected gesture, which he could only interpret as approval. *Why didn't I see it before? I've been so focused on persuading Mr. Anderson.* He understood that she didn't want to undermine her husband, but he also knew she wished her daughter to be happy.

Peter took in his surroundings as if for the first time. He could see the pebbles on the ground as it disappeared behind the carriage. The jagged roots of the trees seemed to stretch and reach for the road, seeking direction. At the base of one tree that he knew he had passed countless times was a deep tree well he never noticed before. Just inside the opening looked the shape of a small animal that appeared to be trapped.

He yelled to Isaiah to stop. Peter exited the carriage and slowly approached the figure. The rain began to form a light mist on his face. Dry, brown pine needles crunched beneath his feet. The small form crouching beneath the tree was no animal but a small child. His knees were pulled up to his chin, and he was whimpering. *He's lost*, Peter thought with sudden clarity. His mind flashed to the dock at City Point, where he had been left alone. Everything had been foreign. The place. The people. The language. He had no idea just how far he was from home. In that moment, he had felt so lost and scared, he remembered wishing briefly that he was actually back on the boat with his kidnappers because at least that was familiar to him. Peter immediately identified with this young boy's plight.

"Are you lost?" Peter asked.

The boy remained silent.

Peter knew he must be reluctant to trust a stranger. He squatted down in the dirt, so he seemed less intimidating. "I'm Peter," he said and held out his hand. "I was once lost, too," he went on, "and a nice man helped me, so I want to do the same for you."

The little boy timidly extended his hand. He pulled it back for a brief moment, as if withdrawing his willingness to trust. Yet as soon as his hand disappeared inside Peter's, the boy relaxed and his body kept moving until it was nestled next to Peter. Peter took him to the carriage and after some prodding was able to determine where the boy lived. He instructed Isaiah to steer the team in that direction. Along the way, he told the story about the day he was lost on the dock. He was so engrossed in this rescue mission, he lost track of time.

★

Prince Edward Tavern sat on the upper edge of Prince Edward County known as Clover Hill, overlooking the James River. The lavish, two-story inn rivaled the most elaborate stays in the major cities. But rather than encroaching buildings and cobblestone streets, it was surrounded instead by shady trees and an expansive hillside and peered out expectantly through tall, shady trees. The building itself, white punctuated with six gables and black shutters, nestled there naturally like an extension of the earth.

In an annex off the upstairs room, Susannah congregated with Sarah Winston and a few of their female friends to tidy up their toilet. Among the young women was Susannah's lifelong friend Catherine Brooke, who was also being formally presented here in Buckingham. Her father had selected this event so the childhood friends would be together.

Catherine, George and Susannah shared many childhood memories in Richmond when their fathers had worked there together. Even then, Susannah knew she wanted nothing to do with George. She thought him obnoxious; always going around presuming the world and everything in it belonged to him. She could recall countless instances of bossy George trying to get his way.

Once, about a month into the summer when she was nine, the Carringtons and Andersons had been invited to the Brookes at Farmer's Hall. The children were in back in the late morning sun imagining the garden off the terrace was a battlefield. Susannah and her brothers James and Thomas against Catherine, her brother Humphrey, and George and his younger brother Paul. They hid behind rows of neatly trimmed summer boxwoods on either side of the courtyard to shield themselves from faux shots while attempting to infiltrate the other's camp. Thomas had already captured Catherine, while Susannah stood guard. She could see George, Humphrey, and Paul huddled together behind a large oak tree, clearly planning some sort of ambush.

"You go left," George whispered to Humphrey in a bullish tone. "Paul, you go right. Make them think you're going back in for Catherine and cover me. I'll go up the middle and take Susannah. Once I'm out of there, and they realize they've been outsmarted, they'll come for me. That's when you go in for Catherine. Got it?"

Too bad I can't warn James and Thomas, Susannah thought feebly. But they were nowhere to be seen. Instead, she took advantage of the opportunity to talk to Catherine, who also didn't feel trapped at all standing next to her friend. "I wonder how long I'll stay captured?" she said. "With any luck, the rest of the morning!" Susannah exclaimed with a giggle. "Maybe the boys will get lost!"

Neither had to wait long for an answer. Before they could react, George was behind them and had grabbed Susannah's arms. "I'm taking you prisoner, Susannah!" he shouted, tilting his head upward so his voice would carry across the garden. Susannah and Catherine looked at each other dismally, each wondering why they ever went along with this.

George tightened his grip on Susannah's arms and paraded

her down the center of the garden. James and Thomas took the bait but couldn't reach George before he had Susannah behind the line. "Ouch! You're hurting me, George! Let go!" Susannah yelled, trying to wriggle free.

Lowering his voice, he whispered near her ear, "You know, you won't always be able to get away, Susannah." Then, with finality, he announced, "We win!" Naturally, he expected everyone else to go along.

"Oh, yeah? What makes you think you get to decide, George?" Thomas taunted. George looked around to see where the voice was coming from, but was too late. Thomas had sneaked up behind him and yanked his knickers clear to the ground. The rest had gathered around and laughed hysterically. No longer able to tolerate their jeers, George sulked off toward the house, pulling up his knickers as he went.

"Do you remember the look on George's face?" Susannah said, reminiscing with Catherine, as the two sat in front of the mirror.

"Do I! He was never good at taking a joke, was he?" Catherine asked, checking that no loose strands of her auburn hair were visible beneath the spangled feathered headdress. "I can't believe he said that to you. How can your father expect you to marry him?"

"It's awful, isn't it?" Susannah agreed with disgust in her voice, then shifting to a wistful, dreamy tone, "Peter is nothing like George. He has such a kind heart."

"You've written of little else for the last year! I am looking forward to seeing him again. It's fortunate he can be here. So many can't be," Catherine lamented. "Makes me wonder why we're even doing this now. Seems so futile."

Susannah covered her friend's hand tenderly with hers. "I know. I am missing my brothers, too, but they will all be back soon. We know you belong with Andrew. Try not to worry." Addressing the room, she asked, "Shall we go?"

The ladies entered the main room in formal fashion—Sarah Winston leading with Catherine and Susannah behind. They stopped and gave a short curtsy before finding a place to look inconspicuous among the other guests. She scanned the rest of the room hoping she might see Peter.

Eligible gentlemen, dressed in satin-trimmed jackets, their tidy wigs adorned with velvet ribbons, skulked around the room. Ladies in their stately polonaises clutched matching fans, visibly attempting to feign comfort. Ben Ward, proprietor of another local tavern in Amelia, clearly enjoying a night off, occupied his usual spot at the bar, throwing back a tankard of rum. John McGraw, the local schoolmaster, conversed animatedly with local farmer and soldier Joseph Curd along with several other furloughed soldiers who had been serving in the area. Others, including George and Humphrey, ogled Mrs. Anderson's rich, six-layer cake, hoping that being first in line would somehow give them an advantage. As she sliced and served, Mrs. Anderson hovered protectively, not about to let all her hard work end in spoils.

Susannah took note of George's location. Knowing an encounter with him was all but certain, she still intended to avoid him as much as possible for the duration of the evening.

The second-floor room, usually spillover for diners or commercial travelers, had been transformed for the social event. Windsor chairs with their myriad cherry-finished spindles had been skirted and pushed to the walls, allowing ample room for dancing. The spicy aroma of the traditional Twelfth Night fare was intoxicating. In one corner, a guitarist and fiddler swayed in time with their instruments as they played a buoyant version of "Over the Hills and Far Away."

As the prior year's king, now this year's host, James Anderson announced it was time for the changing of the flag. Traditionally, the flag would be changed to the King's colors, but this year, just as the last, two furloughed soldiers assisted James in raising the new flag of the United States. Cheers and applause erupt across the room.

While Susannah clapped, she stole a glance toward the door worried that Peter still hadn't arrived.

George took advantage of her momentary distraction and swaggered over to her from the side. Couples lined the floor for the first contra dance. With cake in hand, he leaned into Susannah and addressed her in a casual, innocent tone, his hands clasped behind him. "So, where is our friend Peter tonight?" George asked.

"He will be here," Susannah said evenly, looking straight ahead. She didn't want to let on that his words had any effect on her.

"It will be expected for us to dance, you know," he said, half-expecting she would protest.

"Then, by all means, let's," Susannah said coldly, her countenance unchanged. Noticing that her father's gaze in their direction, she exchanged a wordless glance with him. With a single nod, he beckoned her to acquiesce to whatever George might have said.

307

Her thoughts were interrupted for the moment when George suddenly cheered, "I've got the bean!" As he produced the vegetable from his mouth, he lifted one side of his mouth in a smug half-smile.

Susannah looked at her feet to avoid any shifting glares. She suddenly lost her appetite for cake, even her mother's.

"I'll give you the honor of the first dance with the King," George said, now overconfident. As he led her out onto the floor, he added, raising his eyebrows, "Then, we'll see about getting you some cake."

"The King dances!" someone shouted from across the room. It was customary for guests to imitate any action by a member of the royal pair. The royal pair would respond in kind, assigning ridiculous tasks to the revelers.

On the floor, her body was stiff and awkward in his arms. She evaded his eyes. She deliberately kept space between them. She kept her gaze on whatever was just over his shoulder. She exchanged a wordless look with Catherine as if to say, "Please let this be over soon."

After a few turns, they found themselves at rest. George reached up to stroke Susannah's cheek, more for the benefit of onlookers than for his dance partner. His finger burned to the touch. "Need I remind you of the arrangement between our parents?" George asked more kindly than he meant.

"I'm well aware of it," she replied flatly, keeping her lips tight as she spoke.

"That oaf of yours has nothing to give you. His hands are empty," George said, derisively.

"He's given me more than you could ever hope to in a lifetime,

George Carrington," Susannah fired back, as they re-entered the line. Again, she looked toward the door, her head shifting from side to side with each turn. She yearned for relief from more than just the dance.

As if on cue, Peter slipped through the door. He immediately spotted Susannah, who felt instant relief at the sight of him. She had to look twice to make sure it was really him. The dark-colored suit he wore complemented the bronze tone of his skin and accentuated his build. It fit him so perfectly, like it was made just for him. *He looks amazing!* She thought, starting to feel lightheaded. Sensing the tension fall from Susannah's posture, George followed her gaze to the door, bristling at the sight of Peter. Then, he remembered the bean in his pocket. A slow, wry grin spread across his face.

When the music ended and those on the floor dispersed, George moved to the front of the room to assume his role as King. Several of Mr. Anderson's guests greeted Peter, soldiers among them, who identify him first by his size, then his recent fame.

"The crowd dances!" George directed.

Staying true to his word, Peter did not approach Susannah. Instead, he spotted Sarah Winston and, after she agreed, he led her out to the floor. He was conscious of everyone's stares, including those from George. Those who knew him had never seen him dressed this way before, let alone seen him dance.

"The revelers drink!" George instructed, raising his glass, at the end of the song. "The King lifts his glass!" yelled another guest.

Peter accompanied Sarah to get a bit of spiced ale, where Susannah had been standing with Catherine. Sarah and Susannah exchanged a slight embrace, careful not to disturb the other's caparison.

"I was wondering if you would be able make it," Susannah intoned formally, looking at Peter.

"I almost didn't," Peter said. "We happened upon a boy who had wandered a little too far from home. I couldn't leave him."

"That certainly sounds like something you would do," Sarah commented, slightly amused. "I'm sure his family is grateful."

"You look dashing," said Catherine, expressing what she knew Susannah could not.

"Thank you, Catherine," he said. Gesturing toward the floor, "Then I guess you wouldn't mind being seen with me out there."

"Not at all," she said, knowing Susannah wouldn't mind.

Peter felt a measure of comfort and familiarity with Catherine that he couldn't explain. Her elegance and charm were captivating. He was grateful to have another who supported his personal ambition, especially one so close to Susannah. They conversed and laughed with ease, especially after George started directing some of them to contort their bodies contrary to what the dance dictated. Soon, they were all hopping and twisting about on the floor.

George had already issued several individual commands, so it was no surprise when he singled out Peter. "Peter sings!" Certain this would humiliate the giant, George crossed his arms in front of his chest and waited.

Quickly picking up on George's intentions, Peter cleared his throat. "I sure hope I don't embarrass myself," he pronounced deliberately, as George sniggered, "but here goes."

The deep, smooth sound that emanated from Peter's mouth

as he sang was melodious. His voice surprised everyone with the exception of the Andersons. When Peter finished, the room erupted around him in whistles, claps and cheers. The shock that registered on George's face quickly transformed into annoyance. He was not about to let this ogre humiliate him.

"Peter eats cake," George barked, then added, "with only his face." A few gasps escaped the crowd at the audacity of his request.

Taking it in stride, Peter waltzed over to the cake, spinning a few times as if he looked forward to the challenge. Only one uncut layer of the cake remained. Peter crossed his arms behind his back and leaned forward, sinking his face deep into the center of the cake. As he emerged, his entire face masked in gooey white confection, he chewed and swallowed the bit in his mouth. A few pieces dropped onto the floor. "Mmmm…delicious cake, Mrs. Anderson," he said. Then, with dramatic flair, he stuck out his tongue as far as he could, holding it there for a moment before sending it around his mouth to lick as much off as he could, bemusing the intimate throng.

George began to utter his next order, "Peter——"

But Peter held up his hand, signaling everyone to wait. With two fingers, he fished around inside his mouth and produced a small green pea, which any of the women had yet to discover. Cheers again erupted around the room, for they knew this meant George had lost his position as King.

With the pea in hand, Peter quickly realized he now had a way around Mr. Anderson's specific request. He walked toward a disbelieving George and took his place at the front of the room. He was quiet for a moment, waiting for George to take leave.

"George sits down," Peter said, delivering his first proclamation. More cackles exploded from among the gathered coterie. Refusing to take orders from a former slave, George stomped to the back of the room and stood with his arms folded across his chest.

"I'm honored…fate…has selected me as King of the ball," he said, using part of his handkerchief to wipe some of the cake from his face. He paused deliberately at the word fate and looked directly at Mrs. Anderson. He suspected, after her involvement in the tailoring of his suit, that she had baked the pea in the bottom layer intentionally, knowing he might be one of the last to arrive and, thus, the last to eat cake. There was no doubt now in his mind of her opinion towards him. "I'm even more delighted that my…charade has come to an end." Laughter filled the room. "But," he continued, "I am more than humbled by the prospect of selecting a Queen."

Peter recognized his unique opportunity to have the attention of this many townspeople at once and to speak about his beloved Susannah publicly. *A chance I am not likely to get again,* he thought. He knew he must strike a delicate balance, carefully choosing his words in attempt to convey many messages. "But, before I do, there's something I'd like to say."

"The King speaks!" shouted a gentleman standing near George. A few others holler, chiming in with agreement.

"Today, as I look around this room, I see lovers." Some were visibly uncomfortable with Peter's opening, but he knew he at least had their attention. Then, he explained.

"We are all lovers. Lovers of God. Lovers of freedom. Lovers of family. Lovers of learning. Lovers of self." As he pronounced each definition, he looked around at the people whom he thought might fit them. "To live we must love. Love is born from desire, from passion, from loyalty. It is love that establishes and preserves nations, sacrifices fortunes and protects families. Love fights for what it believes in and for what it holds dear. When all is lost, only love remains. I've known great loss. I've also known great love. I know it now. Just as all of you. Fight for it. Fight to earn it. Fight to keep it." He ended by pronouncing, "The revelers love!"

Peter's words were met with thunderous applause, garnering instant approval by many. He wondered briefly if this was in any way how Patrick Henry must have felt after his rousing speech at St. John's Church.

"Without further ado, I'd like to select this year's Queen." Some had seen him dancing with Sarah and Catherine. They naturally expected one of them to be his choice. "Ball or no ball, this beautiful lady is, in my mind, already royalty. She needs no introduction. It is my great privilege to select..." he said, pausing dramatically, "...Miss Susannah Anderson as the Queen of the Twelfth Night Ball. That is, if she doesn't mind a King with a little cake on his face."

His announcement was met with mixed reaction. There were a few gasps amid a few cheers. Susannah did not hesitate. She walked right up to Peter and boldly swiped one finger across his face, collecting a bit of cake and licking it clean. They clasped hands and raised them above their heads.

Mr. Anderson stood off to one side, momentarily slack-jawed at what had just unfolded. He was so startled by the sudden turn of events that he fumbled as he formally yet somewhat reluctantly announced the couple to his guests.

Peter knew that as King, he was entitled to one dance with the Queen. "You won't mind if I borrow her just for one dance, do you, George?"

With cake still covering part of his face, he led Susannah the Queen out onto the floor. All eyes are on them as the music starts. Eager to prolong their precious minutes together in the spotlight, Susannah slowly slid her delicate hand into Peter's, sending an unmistakable message to every witness. Peter tucked his hand naturally behind her waist. They circled the floor with obvious ease, fully entranced, as if they had practiced just for this moment. They stood close, their posture directed forward, never averting their eyes from the other. Her face glowed radiantly. She could not contain her smile. Her cheeks flushed slightly as he stared at her. They didn't say a word to each other, but spoke only with their eyes, making it evident to everyone around them that all they needed to say had been spoken long before this moment. No one in the room could doubt that the love Peter had spoken of was for Susannah.

There were motley expressions on the faces around the room. Mrs. Anderson clasped her hands together in delight. Catherine was fighting back tears. Mr. Winston seemed genuinely surprised. George was livid, a scowl planted firmly on his face. Mr. Anderson had furrowed his brow, scrutinizing the couple in search of any misstep. Ben Ward was slumped over at the bar, possibly taking George's earlier directive a bit too literally.

Just as the dance drew to a close, a soldier, having received word from his commanding officer, burst through the door and announced in a booming voice, "We've just learned that Clinton is moving a large force into Charleston from Savannah. Cornwallis and Tarleton are with him. They mean to attack."

The announcement summarily dampened the mood, bringing the merriment to an abrupt halt. The New Year seemed to have awakened resolve in the worst of men, an ominous conjecture for spring.

18.

SPRING

WHEN IT CAME TIME for the spring planting, the slaves repaid Peter's humanitarian efforts. Although their numbers had diminished since before the war, they accomplished the work in a timely fashion, because they were anxious to return his kindnesses. As for Peter, he could accomplish the work of four men. He was especially adept at plowing the fields without the aid of a horse and was capable of bearing extraordinary loads. On one such occasion, as a few slaves were preparing to till the vegetable garden, they discovered two large timbers had fallen during the night, spanning nearly the entire length of the fenced area. They surmised both sugar maples had been struck by lightning during the previous night's storm, but were left scratching their heads, wondering how they were going to remove the rotund logs. When Peter arrived, he saw the perplexed looks on their faces.

Without a word, he bent down, cradled the huge trunks with each massive arm, lifting them off the ground; then he pushed them upward until both were perpendicular to the ground. Bending his knees slightly, he lowered himself and wrapped one arm tightly around each limb. With almost no effort, he hoisted the logwood onto each shoulder and carried them out of the garden and behind the barn to be axed.

The slaves couldn't believe what they had just seen. When Peter returned, he saw them gaping at him, open-mouthed. "Well, what are you waiting for?" he asked, smiling wryly as if nothing happened. "The ground won't till itself."

★

One morning in early May, Peter came downstairs to find Susannah already sitting in the kitchen. He immediately noticed she was dressed for an outing. A lace neck kerchief was tied neatly around her shoulders, its translucence revealing the rosy color of her skin. The blue-gray dress she wore wasn't one Peter had seen before, so he assumed she reserved it for special occasions. The sleeves ended at her elbows then flared out like cascading bells down to her dainty wrists. A lace cap covered her golden curls, which was fastened neatly in back. She wore a white, wide-brimmed hat adorned with flowers made from some kind of bristly-looking fabric. Next to her, a large, woven basket rested on the table. "Susannah, what are you doing up so early? Where are you going?" Peter asked.

"You and I are going on a picnic today," she announced.

He shook his head. "I can't go. I have far too much to do

today."

"Nonsense. You have worked seven days a week for the past three months. Today, you are taking me on a picnic, and there will be no more discussion about it." Her tone was decisive.

"But what about your father? We had plans to go into town for more supplies."

"My father knows of my plans, and he approves."

"But what about breakfast?" Peter was running out of reasons to object, although he couldn't deny that the thought of spending the day alone with Susannah was appealing.

"I have made some biscuits and preserves for us to eat along the way."

Giving up on his half-hearted protests, Peter only had one more question. "Would you prefer an open carriage or an enclosed carriage?"

"If you think for one minute that I want to ride in the back of an enclosed carriage while you drive us to a picnic, you are sadly mistaken," Susannah playfully retorted.

Just before Peter exited the back door to hitch the horses to a carriage, he bent down and kissed Susannah gently on the top of the head. As he did, he took a deep breath, inhaling the sweet florid scent of her hair. *This was going to be a wonderful spring day,* he thought, wistfully.

When Peter had the carriage ready, Susannah went to meet him outside. He was adjusting a harness on one of the horses. He had rolled up the sleeves of his shirt, revealing his powerful arms. She imagined the feeling of them around her, protecting her. Just the sight of him made her heart race. *He is so handsome.* His dark skin and wavy, black hair were like that of Romeo Montague.

His deep, chocolate-brown eyes looked right through her, pene-
trating her innermost thoughts, rendering her weak. She thought
of his scent—often a blend of sweat, residue of horses' hooves
and coal-smoke from the forge. She didn't mind. She had come
to associate the distinct smell with him. Whenever it reached her,
she knew it meant he was near. Sometimes, in social situations,
she found herself having to take leave just to collect herself. This
was no exception, but she knew that they would soon be alone.
The prospect excited her. She walked over to him, and he took
the basket from her, placing it on the floor in the back. *I wonder
what else she made,* he thought, fleetingly. Standing beside the open
door, he looked at Susannah expectantly and gestured toward it
with his hand. Susannah glared at him. "I told you I wanted to sit
up front with you."

"Indeed, you did." In a single motion, he swept her off her
feet and deposited her ever so gently on the passenger side of the
bench seat.

"Peter! You could have thrown me clear to the other side!"
she exclaimed, slightly flushed.

"Yes, I could have...but I didn't," he joked, and the two of
them exchanged wide smiles. *There's that cute dimple,* Peter thought.
As he climbed up next to Susannah, he was suddenly hit with a
reverie he'd had while mending the wagon wheels. *I never thought
I'd be riding next to her this soon.* Peter steered the horses down the
path and away from the plantation.

As they were traveling, they came to a patch of mossy ground
Peter recognized immediately. It was where he had sought refuge
the night he had been caught in that brutal winter storm on the
way back from Hunting Tower. The tree limb he had tethered his

horse to still lay in the same spot. He drew the horses to a halt and went around to the other side of the carriage, where he lifted Susannah out of her seat and set her down softly as though she were a feather in his hands. As Peter reached into the carriage to retrieve the picnic basket, Susannah looked around and inquired teasingly, "How did you know about this spot? Is this where you bring all of your lady friends?"

"Not at all!" He said, somewhat defensive, then softened his tone. "This is where I slept that winter night when you wondered where I was."

"Peter, I was only joking with you," Susannah replied, realizing her offense.

"Oh," he said sheepishly. After a few moments, he added, "Thinking of you is what got me through that awful night."

Susannah's cheeks reddened.

He grabbed a blanket from under the carriage seat and spread it out over the grass, so the two of them could sit. Susannah began to remove items from the basket—bread, cold turkey and lettuce to make sandwiches, spring peas, a variety of muffins, and a rhubarb pie she had baked just for the occasion.

As Peter helped himself to a muffin, he stretched out on the blanket as best he could. The lower half of his legs stuck out over the edge onto the grass. They both noticed his awkward position and chuckled. Peter shrugged, "There's never a blanket long enough for me." He propped his head up by resting his elbow on the blanket, watching Susannah as she constructed the sandwiches. She sat cross-legged, the basket beside her. As they ate, they talked. About the plantation and all the work Peter had done. About Peter's time in the Army and all that had happened.

Enough time had passed that he could relive the memories without feeling tormented.

"It's so easy to talk to you," Peter said, recalling momentarily some of his more intimate conversations with Arthur. The feeling was similar, but with Susannah the words came freely, like he was thinking to himself instead of talking to another person.

They revealed simple, everyday things about themselves the other had never known. They also laughed more than either had in a long time. Susannah watched as Peter made several attempts to catch a pea in his mouth after tossing it into the air. She bet he couldn't do it, but finally one landed in his mouth. "Oh, that was just luck!" she scoffed. Determined to prove her wrong, Peter started tossing peas into her mouth. In a fitful of giggles, she finally begged him to stop.

She couldn't wait for Peter to taste the rhubarb pie she had made. She prided herself on her baking skills. She cut two slices, and then fed Peter a small piece. Peter let its sweet-tangy flavor fill his mouth.

"Delicious," he complimented her, trying to memorize its taste. "You know what this tastes like?" He waited for her response, but she just shrugged. "More!" They both laughed.

"Well, if it's more you want..." Susannah said, breaking into a mischievous grin. She tried to conceal her hand while she finished her thought, "...then it's more you'll get!" At that moment, she shoved a handful of pie into Peter's mouth, smearing it all over his face in the process.

"Oh, I'll get you for that!" he said, salvaging what he could of the pie with his tongue. He reached for the entire pie and held his arm back like he was going to hurl its contents straight at

Susannah. She fell back in hysterics, held her hand up and pleaded with him not to do it. As her laughter dissolved, he finally relented, and instead pulled a piece of the pie off with his hand and gently placed it in her mouth.

As she chewed gracefully, light streamed through the trees accenting the natural flaxen highlights of her hair. Her skin glowed, causing Peter to stare. He became very still.

Susannah broke the awkward silence. "What are you … looking at?"

Peter paused for a moment to collect his roaming thoughts, never once taking his eyes off her. With a flame in his heart, he said, "Only the most gorgeous creature God has ever made."

Susannah lowered her head slightly in embarrassment, as Peter reached over to stroke her face. An uncontrollable sensation burst inside her the moment she felt his hand touch her face. She leaned into him. He drew her tightly to him. Her lips parted slightly, and he could feel her warm breath. His mouth brushed softly against hers. He traced the full circle of her face with his lips until they came together again with hers. Familiar sensations swept over Peter. Susannah felt lightheaded. Conscious of the intense longing between them, she pressed her mouth tighter to his, which he eagerly returned. She leaned back on the blanket, pulling Peter over her, their lips still joined, hands caressing each other.

After several minutes, with his hand still supporting Susannah's back, Peter rolled over and looked up at the sun through the branches of the surrounding trees. Susannah rolled slightly toward him and placed her hand on his chest. "Peter, I don't know what I would have done had you not come back to us. I hope you know how deeply I love you."

"I love you, too, Susannah, with all my heart. The whole time I was away, thinking of you is what made me go on. If I hadn't known that you were here waiting, I'm not sure I would have had the strength to continue."

Peter sat up and went over to the wagon. He returned carrying his satchel—the one that had been with him every day of the war. He opened it and revealed its meager contents. Inside were the letters Susannah had written to him, read to him with the enlisted aid of his friend Lafayette. Wrapped around his old shoe buckles and Arthur's Bible was the handkerchief she had given him the day he departed for war.

"Whenever I prepared for battle, I held these things, and that gave me strength."

Susannah touched his hands with both of hers, but couldn't help noticing the ragged state of the fabric. "Peter, it's so soiled. I must wash it for you."

"No, I don't want you to do that."

"Why not?"

"Because it means so much to me just the way it is. I always want to remember that."

"Oh, Peter," she breathed, reaching for him. Once again, they found themselves locked in an embrace that they held for some time.

The day they had anticipated had been wonderful, but it was now turning to eventide. They hastened to gather up the remnants of their picnic and headed back to the plantation before dark. Traveling by horseback along the trail at night was difficult enough. Maneuvering in a carriage was next to impossible, and it wouldn't be acceptable for the two of them to spend the night in the forest together. James Anderson may have been softening his regard for Peter, but he knew an episode like that certainly wouldn't win him any favor.

★

By mid-summer, the Anderson plantation had bustled back to life. Peter, James, the slaves and even Susannah and her mother all worked long and hard days, but the effort was well worth it. It was apparent to everyone that the plantation would produce the most bountiful crop in several years.

During this time, James and Peter had many opportunities to deepen their relationship. Working with Peter had been good for the elder Anderson physically and, emotionally. He had sprung back to his old self and looked forward to what each day would bring.

One evening, James came into the barn to find Peter tending to the horses. "Peter, I…you…we've…" he said, struggling to find the right words. "What I mean to say is, you coming to us when you did has been nothing short of a blessing from God. I don't think we could have brought the farm back if it hadn't been for you."

"Thank you, sir. It's been a privilege to work at your side. You've treated me like a member of your family, and…and… well." Now it was Peter's turn to stammer.

"What is it, my boy? What is it?"

"Mr. Anderson—I wish to marry your daughter, Susannah. I am asking you for her hand in marriage."

325

"Well, Peter, I thought you might bring this up one day. I do regard you as a son, but Susannah's future is set for her. I told you that she is to marry George Carrington as soon as he returns from the war. He comes from a good and prominent family. Besides, what have you to offer her? You have almost no possessions. You own no land. You have no work other than here at the plantation. Why, you don't even know how to read or write."

"But I will have land. The government has promised one hundred acres to all who served. And I am to get a pension. And I will learn to read and write—I promise that I will."

"Peter, I absolutely forbid it. I don't see how you can make it work. I really don't. I know that Susannah has feelings for you, too. I may be old, but I'm not blind. And what I want for her most of all is a comfortable life, free from worry. I hope you understand that it's for her good."

Peter opened his mouth to object, but stopped himself and instead acknowledged with clenched teeth, "yes, sir." He felt like a scolded child, forced to give in because he doesn't know how to win. He was dejected and torn. But more than that, he was incensed. *What would it take to prove myself? Aren't my skills and determination enough? Isn't that all our forefathers had when they first came to the New World? Where was the man's faith? What about love? Isn't that enough?*

"Very well, Peter. Now, let's go into the house. Supper is ready."

James left the barn, leaving Peter to finish his chores with mixed feelings. He was crestfallen. He walked around the barn in circles, his hands buried deep in his pockets, brooding. He and Mr. Anderson had become so close that he was certain he wouldn't possibly refuse his request. *I thought for sure he would concede.* He shook his head in disbelief. *Even after all I've done, to them, I'm still nothing more than a farm hand.* In frustration, he kicked the chaff box with his right foot knocking it onto the dirt floor. *Why is nothing ever easy? Ever since I was kidnapped, it's been one trial after another. But I have battled worse,* he reasoned. *And I have Susannah's heart. That much is true. And more than I can say for George.* Just the thought of George with Susannah made his blood boil. He determined to do everything in his power to overcome the obstacles now placed before him. *But where do I go from here?* He wondered.

Peter spoke no further on the subject with James Anderson, nor did he mention it to Susannah.

The next day, he took a wagon to town to fetch some badly needed supplies. After he had made his purchases and loaded them onto the wagon, he stopped at one of the local taverns, recalling pleasant memories with the Marquis de Lafayette. As he entered, he noticed several patrons gathered around a man wearing a Continental Army uniform. It was obvious that they had all been drinking a generous amount of rum. Peter approached the edge of the group and listened from the back for a while. The soldier was obviously a recruiting sergeant trying to persuade the patrons into signing up for militias to fight in the Southern campaigns. As he was talking, the sergeant caught a glimpse of Peter, his head towering above the others.

"You're Peter Francisco, aren't you?" he queried.

"Yes … I am. How did you know?"

"Mr. Francisco, we've never met, but you've quite a reputation, especially at your size."

Chants of "Peter, Peter" rang out from the men who had

gathered there.

"Then, I guess my secret's out," Peter said with a twinkle in his eye. "You've found me. I am Peter Francisco."

The sergeant continued. "I was just telling the lads here what an honor it is to serve, as well as some of the side benefits."

One of the others spoke up, "Peter, this guy says we'll get all the rum we want and women, too."

"Well," Peter responded, "you do get a ration of rum, though I doubt it's as much as you can consume, Tommy." Peter had met Thomas White on numerous trips into town, and he seemed to be in a perpetual state of drunkenness, no matter the time of day. "As for the women, some of the men bring their wives. There are a few unattached women as well, but..."

Peter's voice was drowned out by a rallying cry of "huzzahs" from the men.

"Tell the lads about what a great life it is," the sergeant spoke up again.

Peter's loyalty to the Continental Army took over. He told the men of campfire tales and tall stories, of friends made—omitting friends lost—of the bravery he had witnessed, excluding the stories of men in fearful retreat. The men listened intently as if Peter was delivering a Sunday sermon. When Peter finished, the sergeant spoke again.

"Men, General Gates is raising an army to fight in the Carolinas, for if we do not fight there, surely the British will bring the fight to us right here in Virginia. Charleston is under siege. And I don't know if you've heard, but the ruthless Colonel Tarleton, whose men are savage and brutal, does not abide by the accepted rules of war, killing and pillaging all in his path. Now, I don't know about you, but I don't want our womenfolk to be anywhere near the fighting. I'm going to South Carolina. Now, who's going with me?"

Every man in the tavern began to hoot and howl. Even Peter got caught up in the moment, his mind reeling. Anger welled up inside him. *Those God-forsaken Tories! Who do they think they are? I'm sick of them! I'll die before I let them push me around. Not like that self-righteous James Anderson. Does he think I'm going to just stand aside and watch him sell Susannah off to that confounded George Carrington? I won't do it! I can't do it. But how would she react if I went back to the fighting? On the other hand, what would happen if I stayed? I can't marry her.* He thought about what the sergeant had just said, and about Susannah, and about the Anderson plantation, even Hunting Tower. *What do I have to lose?*

As men began signing papers to join the militia, the sergeant clapped Peter on the back, "How about you, Mr. Francisco? Will you join us, too?"

Before he could stop himself, Peter was making his "X" on another piece of paper.

As the late day sun started its slow descent in the West, Peter began the ride back to the Anderson plantation. *How will I break the news to Susannah? Will Mr. Anderson be glad or will he wish I would still be around to help?*

When he arrived home, Susannah burst out the front door, her customary way of greeting him. "Peter, Peter," she called. "Wait till you hear! Thomas has completed his duty. He's coming home! Isn't that the most wonderful news?" She said excitedly, throwing her arms around him.

"That is wonderful news, Susannah," Peter said rigidly, keep-

329

ing his arms loose around her. *At least Mr. Anderson would have one of his sons to help with the fall harvest,* he thought. "I have some news, too."

"What...is it?" Susannah asked warily, pulling away from him. She sensed something had changed.

"News has come that the British are concentrating their efforts in the Carolinas," he said, pausing for a moment before saying, "And I have just enlisted in the militia." Peter read the stunned look on Susannah's face and immediately defended his decision. "I must go, Susannah. If we don't stop them there, we'll be fighting them right here in Virginia." He wanted to give more of an explanation, but Susannah interrupted.

"No, Peter. No. You can't go. Not now. Not when we are making our plans. I won't hear you speak of it. No, no, no!" She buried her face in her hands, whirled around and headed for the front door.

Peter went inside the house, but she had already gone upstairs, where she had flung herself on her bed and wailed. He walked back to the kitchen and found her father sitting in his familiar spot at the table. He went over and sat down opposite him.

"What is it, Peter?" Anderson inquired. "What has sent my daughter upstairs to cry? The last time that happened, you were going off to war."

Peter relayed the details of his visit in town and his decision to rejoin the militia. "I'm to report tomorrow."

"Well, Peter, I understand. I know you feel duty bound. I know Susannah's heart is breaking at this very moment, but I am resolute in my decision for her to marry George Carrington. I bid you. Go to her and comfort her as best you can. We shall miss you here. Only God knows how we would have managed without you. You were truly heaven-sent, but Thomas comes home any day now, and we shall try to get along the best we can. Now go, Peter. Go to Susannah."

Peter crept up the stairs and paused at the door to her room. The wailing had stopped, and now just soft sobbing echoed through the hall. Peter knocked, but she did not answer. Knocking again, he only heard Susannah's voice order him, "Go away."

He persisted. He knocked once more, then opened the door and entered her room. It was the first time he had ever been in there, and it felt like he was standing in forbidden territory. When he stepped inside, she was lying on her stomach across a blue calico duvet spread over the four-poster bed. She was facing him, but, when he approached her, she rolled her head to look away. Peter spotted boneca de trapo perched on the bedside table. He walked over, sat on the edge of the bed, and placed his hand on the small of her back.

"Please don't cry, Susannah. Please don't."

She rolled back over and looked up at him. The rims of her eyes were red, and he could see the stains of tears on her cheeks.

"How can you do this to me, Peter Francisco? How can you do this to us?" she howled. Fresh tears fell in rivulets down her face. She tried to wipe them away with her hand, but they came too fast.

"Susannah, listen to me. I don't want to fight anymore. But if I don't go to war, the war will come here, and I don't want you anywhere near it. If anything were to happen to you…." Peter wanted to say "My life would be over." But instead, he finished with, "I would never forgive myself."

331

"But, Peter, I feel the same way. All the while you were gone, I feared for the day when we would get a message saying you had been killed. I don't think I can stand that again."

"I promise I'll be gone no more than a year, just one year. If the conflict is not resolved by then, I'll come home."

Susannah rolled over on her back, reached up and wrapped her arms around Peter's neck. "You promise? Do you really promise?"

"I promise, now let me go get my things," he said, removing her arms. Peter got up, went into the house and gathered the few things he would take with him. He had two satchels. A large one for his clothes and a smaller one for his valuables.

Peter stepped out onto the porch. The cool evening air felt fresh and clean in his lungs.

Just a few moments later, Susannah appeared in the doorway, wearing the same green dress that she had worn when Peter had left more than three years earlier. The sight of her in that dress wrenched Peter's heart. He couldn't leave her thinking nothing had changed, waiting in vain for him to return. "Susannah, I asked your father for your hand in marriage," he confessed. He didn't wait for her to respond. "He forbade it."

"What?" Susannah said, his words not sinking in.

"Your father still wants you to marry George Carrington. He said I don't have anything to offer you."

"That's not true! I don't care about George, Peter, I—"

Peter cut her off. "He's right," he said, disbelieving his own words.

"What...do you mean?" she said, certain her ears were deceiving her.

"Susannah," Peter began, with torment in his heart, "you deserve the best life possible. A life filled with every happiness, every comfort. Without worry. I can't offer you that. At least not now."

Susannah was silent for a moment. She spoke softly. "Peter, my one and only happiness is you. All I need is you."

"My feelings for you haven't changed," he said, fighting the urge to pull her into his arms, "but your father is adamant. I don't want you to defy him. He only wants what's best for you. And so do I."

Susannah lower lip began to quiver, and her face contorted into anguish. "Why are you doing this to me, Peter Francisco?"

"Some things are beyond our control," he replied, trying to conceal his own heartache. "I had best be going. We leave for South Carolina no later than mid-morning."

"You ... have my handkerchief ... and your buckles?" she asked through a torrent of tears and sobs, touching the smaller of the two satchels.

"Of course, I do," he replied. "I will still hold them the same way I did before."

Peter descended the steps, went to the barn to get his horse, and returned to the front of the porch where Susannah waited. He kissed her softly on the cheek, then put his foot in the stirrup and settled onto the saddle. She reached for his arm, but before she could touch him, Peter leaned down, picked her up, kissed her one last time, and said, "No matter what, I'll always love you."

As he gently returned her to the ground, she looked at him with tears streaming down her face. "My heart belongs to you, Peter Francisco. It always will."

Peter could take no more. Fighting back his own tears, he

jabbed the horse with his heels, and she bolted for the edge of the property. Once again, he looked back at Susannah and saw her standing there. She didn't move. She didn't lift her hand to wave. Before he turned around, his last image was of her crumbling to the ground.

19.

COLONEL MAYO AND THE CANNON

As PETER JOINED the Virginia Militia in mid-July 1780, he recalled the training that he and his fellow soldiers had been through under the watchful eye of Barron von Steuben. Until that point, the Continental Army had been little more than a rag tag bunch who hadn't the slightest idea how to fight as a unit. Von Steuben had changed all that, and Peter was certain that the more disciplined mindset would be in place for these newly formed militias. Furthermore, the Southern Campaign would be led by none other than General Horatio Gates, who had garnered a good deal of well-deserved fame at the Battle of Saratoga.

But Peter was greatly disappointed when he saw his comrades drilling and preparing for battle. Like those he had met at the tavern where he had been persuaded to re-enlist, most of these men barely knew one end of a musket from the other. *They have no idea about lines of authority. Or military discipline. Or what battle is all about. To them, this is nothing more than a late summer escapade.*

Thinking back, Peter recalled the words of the recruiting sergeant, who had painted a much less demanding and less threatening picture of war than was the truth. Peter had inadvertently become part of the ploy. *I wish the recruiter's description had been more accurate. If it had, maybe some of the enlistees would have realized that war is less about glory than gumption and guts.* Peter was grateful for one thing, and that was the chance encounter with his old friend John Allen, the western Virginia mountain man he had parted company with on the way home from the Northern Campaign. Colonel William Mayo was to be Peter's commanding officer in the field. He was well respected as a field officer who took care of his men and was more than willing to fight right alongside his troops rather than ride his horse at the rear, barking commands. Colonel Mayo had also been a friend to Major General Lafayette, who had related stories about a huge Virginian named Peter Francisco. Thus, when Peter reported for duty, Colonel Mayo immediately tapped him to be his personal aide. Peter was with the colonel when a group of buckskin-clad men with long rifles rode into camp to report for duty. Heading the group was none other than John Allen.

Seeing Peter standing next to the colonel, Allen literally leaped off his horse and ran to greet him. "Peter Francisco, how are ya, ol' friend?"

"I'm fine, John, just fine. But what brings you from your cozy little home in the mountains? When I last saw you heading west, I thought you'd never leave the comfort of the Shenandoahs ever again."

"Aw, you know how it is, Peter. I'm sure it's the same thing 'at brought you here. We got word that if we didn't face off with the Redcoats here, we'd be fightin' 'em back home. Now, tell you the truth, personally, I'd love to get them lobster backs to fightin' in the mountains. Why, we'd just pick 'em off by the dozens. But here I am, ready to fight. I shore am glad you're here, too."

"It's good to see you again, John. Hey, Let me go with you to get your horse," Peter said, trying to discreetly steer them out of earshot of the colonel. "John, don't be so happy. This won't be easy," he cautioned. "I've been here a week now, and by the looks of our troops, we're in for some tough times. They aren't even getting the training we got in the Shenandoah Valley. I fear for the first time we go into battle. I truly do. The only good thing is that we've got some boys from Delaware and Maryland, and they've had some solid battle experience."

"That don't sound very good. Not good at all."

"It's not, my friend. When some of these fellas showed up, they didn't even have muskets, and the word is that we're to break camp and head for South Carolina any day now. I don't know when supplies will catch up with us."

The rumors Peter had been hearing soon materialized, and the gathered militias broke camp a few days later, heading south through North Carolina to South Carolina. *Ill-equipped and partially trained, surely,* Peter thought, *we are heading for disaster.*

Of course, General Gates had fared well in a battle over a fixed fortification, but he was not well-suited for directing his troops over miles and miles of marching and maneuvering. As a result, his forces meandered all over the Carolinas to the point that they seldom even had enough to eat, save a few ears of corn and some turnips. The situation reminded Peter of Valley Forge, when their diet had consisted of little more than fire cakes. *At least now we aren't cold,* Peter reasoned. *Then again, maybe that would be better.* General Gates, who was not very familiar with the southern terrain, would often camp his forces near swamps and marshes. Those areas were breeding grounds for mosquitoes, and they made life miserable for everyone. Poor diet and lack of sleep made many of the soldiers sick, and dysentery was not at all uncommon.

Gates also miscalculated his troop strength. Other militias and soldiers had joined Gates' forces along the way, which led the general to calculate that he had perhaps 7,000 troops at his disposal. Actually, he had less than 5,000, and some of those men simply left and went home, since army life was not at all what they had imagined or, in some cases, had been promised.

As for the British, having seen the Northern Campaign disintegrate from one disaster after another, they bet the rest of their chances on stamping out the rebellion in the South, where they felt they could depend on a stronghold of loyalists. Indeed, there was a large segment of the population that had remained loyal to British rule, but not in the numbers that the English had hoped would swell their ranks. However, the British had been successful in capturing Charleston earlier in the year, at the expense of a large number of American casualties.

Thus, the British, under the command of General Lord Charles Cornwallis, were now attempting to gain control of the South Carolina backcountry, and Camden had become a major base of operations where men and supplies were amassed. On August 14, Cornwallis received word that the Americans were approaching Camden, but rather than simply wait in a defensive position, he decided to take the fight to the Americans. Having sent out some advanced scouting parties, the British general would be sending the balance of his forces to meet Gates' army head-on.

On that same night, Colonel Mayo was carping to Peter about the lack of essential supplies. "Peter," he said, "do you realize that we go into battle within days, perhaps hours, and we don't even have enough weapons or clothes for all the men?"

"Yes, sir, Colonel Mayo. Several of the boys will have to fight hand-to-hand if they are to fight at all."

"This is intolerable, absolutely intolerable. It's bad enough that these lads are not yet properly trained, but to send them to battle without muskets…unconscionable, I tell you." Then, as if accepting the inevitable, he said, "Very well, Peter. That will be all. You go and get some rest now."

"Yes, sir. I'll do that."

Peter did not do as instructed, however. Rather, he wandered about the campfires until he found his friend, John Allen. As he approached the group of men, Peter asked John to come and speak with him privately. "John, you know we go into battle soon," he spoke gravely.

"Yes, o' course I do," John responded.

"You know that a number of our boys don't even have muskets."

"Yes, I know. What're you gettin' at, Peter?"

"Well, we know that the Redcoats always send out some advanced scouts. Suppose we choose for ourselves a soldier who has had special training for sneaking around, and another soldier who's a crack shot to give him cover. And suppose those two fellas sneak into one of the enemy's camps and make off with some of their supplies. And suppose they brought those supplies back here to give to our boys."

"And, I'm supposin' you figure we're the two fellas to do that job?"

"Suppose I am."

"Then I guess we better get to it."

As Peter and John set out, it wasn't long before the glow of a distant campfire caught their eye. The British were camped just across a small stream, and the two men sat among some Palmetto scrub to watch. There they noticed that the British weren't being very attentive. By the number of horses that had been hobbled off to one side, Peter estimated that there were only ten troops among the party. They had pitched a few tents, and most of them must have been asleep, as there was only one sentry that Peter could see. Thinking that the stream provided a natural shield, this lone guard was concentrating on the opposite side of the camp away from the scouts' position.

Peter looked over at John Allen and whispered, "I'm going to head back upstream and cross the river so they can't hear me splashing around in the water. You stay here, and when you see me on the other side, you watch for any alarm in the camp. If they sound the alert, you pick off the sentry first. With any luck, I'll already have their guns, but I'll leave my musket with you in case you need a second shot."

"Peter," John said, "you must be crazy. You can't possibly sneak into the camp, get their guns, and get outta there without gettin' caught."

"Yes, I can, John. You just wait and see."

"Well, it's yer funeral then. I can't help ya much after my two shots."

"You won't be taking *any* shots. Just watch."

Peter maneuvered his large frame quietly through the woods, neatly sidestepping twigs and overgrown brush as he made his way upstream. When he figured he had gone far enough, he removed his boots, entered the waist-level water and crossed to the other side. The embankment was steep, and, since there was no path, he decided to stay in the water until the last possible moment.

This marshland tributary was full of critters, but the surreptitious scout decided not to think about that with his bare feet exposed. Mud and natural debris oozed through his toes as he made his way along the edge of the stream. A few yards before he reached the point where the stream flowed next to the British camp, he reached down, grabbed a handful of mud, and smeared it all over his face.

On the other side, the glow from the campfire danced on the water, revealing to John Allen the silhouette of his friend creeping closer to the camp site. He raised the musket to his shoulder and placed his finger on the trigger, ready to fire.

The smell of burning wood filled the air. When Peter felt he had reached just the right spot, he grabbed at the sides of the embankment and deftly pulled himself up onto the ground inch by inch. Every once in a while, he would lose traction and slip backwards, but within a few minutes, he was fully out of the water, lying prostrate at the edge of the camp. Fortuitously, the British had decided to stack their muskets in the standard tripod arrangement near the water's edge—three groups of three muskets.

Peter was careful in disassembling each of the tripods, making sure that none of the weapons clamored to the ground, which certainly would have roused the sleeping troops, bringing their plan to a disappointing, probably dangerous, conclusion. Each time he had gathered three more muskets, he eased them over to the bank of the stream. When all nine were lined up along the shore, he became even more daring. Near one of the tents he had spotted a wooden crate of musket balls about three feet wide and encircled by metal rings. Allen, stationed on the opposite bank, had kept his long rifle trained on the sentry the whole time, while Peter secured the muskets. Then he saw him making his way over toward one of the tents. "Peter, you fool, leave well enough alone," John muttered under his breath.

Francisco crawled on his belly until he neared the crate, then extended one of his long arms and grabbed hold of the rope handle. Peter estimated the crate weighed nearly fifty pounds, and when he tried to drag it, it made a scraping noise in the dirt. Holding his breath, Peter glanced up quickly to see if the sentry had heard. John Allen leveled his rifle and took better aim. The moment hung frozen in the air as the sentry stood oblivious to the action behind him.

Satisfied that the sentry had not been alerted, Peter lifted his body to a crouching position without taking his eyes off the guard. Still the lookout kept his back to the stream and Peter, who grabbed the rope with one hand, easily lifted it off the ground and swiftly made his way to his stash of weapons. Silently, he slithered back into the water. With one hand, he let the heavy crate sink slowly below the water line until the water seeped into its crevices. Then, with his massive hands, he gathered all nine muskets at once and pulled them gently into the water, letting them rest diagonally on top of the crate in front of him. Carefully, he lifted the crate and muskets as high as he could without letting the base of the crate clear the surface. The handles of the muskets stuck out underneath his arm.

Ever so slowly, he made his way back upstream. John Allen let out a deep breath, for what seemed like the first time since arriving at the water's edge. He also started to make his way upstream, creeping along a parallel course with his partner. After skulking about for a few hundred yards, Peter crossed the stream.

John Allen addressed Peter in a hushed tone. "There for a minute, I thought you'd be caught. That was too close for me, my friend. Next time you wanna do this, forget I'm in the same army with you."

Peter smiled. "We got what we needed, didn't we?"

The two of them stole back to the American camp, Peter carrying the crate of balls with five of the muskets slung over his shoulders, John Allen bearing the other four weapons. When they arrived, Colonel Mayo, who hadn't been able to sleep, was standing next to the fire closest to his tent, watching Peter and John approach. "What have you there?" the colonel asked.

"Oh, just a few supplies the British have generously decided to donate to the cause," Peter replied nonchalantly.

The colonel stood in amazement as the two friends recounted what they had done. "I thought I told you to get some rest," the colonel scolded Peter. "I should have you court-martialed for disobeying a direct order." He winked at Allen.

"Yes, sir." That was all Peter could muster in response. He

thought they had done well.

"Good job, boys. Good job. Now, get some rest with what little remains of this night. And that's an absolute, direct order."

"Yes, sir. We'll do that," Peter said. He would have liked to see the looks on the Redcoats' faces when they discovered that all their muskets and fifty pounds of ammunition had up and vanished in the night. That alone might be worth a court martial.

The next day, after Colonel Mayo had assigned the stolen weapons, men kept coming up to Peter to congratulate him. He insisted that Allen had played a major role, too, but everyone knew Peter was the hero of the hour.

That evening the word went out to prepare for march. Camp broke, and at midnight, General Gates and his forces advanced toward Camden. Concurrently, British General Cornwallis ordered his troops to do the same. Since the two armies were progressing directly toward each other, advanced columns collided around 2:30 in the morning. A few small skirmishes broke out, but both commands withdrew to await the dawn.

At sunrise, the respective armies realized that their battlefield was much smaller than they had anticipated. The killing ground was flanked by marshland which made it nearly impossible for a man to stand, let alone fight. This was a huge advantage for the British, for, even though they had less than half the men of the American forces, they knew the lines would be impregnable much like the Spartans hundreds of years earlier at the Battle of Thermopylae. Defending their position would be far easier than anyone would have anticipated.

Unfortunately, General Gates proved to be a poor tactician on the open field of battle. When he deployed his troops, he positioned the rawest men on the front lines, directly facing the guns and bayonets of the well-trained British soldiers. To the flanks, he stationed more skillful soldiers such as Peter Francisco's band. The last line of Gates' forces—the Maryland regulars—was by far the most experienced.

By contrast, Cornwallis' men were all battle-hardened veterans, reinforced by the cavalry led by Colonel Banastre Tarleton's Legion, a unit of barbaric men with an equally bloodthirsty leader.

Tarleton was a brutal tyrant, whose mission, it seemed, was to ensure that war arrived at every American doorstep. He delighted in ransacking villages, ravishing women and slaughtering the innocent. Their devastation and shame were an imbuement for his soul.

His complete disregard for humanity drove him and his merciless minions in their unmistakable green coats to set houses, barns and outbuildings ablaze. He butchered livestock and obliterated crops, rendering fields permanently barren. He dined in the homes of dignitaries, indulging in their opulence and making general merriment, yet all the while plotting their demise.

In battle, he ignored white flags, viewing them as an opportunity to attack and massacre men in their weakest moments. At Waxhaw Creek, when the loyalists thought Tarleton had been shot during the opposition's call for surrender, they charged upon the colonialists in a furious rage, stabbing many of the wounded as they lay defenseless on the ground. Following that carnage, "Tarleton's quarter!" became the colonies' rallying battle cry.

Rather than demoralizing the enemy, as was his intention, Tarleton's flagrant savagery spread like wildfire through the camps and enflamed the passion for freedom among neighboring communities, causing many who were still undecided to join the effort. After hearing about the atrocities at Waxhaw Creek and many other rural towns, the revolutionaries were hungry for retribution, and they hoped to get it at Camden.

The front line Americans were ordered to get off at least two volleys of fire before withdrawing rearward, where they would join the troops from Maryland. In fact, they were threatened with being shot if they disobeyed the order.

Peter was sitting on his horse next to Colonel Mayo. Hastily, he reached inside his satchel and took out the handkerchief-wrapped buckles. Quickly, he recited his Portuguese prayer and returned the buckles to their protective place. He knew the battle would soon commence.

The British attacked the left flank first, where Peter was still stationed alongside Colonel Mayo. Most of the Virginians had no stomach for the fight. As the first British volley rained down upon them, they turned and ran, many of them throwing their weapons down while fleeing. The colonel and Peter did their best to rally the troops, both of them waving swords over their heads as they rode their horses up and down the lines. A few of the men turned around to fire at the British, but their shots lacked aim, and most ricocheted off trees or burrowed into the ground. When the fleeing soldiers reached a secondary line of North Carolinians, matters became worse. Rather than standing their ground, the North Carolina boys simply joined the retreat.

Peter and the colonel were left with very few troops as the British advanced for close combat. The Virginian slashed at a British trooper and opened a wide gash in the man's neck, but, at that moment, his horse took a musket ball in the dead center of his chest. The horse's front legs buckled, catapulting Peter head first onto the ground and causing him to lose his sword in the process. He reached around and grabbed the musket strapped to his back. A grenadier rushed forward intending to bayonet him, but Peter firmly planted his right foot on the ground and deftly stepped to his left. The soldier passed right by before losing his balance in the lunge. Peter drove his own bayonet deep into the man's back.

Amidst the chaos, Colonel Mayo shouted something that Peter couldn't hear. Ignoring his own safety, he turned his head in Mayo's direction so that he could hear what the colonel was shouting. "The artillery! We must save the cannon!" Mayo yelled.

Seven pieces of artillery had been spread among the front lines. Two of those cannon were assigned to the Virginians, but the soldiers in charge of them had joined the retreat, and the horses that had pulled the cannon into position had been shot dead.

With cat-like dexterity, Peter sprinted to the artillery pieces. Instantly seeing that both sets of wheels had sunk into the soft earth bordering the swamp, he cut loose the leather straps that lashed one of the cannon to its barrel. Without thinking, in a show of unbelievable strength, Peter Francisco lifted the 1,100-pound weapon out of its cradle and hoisted it onto his shoulders. Colonel Mayo and other soldiers in close proximity couldn't believe their eyes. Even the British soldiers stopped charging, in awe of the feat.

Colonel Mayo rode alongside Peter as he carried the cannon to a wagon near the rear lines. *There*, Peter thought, *at least the*

347

men of Maryland are fighting valiantly along with their brothers from Delaware. Heaving the cannon safely onto the back of the wagon, Peter turned around to find that Tarleton's Legion had been unleashed and were about to join the fray. Surrounding them were advancing grenadiers, one of whom aimed a bayonet thrust directly at Mayo's midsection. Still not having fired his weapon, Peter brought his musket to bear and put a ball and three pellets into the British soldier's body.

Smoke and gunfire filled the air. A musket ball found its home in the left flank of Mayo's horse, collapsing the animal. Peter ran to assist his superior officer, who obviously was shaken.

"Come on, Colonel, we must join the others in retreat," Peter yelled, over all the sounds of battle. The colonel nodded in agreement, and the two men set off toward safety. However, in the fall from his horse, Colonel Mayo had twisted his ankle, and he couldn't run fast. Behind him, Peter could hear the sound of hooves pounding the ground, and he turned around to see one of Tarleton's men bearing down on them on horseback. In order to give the colonel more time to get away, the Virginian stood his ground and faced the charging legionnaire. The enemy closed in and swung wildly with his sword, a move that Peter was able to narrowly sidestep. The man wheeled his horse back toward Peter, charging again. But Peter was ready. Once more he stepped quickly to the side, at the same time brought his musket, with bayonet still firmly attached, up toward the trooper's stomach. The blade sank clear to the hilt. As the horse continued its run, Peter was left standing there with a British soldier fully impaled, dangling from the end of his weapon. The man wriggled about for just a few more seconds and then went limp.

348

The legionnaire's horse only continued a few more paces before she stopped. Peter went over and took hold of her reins, mounted, and returned to the fallen soldier to grab his rather distinctive, pluming headdress. Placing it on his own head, the Virginian prodded the horse into a gallop, all the while encouraging the British to give chase, bellowing for all he was worth in a self-protective ploy, "After them, boys! Don't let the rebels escape!" *At least they won't shoot at me if I make them think I'm one of them.*

He had ridden about a half-mile when he spied Colonel Mayo taking refuge among some trees. Peter rode over to his superior and looked down from atop the horse. "Colonel Mayo? Are you alright, sir?"

"Peter, I'm afraid not. I don't think I can go on. I just can't. Now you get out of here before they catch up to both of us. That's an order."

"Well, it's another order I must disobey," Peter confessed, as he dismounted. "Take the horse and ride to safety as fast as you can. Tarleton's Legion is fast on my heels."

The colonel, struggling to stand, allowed Peter to assist him into the saddle. "I should have you court-martialed for this, for disobeying another order. Either that, or I shall be privileged to pin a medal on your chest. I shall never forget this, Peter... never."

"Ride!" Francisco commanded, slapping the horse on its backside. "I'll be close behind." Peter wasn't able to keep up with Mayo's horse, and barely escaped Tarleton's cavalry.

The battle ended in a major defeat. Everything General Gates could have done wrong, he did it in this battle, and in the process lost almost half his men. For Peter, this was a signal to never, ever go to battle with so many untrained soldiers. He had also come to another conclusion. He much preferred going to battle sitting on a horse.

20.

BURYING A FRIEND

WHEN PETER FINALLY MADE IT to the rear lines, he saw a group of men standing around Colonel Mayo, who was telling them about Peter rescuing one of the cannon. As Mayo saw Peter approaching, he pointed out the oversized soldier to the listeners. For several seconds they just stared at him. He was huge, compared to the average young soldier, but to have hoisted an 1,100-pound cannon was beyond their comprehension.

On the heels of a defeat, one of the men began to shout, "Hooray for Peter Francisco!" Others joined in until the chant became a chorus. The group surrounded him and planted several congratulatory slaps on his back. As he continued into camp, he couldn't help but notice several of the distinctively-clad mountain men gathered around one of the hospital tents. He approached with cautious curiosity.

"Is somebody hurt?" Peter inquired.

"It's John Allen," one of the men spoke up. "You friends with him, ain't ya?"

"Yes. Yes, I am. Is it bad?"

"Ol' Johnny took a ball to the chest. It ain't lookin' good."

Immediately, Peter pulled back the flap of the tent. Allen was lying in a crimson-stained shirt, stretched across several boards. He appeared to be unconscious and was waiting to be seen by a doctor. Peter approached and touched his friend's hand.

The wounded soldier opened his eyes slightly, looking directly at Peter. "You was right, big fella. We wasn't even a lil' ready for battle." He coughed, grimaced in pain, as a stream of blood left a trail down his chin. Finding it too difficult to talk, in a raspy voice little more than a whisper, he breathed, "Come 'ere, Peter. I got a favor to ask." Peter took John's hand in his and bent down close to his face.

"Peter," he spoke haltingly, "take me home...promise me... you'll take me home. I want to...go back...to the mountains."

Peter looked at his friend. "Hey, mountain man, you'll be taking yourself home in no time. These doctors will fix you right up, and you can ride back to your glorious mountains."

"I don't think so, Peter. Not this time." John's voice grew weaker. "I know the boys...they would take me back...but you 'bout the best friend I got...Peter...please promise me...you'll take me home...promise me." His friend's labored pleading pierced the giant man's soft heart.

"I'll take you home, John. I promise...I promise."

Those were the last words John Allen would ever hear. He rolled his head to the side and a gurgle escaped his throat. Just then a doctor came over, took hold of his wrist and felt for a pulse. Looking at Peter, not callously as one who had seen so much death but sorrowfully, he said, "If this man was your friend, he's gone."

As the doctor walked away, Peter bent low and gave his companion a kiss on each cheek. "I'll take you to your earthly home, mon ami, and bury you in the mountains that call out your name." Peter exited the tent and the other mountain men gathered around him.

"Is he going to be alright?" one of them asked.

"No, he's better than alright. He's in no more pain. He's in heaven with the Lord," Peter said, walking away. Spying Colonel Mayo, Peter headed over to him to tell him of his plans.

"You don't seem like you're taking to your role as a hero, Peter," the colonel intoned.

"Being a hero doesn't mean much when you lose a good friend," he responded solemnly. He went on to explain what had happened to John Allen.

"I'm sorry about your friend, Peter. I didn't know him, but what you two accomplished the other night was impressive."

"Colonel, I need to tell you something else. I'm going to take John's body back to the Shenandoahs to bury him. I promised him I'd do that, so I'll be needing a wagon and a team of horses."

"Peter, with what you've done, you've earned at least that privilege. I'll make the arrangements."

"There's something else, Colonel."

"What is it, soldier?"

"I hear that they've been organizing cavalry units, and I'll be joining up with one of those. I don't ever want to fight a battle like I fought today, so I won't be coming back to this militia."

"I understand, Peter. I really do, though I'll miss you. What you did for me today, I can never repay. I'll have the wagon sent over to the hospital tent directly."

Peter and the colonel shook hands. Within the hour, Peter had gathered up his few belongings, loaded the wrapped body of his friend in the back of the wagon, and pointed the team of horses north. Even though it would be dark soon, he wanted to leave the camp as soon as possible. In all the battles he had fought, never had the Americans been so thoroughly routed. It was a taste in his mouth that this soldier would not soon forget.

At first Peter had thought about stopping at the Anderson plantation before heading deep into the mountains of Virginia, but that would have extended his task by many days and he wasn't entirely sure he'd be welcome after the way he'd left. He also knew that the body would soon decompose, and he didn't want to subject the Andersons to that.

Initially, the journey itself wasn't unpleasant. The land was fairly flat, and Peter made good time for the first few days, during which he found his mind wandering to all that had happened—battles won and lost, friends found and lost, and love lost. Always his thoughts came back to Susannah. He reached into his satchel and fingered her handkerchief wrapped around the buckles. He brought it to his nose and inhaled deeply. Just the touch and scent of material gave him comfort.

At night, Peter secured the horses, bedded down and won-dered what the future might hold. *How long will the war go on? How many more men will have to die? And will America ever be free? Could she survive without Britain's aid? What about Susannah? Is she safe now? Will any of this fighting reach her? Will Tarleton reach her?*

Because if he did, I would.... His wandering thoughts soon put Peter fast asleep.

★

Several days of heading northwest brought the simple funeral procession to where foothills began and the mountains of western North Carolina lay beyond. The horses began to strain against the weight of the creaking wagon. Peter decided that he might be better off taking an easterly detour before the animals wore out and the wagon fell apart. This went on for several days as he kept the mountain peaks on his left and guided the wagon up towards the Shenandoah Valley.

Eventually, as he crossed over into Virginia, Peter could sense that his last journey with his friend John was coming to an end. He even began to recognize where he was, from his original journey to join the army. He knew he was getting close now, but the ride was getting more difficult, and the wagon was taking a beating from the rocky terrain. Peter could no longer keep the team from traveling a much more perilous course, not if he was to do as promised and take his friend home to the mountains. A trip that would have taken a man on horseback a few days was taking weeks.

Finally, they could go no further. Peter had aimed the team up a rocky incline. The horses were straining, and their breathing had become labored. As for the wagon, it was tilting from one side to the next. Boards began to shake loose. When the wooden wheels could no longer take the pounding of the rocks, the two at the back of the wagon just splintered. The front end tilted up into the air as the back end no longer had any support, and Peter was nearly thrown from his seat. Allen's body slid out the back and rolled down some rocks before finally coming to a rest against an outcropping.

Peter panicked and ran down to check on his friend. As he reached the wrapped body, he was actually a bit amused at his own reaction. *John probably would have been laughing, too,* he thought. Sensing John was still near, and maybe to compensate for his loneliness the last several days, he said aloud, "John, you watching this comedy act?" After all, it wasn't as if John could feel any of it.

Picking up the body, Peter walked the short distance to the collapsed wagon and, laying the body down in a secure place, he examined the two broken wheels. If he had been back at Hunting Tower or The Mansion, he could have repaired the damage. As it was, the wagon had been rendered nearly useless. With dusk settling in, Peter decided to call it a day and make camp right where the wagon had broken down. As he tried his best to sleep, a lone wolf sang its night song like a dirge for John, calmly reassuring Peter that he had chosen the right place.

The next morning, Peter tied John Allen's body to one of the horses along with two roughly cut sections of the broken wagon wheels. Fortunately, he'd had the good sense to bring a saddle and bridle for himself. A rope around the neck of the second horse allowed Peter to lead it up the sloping crag, but even without the wagon to pull, the horses found the going quite difficult, and both labored hard under their loads.

Despite the stress, Peter beheld some of the most beautiful land his eyes had ever seen. In the distance, a warm blue glow emanated from John's cherished mountains, reflecting the sun-lit sky. Majestic peaks carved by the hand of God Himself. Tall, vibrant trees cascaded among them, lapping their feet like gentle waves. Their brilliant sea color reminded Peter of Susannah's eyes.

Straight ahead he spotted a mountain peak that seemed to beckon him, as if it would be just the spot to lay his friend to rest. The horses, however, could not traverse the last several hundred yards, so Peter stopped the animals, got down from his horse and rested for about an hour. He refreshed himself with water from a rushing stream that culminated in a waterfall, drank his fill and took the rest back to the horses. During the journey, he had let them graze on whatever vegetation was available, but both animals had lost quite a bit of weight, almost to the point of emaciation.

Taking John's stiff body on his shoulder, much as he had the cannon in Camden, the Virginia giant began the climb up a jagged rock face. Even for a man as strong as Peter, without the rush of battle, it was a backbreaking task, and he had to stop and catch his breath several times. Upon reaching the summit, he saw a lone pine tree perched on the acme. To one side of the tree, a gray wolf stood, absolutely still. Peter locked on its fire-colored gaze for a moment. Though he couldn't be certain, he thought it might be the same animal with the tormented howl from the night before. Something told Peter the creature was genteel and felt completely unthreatened. Looking around, he saw that the ground was covered in a heavy layer of dirt. Fortunate, since Peter had not given any thought about trying to dig through solid rock. He had slung his bayonet over his shoulder before setting out, though, which would prove quite useful.

Placing the body next to the tree, Peter set about loosening the soil with his blade. Then he scooped out dirt with his bare hands. Even though the temperature was quite brisk at this elevation, he broke out in a sweat, and before long his shirt and trousers were soaked through. Six inches at a time he scraped with his bayonet, and six inches at a time he scooped the loosened dirt by hand. It took hours. Having reached a depth of about four feet, he felt sure that this was deep enough to prevent the mountain animals from disturbing his friend's grave. He walked over to the body, carefully lifted it in his arms, and gently placed his fellow soldier in the bottom of the grave. One last time, he reached out to touch the mountain man, then began the task of filling the dirt back into the grave. Using a bit of twine that had kept the shroud around John's remains, he tied two sections from the broken wagon into the shape of a cross. He dug a smaller hole at the head of the grave and pushed the jagged cross into the dirt. When he was finished, he wasn't sure what to do next. Then it came to him. Softly he said:

> *Com Jesus me deito* (With Jesus I go to sleep),
> *Com a graça de Deus* (With the grace of God),
> *E do Espirito Santo* (and of the Holy Spirit).

"Rest well, my friend. Rest well."

Peter's strength was completely spent and darkness was upon him, so he stretched out next to the grave and fell soundly and dreamlessly to sleep.

Very early the next morning, the sound of birds chirping alerted him to the new day. Looking at John Allen's grave one

358

last time, Peter started his descent to where he had tied the horses. They seemed somewhat better after the night's rest, and after saddling up, he began the next leg of his travel—home to Buckingham, starting with a visit to the Andersons.

Though far less arduous, Peter had mixed feelings about this leg of his journey. *Will Susannah be happy to see me after the way I left?* He wondered. After several days, he laid eyes once again on The Mansion. The sight of it caused his stomach to lurch with anxiety. As he rode toward the main house, he anticipated seeing her, and he didn't have to wait long. It was almost as if she had a sixth sense that he was near, for as he brought his two horses to a halt, she walked hurriedly through the door, stopping abruptly at the top of the porch steps.

Descending from his mount, Peter grabbed the horse's bridle to keep her still. He stood looking at Susannah, unsure what to do next. He wanted nothing more than to scoop her off the porch and cradle her in his arms. He decided he should wait for a signal from her.

"Peter, I had no idea that you would return ... so soon. Is the war over? We've had no news that the war is over."

"No," he confessed, still uneasy. *Should I even be here at all?* He wondered. The silence was too much for Peter. Finally he asked, "Susannah is ... George here?"

"No, Peter. He isn't." Susannah descended the porch steps and walked over to him until she was just an arm's reach away. Looking up at him, she searched his eyes with hers. They told him all he needed to know.

"The war is not over yet," Peter said, the tension subsiding. "If our battle at Camden was any indication, it is far from over."

"Does that mean..." her voice trailed off, pausing for a moment as his familiar rugged scent reached her. Emotion was now evident in her voice. "Does that mean you're going back?"

"Yes, Susannah, it does." He could see the disappointment on her face. It made him long to reach out and stroke her cheek.

"But, Peter, you promised—"

"I promised that I wouldn't be gone more than a year, and I've only been gone a few months," he finished with a smirk.

"But... Peter..."

"Susannah, I am truly happy to see you, but I've just spent some of the most miserable months of my life. We were routed at our battle at Camden. Then, I had to take a good friend home to bury him..." He didn't want to get into the details. "Right now, I just really need some rest."

"I understand. Have you had anything to eat today?"

"I haven't really had a decent meal in weeks."

"Then let's go in. You've arrived just in time for dinner. Mother and Father will be glad to see you."

After some warm welcomes, the Andersons, including Thomas, and Peter sat down to eat. But for weary Peter, famished as he was, the enjoyment of food and company wasn't enough to keep him awake. As soon as he finished eating, he went to sit on the porch swing while Mrs. Anderson and Susannah cleaned up, but by the time she joined him, he was sound asleep. With some considerable prodding, Thomas was finally able to rouse him enough to assist him up the stairs to bed.

The next morning, after truly peaceful sleep in a real bed, Peter woke quite refreshed. Downstairs in the kitchen, he found everyone was ready for the day. Thomas and Mr. Anderson were naturally eager to hear what he had to say about the Southern Campaign. Unfortunately, he wasn't able to paint a pretty picture.

"Do you think that Cornwallis is headed this way?" James asked.

"I do believe that will be his next move," Peter replied. "It's the only thing that makes sense."

"Susannah says you're going back to fight."

"Yes, sir, I am. I rejoined the army because I wanted to stop Cornwallis before he got to Virginia, and if there is any possible way to do that, I want to help." Peter shot a quick glance at Susannah to gauge her reaction, and the anguished look on her face was just as he expected.

"Maybe I should go with you," Thomas pondered aloud, then, barely audible, he muttered, "I don't want to be around for this preposterous wedding anyway."

The color suddenly drained out of Susannah's face as her mother turned around. "You listen to me, Thomas Anderson. You've already done your part, and you know your brother James, Jr. is still in Georgia."

"She's right," Peter chimed in. "Besides, you're needed here at the plantation. But, wait, what wedding are you talking about?" he asked, certain he already knew the answer.

"We need *you* here, too." Susannah's pleading comment was directed squarely at Peter as she quickly tried to mask her brother's slip.

Peter ignored Thomas' comment for the moment. "Don't think for one minute that I look forward to meeting up against the British again. Believe me, I would prefer to stay right here and tend to the farm. But not long ago I saw a British soldier named Tarleton. He's as mean as they come, and if he gets the chance, he'll kill every patriot he can, and he'll lay waste to every farm and plantation in sight, leaving nothing spared, least of all women and children. He's coldblooded and callous, and he has to be stopped."

"Peter is right, Susannah." said James. "The men back at camp have spoken about this fiend Tarleton. He's the worst and most ruthless the Redcoats have."

"But Peter," Susannah pleaded. "After what you just told us about Camden and all those soldiers who ran away, why would you want to go back and fight another battle with them?"

"I'm not. I'm joining a cavalry unit that Thomas Watkins is getting together. It's made up of only experienced soldiers, so that should make a difference." Peter didn't bother to say that new soldiers would also be on the battlefield.

"I don't care! Let the British take it all…let them take it all back." Not waiting for any response, she bolted out the back door. Peter stood up to follow her.

"Let her go, Peter. Let her go," Elizabeth said. "She just needs to pout for a while. She was always like that, even as a little girl. Just let her be for a while. She'll be all right. You'll see." Mrs. Anderson seemed less defensive and more understanding of her than he expected.

Peter spent the rest of the day in the barn with Thomas, talking about what Thomas had been doing since he returned. He still wasn't quite sure how to use all the tools that Peter and his father had purchased while he was away in Georgia, but he was a quick study. While he showed Thomas how to use a fuller to draw out a piece of metal, he asked, "Thomas, what wedding were you talking about at breakfast?" Not waiting for him to reply, Peter continued, "It's George and Susannah, isn't it?"

Thomas stopped fullering from the tool for a moment before saying, "Aw, Peter, I've already got myself in trouble. I'd better leave well enough alone. You should probably talk to Susannah." Then, lowering his voice, he said, "But just for the record, I'm not looking forward to having that bloody chap for a brother in-law."

A few minutes later, Susannah came to the barn. She glared at her brother—a look he had been recipient of before—so he relegated the barn to Peter and his sister. Susannah walked directly over to Peter and tried her very best to look up at him apologetically. It didn't work. She extended her hand outwardly toward him, letting one finger rest gently on his chest, but it was too much for Peter. Before he allowed it to go any further, Peter gently pushed her hand away and walked across the barn. Not knowing what to do, Susannah started talking.

"I'm so sorry I spoke to you that way," she said softly. "I don't want you to go. I fear for you, but Father says you have to do this."

Peter was silent for several minutes. He didn't look at Susannah. At that moment, he wasn't at all interested in discussing the war or his pending return. In a stern voice, he asks, "Susannah, what wedding was Thomas talking about?"

Susannah looked as if she was on the verge of tears. "George wants us to marry before the war reaches Virginia. He says it's for my safety. Father agrees." Susannah hesitated before adding, "Our engagement has been formally announced."

Peter closed his eyes. He gritted his teeth in attempt to control his angst. *Is that really what it's about? I can take care of that! I'll go back to war and take care of Tarleton myself! That'll keep her safe.*

"I could tell something had changed. But I thought it might be because of the way I last left you, returning to war. I suppose I knew this day would come." Peter was silent for a moment. "When are you planning to be married?" he asked, not entirely sure he wanted to know the answer.

"The date hasn't been set, but I don't think it will be long," Susannah said, melancholy in her voice. "I'm so sorry, Peter. How I wish things were different, but I don't know what else to do."

Peter paused for a few seconds looking at Susannah with a blank stare on his face, and walked out of the barn. Susannah just stood there wondering what had just happened. *Where is he going?* She wondered to herself.

James Anderson was sitting on the front porch taking a break from his morning chores when Peter came walking up the stairs, intent on petitioning the man one last time for Susannah's hand.

"Mr. Anderson. Sir. I would like to have a word with you."

"What's on your mind, son?" James said as he peered up at Peter looking directly into the morning sun. "Have a seat over here so that I'm not blinded by the light."

He sat down in one of the empty wooden chairs. With firmness in his voice Peter began, "Well, it's about Susannah."

"Peter." James said sternly. "We have been over this and my answer has not changed."

"But, sir." Peter said, keeping his voice even. "I've been thinking a lot about our last conversation and I think you are overlooking an essential component of marriage. Love. Susannah and I truly love each other, and I know that everything will work out because we have that. We may not have everything at first. You did, but you nearly lost it! That can happen to anyone. Something saw you and Mrs. Anderson through that hard time. I'm convinced that something was love. Even if Susannah and I started with something, we could still end up with nothing. I'm not saying that it will be easy or perfect, but I'm going to make something of my life with the land that the government will be giving me. And in the meantime… I'll get an education. You can't let Susannah marry George. She doesn't even have feelings for that scrawny little nuisance!"

Peter was surprised by his own dogma and by the passion that drove him to speak about the love they shared. *I'm not going back to fight in battle until I've won the most important battle of my whole life.*

"You're young, Peter." James rebutted, removing his spectacles and rubbing his eyes. "I know you think that love is all you need, but there is a lot more to making a marriage work than love.

"Besides, only God knows who will win this war," James continued. "You just told us about the dismal defeat in Camden, and if the British win you will never see one hand full of soil from the land that the government has promised you. You could likely be hunted and killed now that you're a famous soldier in the cause for freedom. George comes from a prominent family who still maintains ties with England, so regardless of the outcome, I know she would still be provided for."

Peter feared that he might be fighting a losing battle.

"And what if the battle comes to Virginia?" Peter continued to argue. "Then what will happen to Susannah? What if Tarleton's men get a hold of her? Have you thought about that, Mr. Anderson?" Peter paused to let the gravity of his words sink in. "Do you really think that George can protect her?"

James sat very still contemplating what Peter had just said.

Seconds turned to minutes as the two of them just looked at each other. Peter tried not to blink, as if he were staring down a rabid dog. He knew that the man who broke the silence would have just lost the battle.

Finally, James cleared his throat. "Well, Peter. If you could keep this war from coming here to Virginia, I would be greatly indebted to you."

With sincere humility, Peter said, "God made me tall and strong for a purpose, and I intend to use every ounce of it against the lobster backs that are trying to rob us of our freedom. They are gripping us with fear and forcing us to make unwise plans for the future. With God's help, I won't let it continue. I'll be going back into battle this spring and taking care of Tarleton myself."

Peter stood up, took off his tri-corn, and tilted it forward in his hand. "Good day, Mr. Anderson."

Peter smiled as he walked down the steps of the porch, knowing that he now had a glimmer of hope in the fight for Susannah's hand.

★

As winter set in, Peter and Susannah spent time together whenever they could. Peter also spent a good deal of time with Thomas, keeping up with the never-ending needs around the plantation as well as the preparations for the next season's planting. Following Judge Winston's lead, the Andersons also devoted a vast majority of their acreage to planting hemp that could be converted to rope and used on American ships.

As anticipated, news arrived that Lord Cornwallis was raiding across the Carolinas, wreaking havoc and destruction. The utter defeat of the Colonials at Camden had set the war effort back a good deal. In fact, the Continental Congress was so upset by the loss that they authorized General Washington to appoint a new commander to lead the army in the south. This was good news for Peter, for although he admired what General Gates had done at Saratoga, he viewed what took place at Camden as simply inexcusable. In Gates' place came General Nathanael Greene, who was a New England Quaker.

Word eventually came that Captain Watkins was ready to put his unit in the field, so Peter once again had to bid farewell and set off for war.

As Peter was readying his horse in the barn, Susannah came in carrying a small bundle in her hands. Even though he was aware of her presence, he didn't look up. He was afraid she'd see the tears forming in his eyes.

She walked over to him and presented the small parcel. "I wanted to give these back to you before you left. I ... It's not right for me to have them."

Peter looked at the package, then at her. He knew what was inside without asking. He pushed it back. With pain in his heart, he said in a hushed tone, "I first gave boneca de trapo to you as a way to remember me, to keep me close when I couldn't be here. That key, I forged as a pledge to you. A promise. One I don't intend to break. I want you to keep them, so you don't forget."

Susannah was so consumed with feeling, all she could manage was a slight nod.

"May I ... still keep your handkerchief?" Peter asked.

"Of course," she breathed.

He kissed her forehead softly, lingering for a moment, then mounted his steed, uttered a simple command and galloped down the path, the pain in his heart—worse than any bayonet—piercing him with every pace.

★

On January 17, 1781, the Virginia giant was back in South Carolina for the Battle of Cowpens. His cavalry unit, among dozens of others, would be facing the Legion of Banastre Tarleton.

Lord Cornwallis had learned that American troops, under the command of General Daniel Morgan, were traveling in the western part of the state. His plan was to lure the colonials into a trap by having Tarleton and his troops either crush the patriots or push them toward his army stationed at King's Mountain.

But Morgan was a marvelous tactician, skillfully luring Tarleton into a trap of his own. Each of the armies had about 1,000 men. Peter was among eighty cavalrymen in this battle that began at seven in the morning, but it wasn't much of a battle. In a little less than an hour, over one hundred of Tarleton's men had been killed and the rest, mostly captured.

At one point during the battle, Peter espied Lt. Colonel William Washington, a relative of the great general, dueling on horseback with Tarleton himself. Peter seized the opportunity. The ache in his heart from leaving Susannah was still fresh. He was still fuming at Anderson for rejecting him in favor of that sick Carrington. And even more enraged that George had beaten him. He was determined to conquer something, so he channeled these churning emotions into a mad force and drove straight for

Tarleton as hard as he could, yelling at the top of his lungs. The continental defender charged the animal right into Tarleton's mount, just as he was about to land a blow to Washington. Tarleton's steed regained its balance, and the British colonel slashed back at Peter. Their swords met in midair and sparks flashed as the two blades gleamed in the sunlight. Peter looked directly into the eyes of his opponent's lifeless, unfeeling eyes, as black and hardened as coal. Spittle flew from Tarleton's mouth.

Peter knew Tarleton's reputation. He knew what the swine was capable of. He wanted desperately to keep him from ever getting to Virginia or anywhere near the people he loved. "I'm going to end your military career right here, right now, you bloody lobster back." Again, their swords clinked and flashed, each parrying the other's attempted blow. Their horses flanked, both men threw all their strength into every swing, and their vociferating shouts seemed to echo the cacophony of the cannon. The earth exploded around them, and drifting smoke from the musket fire nearly obscured them from view.

"What's wrong, slave?" Tarleton bellowed with sarcasm. "Didn't your master teach you how to swing a sword?"

Peter's mind raced. *Slave? How would he know that? Who has he been talking to? Does he know about the Winstons? The Andersons? Susannah?* Panic quickly turned to rage at the mere thought that Tarleton might know where the people he loved lay their heads.

Their swords clashed violently, as Peter snarled back, "I would drive this sword right through your heart, if you had one, you callous bastard." Peter waited, squinted his left eye, clenched his teeth, and glowered into Tarleton's eyes down to his hardened soul. "But don't worry," he seethed. "I'll still kill you."

369

The two men bore into each other with antagonized hatred then wrenched back their swords. Swinging with every ounce of muscle and force behind them, their swords collided in one final blow and snapped clear at the hilt. Without the swords to bear their weight, the inertia from the impact kept their bodies moving forward, propelling both men off their horses and landing them prostrate in the dirt.

Pain shot through Peter's face, and he noticed blood dripping from his nose as he slowly picked himself off the battlefield. *Is it broken?* He wondered. Before he could stand straight, he felt a boot smash into his rib cage, sending him back to the ground.

"I hope you've made peace with God, slave, because you're about to go meet Him," Tarleton sneered, producing his pistol, cocked and aimed at Peter's head.

Lying there doubled over in pain, Peter knew he had to act fast or Tarleton would make good on his promise. His fingers still curled around the handle of the sword, he quickly let go. With instinctive reflexes, Peter rolled to one side and extended his right arm, grabbing a rifle recently orphaned by a dead soldier. In one swift motion, he gripped the barrel of the gun and with all his strength swung the butt into the calves of his enemy, breaking his balance. Tarleton's pistol fired once as it sailed into the air, launching a musket ball into heaven as he landed flat on his back.

Peter jumped to his feet. *Now, I have the advantage,* he thought. But Tarleton's reflexes were just as quick. Without weapons, both men were reduced to dueling with their fists. Within moments, Peter realized his height was raining his punches down on Tarleton like cannon balls. *Maybe if I swing down and up, I'll knock him off his feet,* Peter thought. He knew he must outweigh his nemesis

370

by nearly one hundred pounds, and his next hook lifted Tarleton clear off the ground and threw him at the feet of another British soldier who had been dodging musket fire and wading through thick smoke to deliver an urgent message.

"Lieutenant-Colonel, sir! This battle is disastrous, and your men are retreating. If you don't rally the troops, we will surely fail the King!" the young man blurted.

Fearing his military career was in jeopardy, Tarleton picked himself off the ground with the help of his messenger. Wincing in pain from Peter's blow, he touched his ribs to see if one of them was broken, then slowly mounted his steed.

"There'll be another day, another time, another battlefield, giant," Tarleton snarled, spewing vitriol. "I'll not rest until I have you and everyone who has ever meant anything to you at the end of my sword." Tarleton pulled the reins to the side and galloped off as Peter mounted his horse, which he reared up on its hind legs.

Before Tarleton was out of earshot, he shouted, "I'll hunt you down and have your head on a platter before that happens, you bloody coward!"

Despite Tarleton's successful escape, the Americans, having lost only twelve men, were rewarded with a resounding victory. Peter, still on his horse, was feeling far from victorious. Regret and disappointment flooded his heart not only at his failure to end the life of that vile tyrant but also at his inability to spare the innocent lives that would now suffer under his evil hand.

After the Battle of Cowpens, Peter was assigned as the personal aide to Lt. Colonel William Washington, the second cousin of General George Washington.

Both the British and American armies were quite low on supplies as they played a cat and mouse game throughout North Carolina. General Nathanael Greene faced the never-ending dilemma that had haunted colonial forces since the war began—a shortage of supplies and, more importantly, men. As for the British, Lord Cornwallis wanted to seek out and destroy the Americans before his supplies were depleted.

After Cowpens, Cornwallis had been furious. He became absolutely bent on razing the army that had inflicted such a painful loss on his forces. Greene, on the other hand, knew he had to somehow re-supply both troops and necessities. In order to further thwart Cornwallis' efforts, he decided to split his forces between himself and General Daniel Morgan, who had masterminded the Cowpens victory.

Cornwallis became so frustrated with American tactics that he decided to make his army even lighter and faster, so even though he was short on material, he ordered his supply wagons burned, along with many of the badly needed stores that they carried.

Meanwhile, Greene had his armies cross back and forth over the border between North Carolina and Virginia. Once again, the call went out for men to volunteer for local militias, and the call was met. After a few weeks, hundreds of militia from both North Carolina and Virginia helped swell Greene's strength to nearly 4,500 men, although the exact number was never known, since volunteers could come and go as they pleased. Many of them did just that. There was, however, a core of 1,600 Continental Army regulars, as well as members of the militia, who had seen extensive action in other campaigns. Peter Francisco was among them.

All of this casting about soon came to an abrupt end at a

place called Guilford Courthouse in North Carolina. On March 12, 1781, General Greene marched his troops to within twenty miles of the fateful battleground, having heard that Cornwallis had withdrawn his army to a location near there. A new camp was set up, but everyone knew that they would not be there long. That evening, among myriad campfires and tents, each man prepared in his own way for the events that were about to unfold. Some of the soldiers bedded down early to get some extra rest. Others sat around the warming fires and told stories and jokes. Peter took advantage of the quiet time and went off in solitude to pray. Cradled in his right hand was Arthur's Bible. He found a spot near the trees and knelt down. He tilted his head forward, letting it rest on his thumb and index finger.

"Father, thank you for your many blessings. Thank you for keeping us safe thus far. Please be with each and every man in this camp who has fought so valiantly. Continue to give them the strength to press on. May the outcome of the war be as you desire. Please watch over the innocent lives back home—the Andersons—especially Susannah. Please protect those who will come to suffer at Tarleton's hand. And, if it be Your will, Lord, I ask that you grant me personal victory over Tarleton himself. Amen."

Before he settled in for the night, Peter put the training he received under Baron von Steuben to good use as he prepared for battle. He made sure that his musket was clean and ready for action, that the barrel was dirt free, and that the firing mechanism was in good working condition. Additionally, Peter checked his ammunition satchel to make sure that he had plenty of musket balls and pellets. He wasn't anticipating that he would use his musket much, but it was always best to be prepared because in his experience, battles seldom went exactly as planned. Then he set about shining and polishing his bayonet. Long ago he had noticed how the British troops, with their bayonets gleaming in the sunlight, could be so intimidating, especially to those colonials who had never seen battle before. Although he hated the British, he admired their tactics, right down to the last detail. Therefore, he put a high sheen on his saber. He figured he would soon be using it to cut down enemy soldiers from his position on horseback alongside Colonel Washington. He only wished he hadn't lost his sword during the Battle of Cowpens. He had searched the weapons supply in vain for something more substantial, but every sword he found was even smaller than his last.

21.

A GIFT FROM WASHINGTON

THE NEXT MORNING, everyone in camp was surprised and thankful to see that General George Washington had sent a supply wagon train to General Greene's camp. Among the supplies were food and clothing, for which the men were most grateful, because many were barefoot and shirtless.

One item was of particular interest. It was a crate, small in every dimension except length—it was nearly seven-feet long—and was addressed to Lt. Colonel William Washington. He was in his tent when the item was delivered to him, and several men gathered around to see what it was. Before long, Colonel Washington came out joined them.

"What's in the crate?" one of the men asked.

"Yeah, what did you get, Colonel?" another inquired.

Colonel Washington didn't respond but instead inquired after

Pvt. Peter Francisco.

"After he helped unload the supply wagons, I think I saw him go up to the horse pen. Peter loves his horses, you know," one of the men acknowledged.

Colonel Washington headed off in the direction of the horse pen, and, sure enough, there stood the Virginia Giant, currying his horse and talking gently in one of her ears.

"Peter," the Colonel called as he approached. "Peter, I need you to come with me. I have something I'd like you to see."

Peter left the horse pen, taking care to replace the rail through which he had entered. "What is it, Colonel? Have I done something wrong?"

"No Peter, you've not done anything wrong. It's just something I'd like to show you. I need your opinion."

As the two men walked back to Colonel Washington's tent in silence, Peter had a dozen questions he wanted to pepper the colonel with, but, out of respect for his superior officer, he held himself in check. *What on earth could it be?* He wondered. The colonel provided no clues.

When they arrived back at the colonel's tent, Washington pulled back the flap to allow Peter to enter. This was unusual since officers always entered first, especially before privates. Being full daylight, it took a few moments for Peter's eyes to become accustomed to the dark shade, which the tent provided.

Lying on Colonel Washington's cot was a five-foot blade, six feet in length. *The sword that Lafayette had spoken about when we were recovering at Brandywine! General Washington has sent me a proper fighting weapon! Never again will my sword shatter like it did in the duel against Tarleton.* Peter was speechless.

"What do you think, Peter?" Colonel Washington asked, breaking the silence. "My cousin, the general, had this especially made for you."

In a somewhat hypnotic state, never moving his eyes from the stretched sword, Peter blurted, "Oh, she's a beaut." With respect and a fierce resolve, he continued, "Colonel, I'll use this weapon to eliminate our enemies. I'll proudly carry it into battle. I swear by all that's holy, I cannot wait to meet Colonel Tarleton again on the battlefield, where he'll taste my steel. And I'm humbled that General Washington would take the time to have this made for me, a simple private."

"That's something else I wanted to talk to you about, Peter. General Greene has seen fit to offer you a battlefield commission. You are to be an officer, Peter. What do you think of that?"

"It is a great honor, truly it is. But," Francisco spoke with a pang of regret, "I must decline, sir."

"But why, Peter?"

"I know that officers need to read and write reports, but I have the skills for neither."

"Peter, I had no idea. What I do know is that you have served our new country well. You have been valiant in every respect. You have won the admiration of everyone with whom you have served, and your name shall be recorded in the annals as a true patriot. As I've heard my cousin say on more than one occasion, you really are the Hercules of the Revolution, and now you have the sword to prove it."

"Thank you, sir. Your words mean a great deal to me. I have sought no honor, only freedom from tyranny and protection for my family and friends. And now, with this sword, I'll no longer be waving a little stick at my enemies." A sinister smile spread across his face as he ran an admiring hand carefully, over the gleaming blade and the well-crafted handle and imagined his next encounter with Tarleton.

The colonel and Peter exchanged handshakes. When he opened the tent flap to go outside, a large crowd of men had gathered still wanting to know what was in the crate. Proud of his sword, Peter held it high above his head. His height combined with the length of the sword seemed to reach up and touch the sun that reflected in a flash of light off the blade, dancing brilliantly for all those assembled to see.

"Good Lord, do you see the size of that thing?" one man was heard to say.

"This must be a sign from God that victory is ahead," gloated another.

"Hooray for Peter Francisco!" Just as at Camden, the chant, started with one man, but soon dozens chimed in, all cheering simultaneously. "Hooray for Peter Francisco! Hooray for Peter Francisco!"

For the remainder of the day, soldiers from all around camp approached Peter, wanting a look at the sword. It was by far the biggest that any of them had ever seen, and they marveled at how easily he could wield it. He practiced repeatedly, whipping tightly it back and forth through the air, preparing himself for the time when he could unleash it on the British and that wretched Tarleton.

That night Peter slept with his new sword at his side, waking the next morning with novel purpose. He asked one of the mountain men, whom he had met through John Allen, to help him

378

craft a scabbard from a tanned cowhide to strap across his back to carry the prized blade. He polished the sword until he could see his own mirrored reflection split across the two edges of the blade. Something he didn't often have the opportunity to do. He tilted it back and forth to see as much of himself as he could. He pondered his size—his thick, sinewy neck and broad shoulders. *Am I really as big as everyone says?* He honestly didn't think of himself that giant. He just thought everyone else was really small. Regardless, he knew he had what it took to beat Tarleton, and he hoped to get the chance.

The next morning, the newly-supplied Americans bolstered their strength and endurance by consuming a hearty breakfast. Additionally, each soldier received a measure of rum. The hard ground, covered in thick frost, crunched beneath the soldiers and horses, amplifying their footfalls as they took their places for battle. In the chilled morning air, their warm breath ascended toward heaven like silent ministrations.

General Greene deployed his forces in three lines that stretched across New Garden Road, which ran through the center of the battlefield.

For the Americans, the first line consisted of North Carolina militia. These men found some protection behind a rail fence from which to fire upon the advancing British. On their flanks were the mountain men with their long rifles, as well as the cavalry units, including Peter Francisco and Colonel William Washington on the right. Two six-pound cannon sat on either side of the road.

The second line of colonials—about three hundred and fifty yards behind the first—was made up of the Virginia militia as well as some Continental army veterans. The most seasoned troops, some 1,400 of them, from Virginia, Delaware and Maryland, were the third and last line. This line also had two more cannon.

The plan was to have the mountain men use their long guns to pick off at a distance the advancing British, a tactic that the British could not counter. Then, once the English were in range, the first line would fire two volleys and fall back in an orderly fashion. As before at the battle at Camden, these troops were told to fire twice and hold their ground until the retreat was called or they would be shot by the defenders in the second line. Although the threat had not been taken seriously at Camden, most of the front line soldiers were convinced that the orders would be carried out this time. The cavalry would remain in reserve unless needed. They, too, were to fall back with the first line, thus supporting the second and eventually the third line of defenders.

As General Greene took note of his troop placements, he was quite pleased and secure in his battle plan. One other aspect gave the general cause for confidence, and that was that the terrain offered an unexpected advantage. Each of his lines was at a slightly higher elevation than the one preceding. Therefore, the British would have an uphill battle every inch of the way.

As for Cornwallis, even though his forces were far inferior in numbers, he was confident that his proficient soldiers would carry the day. With information that his opponent was just ten miles away, the British general ordered his troops to begin their march at 5:30 in the morning. Unlike the Americans, they had little food for breakfast. At about noon, Cornwallis arrived to take stock of the battlefield. He could see the rail fence behind which Greene's first line was hiding. He saw the wooded area on either side where the mountain men and cavalries were lying in wait.

Peter, donning his new sword strapped across his back and sitting astride his horse next to Colonel Washington, reached into his satchel and took out the buckles that were wrapped in Susannah's handkerchief.

Com Jesus me deito (With Jesus I go to sleep),
Com Jesus me levanto (With Jesus I awake),
Com a graça de Deus (With the grace of God),
E do Espirito Santo (and of the Holy Spirit),
Eu vou para a batalha (I go into battle.)

Placing the items back in his pouch, Peter readied himself mentally. Summoning the angst he felt toward Tarleton and the freedom that was ripped from him so long ago—the same freedom that the British were trying to take from him now—and thinking about his Susannah soon becoming the wife of that blasted Carrington, he channeled all his energy into focusing on this important battle.

It was one o'clock in the afternoon. Cornwallis, in an attempt to draw some fire so that he could better determine exactly where the Americans were, brought up his artillery, but the Americans beat them to the punch and fired their cannon first. The British responded in kind and the resounding boom echoed across the field, which seemed to penetrate straight through the earth beneath them. Cornwallis' men formed their ranks and began their traditional attack, marching in step as they moved toward the American front lines. As these troops drew within one hundred and fifty yards of the fence, shots rang out from both flanks as the mountain men took careful aim and drew down on their targets. British soldiers, pawns in the cruel game of battle, began to fall. The front line of Americans used the fence rails to steady their aim and cut loose with a fusillade of musket fire. Wide gaps began appearing in the British line, but still they kept coming.

As the 33rd Regiment of Foot neared to within thirty yards, they fired on the Americans with their own volley. Smoke and musket balls filled the air. Some of Greene's troops fell under the withering fire. Unlike in the past, however, most of the militia stood fast, reloaded and got another volley off at the enemy with deadly accuracy.

Then, unfazed by the number of their fellow soldiers who had already fallen, the British regiment initiated its classic bayonet charge, a most formidable sight. Much to General Greene's dismay, the center of his first line disintegrated in fear and cowardice and made a mad dash rearward. The riflemen and cavalry on the flanks, including Peter's unit, were far more orderly in the planned retreat and also provided deadly covering fire for those troops heading for the second line of defense.

The British, under the command of Colonel James Webster, were suffering terrible casualties, but they continued their forward advance. As the infantry approached the second of Greene's lines, they quickly realized that they would be facing a far more defiant foe. The Virginia militia was considerably different than the first line North Carolinians. Many of them had been regulars, and there was a smattering of long-riflemen sprinkled among them.

As before, the long rifles spoke first as the English came within range. The Redcoats continued to see their ranks thinning, but they were powerless to remedy the loss. Some, both on the far left and right, sought shelter in the woods. Colonel Washington, along with Peter Francisco and the cavalry, sprang into action.

As was his custom, Washington led the charge with Peter to his immediate right, who had unsheathed his massive broadsword. Within moments, he had cut down two of the British troopers with crashed blows. A few of the lobster backs, seeing the massive sword, did their very best not to confront the giant Portuguese, preferring instead to choose lesser targets to fight.

As seconds turned into minutes, the fighting became so intense that soldiers on either side, confused in the fray, could scarcely make out what was going on. The second line kept firing unlike the first line with its fire-two-shots-and-run scheme. Men were shooting and reloading again as fast as they could, some as many as fourteen times, clouding the field and obscuring their vision with thick smoke. When visibility became next to impossible, Greene ordered the orderly retreat that would meld his second line with his third.

Peter's cavalry withdrew as ordered, but not until the six-foot sword had eliminated yet two more of the enemy. As they reached the third of General Greene's lines, the cavalry pulled their horses about and prepared to clash once again with the advancing British. One trooper charged at Peter with his bayonet raised. Peter brought his sword down and shattered the man's musket. Then with a swift backhand motion, the steel in his hand cruelly removed the soldier's head. The man's body fell onto Peter's horse, leaving a trail of blood down the side of the animal.

Another of the enemy charged at Peter's horse, causing the animal to rear up and throw its rider to the ground. Incredibly nimble, Peter was on his feet before the soldier could finish him off. As the Redcoat charged at him, the Virginian brandished his weapon and pulled it through a wide arc; the blade cut entirely through the man at mid-torso. His upper body fell to the ground, before his legs, in a ghostlike manner, took a few more steps.

Observing a number of British infantry crowded around Colonel Washington, Peter sprinted to protect the officer for whom he felt great personal responsibility. His blade rose and fell, swirling through the thickened gun smoke as he charged across the battlefield on foot. One blow removed the arm, shoulder and a portion of the upper chest of his opponent. Another, not quite as well-aimed, caused the sharp blade to be off-target. The mass of the blade itself, having been swung with such ferocity by such a large man, seemed to break every bone in the soldier's upper body. Anyone nearby could hear the sound of bones crunching.

Seeing that his colonel was at least temporarily out of harm's way, Peter found his horse and mounted in order to more effectively fight and chase the British. Just as he fastened his seat into his saddle, a grenadier appeared out the smoke and drove his bayonet deep into Peter's left calf, so far that Peter was actually pinned to his horse. Fearing that a sudden move would cost him his leg, he motioned for the Redcoat to step back. But the soldier had not seen the fearsome weapon Peter held on the other side of the horse, which he had already dexterously used to dispatch eight of his opponent's compatriots. As the British soldier withdrew his blade, he stepped back and positioned himself to make another thrust. Peter's sword, however, caught a narrow stream of sunlight that had somehow found its way through the smoky air, and for the briefest second, the Redcoat looked up and spied that which would end his life. Peter, using just one hand operated by the power of his huge forearms, brought the sword down with such force that it struck the soldier on the crown of his head, splitting the skull open and continuing into the shoulder. When he lifted it away, the man's body continued forward for a moment before collapsing to the ground.

Through the haze, Peter could see that the British cavalry had been ordered into the battle, no doubt led by bloodthirsty Colonel Banastre Tarleton. Squinting through the dissipating smoke, Peter scanned the scene for the man he sought to eliminate. In the distance, he spotted his target wearing his legion's distinctive headgear and officer's coat. Peter's eyes narrowed. The wound in his lower leg pounded furiously, but the pain dulled at the sight of Tarleton. Anger shot through him. Though his breathing was already labored, Peter's chest heaved as he exhaled with considerable force. He could feel the blood coursing through his veins. Ending Tarleton's life became Peter's only goal. Weary as he was, his leg throbbing, he summoned the strength from somewhere deep within, channeling his anger like a wave crashing to shore. He heard his own blood-curdling cry as he charged his horse in the direction of the British officer. Two of Tarleton's men saw where he was heading and together charged him from the side. Their horses rammed his steed. Peter grasped his sword with two hands and brought it around, cutting through the air deftly. In one flash of steel, the Virginia giant simultaneously cut the heads off both attacking members of Tarleton's legion.

Remembering his objective, Peter realized that he'd lost sight of Tarleton. In a panic, he scanned the field. As quickly as he had disappeared, Tarleton came back into view, challenging Peter to a duel, a dare which Peter was more than ready to accept. He jammed his heels into the sides of his horse and goaded the animal on toward the British colonel. Being so focused on his intended target, however, he hadn't noticed a group of British infantry with bayonets pointed upward, forming a traditional square of defense between Peter and Tarleton. As Peter reached them, one lunged forward, driving his bayonet into Peter's flesh just above the right knee, and the momentum of his horse drove the blade up his leg near the hip. His horse toppled, and Peter was thrown to the ground.

Though the battle raged on, time for Peter stood still. He buckled under the intense pain, unable to focus on anything else. The offending trooper was looming over him ready to make a final thrust into the massive chest of the Portuguese. Under his breath, Tarleton muttered, "Kill him. Kill him." Mentally, Peter prepared to die. But as the man lifted his weapon for the final plunge, his own chest exploded.

Cornwallis, seeing that his forces were badly slaughtered, had ordered his cannon loaded with grapeshot and fired into the midst of the fiercest fighting. His own officers had argued against this action, but the general thought it was the only way to end to the carnage. Both American and British soldiers were mutilated by the onslaught, but the British rearguard was able to retreat, including Tarleton, who was determined more now than ever to eliminate all those for whom Peter ever cared.

General Greene decided to abandon the field rather than risk losing any more of his forces. With such serious injuries, Peter was left to die. Drifting in and out of consciousness, he intermittently felt the overwhelming pain in his leg. None of his previous wounds compared to this one. Not the musket ball at Germantown. Not the ball that he still carried in his thigh as a result of action at Monmouth, not the nine-inch slash that had cut his belly open, not the bayonet by the grenadier that he had taken in his left calf while on the horse. The slightest stir of the breeze against the open wound was enough to make Peter to cry out, yet he could not find the voice or strength to do so. After a while, he noticed a large oak tree several yards away. He mustered what little strength he could and slowly, inch-by-inch, dragged himself over to it and leaned against its trunk, waiting for death. The sounds of battle receded. Pluming clouds from the musket fire had dissipated into a translucent haze lingering with the smell of burnt black powder and a rusty odor that Peter could only assume was blood.

Both of the armies had given up the field, though the British remained in close proximity. Technically, the British were the victors, but Cornwallis had lost better than a quarter of his men. The reality was that the conflict would serve to signal the beginning of the end, as Cornwallis would embark on a course that would lead to the closing stages of British colonial occupation.

Bleeding next to the oak tree, all Peter knew was that death was all around him. Bodies spotted the field, in some places, atop one another. Every so often, he heard high-pitched moans coming from somewhere on the field, as some tried to stay alive and others succumbed to encroaching death.

As more cries reached his ears, haunting him in the silence, Peter could take it no longer. In his exceedingly weakened condition, he crawled in the direction of the loudest moans, reaching one of his fellow cavalrymen. With his long arm, he reached out and fumbled to grab some material of the man's uniform. Finally, with a fistful of shirt, he slowly, painfully pulled the man over to the oak. He was more than spent, but he couldn't ignore the groans and cries escaping around him. He repeated this rescue mission three more times, and, each time, he returned to the same tree with another brave soldier.

The afternoon wore on until dusk began to settle over the hundreds of decaying and dying bodies. Peter drifted in and out of consciousness. He saw himself as a little boy in the Azores Islands with his momma and papa; Edna Watkins, the kind lady who had fed and clothed him when he was abandoned on a Virginia dock; and Arthur, who had not only become an earthly father to him but also introduced him to his heavenly Father; he could see Judge Winston, who had given him a home and a purpose for almost a decade; he saw the Marquis de Lafayette, who was almost like a brother; and John Allen, the mountain man who had befriended him. Most of all, he thought of beautiful Susannah, who would always be in his heart. How he wished he could compose a letter to her now as he took in his final breaths. *What would become of her? At least she will be well taken care of.*

Rain showers began to fall softly, as though tears from God's eyes. The downpour followed. Peter's head slumped on his chest. Rainwater saturated his hair and garments, eventually trickling down his face to his lips, and the same gurgling sound that had signaled the end for John Allen slipped from his mouth.

388

22.

LEFT FOR DEAD

ALTHOUGH THE BRITISH had maintained control of the battlefield, for them, it was a hollow victory. Charles James Fox, a vocal critic of the war, would later proclaim, "Another such victory would ruin the British army." Eventually, with Greene's forces in pursuit, Cornwallis would retreat all the way to Wilmington, North Carolina.

In the meantime, General Greene had been aware that there was a large number of Quakers, much like himself, who were living in the area. From his own upbringing, he knew that those of his faith were widely recognized as caring and empathetic and adept at tending to the ill and injured. He sent out a request that those nearby farmers search the battlefield and offer aid and comfort to any wounded soldiers, regardless of their affiliation in the conflict. They did so by the hundreds. Almost every farmhouse in

the vicinity, in addition to the Guilford Courthouse, was converted into a makeshift hospital.

One Quaker by the name of John Robinson came across a
gruesome sight. A giant man lay propped up against an old oak
tree. Based on his readings, he wondered briefly if this man suffered from elephantiasis. The wound on his left leg oozed, but
it was not very large. His right leg, however, was laid bare to
the bone. Around him were the bodies of four men. Robinson
checked on the four smaller soldiers, and then turned his attention toward Peter. As Robinson shook him by the shoulder, Peter
was in a deep state of unconsciousness. He felt the hand on his
shoulder. *I must be in heaven,* he thought. *Is that God waking me?*
Will I see John Allen? Arthur? The shaking continued and eventually he opened his eyes to see a man with a narrow face and a
long nose peering down at him. His face was clean-shaven, and
his long, wispy hair was held in place by a short, wide-brimmed
hat. He had what looked like a scarf tied around his neck. His big
gray eyes seemed kind. The man uttered words that Peter didn't
think he would ever forget. "My name is Robinson, and I have
come to comfort thee."

Peter could not speak. Even if he could have summoned the
energy, he had no words to say. He felt several men lift him and
carry him to a nearby wagon. Peter wanted to ask about the men
he had tried to save. He wanted to ask about his sword. But he
couldn't find the strength. Instead, he drifted to a world of darkness, where pain was the only constant.

Robinson transported him to their nearby farm where Martha Robinson was preparing to receive the wounded. She had
cut bed linens to serve as bandages, and she had boiled water on

the surface of the wood stove for cleansing wounds and bathing the injured. Several barrels had been brought in from the barn. Spanned across them were heavy wooden planks, which were provisioned as beds. When several men entered carrying Peter, Mrs. Robinson gasped at his size. She quickly located a few extra planks and stacked them on an existing set to reinforce their ability to bear this huge man's weight.

Looking at Peter's leg, she frowned. Saying to no one in particular, "I know not if I possess the skills to stem the blood from a wound this size." Despite her misgivings, she set about to cleaning the wound with cloths dipped in hot water to limit the possibility of infection. Though she did so as gently as she possibly could, with each touch to the gaping gash, Peter cried softly in his stupor. Mrs. Robinson instructed two men to hold the Virginia giant still, and she covered his face with a cloth for fear that he might fully wake and go into shock. Working feverishly, she ignored lesser-wounded men to attend to Peter. She tried her best to move muscle and tissue into their proper places. Every now and again, she would use simple needle and thread to cinch vital parts together. Once she was satisfied with her progress, she began to sew the entire wound closed, using little more than the skills she had acquired making clothing for her family. She had also attended to the less serious wound in the calf of his other leg. Before she was finished, Martha Robinson had spent almost as much time on this one patient as the battle itself had taken.

Again, it took several men to lift Peter's bulk and move him to a bedroom in the rear of the house. Lying on that bed, which once more had to be rigged to accommodate his height, Peter fell into a deep and long-lasting slumber. For three days, Mrs. Robinson regularly checked on her patient.

Since taking care of him, John Robinson's wife had tended to and sewn all sorts of wounds, but none as serious as Peter's. She had dug musket balls from the bodies of soldiers, both American and British, but none of their injuries had been as challenging. As a result, she had taken a special interest in the tall soldier.

By mid-afternoon on the third day, Peter started to rouse from his peaceful state. Martha noticed this and kept checking on him even more frequently. At long last, he struggled to open his eyes, and he saw yet another strange face looking at his. Her wide, friendly smile caused her eyes to narrow behind her spectacles. A delicate-looking bonnet loosely surrounded her face and tied neatly under her chin. He sensed she had a gentle spirit. Attempting to speak, he felt as though his throat was full of sawdust. Martha pulled a chair near the edge of the bed to listen and placed a soft hand on his arm. Her voice was so subdued, it was nearly a whisper. "Speak not, for thou hast suffered a great wound. Thou needest all thy strength to heal, so rest if thou wouldst."

Peter could not resist. His head was filled with questions and they spilled out of his mouth before he could stop them. "Where am I? What happened? What of the soldiers I dragged from the battlefield? Where is my sword? How is my horse?"

"I see thou art not accustomed to following instruction, so I shall answer thy questions, but thou must promise to rest and not become excited."

"I promise," Peter spoke hoarsely.

"Thou art at the farm of mine husband, John. Thou wert brought here three, perhaps now four, nights ago. It seems that I have lost all sense of time. Thy leg wound is one of the worst I have seen. With the grace and guidance of God, I do pray I have been able to provide proper care to help thee heal. As for the soldiers whom mine husband found gathered 'round thee … none survived. Thy horse, I cannot say, but a vast many lay dead on the field. Even now, men are gathering their remains for proper disposal before they decay. As to thy sword, one of our neighbors found one; 'twas taller than he! He brought it here thinking thou wert the only man large enough to carry it. I will have it brought to thee, but now I ask thee to recall our agreement. Rest for now, and I shall bring thee some broth."

Peter did as instructed and rested his wounded body. Even though soup wasn't his favorite, he was grateful for anything. He was even more grateful to these kind people for saving his life.

In only a few minutes Martha returned with a bowl of steaming broth. He shifted himself into a nearly seated position, but Mrs. Robinson insisted on spoon-feeding him. She was obviously quite skilled in the practice, for she didn't spill a single drop. This gave Peter an opportunity to further study her appearance. She was slightly rotund. Her hands were aged beyond her years. Over her plain brown dress, she wore a white apron, which Peter saw had been mottled with bloodstains that wouldn't wash out. Just as she finished, a man entered the room. The long, narrow face belonged to the man who had found Peter leaning against the oak tree on the battlefield.

"I believe this belongs to thee," James Robinson said as he carried Peter's broadsword and laid it next to the bed. "I have taken the time to clean its blade of all the blood which rested upon it."

The effort of eating had expended what little energy Peter

could muster. All he could say was a weak, "Thank you." Sliding back down in the bed, he again fell sound asleep.

Over the next several weeks, Martha Robinson nursed her patient back to health. After nearly a month of bed rest, he started to walk around the Robinson farm, slowly regaining his strength. Most of the time he'd walk alone, but, occasionally, he'd join other recuperating soldiers. During one such walk, Peter overheard two of the men discussing a letter one of the officers had received.

"Who could even think about getting married during a time like this, when the war is so close to home?" one soldier scoffed, limping with a crutch at his side.

"True," his friend agreed, "I can't see many people attending when all they can think about is protecting their families, their livelihood."

"From what I understand, it was all somewhat rushed. John said in his letter, in so many words, Carrington indicated that he wanted it to be a done deal before the war came to Buckingham. The rest was cryptic."

"So, when is the wedding? Did Carrington mention a date?"

"Yes, that part I do remember because John showed me the invitation, saying he probably wouldn't get back home in time. And I recall the date being somewhat cryptic." The man tapped his finger against his lips in concentration. "Three cycles past new moon, for the first day of celebration."

"So, approximately twenty-six May," he concluded, doing a quick calculation based on the current phase.

Peter's mind spun upon hearing this news. There was no need to inquire who they were referring to. He wasn't sure he would make it back in time, either. *So, it's really happening*, he thought, letting the finality of it sink in. *There has to be something I can do.* He thought, enraged. *I'll work harder to rehabilitate myself. I'll leave early if I have to. I have to find a way to stop it.* He would never be the same if Susannah married George. Peter was concentrating so hard on finding a way to reach Susannah, he missed part of the soldiers' conversation.

"And this part I remember," the soldier continued. "The invitation-letter suggested the wedding would take place in a clandestine location in the morning and kept referring to it as the 'gathering.'"

"Probably intentional in case it got intercepted," his friend said, offering an explanation.

"John said that in the letter, information on the location would 'follow,' but I suspect the 'gathering' won't be at Anderson's plantation," he replied.

After contemplating it for several weeks, Peter resolved to make it back in time before he lost Susannah forever. A month later, in mid-May, after bidding farewell and expressing much gratitude to the family that had taken him in and compassionately cared for him, Peter set out on a two-hundred-mile journey back to Virginia. Walking all the way in the direction of The Mansion, Peter was able to regain strength in both legs, which had been mutilated and scarred in so many battles. His pace was steady and measured, and a trip that would ordinarily take him weeks, he was able to shave down to just ten days. He slept less. He trudged through heavy downpours, pushing through the pain in his leg. All the while, he told himself over and over, *I'm coming for you, Susannah.*

★

The war continued. Cornwallis, after retreating to Wilmington, determined that his best course of action was to march his remaining troops up the East Coast of North Carolina and into Virginia. He had also given Tarleton orders to go in advance of the main body of troops. Specifically, Tarleton's instructions were to destroy food stores but leave enough food so that the civilians could continue to at least feed themselves. The point of the directive was to deny the American forces of food and supplies that could be used to strengthen the colonials.

However, Tarleton had always had his own way of interpreting orders. He had shown such a bent in the past when he allowed his men to indiscriminately kill those who were unarmed, even women and children. Thus, Tarleton and his men set about ravaging the Virginia countryside. Six weeks after the Battle of Guilford Courthouse, Tarleton and his men swept down on Cumberland County. He had not forgotten the Virginia Giant and had learned that Peter lived on a plantation called The Mansion. After a few days of searching, Tarleton was satisfied that he knew the location of The Mansion. He intended now to make good on his threat to destroy his hated opponent as well as all those he cared about.

Arriving at the plantation in the early hours of the evening of May 22, he conducted a personal search. He and his men crept up the stairs, rummaged through every room, opened every door, and turned every mattress. The house, barn, and slave cabins were completely empty.

Tarleton was livid. His prey had escaped his sword, but he

396

had no knowledge that Peter Francisco had not even been at The Mansion for months and that only now was he making his way there from North Carolina. Finally satisfying himself that the plantation was vacant, Tarleton ordered it put to the torch.

The night sky grew lurid with the ginger glow cast by the flames as every building was burned to the ground. Fires were also set throughout the fields to singe the first shoots of crops rendering them useless. Tarleton sat astride his horse on the very spot where Peter had bid farewell to his dear Susannah. He was not pleased that his personal objective had not been achieved, but there was a certain satisfaction as he watched the conflagration with a sinister smile on his face. His narrow eyes filled with hatred so intense it was as if he controlled the fire with nothing more than his malevolent gaze.

Turning his troops north and westward, Tarleton continued his raids through the countryside, exacting a mean-spirited revenge for a war that even he had already concluded was lost.

★

A few days later, shortly past Noon on May 26, Peter arrived at The Mansion, weary and haggard. His shoulders were hunched over. His hair was thick and matted. The growth on his face had formed a short beard. His eyes were drawn from lack of sleep. His clothes were stiff and clung to him from the rain. He smelled like he hadn't bathed in months. His knees bent slightly in an involuntary way that suggested he would crumble to the ground at any moment.

At the plantation, where he thought he would find revelry and

397

merriment, instead he was met with destruction and devastation. Everything lay in ruin. Only one word escaped Peter's lips, "Tarleton." The thought of what had occurred filled Peter with rage, not just at that vile militant but at himself for not ending his life when he had the chance and keeping him from reaching Susannah. He shuddered as he imagined the fire. The orange flames dancing around the timber, feasting on everything in its path, as if celebrating a release from a long slumber. Thick smoke swirling towards the sky like gray ghosts, then disappearing among the darkening clouds. The heat pushing outward, trying to make room, robbing anyone of air....

Oh. Oh my. What if they were still here? He thought. *What if Tarleton locked them all inside before he....* Struck with terror, Peter was unable to finish the thought. Mustering what little strength he had left, he pumped his burly legs and ran as fast as he could, gaining purchase against the path that led straight to where the main house once stood.

Feverishly, he tore at timber and boards that felt, even now, warm to the touch, some painted white with ash and seething with a pulsating red-orange glow. He frantically looked for Susannah and her family, hoping beyond hope that he would find no sign of a charred body. Smoldering ashes seemed to be all that remained.

So, where could they be? Did Tarleton capture them? Peter wondered. Continuing to survey the destruction, Peter was naturally drawn to where the barn once stood. The only thing recognizable was the anvil that he and James Anderson had purchased together. The smell of the still-smoking lumber was becoming oppressive. Peter felt his temper rise. *Fire turns people into slaves,* he thought. *Slaves to circumstance. Slaves to misfortune. And Tarleton is to blame.*

At that moment, thunder cracked and the dark sky opened up, dropping heavy pellets of rain all around him, soaking him in minutes. Weakened from the long journey and the reality of what lay before him, Peter sunk to the ground on his knees. He gritted his teeth as the pain in his leg surged up his side. His sword, still slung over his shoulder in the scabbard, pierced the earth as he fell. Tears streamed down his cheeks and his chest heaved. He yearned for revenge. He felt as misplaced as he did on the wharf as a boy. Overcome with grief and anger, his face contorted as he lifted his arms toward the sky, fists clenched, and let out a blood-curdling cry, "Noooooohhhhh!" Weeks of tension released from his body. For a moment, he was still. Then, as though surrendering his spirit, he fell forward, his forearms splashing onto the muddy ground. In a low, raspy voice, he said, "God help me. I'll get you, Tarleton!"

He reached inside his pouch and touched Susannah's handkerchief. For the moment, it was his only remaining connection to the woman he loved so much. *Wherever she is, I don't care if she is married,* Peter resolved, *I won't rest until I find her.*

After gathering himself, not knowing where to turn next, he set a course for Hunting Tower, wondering if that, too, had been destroyed. Unsure of how he might be received, he was more than willing to swallow his pride in search of any information as to the whereabouts and safety of Susannah and the Andersons.

Two days later, grimy and fatigued, he arrived at Hunting Tower, the house where he had spent the formative years of his life. Hesitating to approach the door, he stood for about fifteen minutes remembering the way he and Judge Winston had last parted, how he had been ordered off the property. Peter didn't have long to contemplate. The front door opened, and Judge Winston came out onto the porch. A haversack hung from his shoulder across his chest and rested against his hip.

The judge was momentarily stunned to see Peter, the once-little boy he had purchased at an orphanage, now a weary and worn defender of freedom, standing before him. Finally, the judge cleared his throat and spoke. "Peter? My goodness. Peter. I almost didn't recognize you," he said, taking in Peter's gaunt appearance. Have you just come from battle?"

"Judge...sir...I...I just came from the Anderson farm. The Mansion has been burned to the ground. Nobody was there. I can't find ... I can't find Susannah or her family," stammered Peter, trying to hold back his emotion. But the judge could see that Peter was visibly shaken. "Calm down, Peter. Calm down. As far as I know, all of the Andersons, including your Susannah, are alright. I received word that some British cavalry officer by the name of Tar—"

"Tarleton!" Peter broke in. "Tarleton! I knew it! He's an animal! That swine! I hate him with every fiber of my body. He's here in Virginia? He's here in the area?"

"He was, but I don't know where he is now. He was looking for you, Peter. You have made a real enemy in that man. Anyway, when I heard he was looking for you, I thought he might go to the Anderson plantation, so I sent Alfred to warn them."

Judge Winston, through his nephew, Patrick Henry, had learned what Tarleton had planned. When Alfred had arrived with his warning, the Andersons gathered up essentials and as many belongings as they could that had value, loaded them into wagons and carriages, and made good their escape.

"I do thank you for warning them. I know we have not always seen eye-to-eye. As for Tarleton, it is *he* who has made an enemy of *me*... more than once. I swear, I'll hunt him down, and I'll kill him." Instinctively, Peter reached above his head and touched his broadsword.

"What have you there, Peter?"

"It's a sword. General George Washington himself had it made for me."

"From everything I have heard, you deserve that and much more. Word of how you have fought has reached all around these parts. Everybody says you're a war hero, and they speak of you as the Virginia Giant and the Hercules of the Revolution." The judge stepped back as if to go into the house, then turned again toward the tall man on his lawn and spoke words Peter had never expected to hear. "I'm so proud of you, Peter. I really am. But where do you go now?"

Trying to absorb what he had just heard, he responded, "I'm not sure. I owe that cursed Tarleton a vis—"

"Now hold on, Peter," the Judge interrupted, "I'm told that Tarleton has as many as four hundred troops in his command. I don't think that even you and that large sword strapped to your back can match those odds."

"You may be right, judge, but I have to make my plans. But, first, I need to find Susannah, but I don't even know where to begin to look. " He hesitated, uncertain he really wanted to hear the response to his next question, but he knew he had to. "I understand... she's married." Somehow, articulating his thought made it seem more likely. "Judge… did you attend the wedding?"

"No, I had business in Richmond and Mrs. Winston wasn't feeling well enough to make the journey to Goochland," the Judge replied, then, reaching into his haversack, he added, "But I still have the invitation right here." He pulled it out and handed it to Peter. "I was going to have a gift ordered and sent to them today when I was in town."

Taking the parchment from the Judge, Peter felt as though he were being handed a death sentence. It read just as the soldier back at the Robinsons had described. "So, that's where it was. Then it really is true," Peter said solemnly, closing his eyes for a moment. "I still need to know she's safe and well. Judge, if you can think of anyone who might know or hear anything, please…"

"Will do, my boy. In the meantime, I recall telling you that you would always have a home here at Hunting Tower."

He calmly reminded the judge, "And I recall you telling Alfred to escort me from the plantation."

"You're absolutely right, Peter. I did. But those were the ravings of a bitter and jealous man. Your room behind the main house is still empty. You are welcome to use it for as long as you want, and to come and go as you please."

The judge offered his hand. Peter hugged him instead. "My life would not be what it has become were it not for you. For that, I am forever grateful."

"It is I, and all who may one day be free of the English yoke, who should be grateful to you, Peter Francisco."

A look of humility swept across Peter's face, for since he did not seek praise; neither did he accept it well. He viewed himself as just another man doing what he knew in his heart needed to be done.

He did stay at Hunting Tower for several weeks and even re-sumed his former blacksmithing duties to help out. Occasionally, he would go to Buckingham and spend time exchanging stories in taverns with the very people who held him in such high regard. By then, almost everyone knew of the Virginia Giant. During one of these excursions, Peter encountered the local printer Edward Hunter. He mentioned a letter was being held for him at his office since it couldn't be delivered to The Mansion.

Peter nearly jumped out of his skin. "Really?" he said excit-edly, leaping out of the chair, which sent it spilling backward onto the floor. He thought the letter could be from Susannah. "Thank you for holding it," Peter said, clearing his throat, his tone much more subdued. "I'm back at Hunting Tower. Could we... could we possibly get the letter now?"

"I don't see why not," Edward said. "Follow me."

Both men walked in step together toward Edward's office. At times, Peter had to deliberately slow himself down to prevent getting too far ahead of Edward. Fortunately, the office was just across and down the street a little ways from the tavern.

Once inside, Edward pulled out a small basket from under-neath the waist-high desk and thumbed through its contents. Peter could barely contain himself. *She's okay!* He celebrated inwardly, a bit premature. *After I read this letter, I'll know exactly where she is!*

Edward scanned the envelope. "Looks like it's from a Colonel Washington," he said, handing the letter over to Peter.

"Oh, that's right," Peter said, dejected. "It's probably my or-ders." Peter tore open the letter. What he read surprised him. He wouldn't have to return to battle. Instead, in lieu of raids being made by the British under Tarleton, he was being given a recon-naissance mission to gather what information he could and to alleviate the conditions close to home. His first assignment would be at Ben Ward's Tavern in Amelia, Virginia. Peter spent several nights at the tavern, talking with other guests and patrons while watching for any suspicious activity.

Early one morning, he and Ward were eating breakfast and talking. A few others milled about. Every once in a while, Peter casually scanned the place with his eyes. Once, a young woman with light-colored hair walked into the tavern, and, like countless times in the last several months, he mistook her for Susannah. *Will I ever find her or will I go mad first?* He wondered. He absent-mindedly fingered his silver buckles that he'd asked Petunia to sew onto the knees of one pair of his breeches. Ward had always been an affable fellow, although Peter did not trust the man because he seemed much like a willow tree that bent with the wind. As the two chatted, they heard some riders approached and looked out the window.

Nine of Tarleton's legion, along with three Negroes, rode up to the tavern. Having left his sword upstairs in his room, Peter had no choice but to attempt an escape out a side door, but when he opened it, there stood one of the Dragoons with his sword drawn and ready.

"You're not going anywhere," the British cavalryman said, bearing his sword.

Sensing that this was a fight he could not win, Peter threw up his hands and surrendered. Fortunately, none of the raiders sus-pected he was the one man their leader Tarleton so desperately sought to kill. Assuming their comrade had the situation well under control, the rest of the Dragoons walked into the tavern and ordered up gills of rum.

The instigator who had cornered Peter looked him over, his lip curled in a hateful snarl. "You don't look prosperous, but I'll be asking you to empty your pockets and give me all you have."

Carrying nothing of value, Peter relinquished what little money he had along with a pocket watch. As he admired the simple timepiece, the soldier spotted something shiny on Peter's breeches. His worn buckles had produced a dull reflection of the sun.

"Hand those over!" he said, pointing at Peter's knees, jabbing his sword at Peter's chest. I'll bet they have some value… in trade," said the soldier.

The raider had suddenly made it personal. Peter's mind flashed with images of the places these buckles had been. *They are who I am. They have been with me everywhere. Sometimes, my only means of comfort. My only source of identity,* Peter thought, his breath growing quick and his mind raging wild at the thought of giving up his beloved buckles. This gave him an idea. He had almost lost them before. He would not lose them again. "These buckles are a part of me, and I'm not just handing them over to anybody. So if you want them, you'll have to take them."

In spite of his size, the guard naively sensed no danger, especially since his fellow troopers were just inside the tavern, so he set about removing the buckles from Peter's britches. As he did, he placed his saber under his right arm with the handle and hilt extending toward Peter.

Just as the man reached out to remove the buckle marked with a "P," Peter grabbed the handle of the sword. He raised the weapon and brought it down on the Dragoon's head. As the man dropped to the ground, he pulled out his pistol and aimed it at Peter. Peter reacted, swinging the Dragoon's sword and nearly severing his hand. The man gaped at the remnants of his arm in shock. His hand dangled from his wrist by only a ligament. When the pain set in, the man yelped loud enough for the rest of the soldiers inside the tavern to hear.

Expecting a rush of soldiers, Peter moved towards the front door to get into position. A hand holding a cocked pistol slowly emerged. Peter had his eyes trained on the threshold and didn't notice the gun just inches away from his head. The soldier pulled the trigger just as Peter lifted his head, looking right down the barrel. Peter heard a faint click as the pin hit the chamber without sparking the flint. *It hasn't been cleaned! Thank you, Almighty God!*

Peter took the Dragoon down quickly. Surmising that the rest of the soldiers would soon follow, he took off toward the back of the tavern. As he came charging around the corner, he stumbled upon a soldier on his horse who was frantically trying to straighten the fiador before galloping away. Seeing his opening, Peter charged the mounted soldier, deftly plunged his saber just beneath the man's ribcage, and lifted him off the horse.

The remaining Dragoons were in a panic trying to mount their horses, but the animals themselves were panicked. At the same time, Tarleton's men sensed that they were under attack by a superior force. When Peter realized that these soldiers were looking in the direction of the woods, he seized on an idea.

"Come on boys. Help me finish them off," Peter shouted to no one. "Don't let them get away." In fear for their very lives, the remaining Dragoons abandoned all hope of remounting and started to escape on foot, but unknown to Peter, a much larger force of Tarleton's men were just a quarter mile away. When he finally saw swirling dust ascending into the air behind the running men, he knew he needed to make a hasty retreat himself.

Standing near the nine horses still tethered, he easily drew together the reins, then mounted one sizeable white stallion. With no time to waste, Peter goaded the horse and galloped off in the opposite direction from the approaching column of men led by none other than Tarleton himself.

Seeing that the American's head start could not be matched, Tarleton drew his horse to a halt and dismounted. As the vanquished troopers later recounted their story, Tarleton soon realized that just one man had outsmarted nine of his Dragoons, and not just any man. Peter Francisco.

"Have none of you even the courage of a river rat?" he shouted. "I should hang you all." In a fit of rage, Tarleton drew his pistol, aimed it at the face of one of the soldiers and pulled the trigger. While reaching for his own saber and intending to take down the rest, he was pulled away by some of the Dragoons. It took several minutes for him to regain any sense of composure after being humiliated by the escape of the one American he hated most.

Assuming that Tarleton's men were in pursuit, Peter ran the group of horses as fast as he could deep into the forest. After a time of meandering to cover his trail, he circled back to the tavern to see what had happened, leaving the horses behind in the woods. When he was sure that Tarleton and his men had moved on, he rode up to the tavern, wanting to retrieve his sword. Cautiously, he walked in to find Ben Ward standing next to the bar, a dark stain spread between his legs and down his pants.

"I see the excitement was a bit too much for you, old man," Peter laughed heartily.

"Peter, thank God you're alright. I told them British that you would head straight north, and they believed me! I even watched as they rode off in that direction."

"Yes, I'm sure you did. I'm sure you did just that," Peter said with a bit of mockery. Then glancing around, he added, "I'm here for my sword and belongings."

"Sure, Peter. But ... don't you think I'm due something for my trouble? After all, I sent them in the wrong direction, didn't I?"

Peter didn't believe a word that left Ward's mouth. *On the other hand,* he thought, *it might be worth something to keep the man quiet.* Should Tarleton's men return, Peter didn't want old man Ward pointing out the direction to Hunting Tower.

"Would two of the horses be enough to satisfy you and purchase your continued loyalty?" Peter asked.

"Absolutely. You can trust me," he answered somewhat disingenuously.

"I'm sure I can," Peter replied, not buying the commitment. "But if I learn otherwise, I'll return and our conversation will be a bit less friendly, as it will be my broadsword that'll lead the discussion. I'll make sure the horses are delivered." He wasted no time gathering up his things and returned to the woods to head the remaining horses toward the Winston plantation. When he arrived, Judge Winston was just coming out of the barn.

"My word, Peter, where did you get all those horses?" the judge inquired.

"Just a little donation from Tarleton's men," Peter answered, recalling with a smile the response he and John Allen had given

Colonel Mayo in reply to a similar question.

"Well, what are you going to do with them?"

"I thought you might like to buy them, since some of your Canadians have died."

"Indeed, I would, Peter, and I'll give you a fair price for them."

"I never once thought that you wouldn't, Judge. But this one," Peter said, indicating the steed he rode, "This one is not for sale. He seems a sturdy mount, and I'll name him Tarleton. If somehow my destiny is not to kill him, then I'll surely ride on his back."

23.

THE END IS NEAR

THE SUMMER PRESSED ON, and Peter was quick to jump back into a variety of duties at Hunting Tower, if for no other reason than to keep his mind off of Susannah's whereabouts. *She's probably settled into married life by now,* he reasoned. He had resisted the urge to go on an all-out manhunt for her, not wanting to intrude or cause any problems.

On the plantation, he was no longer viewed as a slave, an indentured servant, or as property. In fact, Judge Winston, in addition to allowing him to stay in his old room, even paid him a small sum for his work.

On one sun-filled day, Peter knocked on the door at the main house, and Mrs. Winston answered. Her feelings for Peter had not really changed since her husband had first brought him home from the orphanage those many years ago, though she couldn't help but admire the reputation Peter had gained from his action in the war.

"Peter, what brings you here?" Mrs. Winston said, gazing up at the man standing at her door.

"I've come to fetch the judge, but I'd also like the rest of the family to see what I have to show him."

"Come in, then. I'll go see where everybody is."

"If it's alright, I'll just wait here on the porch." Peter knew how Mrs. Winston felt, and he preferred not to come into the house. A few moments later, the entire Winston family including the children, none of whom were children anymore, gathered on the front porch.

The eldest, Sarah, had married, but her husband had been killed in the southern campaign at Charleston. After his death, she had moved back home. Anthony, Jr. had also been at Charleston where he had lost an arm when the cannon he was manning exploded. Alice and Martha had grown into lovely young women but had yet to marry, since most able-bodied men had gone off to fight.

Judge Winston was the last to come out onto the porch. "What's this all about, Peter? My wife says you have something to show us."

"Yes, sir, I do. I'd like you all to follow me to the barn."

The family followed him, but when they got to the barn, they saw nothing out of the ordinary.

"I don't see anything different," Sarah said.

Without saying a word, Peter pointed to the barn roof about thirty feet overhead. There, at its zenith, in a shape that resembled a sailing ship, perched the largest, most magnificent weather vane any of them had ever seen. Supporting it were several concentric circles that formed the Earth. Compass directions were marked along its equator. At that moment, the wind gently guided the vessel's bowsprit toward the southwest, reminding them all of the way Peter had come.

As the little group gazed silently into the sky admiring his handiwork, Peter broke in. "I don't know how long I'll be staying at Hunting Tower, but I wanted to give you something to remember me by."

Judge Winston finally spoke up. "Why, it's wonderful, Peter, just wonderful. I've always wanted a weather vane. I just never got around to having one made. Thank you. I can assure you that whenever I look up at that barn, I shall always remember the scared little boy I brought here and the fine gentleman he has become." The rest of the family congratulated Peter on his work, and even the judge's wife had some kind words to offer.

That evening, as had become his custom since reestablishing residence at the Winston plantation, Peter visited Arthur's rock. During these visits, he poured his heart out to the old Negro who had meant so much to him. He spoke of some of the men he had fought alongside in the war and of the battles. Somehow, these conversations always worked around to Susannah.

"You would have liked her, Arthur. Really, you would. She is probably married now and has begun a new life, but I can't stop thinking about her. Is that wrong? I think I would feel better at least knowing she was okay. But now, I don't even know where she is. I don't know if she's safe or not."

He paused for a long time. Then he turned to God, whom he had first learned about as a little boy and to whom Arthur had led his heart. "Please, God, if there are angels in Heaven, could you ask them to look out for her and protect her from any harm? You've given me great strength, but I'm powerless right now, and I don't know what Tarleton's men may have done to my Susannah. Please protect her… I beg of you."

★

In late August, word came to Hunting Tower that Cornwallis had marched his troops toward Yorktown. His latest strategy called not for defeating the colonialists in the north, nor for defeating them in the south. His goal was to sweep across Virginia and split the colonies in two.

In the meantime, Lafayette had been harassing British fighting forces wherever and whenever he could find them. Most of these troops, however, had withdrawn with Cornwallis, who was amassing his army in Yorktown. General Washington saw an opportunity to bottle Cornwallis up and perhaps even drive the British into the sea. Thus, on August 19, he and more than 7,000 of the Continental Army began their march to the south. Other colonial militia and regular forces were also told to rally there, and their strength eventually numbered nearly 20,000.

Through an aide of Colonel Washington, Lafayette was able to find out that his old friend, Peter Francisco, was at Hunting Tower. Sensing that this was to be the last action, he sent a messenger to the Winston plantation to ask Peter to join him in what he was certain would be victory.

So after taking leave from the Winstons, Peter mounted his steed Tarleton and headed toward Yorktown, arriving there on

September 6, 1781. He was a bit concerned when he rode into the American camp, for he could only account for some 4,000 troops, not nearly enough in his estimation to finish off Cornwallis and his men. Reaching Lafayette's tent, Peter climbed down from Tarleton just as the general was coming out of his quarters.

"Luso," Lafayette shouted. "Peter! I cannot tell you 'ow good it is to lay eyes on you at last. Victory is in ze air, and I did not want you to miss it."

"Victory? Did you say victory? You must have had far too many gills of rum to be claiming victory. Why, you haven't even the troop strength to put up a good fight."

"Ah, you worry too much. General Washington should arrive wizin ze week. He 'as a magnificent plan to bottle up ze English and put an end to zem. Trust me, Luso. We shall drive Cornwallis into ze ocean. But 'ow 'ave you been? I 'eard about your little... 'ow shall I say... adventure wiz Tarleton's men. 'Ow is your lady friend? Are zere plans for marriage yet? Remember, I am to be invited." As usual, Lafayette fired his questions like a musket volley, he was so happy to see his Portuguese friend.

"Lafayette, I honestly don't know of Susannah or her whereabouts. Her family was warned about a raid by Tarleton, and they fled their home just a couple days before he arrived and burned their home to the ground, destroying most of the surrounding land. The Andersons also left before I could reach home. Her father wished her to marry George Carrington, and, from what I have learned, their wedding was to take place a few days later."

Lafayette could see that his friend was quite upset. "Ah, I am sorry, Luso." He decided to change the subject in attempt to steer Peter's mind away from his obvious misery. Noticing the sword strapped to Peter's back, he said, "So, zat is ze sword ze good general 'ad made for you?"

"I almost forgot," replied Peter, drawing the sword from its scabbard to show it off.

"It is even more magnificent zan I 'ad imagined. I know it took a while to get it to you, but I 'ear you took ze lives of a good many Redcoats down at Guilford."

"Indeed. She has served me well, and I pray to use her next to put an end to Tarleton before this war comes to an end."

"Perhaps you shall. I 'ear zat 'e is 'ere wiz Cornwallis, so perhaps you shall. Now, come," said Lafayette as he reached up slightly and dropped an arm around Peter's shoulder. "Come tell me all zat I ask."

The two of them retired to Lafayette's tent and talked well into the night, reminiscing about their shared adventures and catching each other up on what had transpired since Lafayette had last bid farewell to Peter so long ago. Lafayette had ordered an extra cot placed in his personal tent so that Peter could stay with him that night.

Peter told Lafayette that he had turned down the offer of a commission because he still could neither read nor write.

"Zere will be time for zat once zis war 'as concluded. For now, 'owever, I wish to name you again as my personal aide. Will you accept zat responsibility?"

"I've served many in the same role—Colonel Mayo, Colonel Washington and others. I would consider it the highest honor to serve as such with you, General Lafayette."

"Call me general one more time when we are alone togezer, Luso, and I shall 'ave you executed for insubordination." The subsequent guffaws coming from the tent compelled several high-ranking officers to peek in to see what was going on.

Nearby where the war continued, a few remote skirmishes occurred on a daily basis, but none were of any consequence. Peter and Lafayette did not participate. True to Lafayette's prediction, on September 29, reinforcements led by General George Washington arrived, having spent three days in Williamsburg. Cornwallis, sensing the Americans' intentions, had pulled his troops even closer to Yorktown proper in order to further concentrate the strength of his defenses.

As Cornwallis continued to draw his men into a tighter circle, they were abandoning defensive trenches that they had dug previously. Washington ordered artillery placed there, his plan to lay siege on Cornwallis and bombard the British general into submission. However, Lord Cornwallis had left a number of redoubts to remain on the flanks of the entrenchment, so that they might harass the Americans as they prepared their cannon emplacements. At one of these redoubts, Peter Francisco would see his final action of the war.

Realizing that those British positions had to be eliminated, Washington asked for volunteers to overrun the English outposts. Lafayette was quick to accept the challenge, so Peter and his sword entered one last battle. It was to be a night attack, similar to Stony Point, and guns were not to be loaded. Lafayette's group totaled about four hundred men. A similarly sized force of French troops was assigned to take a nearby redoubt.

There wasn't much action, as Lafayette's men easily stormed the position and took it at bayonet point with almost no resistance. Peter's participation was primarily to stand by Lafayette and serve as his bodyguard, and that proved to be a wise decision. As Lafayette entered the redoubt, a wounded officer lay on the ground and brought his pistol to bear on the Frenchman. Peter saw what was coming and deftly stepped between Lafayette, putting himself in harm's way, and drove his sword into the British officer's chest.

"Luso," Lafayette said from behind Peter's massive shoulders. "I see zat I shall owe you an eternity of favors. I hate owing favors, but in zis case, I shall make ze exception." Peter turned around just in time to catch the grin on Lafayette's face.

The general then sent a message to the leader of the French group, which had been assigned to take the other redoubt. It said: "I am in my redoubt. Where are you?" It took several minutes, but the French also reported that they had completed their mission.

After further maneuvering and digging new trenches, even closer to Cornwallis and his forces, the bombardment began on October 9 and intensified on October 16 by yet more cannon. The British were taking a terrible pounding, and French ships had closed off their potential escape by sea.

On the morning of October 17, Peter and Lafayette were sitting horseback on a hilltop overlooking the trenches, cannon and the city. Without warning, out of the early morning mist appeared a drummer and a British officer waving a white flag. Lafayette, in somewhat disbelief, reached over and gave Peter a hard slap on the arm. "Do you see, Luso? Do you see zat? Zey are giving up. Cornwallis is surrendering. We 'ave won. We 'ave won. We 'ave won!"

While that should have been Peter's most gratifying moment,

the very moment he was fighting for, the surrender did not bring celebration. His mind quickly shifted to Susannah. *She was what I had been fighting so desperately for, and now that she is nowhere to be found, victory is less sweet. Where could she possibly be and can I even hope to find her? And what of Tarleton? Now that the war is over, I will never have the opportunity to meet Tarleton again on the battlefield.* Lafayette's words jarred him from these thoughts.

"Peter, you 'ardly look like a man should on such a victorious day. What is it zat dulls your celebration?"

"I was just thinking about Susannah. I *am* glad the war is over, but freedom spent without knowing the love of my life is safe and well would be hollow, indeed."

"Zis I promise you, Luso. We shall find her. You and I, togezer. I shall not retire from zese shores until we do. I owe you at least zat much."

The negotiations for surrender went on for two days until, on the afternoon of October 19, the victorious troops lined both sides of the road leading from Yorktown to a makeshift table where the papers of capitulation were signed. The French were on one side of the road, the colonials on the other. In the distance, everyone could hear British drums begin to roll. Then their band started to play a somber tune called "The World Turned Upside Down," which was appropriate for the defeated English.

Surprisingly, General Lord Charles Cornwallis did not lead the British. Rather, at the head of the column came General Charles O'Hara, as Cornwallis claimed to be too ill to attend the ceremony. Also conspicuously absent was Colonel Banastre Tarleton. Perhaps the British realized that the Virginia Hercules would stir up such sentiment that a riot might ensue.

The British troops refused to look directly at the Americans, preferring instead to focus their attention on the finely uniformed French. Interpreting this as an insult, Lafayette sent instructions for the American band to strike up a rendition of "Yankee Doodle." This was originally a song of mockery directed by the British troops toward the Americans in forgotten and far away Boston. American soldiers up and down the lines now snickered at the turnabout.

At the conclusion of the treaty signing, the British soldiers withdrew. General George Washington mounted his horse and rode along the columns of men to review his troops. When he arrived at the point where Lafayette and Peter Francisco were sitting on their mounts, the general stopped and approached Lafayette. He nodded toward Peter, and then spoke directly to Lafayette. "Without him," he said, tilting his head in Peter's direction, "we would have lost two crucial battles, perhaps the war and with it our freedom. He was truly a one-man army."

As Washington left, Lafayette, with a smug, proud smile on his face, looked over at Peter. This time Peter was smiling, too.

24.

EPILOGUE

A MAN OF HIS WORD, Lafayette joined Peter, and the two of them set out to find Susannah Anderson. They even stopped at Hunting Tower for an evening, where Lafayette regaled the entire Winston family with tales from the war, always making sure they fully understood what a hero Peter Francisco had been. They were invited to spend the night, and when the evening drew near, Peter began to proceed to his old sleeping quarters. General Lafayette was expected to stay in the main house.

"Where are you going, Luso?" Lafayette asked.

"To my room out back," Peter replied.

"Zen I shall sleep zere as well."

"Now wait just a minute," Judge Winston insisted, "My wife has set up a room to accommodate both of you. No one is expected to sleep behind the house tonight." That was the very first time

Peter had been welcomed to sleep in the main house at Hunting Tower, and it felt good.

The next morning, he and Lafayette stopped by Arthur's rock. Peter climbed down from Tarleton and spent a few moments in quiet contemplation. As he remounted, Lafayette noticed that his friend had tears in his eyes.

"He must 'ave been quite a man," Lafayette commented.

"He was. He most certainly was," replied Peter.

Having read the inscription Peter had put on the rock, Lafayette said "Well, 'e raised a fine son, and 'e would be proud of you, Peter Francisco."

After passing by what remained of The Mansion and the Anderson plantation, Peter and Lafayette scoured the countryside for any word on where Susannah might have gone. In mid-December, they spoke with a merchant who had had several business dealings with James Anderson, and he told the pair he had heard that the family was staying with friends in Richmond. Peter and Lafayette rode as quickly as they could toward Richmond.

Arriving late that night, they took up residence at the very same hotel where Peter and Judge Winston had stayed many years earlier when they went to St. John's Parish Church. Richmond had tripled its population since then. Not knowing where to start, the two spent days going door-to-door, but still there was no word of Susannah. By then, the air had turned bitter cold, and a wet snow covered the streets as Peter and his friend approached the St. John's Church early one Sunday evening.

"Look there," said Peter pointing toward the church. "That's where I heard Patrick Henry. That's where I first knew I would fight for this country's freedom."

"Zat was most certainly a fateful day, Peter," Lafayette responded.

With the conclusion of the worship service, the church door was opened and people began to spill out, wrapping scarves around their faces and pulling gloves onto their hands in protection against the miserable weather. The scarves made it difficult to see anything besides where they were walking.

Just as Peter and Lafayette arrived at the steps, a young lady, walking briskly, slipped on a patch of ice and began to stumble. As she was about to topple into the street, Peter reached out and deftly caught her before she landed hard on the ground.

The young lady looked up into the eyes of her rescuer. An awkward moment hung frozen in the winter air.

"Peter Francisco!" she uttered in astonishment.

Peter spoke with equal astonishment, "Susannah! I have been looking for you for so long. I'm so glad you are alright." The two held their pose, and Peter flashed his eyes at Lafayette. "We have found her, Lafayette. We have found her!"

Once again the Marquis broke into a smile. "Luso. Zis is providence. Surely, zis is ze 'and of God." He then proceeded down the street to give them a few moments alone.

"How is your family? Is everyone alright?" Peter asked, trying to keep himself from staring.

"Yes, they are fine. They are staying with the Brookes," Susannah said, fully aware that Peter still held her arm.

"I'm so glad," Peter replied. Seeing that she was alone, he hesitantly ventured, "Where … is George?"

For a moment, Susannah looked down at her hands clasped in front of her. She bit slightly at her lip. Without looking up, she explained, "We had to flee so suddenly to escape Tarleton's raid, there was hardly time to think. The wedding was to take place just two weeks later. When we learned The Mansion had been burned, I took it as a sign and called off the wedding. My family had already been through enough."

"So … you're not married?" Peter asked, daring to believe.

All the tension in Susannah's body seemed to release. Emotion was evident on her face as she said, "No, Peter. I'm not married. I've thought about you every day since. Naturally, I assumed the worst and thought you dead. I honestly never expected to see you again."

Peter's mind reeled. *Could this possibly be true?* "Susannah, do you remember what I said to you when I gave you the key?" he asked. Then suddenly realizing the key must have been destroyed in the fire. *No!* He thought, then exclaimed, "The key! It's gone, isn't it?"

As his words echoed around them, Susannah reached into her coat pocket, revealing the iron key with a heart-shaped grip that Peter had forged for her that Christmas they shared. "I never let it out of my sight. I took it with me when we fled, along with boneco de trapo. They were my only mementos of you."

Peter wrapped his hands around Susannah's and together they cradled the key, a symbol of their future. Looking down into Susannah's green eyes, he said, "Susannah, I have never stopped loving you. Now that this war is over, I promise you I will earn your father's approval." Then, not wanting to be presumptuous, he added "That is, if you'll still have me."

"There is nothing in this world I want more," she said, tears in her eyes.

Looking down at Susannah, Peter smiled in agreement then pulled her closer until their lips met. It was as if not a moment had passed since they had first sat together on her front porch swing. Not a sound could be heard as the couple stood in embrace, snow falling gently around them.

CPSIA information can be obtained
at www.ICGtesting.com
Printed in the USA
BVHW030310230720
584324BV00002B/3/J

9 781495 170461